# An Untrustworthy Army

## Book Five of the Peninsular War Saga

By

# Lynn Bryant

To Richard Dawson

For 25 years

With love

# About the Author

Lynn Bryant was born and raised in London's East End. She studied History at University and had dreams of being a writer from a young age. Since this was clearly not something a working class girl made good could aspire to, she had a variety of careers, which included being a librarian, an NHS administrator, a relationship counsellor, the manager of an art gallery and the owner of an Irish dance school before she realised that most of these were just as unlikely as being a writer and took the step of publishing her first book.

Two of Lynn's books have been shortlisted for the Society for Army Historical Research fiction prize.

She now lives in the Isle of Man and is married to a man who understands technology, which saves her a job. She has two grown-up children and two Labradors. History is still a passion, with a particular enthusiasm for the Napoleonic era and the sixteenth century. When not writing, she walks her dogs, reads anything that's put in front of her and makes periodic and unsuccessful attempts to keep a tidy house.

# Acknowledgements

As always, I'm grateful for the help and encouragement I've received from so many people during both the writing and re-editing of this book.

Research is a huge part of the writing I do, and I'd like to thank various historians and writers who have helped me with the maddest questions, especially Jacqueline Reiter, Kristine Hughes Patrone, Catherine Curzon, Rob Griffith, Josh Proven, Eamonn O'Keeffe and many others on social media and in person.

I would like to thank Mel Logue, Jacqueline Reiter and Kristine Hughes Patrone for reading sections of the work and making helpful suggestions.

Thanks to the amazing Heather Paisley, my editor and best friend for more than thirty years, for showing me all the ways in which spell check doesn't help.

Thanks to Richard Dawson, my husband, for another amazing cover, for technical help and for endless support and patience during the writing of this book.

Thanks to my son Jon and his girlfriend Rachael for dog sitting, guitar playing and good humour, Thanks to my daughter, Anya, for making me laugh and for never failing to have an opinion.

Last but not least, thanks to Oscar and Alfie, the stars of Writing with Labradors for sharing my study and bringing me joy.

And in loving memory of Toby and Joey, the original gorgeous stars of Writing with Labradors who are swimming and playing somewhere over the Rainbow Bridge. I'll never forget either of them.

# Chapter One

It had been hot for weeks, a blistering heat which battered down onto the Anglo-Portuguese army, settled in sprawling cantonments around the city of Salamanca. Colonel Johnny Wheeler of the 112th infantry, baking on horseback, took his place in the triumphal procession into the city wishing that he could be somewhere shady, with a cool drink and his feet up.

"Why us?" he complained to his second-in-command. "Of all the regiments in this army, why are we here, sweating our arses off, while most of them are probably bathing in the river and drinking wine?"

Major Gervase Clevedon glanced at him with a grin. "Cheer up, sir, it's supposed to be an honour. We're here because the 112th distinguished itself during recent actions."

"Well, I wish they bloody hadn't," Johnny said glumly. "Pretty place, this, mind and at least they've the sense to appear welcoming, whatever they might actually think."

"I'm not sure they've been that welcoming to the sixth division these past ten days."

"I can't say I blame them. God knows how it took them ten days to reduce three convents."

Wellington's army had marched north from the Portuguese border earlier in the month and had arrived at the city of Salamanca on the 17th of June. He had received excellent intelligence along the way which had correctly informed him that the French had abandoned the city, leaving a garrison of around eight hundred men in three fortified convents within the city. What Wellington's intelligence sources had failed to describe, was how well-built the fortifications were and what his Lordship had imagined would be a simple mopping up operation had dragged on for ten days. Partly this had been due to the difficulties of reducing these particular defences and partly due to Wellington's lack of resources to do so; he had been obliged to send for extra ammunition and had lacked good siege equipment. Johnny, who admitted that he was heavily biased in favour of his own division, also thought that the sixth division had not been the best choice for the job, having little experience of sieges.

He had mentioned this to his commanding officer and received a basilisk blue eyed stare from Colonel van Daan who commanded the third brigade of the Light Division.

"Do not wish that on my lads, Colonel Wheeler, or I will gut you like an Irish herring. I have seen enough siege warfare this year to last me a lifetime. If they call us up for this, I am inventing an epidemic of camp fever."

Paul van Daan had looked grimly at the orders when they had finally arrived, remembering, Johnny knew, the piled dead in the breaches at Badajoz.

"He's asking for volunteers," he said. "Two from each company of the Light Division to form a storming party. Johnny, I do not want to go out there and ask my lads to put themselves forward for another piece of suicidal lunacy which is going to lose men that I care about."

Johnny stood silently, watching his friend. Eventually, the Colonel came out of his reverie and said:

"All right. Let the company officers know. Two from each company and I'll take nobody with a wife and children. If we don't get enough volunteers, I'll go down there myself, see how he likes that."

"We'll get plenty of volunteers, sir."

Johnny watched the storming party march out with a heavy heart. His commanding officer rode down beside them to see them into position and assess their chances and then rode back several hours later looking considerably more cheerful

"They've surrendered," he said. "Out of provisions and ammunition, I think. Sometimes my prayers are answered. I've just been with Lord Wellington and he has ordered a victory parade into the city tomorrow and wishes the 110th and 112th to be part of it. Better smarten your lads up, Johnny."

Johnny regarded him blankly, thinking about the tattered and patched uniforms of the entire Light Division. "How?" he asked.

"Tell them to clean their weapons and stand up straight. They're soldiers, not actors, it's the best he's going to get."

Despite his reservations, Johnny welcomed the chance to spend more time in the city, although like many of the officers in cantonments outside Salamanca, he had visited several times to look around. There had been little to do during the investment of the forts apart from a sudden flurry of activity on 20th June when it had looked for a while as though Marshal Marmont might launch an attack on the Allied forces gathered on the heights of San Cristobal. Otherwise, Wellington's officers spent their time playing cards, visiting the city and speculating on their commander's next move.

"I suspect one or two wine shops might lose half their stock tonight," Gervase Clevedon said tolerantly. "But if they've any sense at all, the taverns will do a good trade. The brothels certainly will, I'm not expecting many of my lads to go back out to camp tonight, they've bloody earned this. They'll spend what's left of their pay and be broke for months, but it'll be worth it to them."

Johnny grinned, knowing it was true. "Gervase, what happened to us? We used to be such correct young officers. I swear to God I once had a man flogged for drinking on duty."

"They still don't drink on duty, sir, he'd kick them into the river. And I for one wouldn't go back. We were a regiment of outsiders, the 110th, new-fangled and pretty much laughed at by half the army back in India. Some good lads, mind, but no identity to speak of. As for the 112th it was in so much disgrace when it came back from the Indies, most people thought it was going to be disbanded."

Johnny ran his eyes over the neat ranks of the 112th and felt a lift of pride. He had taken over command of the regiment just over a year ago and after many years in the army when promotion had seemed an impossible dream, well beyond his purse, he had not learned to take it for granted. "I know. Look at them now, up here with the Light Division's finest. Jesus, it's hot. I wish they'd get going."

Clevedon was peering back along to column. "I think you might find," he said cautiously, "that the victory parade is being held up, while Colonel van Daan's wife's maid locates her missing hat."

Wheeler broke into laughter as a pretty brown-haired woman in a sprigged muslin gown sped past them carrying a fetching straw hat trimmed with silk flowers. "Get a move on, Teresa, we're dying of heat stroke out here," he called.

Teresa Carter looked back over her shoulder. "I do not know why he bothers, she will have lost it before they get into the Cathedral," she said.

At the head of the 110th, Colonel Paul van Daan took the hat from Teresa with a smile of thanks and turned to his wife.

"Put it on," he said in tones of considerable patience. "Keep it on, I am not having you with sunstroke. Or I will spoil Lord Wellington's lovely parade by tipping you off that horse into the river."

"I'm not sure I'd mind that just at the moment, it might be cooler," his wife said, tying on the hat at a particularly fetching angle. "Jenson, would you ride up and present our apologies to Lord Wellington for the delay? The Colonel has a mania about my hats, I cannot tell you what a bore it is."

Paul's orderly grinned and spurred his horse forward. The victory parade would lead to a Te Deum in the Cathedral and the Plaza Mayor would be illuminated during the evening while Lord Wellington and his officers were entertained by the Spanish grandees of the city to a civic banquet and fireworks. Paul had given the men of the 110th and 112th leave to spend the night in the town, providing they behaved themselves, and were back in camp by noon the following day. By now, his veterans had learned to trust his promise that he would go through the town in search of them personally if they failed to turn up and he was not expecting any trouble.

"You would think," his wife commented, drawing up beside him, "that the Spanish would have had enough of fireworks, given that the French seem to have blown up entire sections of their city to build fortifications. Since being with the army I have found that things exploding in the sky have taken on a whole new meaning for me."

Paul laughed and turned his head to survey his wife. They had marched north from the border after several weeks of awaiting reinforcements

3

and provisioning their army. Lord Wellington's previous sortie into Spain in 1809, which had culminated in the bloody field of Talavera, had been cut brutally short by the inability or possible unwillingness of his Spanish allies to provide the supplies for men and horses that had been promised, and Wellington had been determined not to risk the same thing happening again. Improvements had been made since then, to the commissariat and the quartermasters departments and there were no problems in supplies coming into Portugal or being sourced locally. The difficulty was in transporting them to where they were needed when they were needed. Troops marched quickly, considerably faster than the ox-wagons which were often used to bring up supplies, and it was not unheard of, for Wellington's army to arrive at their destination and find no provisions or baggage.

It was relatively unusual for the third brigade of the Light Division, which Paul commanded, to find itself without food. He was known as a perfectionist in the management of his regiment and had extended this attitude to running a brigade. It was more of a challenge given that he now had eighteen hundred men under his command, but he had been remarkably successful so far, although he suspected it had made him no friends in the commissariat while his young wife, who assisted him with the administrative aspects of running his brigade, was probably even less popular than he was.

Paul watched Anne who was looking around at the glorious soaring buildings of Salamanca with obvious appreciation. She was attracting considerable attention from the crowd, being the only woman in the parade at the specific invitation of Lord Wellington who was her constant admirer. She was twenty-two and they had been married for two years, although he had known her for two years before that, but he was not sure he would ever become complacent about having her beside him. He had been deeply attached to his pretty, gentle first wife who had died bearing his daughter, but he adored Anne in a way that he could never have imagined feeling about any woman and it had very little to do with her startling beauty.

It had been an appalling year for them so far. After the heady first year of their marriage, Anne had given birth to a son, his fourth child and her first, and Paul could remember thinking in those days after William's birth that he had never felt so happy and so secure as he did with this unconventional young woman with the black eyes of a gypsy and the courage of a lioness. She travelled with his regiment without apparent concern for her own comfort or safety, but she was less sanguine about her small son in an army camp, where sickness and fever killed many of the children born to the army wives and camp followers. They had agreed reluctantly that he should be sent home to be raised by Paul's family along with his other children. In Lisbon Anne had met his older children for the first time, and Paul had been surprised and delighted by how quickly she seemed to have developed a bond with them. He would never have thought of Anne as particularly maternal, but she had taken Grace, Francis and Rowena to her heart as if they were her own. And then travelling back to join him at Badajoz where the English were besieging the city, she had been taken by the French, and for two long weeks Paul had thought that he might never see her alive again.

Anne turned her head to look over at the crowd where a group of Spanish girls had made garlands of brightly coloured flowers. They were running forward to decorate the officers and men of the army and in some cases their horses. As Anne and Paul watched, a pretty girl of around sixteen threaded her way through the ranks to Sergeant Jamie Hammond who was young and dark and good-looking, marching easily at the head of the 110th light company and draped a garland of white flowers about his neck, reaching up to kiss him. Hammond smiled and scooped her to him, kissing her with obvious enjoyment and then waving to her as she ran back to her giggling friends.

"I suspect that Michael is wishing he was still on foot just now," Anne said. Paul grinned. Captain Michael O'Reilly who commanded the light company of the 112th. had formerly been his sergeant and had developed something of a reputation with the local girls although since he had taken up a commission, he had been a little more circumspect.

"It's a shame we won't be here longer, it won't be long enough for him to find himself a girl," Paul said.

"I'm not so sure. He's an extraordinarily quick worker," Anne said, and Paul gave a choke of laughter.

"A completely unsuitable conversation for the colonel's lady, girl of my heart."

Anne turned her head and smiled impishly at him and Paul felt his heart turn over. Her resilience was astonishing given her ordeal at the hands of a French colonel only three months earlier. She glowed with health and vitality and enjoyment of the day and Paul thought ruefully that she seemed to have recovered faster than he had. The image of his battered, abused wife standing in her shift when he had fought his way through to find her was burned into his brain and Paul was not sure he would ever forget the expression in her eyes when she had told him that she had been raped. Paul was trying hard not to be over-protective with her, since he knew it would drive his independent-spirited wife crazy if he fussed over her or tried to restrict her movements, but her ordeal was too recent for him to forget how it had felt to know that another man had hurt her so badly and he had not been there to protect her.

Around them the people of Salamanca thronged the ancient streets. The buildings were graceful, in a variety of ochre and pink stone, soaring arches and towers giving way sometimes to a crumbled heap of stone where Napoleon's troops had destroyed some historic foundation to use as building stone for the makeshift fortresses which had held the town.

"It's lovely. Such a shame about the destruction," Anne said, fanning herself. Paul surveyed the fan with some amusement. His wife, who had little interest in fashion, regarded fans as purely functional objects and he was sure he had never seen the elaborately painted article before.

"It is. A lot of these buildings were part of the university, but it's mostly been closed down by the French. They've destroyed some of the buildings and used others as barracks which will mean they're wrecked inside.

The place we're billeted in tonight was one of the old colleges. I've got some of the lads clearing it out now. It's big and very elegant but they'd left it like a pigsty."

"They probably left in a hurry," Anne said, looking around her. "I wonder what happened to the students?"

"Probably most of them ended up either in the French army or the guerrillas," Paul said.

"Or dead," his wife said quietly.

"Yes, poor bastards. It's funny, this place reminds me of my student days in Oxford. Hard to imagine Magdalen and Balliol ripped apart by French infantrymen. It puts it in perspective, somehow."

Anne glanced at him. "Which college were you?"

"Balliol. Have you visited Oxford?"

"No, love, I'm a Yorkshire lass, I'd never been anywhere until I married Robert, apart from York, Harrogate and a trip to London when I was fifteen."

Paul laughed aloud and reached for her gloved hand, raising it to his lips with great formality. "And now you speak five languages, bully the local merchants in two countries and have an Earl languishing at your feet."

"Lord Wellington does not languish, he is far too busy," his wife said repressively. Their byplay had been noticed by a section of the crowd. The population was cheering wildly, with more and more of them running to hand flowers and fruit to the officers and men. At the head of the parade Lord Wellington's horse was already garlanded and its bridle and saddle decorated with offerings. As Paul and Anne rode past, a woman detached herself from the crowd. She was holding the hand of a boy of about six, a beautiful child with large dark eyes, dressed in Sunday best for the parade. She pushed him forward, a posy of flowers in his hand, but as he ran, one of the horses started up and the child stumbled in fright and fell hard onto the cobbles.

Anne looked over at Corporal Jenson, Paul's orderly. "Hold her," she said, and slid from Bella's back, passing him the reins. Paul reined in, waving to Major Swanson who commanded the 110th first battalion. "Carry on, Major, we'll catch up."

The boy was on his knees, both of them grazed and bloodied, trying hard not to cry so publicly when Anne reached him. She knelt, apparently indifferent to her riding dress in the dust.

"Are you hurt?" she asked quickly in Spanish.

His mother had reached him at the same time. The boy looked up into Anne's face and looked startled as he took in her beauty. Anne lifted him gently to his feet, pulled out her handkerchief and dabbed blood from his knees.

"You have battle wounds of your own, Señor," she said gravely, and he looked down at his legs and then up into her face and laughed. His mother put her hand on his shoulder.

"You speak Spanish, Señora?"

"I do; my friend is Spanish, she taught me. You have a very handsome

6

son, Señora, what is his name?"

"Diego," the woman said. "He is five."

"He is tall for five. And very brave – hardly a tear. Were these for the soldiers?"

Anne picked up the posy of white flowers and gently blew the dust from them. The child studied her.

"They were for you, Señora. Because you are so beautiful."

"Diego, thank you." Anne raised the posy to her face to smell. "So lovely. But if we are friends, there should be an exchange of gifts."

She reached up and detached one of the silk flowers from her hat, twisting the securing wire into a buttonhole which she carefully placed in the child's dark jacket. Diego looked down at it, astonished, and then up at Anne, his face transformed. Anne laughed and handed him the soiled handkerchief. "Keep this also for your war wounds. Thank you for these, they are beautiful."

She turned to find that Jenson had dismounted and was waiting, smiling, to lift her up. Behind her the woman said:

"Thank you, Señora. You have children?"

"Back in England. I miss them."

"May you see them soon, Señora." The dark eyes shifted to Paul. "Your husband is an officer?"

"A colonel. Who is going to be in trouble if we don't catch up with the rest of his brigade before we reach the square," Anne said with a smile. "Enjoy the day, Señora. Adios, Diego."

Anne turned back to Paul and heard for the first time an enormous swell of cheering around her as the crowd acknowledged the small drama. Slightly pink cheeked, she allowed Jenson to lift her into the saddle and looked at her husband.

"Better get a move on, Colonel, before his Lordship starts yelling."

"He won't mind today. You should have married royalty, Nan, you're very good at this."

"Any more remarks like that and I'll slap you," Anne said succinctly, kicking Bella into a trot to move back up the parade to the head of the 110th. "Although it was a good thing you made me wear this ghastly hat, it turned out to have its uses."

"I am so glad," Paul said politely. "Jenson, that fan does not suit your particular style of beauty."

"I thought it was my colour, sir. You dropped this, ma'am."

Anne reached over and took the fan. "Thank you, Jenson. I will undoubtedly lose it before the end of today anyway, but it's been surprisingly useful in this heat."

"Where did you get it from?" Paul asked.

"It was a gift from Don Julian," Anne said demurely, and her husband made a rude noise.

"And what in God's name is Julian Sanchez doing, sending my wife gifts?"

"I was seated next to him at dinner one evening, in Lord Wellington's tent. I think I've received some form of gift every day since, it's embarrassing. He said that he wishes to see me in a mantilla and will find me the best lace he can in Salamanca. Although he was struggling to decide if he thought black or white would suit me better."

"If he has the audacity to send you a mantilla of any colour, girl of my heart, I am going to punch him," Paul said forcefully. "Don't you already have a rather attractive one that I bought you in Lisbon?"

"I do. It is black. I did tell Don Julian that. He was quite poetic about the contrast of black lace against..."

"In a minute, I am going to throw you off that horse," Paul said explosively. Around him, those of his officers who could hear were laughing. The parade was clattering into the Plaza Mayor and Anne looked around her at the glorious array of Romanesque churches and associated buildings.

"This is so lovely," she said. "Paul, it is barely noon and you have already threatened me with violence twice, is it necessary? As for poor Don Julian..."

Paul had dismounted and moved forward to lift her from her horse. Across the square, Lord Wellington was standing on the cathedral steps, surrounded by his staff and an adoring plethora of Spaniards, including half a dozen women who seemed to be vying to be close to him. Don Julian Sanchez, the Spanish guerrilla leader, was with him, a dark man in his thirties in a fur trimmed pelisse which must have been sweltering in the heat. Paul saw Wellington look over and Don Julian follow his gaze. He grinned and lifted Anne from her horse. As her feet touched the ground, he pulled her close against him and kissed her with considerable enjoyment in a manner totally unsuitable in such a public place and in full view of the commander-in-chief.

"Colonel van Daan."

The precise German tones of the commander of the Light Division made him raise his head. Alten was standing before him, his eyebrows raised. Paul laughed and released Anne.

"My apologies, sir. I was just making a point to Don Julian Sanchez about his exact position in relation to my wife. Shall we go in?"

"By all means," Alten said, offering his arm to Anne. "If I offer to escort her, are you likely to hit me?"

"No, sir, I trust you with her."

"I am not at all sure if that is a compliment or not," the Hanoverian said drily, and Paul burst into laughter. They moved towards the steps of the Cathedral and Paul paused by his men, who were lined up neatly outside.

"Sergeant-Major Carter."

"Yes, sir?"

"You can stand them down. After this we go back to our billet to change and then I have to endure around five hours of bad food, long speeches and Don Julian bloody Sanchez trying to put his hand on my wife's leg under the table."

"Make a change from Lord Wellington doing it, sir."

"That is not helpful, Sergeant-Major. You've all got a night's leave in town, but I want them back up to camp and sober by noon tomorrow or I'll be after them personally. Make sure they know I mean that."

"I thought you needed to keep an eye on your wife, sir, in case she runs off with a Spaniard."

Paul regarded his Sergeant-Major frostily. "Your sense of humour is one of the many reasons I promoted you, Carter. Don't get too drunk."

"I won't, sir. I'm off to collect my wife and my daughter and I'm going to spend what's left of my pay. Teresa's dying to show me around, we're close to her childhood home here, so she knew the city as a girl. I thought we could have supper in one of the taverns, take some time..."

Paul smiled. The marriage between his Sergeant-Major, a former pickpocket and cut-purse from the slums of Southwark and his wife's Spanish maidservant who had been both a nun and a prostitute, seemed to be turning out very well. Paul was ridiculously sentimental about Carter's obvious devotion to his wife. He fished into his pocket and took out two coins.

"On me," he said.

Carter looked down at the money and then up at Paul. "That's more than even a Spanish innkeeper can charge, sir."

"Spend the rest on a gift for your lass, Danny. Christ knows she earns it."

"I'm not that bad, sir. Hammond is going into town tonight, but he'll be back up and sober tomorrow, he'll chase up any stragglers."

"Carry on then, Sergeant-Major. Oh Jesus Christ, can I not trust Charles Alten to do anything? He's let Wellington get hold of my wife."

Carter was laughing. "Go and rescue her, sir. Thank you."

Paul marched up the steps to where Lord Wellington was placing Anne's hand onto his arm and saluted. "Did you enjoy the parade, sir?"

"No," his commander in chief said briefly. "Any more than you did. And I am sorry, Colonel, but I am borrowing your wife for a while, I need protection."

Paul glanced at the Spanish ladies, who had withdrawn to take their places in the congregation and suppressed a smile. "There's a fee, sir. If we're marching out in a day or so, I'd like a few hours off with her tomorrow, I need to take her shopping." Paul looked over at Sanchez, whose dark eyes were fixed on Anne's lovely face. "I thought I might buy her a mantilla in white, since she already has a black one. And perhaps a new fan."

Lord Wellington met his eyes in with a gleam of amusement. "As you wish, Colonel. Come my dear. I see that you are wearing my brooch. It looks charming on that jacket."

He moved ahead with Anne towards the cathedral and Paul looked around at Major Carl Swanson who commanded the first battalion of the 110th and was his closest friend. "I bloody hate him sometimes," he said. "Come on, let's get this over with."

The dinner dragged on endlessly with toasts and speeches in several languages which made Paul long to escape to the campfires outside town with a bottle of wine and the scurrilous wit of Corporal Dawson of his light company. Paul was seated too far from Anne to do more than exchange despairing glances with her. Anne looked back, smiling, not breaking off her animated conversation with the two middle aged Spanish dignitaries between whom she was seated. Anne was a natural linguist and had learned both Spanish and Portuguese since she had arrived in Lisbon three years earlier. Paul had always been slightly envious of her ability to study a subject and stick to it; he had the intelligence but not always the application, although his own language skills had improved immeasurably because of his dislike of being outdone by a slip of a girl nine years his junior.

Paul watched his wife through the interminable meal, replying to the voluble Spanish lady beside him when necessary and enjoying the sight of Anne, beautiful in a gown of black lace over a matching underskirt which she had had made for her in Elvas several months ago. Anne's wardrobe was, of necessity, very limited and Paul sometimes wished he could spoil her as much as she deserved. The problem was not money; he came from a wealthy family and could afford to be very generous with his gifts. But Anne's limited interest in fashion combined with the practical need to keep her baggage to a minimum, meant that she attended every headquarters party in the same gown. Anne clearly did not care and from the expression on the face of her dinner partner, who was almost drooling over her, neither did her Spanish hosts.

It was evening by the time Wellington was able to take his leave, and the air was cooler, still warm but with a very slight breeze. Paul collected his wife and led her outside to wait for their horses on the steps of the civic building. Lord Wellington had emerged and was awaiting his carriage, talking to Colonel Fitzroy Somerset, his young military secretary. Catching sight of Paul and Anne he beckoned, and Paul approached and saluted. Wellington bowed to Anne.

"Did you enjoy the celebrations, ma'am?"

"Very much, sir. The cathedral is beautiful, and these buildings..." Anne looked up towards the darkening sky, indicating the graceful lines of colleges and churches on the skyline. "One day I should love to spend some time here, seeing it properly."

"I wish I could oblige you now, ma'am. Sadly, I think we must be on the road tomorrow or the following day. Are your men ready, Colonel?"

Paul thought about the probable condition of his men at present, in the taverns and brothels of Salamanca, and kept his expression neutral. "Absolutely, sir," he said instantly.

Wellington's blue eyes gleamed with amusement. "I wonder if I should send the provost marshals into town this evening?" he said. "Just to make sure we have no strays."

"I wouldn't, sir," Paul said, seriously. "The sixth division are definitely out on a spree and they've had a difficult couple of weeks trying to storm those forts. I'd give them their head for an evening, they'll do better on the march if they feel they've had a holiday. If you wish, I'll send my light company down, they'll keep an eye on things and make sure nothing is getting out of hand and that our men are paying their way."

10

Wellington looked as though he could not decide how to respond to such blatant mendacity. Eventually he simply shook his head. "I will have my eye on them when we march, Colonel."

"Thanks for the warning, sir, we like to know when to expect you. Where next?"

Paul was not sure if his chief would answer. Wellington always kept his plans very close to his chest, but during the past weeks, Paul knew that he was genuinely unsure. He wanted to bring the French to battle and had set out from Portugal with just that intention, but he was also very conscious of the importance of keeping the French armies separated. A swift joining of forces from various parts of the Peninsula could leave the Allied army hopelessly outnumbered.

Paul thought that such a French combination was unlikely. He had been fighting under Wellington in Portugal and Spain for four years now and he knew that rivalry and jealousy between the various French commanders had more than once saved Wellington's smaller army from possible annihilation. In May, Wellington had sent Sir Rowland Hill with his second division, to destroy the pontoon bridge across the Tagus at Almaraz, effectively separating the armies of Marmont and Soult. Hill's assault had been successful, and Wellington had decided that Marmont should be the target of his planned attack.

Wellington was silent for a long time. Finally, he said:

"We'll go where the Marshal goes, Colonel. Towards the Duero, my sources tell me. General Alten has my orders."

"Yes, sir," Paul said. He could see the horses approaching, led by Jenson and the stocky, dark haired figure of Anne's new groom. Isair Costa had been groom and orderly to Captain Juan Peso who had commanded one of Paul's Portuguese companies and who had died in the horror of Badajoz. Paul missed the cheerful young officer from Oporto who had helped him learn Portuguese and joined in fencing lessons with some of Paul's other officers and he was glad that Anne had found a place for Costa. She had never employed a groom before, but her experience at the hands of the French earlier in the year had left both her and Paul slightly jumpy and he hoped that Costa's solid presence at her heels whenever she went out would help her to feel safe again.

"This may not be the easiest campaign for a lady, Colonel."

Both Paul and Anne turned to stare at the commander-in-chief. Wellington's dislike of having wives with the army was well known, but it had been a long time since he had shown any sign of objecting to Anne. Paul opened his mouth to say something, and felt his wife kick him painfully in the ankle. He closed it again and Anne smiled charmingly at Wellington.

"Do you think I should remain in Salamanca, my Lord?"

Wellington looked surprised. "No, ma'am. Not without your husband."

"My Lord, I am sorry, but I don't think I can face the thought of a journey to Lisbon without him. Not after last time."

Paul clamped his mouth shut so hard that his jaw ached. He could not

11

quite believe that his wife had just used the horror of her ordeal so blatantly, but the effect was extraordinary. Wellington's expressive face flushed, and he reached for Anne's hand and raised it to his lips.

"Ma'am, my humblest apologies. I was thinking aloud, nothing more. You must know that I would not ask you to do anything that might make you feel unsafe. My concern is always for your comfort and security, I am an ass to have spoken without thinking."

"I know, sir, I'm very grateful. I'll try not to be a trouble to you."

"You never are," Wellington said warmly.

"I had a letter from Murray yesterday," Paul said, searching desperately for an alternative topic of conversation before he began to laugh.

"I had one myself. Damned nuisance, him not being here. I miss him."

Paul grinned. General Murray, Wellington's long-time quartermaster-general had gone home on leave, and Wellington had received the news that he had been given a post in Ireland and would be replaced by Sir James Willoughby Gordon who was on his way to join the army. Paul knew nothing of the new man apart from rumours that he had been given the posting at the request of the Duke of York, whom he had previously served as military secretary. Wellington did not always enjoy easy relations with his staff, but he had come to trust Murray and Paul, who had once spent a few agonising months assisting the quartermasters' department in winter quarters, had enormous respect for Murray's organisational talent and immovable calm.

"Sir James will do fine, sir," he said soothingly.

"It is to be hoped that your optimism is justified, Colonel, or I will not hesitate to second you to his staff to bring him up to scratch," Wellington snapped. "It is ridiculous the number of men I am losing; they are constantly asking for leave. Murray has gone, I'm losing Picton and Graham..."

"Sir, that is not fair. Picton's wound has broken open three times, he needs time for it to heal and he won't get it out here. And poor Graham is going to go blind if that eye infection doesn't clear up. You'll have Cole back, you like him. As for Picton's division..."

"Picton wants me to give it to my brother-in-law," Wellington said.

"I'd take his advice, sir, he knows what he's doing."

"Possibly. Are you remaining in the city tonight?"

"Yes, sir, we've got quarters in one of the old colleges, but my officers will be up at dawn to ride out to camp and make sure the men are ready to march."

Wellington took Anne's hand and kissed it, then looked at Paul.

"I see no reason for them to take so much trouble, Colonel," he said smoothly. "I imagine if they simply walk up to the city gate, they will be able to catch most of them on their way back from their excesses in the brothels and taverns of Salamanca. Good night, ma'am."

# Chapter Two

The small party of officers ran into the sentries during the late afternoon, their first indication that they were close to the British army. By that time, they had been riding since early morning under a fierce heat and despite several stops to water and rest the horses, all four of them were tired, riding at walking pace and with little conversation.

It was a relief to be challenged by a stocky corporal in a red coat with silver grey facings who stepped forward leaving his three comrades relaxing in the shade of a small cork oak plantation.

"Who goes there, sir?"

"Officers of the British army, damn your hide," Captain Vane snapped and Lieutenant Witham glanced across at Lieutenant Carlyon and rolled his eyes. Ensign Anderson, who was very young and unsure carefully did not look at either of them. On the long journey north from Lisbon, Witham had formed a bond with Carlyon, based almost entirely on their mutual dislike of Captain Vane. The man was rude, arrogant and unpleasant to be around and Witham felt sorry for Anderson who was new to the army and was going to have to serve with Vane in the 117th. Both Witham and Carlyon were from the 115th North Yorkshire, Carlyon fresh from service with the second battalion in India and Witham transferred in for promotion after a spell at the Cape of Good Hope. They had met on the transport from England and had swapped battle stories around the fire during their trip. Vane had joined in with enthusiasm. He was older than both of them, formerly with the 87th and had fought in Portugal and Spain before. Witham personally wondered about some of the stories. If Vane had been half as heroic and daring as his tales suggested, he should have been at least a Major by now.

The Corporal saluted with a smartness that was almost ludicrous. "Yes, sir. Begging your pardon, I'd guessed that you were officers. But it's my job to ask which officers and where you're bound. Army's spread out a bit, you'll need directions."

The other three men had got to their feet and were walking forward. One of them, a long-limbed man in his thirties with a good-natured expression, wore a sergeant-major's stripes on his coat. As they approached, Captain Vane lifted his riding crop and slashed at the Corporal. Witham flinched; he had seen

Vane do it before. Carlyon gave an exclamation of protest, but it was unnecessary; the Corporal moved with unbelievable speed and the crop slashed across the arm he had raised to protect his face. Vane stared in disbelief.

"You impudent, bastard," he said slowly. "Put down your arm and stand still."

The Corporal lowered his arm. Carlyon said:

"Sir, there's no need, he's only doing his job."

"Mind your own business, Mr Carlyon," Vane said softly. "Move a bit closer, Corporal. I don't want to have to stretch my arm too much."

The corporal remained where he was, his expression impassive. Vane raised his arm high.

"Corporal Cooper, step back, would you?" a voice said clearly. "Don't want to get in the way of the officer."

Witham caught his breath. The tall Sergeant-Major was coming forward, his pleasant expression gone. Without any sign of hesitation, he put his hand on Cooper's arm and moved him back out of range of Vane's crop, stepping between his Corporal and the Captain.

Vane's face was scarlet with anger. "How dare you? I'm going to have the skin off your back and those stripes off your arm for this, you piece of scum. What's your name?"

"Sergeant-Major Carter, sir, 110th light infantry. I serve under Colonel van Daan; best take your complaint to him."

Vane had lowered his arm. He looked, for the first time since Witham had met him, slightly uncertain. "Van Daan. Don't know him, but if you're an example of the men he commands, it's a bloody disgrace."

"You can tell him that in person, sir, I'll give you directions," Carter said impassively. "My apologies if I seemed rude, it's just that it's against army regulations for an officer to beat the men and I wouldn't want you to get into trouble. Probably best if you take your complaints to Colonel van Daan and see if he feels it warrants a charge."

Witham realised he was not breathing at all. There was a very long moment of silence. Vane did not seem able to speak. Finally, he did so, and the words came out on a hiss of sheer fury.

"I shall remember your name, Carter, and your face. You'll slip up sooner or later and I will have the hide off you."

"Very good, sir," Carter said. His expression was a study in indifference and Witham struggled not to laugh aloud. "Might I ask which regiment you're searching for?"

Witham decided it was time to intervene. "This is Captain Vane, Sergeant-Major and Ensign Anderson, both for the 117th. Mr Carlyon and I are looking for the 115th."

"Very good, sir. The 117th are with the sixth division, they're with the main army at Medina del Campo, it's about six miles south-east of here. The 115th are serving with the Light Division up at Rueda; it's also where Lord Wellington has established headquarters. It's only a mile or so from here. Our relief pickets are on their way down, if you can wait a short time, I can show you the way up." Carter looked at Vane. "Captain Vane, it's entirely up to you, sir, but you could come up with us and find a billet for the night, set out tomorrow to join your regiment."

"Thank you, Sergeant-Major" Witham said appreciatively. "It's been a long trip."

"I expect it has, sir. Why don't you come through here, there's a stream beyond the trees. It's a bit low but you can water the horses and cool off a bit."

It was pleasantly shady in the small copse and the stream ran clear and clean. Witham watered his horse and tethered him to a tree while Carlyon and Vane's grooms did the same. Witham had brought no servant with him, having grown accustomed to managing his own kit and his horse with occasional help from one of the men of his company.

Witham had gained the impression during his conversations with Simon Carlyon, that his fellow officer was from a similar background to himself. Witham's family, like Carlyon's, were small landowners from old county families, Carlyon's from Yorkshire and Witham's from Sussex but unlike Carlyon, Witham was a younger son with two sisters who would require dowries in the future and he refused to ask his brother for any more financial help than was strictly necessary. He had found, during the journey, that his new acquaintance was more than willing to share the services of the taciturn, middle aged Reynolds and Witham appreciated it, but he did not wish to presume too much.

With the horses tethered, Witham joined Carlyon who was stretched out on the dry, sparse grass by the riverbank.

"Bloody dry here," Carlyon said. "Not good country for cavalry when the supply line fails."

"No," Witham agreed. "I'm glad we're close by, I'd rather not ride another six miles in the morning. Poor Anderson."

"Especially since he's got to ride those six miles with Captain Vane, and without the leavening joy of our society," Carlyon said and they both laughed.

They sat quietly for a while, listening to the gentle rush of the water over stones. Behind them, the men were talking, with an occasional burst of laughter, and further away, Witham could hear the aggressively loud tones of Captain Vane, complaining to Ensign Anderson. Witham glanced at his companion, who was aimlessly throwing pebbles into the water.

Witham had been conscious over the past couple of days that Carlyon's cheerful banter seemed a little forced as they drew closer to their destination. Witham did not think his companion was worried about going into battle; Carlyon had fought for some years in India and had more actual battle experience than Witham. He might, he supposed, be slightly nervous about the transition to light infantry, which was new to both of them.

The 115th had always been a traditional line regiment. It was one of the newer regiments, raised during the long years of the war against France and had a chequered history. There were currently two battalions, one of which was in Spain and the other in India. Witham had been commissioned an ensign with the 120th four years earlier. His first campaign had been the horror of Walcheren and he had then been sent to Cape Town, but he had applied, as soon as he could afford it, for a transfer to a regiment fighting in Europe. The 115th had been cheap and Witham was not wealthy. He had been surprised and delighted to be informed on arrival in Lisbon, that the 115th was now part of the third brigade of the Light Division and that he and Carlyon would receive training in the field to fight as light infantry.

Witham had spent the journey alternately studying Spanish and devouring several second-hand training manuals which he had picked up cheaply in Lisbon where the personal effects of officers killed in action were often auctioned off. He found the subject absorbing and could not wait to see how the theory worked in the field. Carlyon had seemed taken aback by the change initially, but during the journey he had borrowed Witham's books and they had spent hours discussing the various drills and manoeuvres and speculating on their new battalion, which had apparently suffered appalling losses in the bloody storming of Badajoz, including that of Major Stead, the battalion commander. Witham had thought his companion as enthusiastic as he was about learning new skills, but Carlyon's endless flow of conversation seemed to have abruptly dried up.

"Are you all right?" Witham asked, slightly awkwardly. They had never discussed personal matters and he was not sure how to begin.

Carlyon looked startled. "Sorry? Oh - yes, of course."

He did not sound it. Witham studied him for a few moments to see if he would say more. He was trying to decide if their friendship had reached the point yet where he could push beyond Simon's polite denial.

"You don't seem it," Witham said finally. "Look, old chap, it's none of my damned business, I know. But something's bothering you. If you want to talk, I'm here."

Simon Carlyon turned to look at him and gave a somewhat forced smile. "You might wish you'd not asked," he said.

"I won't. It can't be bad news from home, we've not had mail. What is it, Simon?"

The other man sat up from his lounging pose and took a deep breath. "I'd rather not tell you, but I'm going to have to. I should have told you about it before, there's no way to keep it quiet. I believe it was quite the scandal at the time."

"Scandal?" Witham said, bewildered. He had been expecting another polite denial and was somewhat surprised at his companion's sudden willingness to confide.

"Yes. And if I don't tell you, somebody else will. I'd rather you heard it from me," Carlyon said. He sounded depressed and it bothered Witham. "It happened just after I joined. My older brother was in the regiment but moved on to the quartermasters' department and came out to Portugal in 1809 with Wellington – Wellesley as he was then. He brought a young wife with him."

Witham was surprised. "I didn't know you'd a brother in the service," he said.

"I don't, he's dead. He was killed a couple of years ago and we don't really talk about him. He married not long after I joined, a local girl. She's about the same age as me so I knew her better than Robert when we were young - hunting and tea parties and such like. After that, of course, I was away at school a lot and then I joined up. I remember her very well, though. When I heard Robert had married her, I remember thinking how lucky he was. Her father was wealthy, a local textile manufacturer, it must have been a good dowry. But she was so beautiful."

"Was?" Witham asked.

"Probably still is, she can't be more than twenty-two or three." Carlyon gave a painful smile. "Robert did all right, earned a promotion to captain. But I'm not sure the marriage went all that well. My father always said he'd married her just for the money, he didn't entirely approve. Robert was like that; always wanting more. My father has a good little estate and was the local MP for years. Enough for a respectable income. We were all shocked when Robert chose the army; he didn't need to. But he wanted fame and fortune. It didn't come quickly enough, and I think he saw Anne Howard as a comfortable living. Maybe she resented that. We heard all sorts of rumours, but in the end, he was charged as a thief and a deserter, he'd run off with money from the army pay chest. There was a warrant out for his arrest, it broke my mother's heart. And then we were told he'd died – shot while attacking his wife, by another officer."

"Oh Christ, Carlyon, I am sorry," Witham said, appalled. "Bloody awful for your family"

"It was. My father wanted me to sell out. He said I'd never get anywhere with Robert's reputation following me around. But it wasn't so bad, a lot of people don't make the connection, and I liked the army, I didn't want to leave. I served time in India and then was offered promotion to lieutenant in the first battalion. I thought I'd be all right, even out here." Carlyon gave a painful smile. "It was almost a point of pride for me, that I could live it down. Some stupid idea about restoring the family honour, I suppose. I was an idiot, but it might have worked. And then, when we arrived in Lisbon, I heard where we were serving."

"Why does that make a difference?" Witham asked.

"Because she remarried. Very quickly." There was bitterness in Carlyon's voice. "He's now the commander of the third brigade of the Light Division and that's where we're serving, Nick. And I'm fairly sure my former sister-in-law isn't going to want me in her husband's brigade. So I'm rather wondering, if I'm about to be transferred somewhere else or sent home on half pay."

"Surely she can't do that," Witham said. He felt a rush of indignation on behalf of his friend. "It's nothing to do with you, what your brother did, and it sounds as though she wasn't entirely innocent."

"Perhaps not, I don't know enough about it. But it's more complicated than that; the man who shot him is very senior in the brigade. I'm not naive,

Nick, I'm on my way out. I just don't know where."

Witham could think of nothing to say. "I'm sorry, Simon," he managed eventually. "It's so bloody unfair."

"It's army politics, old man. We both know how it works."

Carlyon's revelations cast a slight gloom over Witham, and he was glad when the sound of marching feet heralded the arrival of the new pickets. Sergeant-Major Carter went to meet them, and Carlyon and Witham rose, brushed off their dusty trousers and went through the trees to find half a dozen men in the same uniform and an officer on horseback. Sergeant -Major Carter appeared to be explaining the new arrivals. When he had done, he saluted and went to speak to the new pickets, giving them instructions and the officer walked his horse to where the four new arrivals waited.

He was a pleasant-faced man, probably in his late twenties or early thirties, with mid-brown hair neatly tied back and a pair of shrewd green eyes. A major's insignia adorned a coat which had seen considerably better days. Both coat and trousers were patched and stained, and it made Witham acutely conscious of his very new uniform; he felt like a greenhorn next to the Major's battle stained garments. He saluted and was aware that the other officers had moved forward, doing the same. The Major returned the salute.

"Welcome to Spain, gentlemen. You must be exhausted, travelling in this heat. Major Carl Swanson, first battalion, 110th. I've been riding the lines, checking all the pickets are behaving themselves, but I'll ride back up to the village with you."

Witham was surprised; picket duty was the province of junior officers, with a captain in overall charge. Something must have shown in his expression because Major Swanson grinned.

"It isn't my job, but it's a good excuse to exercise this lad and besides, every now and then I like to surprise them with a visit, it keeps them awake. Names?"

"Nicholas Witham, sir, and this is Simon Carlyon. Both for the second company."

"Welcome to the Light Division, gentlemen. Mount up while I speak to these officers and then we'll have a chat on the way, and I'll tell you what's been going on."

Witham and Carlyon obeyed, and Major Swanson rode over to Vane and Anderson. Witham saw him talking quietly with them for a few minutes, then he turned his horse.

"Major Swanson," Vane said loudly, and Carlyon looked at Witham.

"Oh, no."

"If he makes up some shit to get that NCO into trouble, I am telling the truth, Simon, I'm bloody sick of him," Witham said very quietly.

"I'm with you," Carlyon said. They watched as the Major turned his mount back and looked enquiringly at Captain Vane. Vane stepped forward.

"I have a complaint to make, sir, and a serious one. About that NCO - Carter, is it?"

"Sergeant-Major Carter?" Major Swanson enquired politely.

"If that's what he is," Vane said contemptuously.

"Oh, I'm fairly sure that's what he is, Captain," the Major said cordially. "What's the problem?"

"He was insolent. Spoke to me disrespectfully and interfered with discipline. The man is a disgrace, he should be flogged and demoted. I was shocked; no NCO of mine would speak to me that way."

The Major looked over at Carter. "Is that true, Sergeant-Major?"

"I've no idea, sir, I've never met any of Captain Vane's NCOs," Carter said, straight-faced.

"Don't get bloody clever with me, Sergeant-Major, I have not had my dinner yet," the Major said. "Did you actually do anything?"

"Not intentionally, sir. Bit of a mix up."

"Right. Apologise to Captain Vane for confusing him."

Carter looked over at Vane, and Witham recognised, with dawning delight, that Major Swanson required no explanation and was completely uninterested in Vane's complaint.

"Sorry you became confused, Captain," Carter said warmly. "Sincerely didn't intend it to happen, I'll try to be much clearer in future."

Vane looked nonplussed and Witham did not blame him. Carlyon was leaning forward, pretending to adjust his bridle to hide his laughter.

"Captain Vane. Accept Sergeant-Major Carter's apology."

Vane looked as though he would have liked to argue, but something in the young Major's steady gaze seemed to prevent it. He muttered something which might have been an acceptance. Major Swanson nodded.

"Right. Glad that crisis is averted, let's get going before I miss supper. Danny, I'm going to ride on ahead with these gentlemen, see you back in camp."

"Yes, sir."

They rode in silence for a short while. Vane had dropped back to ride beside Anderson. Eventually, Major Swanson said:

"They'll have told you in Lisbon, I imagine, what happened at Badajoz?"

"Some of it, sir," Witham said. "And that we'd been attached to the Light Division. I was sorry to hear about Major Stead although I didn't know him."

"No, you came in from the 120th, didn't you?"

"Yes, sir."

"I didn't know Major Stead that well myself, he'd only been around for a couple of weeks. The battalion is under the command of Major Corrigan now, newly promoted from the 112th. You'll be under Captain Lewis, who also transferred in from the 112th. I'm not sure if you're aware how badly the 115th got mauled at Badajoz, they're short of officers and men at present so you'll be very welcome." The Major glanced behind him at Vane. "Have you been with him all the way from Lisbon?"

"Yes, sir."

"That must have been a real joy."

19

Witham gave a choke of laughter. "Let's say I'm glad I'm not bound for the 117th," he said cautiously. "Not really my kind of officer, sir."

"I'm glad to hear it, Mr Witham." Major Swanson was regarding Carlyon with a thoughtful expression. "The 115th, Mr Carlyon? Are you from Yorkshire?"

"Yes, sir."

Witham heard the change in Carlyon's tone with a sinking heart. He looked at the Major and realised that he knew, but he said in the same easy, pleasant tone:

"Colonel van Daan did a spell in Yorkshire years ago in temporary command of your regiment. He…"

"I'm his younger brother, sir."

Swanson studied the other man. "I see. Have you heard that question often, Mr Carlyon?"

"A few times. Mostly from men who served out here, but I suppose I'm going to hear it a lot more now."

Major Swanson sighed. "Very likely," he said. "I'm sorry, lad, your life just got more complicated, but then I imagine you've already worked that out."

"Yes, sir. I've been worrying about it ever since Lisbon."

Witham looked from one to the other, feeling uncomfortable. "Look, this feels like something that's none of my business," he said. "I'll drop back…"

"No." Simon Carlyon shot him a quick smile. "It's all right, Nicholas, you already know, and it's clear the Major does too. I imagine Colonel van Daan will see me as soon as possible and let me know where I'm to serve."

Major Swanson gave a little smile. "Don't be so hasty, Mr Carlyon. I told you, the Colonel is short of good officers, he's not going to want to lose you unless he can help it. Wait until you've spoken to him at least."

"That's good of you, sir, but I imagine the Colonel will put his wife's comfort ahead of an officer he's never even met."

"The Colonel will do what's best for the brigade, lad, and she wouldn't ask him to do anything other. Keep your tongue between your teeth and give it a chance, this may not be as bad as you think. Here we are, it's up this way. The Light Division is based in and around the village and Lord Wellington has moved his headquarters up here to be closer to the centre. He's waiting to see what the French do, so we might have a week or two here. Then again, we might be on general alert in a couple of hours. There's been fierce competition for billets in the village, but the Colonel has left that fight to the first and second brigades. We're camped out this way in tents. There's been some sickness among the troops; our men seem mostly clear of it so far and the Colonel wants to keep it that way."

The camp was laid out at the top of a long ridge, with a view over acres of cattle pasture and vineyards and then on to the river. In the bluish light of evening there was a softness to the landscape, but Witham thought it seemed a dry, harsh land although surprisingly fertile. He had seen cattle as they rode up, mostly black or grey with long horns and the hardy build of draft animals. There were flocks of goats roaming the scrubby uplands, but it was clear that the main crop of the area was the vine.

The area felt arid and remote. Unlike the neat rows of vines that Witham had seen in Portugal, these were stubby plants crouched low to the flat ground and spread far apart. From a farming family, he guessed this was to enable the roots to grow deep, essential in such a hot, dry climate which could turn frosty overnight.

"Wine making," Major Swanson said, glumly. "It's one of the reasons I'm out checking up on our men more often than usual. Keeping this lot sober is a twenty-four hour a day task just now. The whole army is as bored as we are with nothing to do, but unlike them, we are sitting right on top of an extensive underground network of wine cellars and caves that go back centuries. The 95th have already lost one man who drowned in a vat of wine, and yesterday Sergeant Duffy of my sixth company hauled two very sorry specimens out of the river half dead because they got drunk and went for a swim. Gave a great laugh to the French watching on the opposite bank."

"They're that close, then?" Witham said, surprised. "The French."

"They're camped on the other side. You'll see them in the morning, it's all very friendly. A lot of the men go down to bathe in the river and they're doing the same. I give them a couple of days and they'll be exchanging rations and splashing each other, I've seen it before."

"Is that allowed, sir?" Carlyon asked.

"Probably not officially, Lieutenant, but I'm not going to stop them. It doesn't do any harm, occasionally, to remember that we're all men. Up this path."

The horses negotiated the rocky pathway with care, and Witham looked down in some surprise on a well organised circle of large tents, around a number of cooking fires. Beyond that, were neat rows of smaller white tents, divided into blocks which might denote companies and battalions. Each section had its share of bigger tents for the officers and the smoke of numerous fires streamed lazily into the stillness of the late afternoon air. Sentries were dotted about in small groups around the edges of the camp, which must have stretched for at least a mile, and there was a smell of food cooking which made Witham's stomach rumble in protest.

Witham was struck by the number of women and children about as they made their way through the lines towards the larger tents in the centre. He was accustomed to the presence of some wives and camp followers with the army but there seemed an unusually large number here. At the edge of the inner circle, Major Swanson reined in and swung himself down from the saddle.

Two men, privates in the uniform of the 110th came forward immediately to take the horses. Witham dismounted uncertainly and was immersed in a small wave of efficiency as other men came to deal with luggage and to speak to Carlyon's groom. Witham stood watching in some bewilderment. He was more accustomed to arriving unheralded into an army camp and scrabbling to find space to put up his tent or graze his horse.

A voice was raised from a tent on the far side of the open square. "Major Swanson," it roared, and Witham jumped. "Where the devil have you been, I thought you'd fallen into the river and drowned yourself. How long does it take to ensure that the pickets are sober?"

"That depends on the pickets, sir," Major Swanson said placidly, beckoning to the newcomers and making his way across the square. "We've got guests for dinner."

"Have we? Well, ship them in then. Although if one of them is planning on hitting my men with a riding crop he's going to end up headfirst in Sergeant Kelly's beef stew."

A tall figure was striding towards them, a fair-haired man of around thirty with an attractive smile and a pair of deep blue eyes. He wore the insignia of a colonel although he seemed young for his rank, but Witham supposed it must be the commander of the third brigade of the light division. He saluted and the other man returned the salute.

Major Swanson was laughing. "How the bloody hell did Carter get back here ahead of me?"

"Apparently there's a shortcut up through one of the wine caves, you couldn't do it with a horse. He's got a funny sense of humour," the Colonel said. "Welcome to the Light Division, gentlemen. Come and get a drink, supper will be ready soon. Bet you're sick to death of travelling. If you're lucky you might get a week's break before Marmont makes up his mind which way he's going."

Major Swanson came forward. "Sir, these are Captain Vane and Ensign Anderson who are for the 117th. I've said they can stick with us tonight and we can find them a guide tomorrow to where the sixth are bivouacked."

"I expect we can find space for them," the Colonel said. The blue eyes rested on Captain Vane thoughtfully. "Vane? The name's familiar, have you been out here before, Captain?"

Vane saluted stiffly. "Yes, sir. I fought with the 87th up until..."

"Talavera," Van Daan said quietly. "Cadiz after that I believe?"

"Yes, sir, although I wasn't aware, we'd met."

"I don't think we did." There was a stillness about the Colonel and Witham was irrationally glad that his new commanding officer was not directing that particular look at him. "I've a memory for names, though." The blue eyes moved to Anderson and Paul van Daan smiled. "Mr Anderson, welcome. Don't look so worried, you'll get used to it."

"Yes, sir."

The Colonel glanced at Witham and Carlyon. "And by your uniforms I think I'll be seeing more of you two. Second company?"

"Yes, sir," Witham said. He was conscious of a feeling of belligerent protectiveness. "We only recently realised we were fighting as light infantry."

"It's a recent change, we're still working on training, so you've not missed much. Apart from Badajoz and believe me, that was not a loss. I'm sorry, I didn't catch your names."

Major Swanson intervened. "This is Mr Witham, sir, recently of the 120th, transferred for promotion. And Mr Carlyon is local to the regiment and has been serving with the second battalion in India."

Witham found that he was holding his breath. Paul van Daan looked at Simon Carlyon for a long moment. Carlyon saluted and stood very still. Suddenly the Colonel smiled.

"You look like him," he said quietly. "Not your colouring, but the shape of your face and your eyes. I don't think we met, did we? Weren't you at school?"

"I'd left by then, sir, I was already with the regiment, an ensign."

"How are your parents?" the Colonel said. Knowing what he did, Witham was surprised by the question and he could see that Carlyon was too.

"They're well enough, sir. Father retired you know."

"I know. My brother-in-law George Howard took over his seat."

Carlyon took a deep breath. "Look, sir, I realise…"

"Not here," Paul van Daan said quickly. "It's personal to both of us." He glanced over at one of the orderlies. "Jenson, will you get Captain Vane and Mr Anderson settled and make sure they've everything they need, then you can bring them over for supper, it'll be ready by then. And get Mr Ashford to escort Mr Witham here over to the 115th. My compliments to Major Corrigan, I'd like them both to dine with us this evening. Oh, and Jenson?"

"Sir?"

"Make sure some of the men set up their tents and unpack for them, will you? They're an idle bunch in the 115th, they won't do it otherwise."

"I'll send Browning with Mr Ashford, sir, he can supervise them."

"Thank you. This way, Mr Carlyon."

***

Simon Carlyon followed the Colonel into a large tent. It was clear that this was the Colonel's headquarters as well as his sleeping quarters; part of it was split off with a makeshift curtain, separating the sleeping area. The rest was scattered with boxes and chests, a portable washstand, a campaign table strewn with paperwork and a smaller folding table with several camp chairs set around it. There was an elegant portable writing desk which appeared to have been abandoned, open, in the middle of the floor. A lace shawl was draped over the back of one of the camp chairs, and a woman's straw hat lay in solitary splendour on top of a chest.

The Colonel grinned and picked up the shawl and hat, moving them to the far side of the tent, then lifted the writing desk out of the way. "Looks as though my wife has been in," he said, and turned as another man entered the tent, a tall dark sergeant in his twenties carrying a ledger. He placed it on the desk and saluted.

"There you are sir. I thought you'd deserted after this afternoon's effort."

"What effort?" the Colonel demanded. "What have I missed?"

23

"You not heard?" The Sergeant grinned. "The fourth company found a wine cellar unguarded and decided to celebrate. Captain Barry has just gone down there now."

Colonel van Daan froze. "I thought the fourth company were supposed to be on picket duty on the north ridge."

"They were, sir. The cave is cut just below it."

"How many of them?" the Colonel said in a strained tone.

"Pretty much all of them, I think, sir. Don't worry, Major Clevedon has sent out fresh pickets from the 112th instead and Captain Barry..."

"No," the Colonel said firmly. "This is the sixth incident in three days, it stops now. Get over there, Hammond, take a guard from the light company and keep them there until I arrive. My compliments to Captain Barry, but I'm dealing with this lot personally."

"Yes, sir."

Hammond left the tent and Paul van Daan went to a bound chest where wine and several cups were set out. "Sit down, Mr Carlyon, and have a drink. When did you realise who you were serving under?"

"In Lisbon, sir."

"That thought must have kept you occupied most of the way."

"Yes, sir. I didn't expect to meet you so soon. I was going to try to talk to Major Stead, first..."

"You've heard about him?"

"I have now, sir. I'm sorry, I didn't know him. It sounds as though it was bad."

"It was a bloody disaster," the Colonel said frankly, opening one of the bottles and pouring two cups. "The 115th had only joined the brigade two weeks earlier. They were intended for the seventh division, but they'd been having a few disciplinary problems and Lord Wellington thought they might do better with me. They weren't trained as light infantry but that hardly matters when storming a town and I'd hoped we'd have time to work with them. They hit a mine going over the wall. There were six companies, around five hundred officers and men. A hundred dead and another hundred and ten wounded."

"Dear God."

"It was horrible. It took out a fair few from my German and Portuguese battalions as well. We've got reinforcements coming in steadily but most of them are raw troops and we're short of officers, so you'll be very welcome."

There was a brief pause. Simon took a deep breath. "Will I, sir?" he asked.

Colonel van Daan folded his long length into a camp chair and pointed to the one opposite.

"Have a drink," he said quietly, and sipped his wine. "I'd no idea that Robert's younger brother had joined up. I'm not sure how that one got past me but I'm hopeless with the gossip, I never listen."

Simon sat down awkwardly. "I joined when I left school. I was in India when the letter came to say that he'd been charged in his absence with

24

theft and desertion. My parents were devastated."

"They must have been. They were good people, I liked them very much. I stayed with them for a while when I was in Yorkshire. The barracks were not fit to live in when I first got there, and it was terrible weather. Your brother was a big help to me, I employed him as quartermaster. We were quite friendly."

"Did you know her then? His…your wife?"

The Colonel nodded soberly. "Yes. He'd mentioned that there was a lass he was trying to court, and I'd worked out it was for money, but that was his business. I've never struggled for money, Lieutenant, so I've never felt able to judge on that score. I met her by accident during a snowstorm."

"I remember how beautiful she was, sir."

"She was seventeen and I'd honestly never met a girl like her before, but I was already married. After I left, she married Robert. I met them again about a year later on a transport to Portugal."

"I never saw either of them again," Carlyon said. "When we heard, my father begged me to sell out. He said I'd never have a career with his reputation following me around and besides, I was his heir now. But I'd always wanted the army, more so than Robert did. And I did all right."

The Colonel sipped the wine. "Can you tell me what you know about what happened to your brother, Lieutenant? I've never been sure what your family was told, which is why I've never written to your parents, although I wanted to."

Carlyon set his cup on the table. "My parents were told that he had deserted and stolen army money, that he would be cashiered in his absence and his effects sold to cover some of the loss. After a time, a letter came to say that he'd been shot dead by a senior officer because he attacked and tried to murder his wife."

"Is that it?" Van Daan asked quietly.

"Not entirely. My parents had a letter from your wife after she married you. It explained the circumstances in more detail. Up until then I had assumed that it was you who had shot him."

"I see."

"I gather there was some mistreatment of his wife, sir."

"He used to beat her. Badly."

"I've run into a few men since then who were out here at the time, they all have their own version of the story. I try not to listen."

"Good man, they'll all be bollocks. Very few people know what actually happened that day. All right, Mr Carlyon, I'm going to tell you the truth. If you're going to find it hard to serve in my brigade, we can arrange a transfer to another. It won't be hard, the army is screaming for good officers, somebody will take my arm off."

"What makes you think I'm any good, sir?"

"Because your brother was. He worked in administration, no real combat experience, but he was very good at what he did. Reliable, clever, quick, got on well with both junior and senior officers and didn't seem to struggle with the men. I liked him when I first met him, but it turned out I was wrong about him. He was a good officer but he'd a problem with women and he beat his wife regularly and brutally. You'll hear, in some circles that it was because she and I were sharing a bed. We weren't. He was jealous of any man who looked at her. He'd deliberately compromised her reputation to force her to marry him because he wanted her money, but within a year he was completely obsessed with her. I will readily admit that I wanted to kill him, but I didn't. He was shot dead by one of my officers while he had a pistol pointed at her head."

Simon Carlyon did not speak. He could feel his stomach churning. He had heard the basics of the story, but it was never spoken of at home, and his friends in the regiment knew better than to mention it around him. He drank the wine and they sat in silence for a few minutes.

"I'm sorry, lad. It's not pretty."

"I know. Look, sir, you've been really good about this, more so than I expected."

"There is a 'but' in there, isn't there, Mr Carlyon?"

Carlyon shook his head. "I don't know," he said. "I don't know what I feel. When I applied for this promotion, I knew, realistically, that I might meet you - and her. But I didn't expect to be serving under you. Besides…"

"Go on."

Carlyon looked up and met the blue eyes steadily. "Is he still here?" he asked. "The man who killed my brother?"

Colonel van Daan was silent for a long time, giving Carlyon the answer he needed. Finally, he said:

"Yes. I could lie to you, but once it becomes known who you are - and it will - some arsehole will tell you."

"I already know his name, sir, it isn't something you forget that easily. Captain Wheeler."

"Actually, it's Colonel Wheeler these days. He commands the 112th and is my second-in-command."

Carlyon felt a flood of pure rage. He set down his glass. "Then I think I had better apply for a transfer, sir. Because I don't feel able to salute the man who shot my brother dead."

There was a painful silence. It was broken by a sound at the tent flap. Colonel van Daan looked around and then got to his feet. "I thought you'd be longer," he said quietly, and Carlyon did not need to guess who was there. The expression on his formidable Colonel's face had warmed and softened. Carlyon rose and turned, and a girl came into the tent.

"Am I de trop? I can go away and come back later…oh dear God!"

Simon Carlyon studied his former sister-in-law. He had not seen her since they were both in their early teens and he had sometimes wondered if his memory had exaggerated her beauty, but it had not. She was tall and slender with shining dark hair which she wore in an unusual style, low on her neck, and almond shaped dark eyes which looked almost black. The perfection of her features was as he had remembered it, made lovelier as she had grown into young womanhood, and her figure was enhanced by the cut of the wine-coloured riding habit. She was a woman male eyes must follow everywhere and for two years she had belonged to his brother Robert who had, if Colonel van Daan's simple story were true, used her brutally. Looking at her, Carlyon wondered how any man could want to hurt a girl as young and lovely as this one.

"Mrs van Daan. I'm sorry…"

The girl came fully into the tent dropping the flap. There was an upheaval behind her, and Carlyon stared at the sound. Anne sighed. "Do you like dogs?"

"Dogs?" Carlyon said, disoriented. "Yes. But…"

"Good." Anne van Daan lifted the flap. "Come in, Craufurd. Don't jump on the Colonel, he's not changed yet."

A huge dog of indeterminate parentage erupted into the room and went straight to Colonel van Daan, shoving its large head into his hand. Paul van Daan bent to ruffle the shaggy ears.

"Good evening, Craufurd. Don't hesitate to cover my uniform in dog hairs, will you, Jenson has nothing better to do than brush it? Bed. Now."

The dog padded to a blanket on the floor and settled down comfortably and Carlyon turned his gaze back to Anne. She was studying him.

"Simon Carlyon. I didn't even know you were in the army, let alone in the 115th. I don't know whether to shake your hand or embrace you. Seeing you takes me right back to those dreadful dancing lessons with the Battersleys' Italian dancing master."

"Oh – I'd forgotten that." The memory brought laughter, the last thing Carlyon had expected from this meeting. "Didn't he…?"

"Yes, he seduced Frances Dearburn, who cannot have been more than sixteen and ran away with her. Shocking man. I must have been about thirteen when he tried to kiss me in the schoolroom. Dancing with him was a constant battle, his hands were everywhere."

"I am trying to imagine you at thirteen, girl of my heart, and I have more sympathy with the Italian dancing master than is at all suitable," the Colonel said, sounding amused. "Why did he run off with Miss Dearburn and not you?"

"Possibly the slap around the face put him off me a little, but I rather suspect he disliked me in the end when I began to question his knowledge of Italian. I had learned a little from my music master, you know. I've always wondered where he was really from."

"There are more Italians in your girlhood than I'm comfortable with. Did you murder the farrier?"

"No, but I supervised him redoing the shoe very carefully. He's competent enough, just lazy. Sit down, Simon. I'm rather guessing this is not a social visit; the uniform gives it away. Are you posted here?"

Carlyon nodded. "I've been with the second battalion in India, got the chance of promotion. Second company. I didn't realise until I got to Lisbon…I am sorry, ma'am."

"Oh, for what, don't be silly," the girl said warmly. "As if anything that happened between your brother and I, three or four years ago has anything to do with you. It is good to see you. I had a dreadful tendre for you that summer."

Her husband gave a splutter of laughter. "No, I am not listening to this. I have no objection to you serving under me on principle, Carlyon, but if she is going to spend her entire time reliving her girlish devotion…"

"Ignore him," Anne said calmly. "How are your parents, Simon?"

"They're well, thank you," Carlyon said. "I'll be honest with you, ma'am, I wasn't expecting you to be so welcoming."

"Well I wasn't expecting you at all, so we're both surprised here. Simon – this can't be easy for you. I think it's incredibly brave that you've stayed in the army at all, let alone come here. It must have been a shock finding out who you were serving under."

Carlyon nodded, his eyes on her face. "I didn't know what to think," he said. "Honestly, I'd have been excited – getting the chance to serve in the Light Division."

Anne studied him with sympathetic eyes. "Do you not think you can?" she asked.

"I don't know, ma'am. I've not had a chance to think. In the short term, I'll do my duty, it's what I signed up to do. In the long term…I don't know."

Anne van Daan moved forward. "I do understand," she said. "So does the Colonel. I'm sorry this is such a rush; these things never happen in winter quarters when we've time. Simon, just think about it. Please don't rush into making a decision. I'm going to call Jenson to show you where your tent is pitched. Unpack, come to supper and give yourself time to think. Don't write us off without giving us a chance. Will you promise me that?"

Carlyon took the hand she offered him and raised it to his lips. He was aware that at that moment, he would have promised Anne the world and he suspected it was a common reaction. "Yes, ma'am," he said.

His former sister-in-law laughed. "That is so formal," she said. "If you decide to stay - and I hope you will - you're my brother, and we were always good friends. My name is Nan, I hope you'll feel comfortable enough to use it soon."

Carlyon could think of nothing to say. He saluted and turned to leave. The Colonel got up. "And meanwhile," he said in grim tones, "I am off to visit the fourth company of the 110th light infantry and hopefully, to put them off wine for life."

# Chapter Three

Rueda was an attractive little town on the left bank of the Duero. In terms of population, it was little more than a large village, but it had a fine selection of buildings, including several churches, a collection of large houses, a convent, a monastery and a huge abandoned building which Paul thought might have some kind of seminary. The poorer houses in the town huddled together in narrow streets and alleyways, a tangle of red tiled roofs, whitewashed walls and small plots and gardens growing fruit trees and a few vegetables.

Beyond the village was a landscape of rolling hills with corn fields and vineyards, dotted with farm buildings. The countryside was in fairly good condition and Paul supposed that the French occupation had been in place for several years here. However the inhabitants of the Duero valley felt about the invasion, they had been free, at least, from the devastation of constant war, with armies marching over the landscape, looting and burning and leaving towns and villages in ruins.

The wine cellars and caves of the Valladolid region were cut into the hillsides, stretching in places for miles underground. Some of them were centuries old, and Paul had been taken on a tour of some of them several days earlier by a local winegrower, with Anne and some of his other officers. The Spaniard had been hospitable and generous with a gift of wine and Paul had promised to do his best to curb the depredations of his troops, which he knew was the point of the gesture.

Paul had called together his officers, given his instructions and sent them out to give the same speech to the men of his brigade. He had known that it would be impossible to stop all looting with the troops spread out in a string of camps. The rest of the light division was quartered in the town of Rueda itself and Paul knew that the officers of the first and second brigades were delighted with their accommodation. His friends in the other brigades had been equally delighted that the third brigade was housed in tents. Paul's brigade had a long-standing reputation for grabbing the best billets wherever they stopped and Andrew Barnard who was currently in command of the first brigade was openly gleeful.

"What happened, Paul, did your quartermaster fall asleep?" he asked, watching Paul's men setting up camp. "It gets very cold out here at night, you know."

"Thank you very much for your concern, Colonel Barnard, I shall remember it in winter quarters when you show up wanting a dinner invitation because your billet is damp and your cook's caught the ague," Paul retorted with a grin. "Anyway, aren't your lot expected to turn out every night in case of an attack?"

"We're on the alert, certainly, but I think we'll still sleep better than you will. My officers are overjoyed. They've commandeered the old college building, it has a dining hall the size of a ballroom. Your officers are cordially invited to join us for a dance this evening, by the way. And probably every other evening while we're here. Kincaid and a few others are touring the area begging the company of every presentable female who can trip a measure."

"Probably a few less presentable ones as well, knowing that lot. I'll pass the word around and when they're not on picket duty they can join in the party. How are your fever patients getting along?"

Barnard pulled a face. "Still a good few down with it; it's why they've let us stay in the town, I think. They're hoping warm, dry billets will help them get over it quicker."

"I wondered if that was it, Hookey isn't usually that generous. Where's he staying?"

"Big house at the far end, they're just moving him in now. Somehow, I doubt we'll see him at the evening hop, dancing with a farmer's daughter."

"You might, if I bring my wife down, Andrew."

Barnard laughed aloud. "Bring her. Wellington might not be there, but I'd love to dance with her."

"I will. In the meantime, I suspect we'll all have a full-time job keeping these drunken bastards out of the wine cellars."

Barnard grinned at him. "Good wine, though."

Paul had not told Barnard that it had been his choice to camp rather than to find billets in the overcrowded town. His brigade was well-equipped, and he hoped to avoid the illness which had laid low too many of the other two brigades by staying away from them. He also knew that it would be easier to keep an eye on the men if they were all camped together rather than split up throughout the town and neighbouring farms. It seemed to be working until the fourth company was sent out on picket duty.

Paul collected his horse and his orderly and rode out towards the river. The sun was beginning to sink, giving the cooling landscape a bluish tinge, with orange and gold streaking the sky and reflecting off the sluggish waters of the river, visible through shrubs and stunted trees. The pickets of the 112th could be seen on the low hill, silhouetted against the skyline and across the river the cooking fires of the French were already lit. The smell of food wafted across the water making Paul hungry.

It was less than a mile to the first of the wine caves, its entrance guarded by a wooden farmhouse and a small yard. The caves were centuries old and had been dug out of the sides of the hills, enormous underground chambers, hewn from the rock. One chamber led into another, some appearing to go on for miles, and they were lined with huge barrels and pipes of wine. It was in one of these, that Rifleman Taylor had breathed his last two days earlier, drowned in one of the large open casks having presumably fallen in while inebriated. Taylor had been a notorious drunkard who must have found the ready supply of wine irresistible, but Paul knew that very few of the men were wholly immune to temptation.

Paul found a small group of officers on the hillside by the cave entrance. Captain Barry came forward, saluting, as Paul dismounted and handed the reins of Rufus, his big roan gelding, to Jenson.

"Sir. Sorry about this. I didn't want to trouble you…"

"You mean you didn't want the bollocking you thought I'd give you, Captain Barry," Paul said grimly. "What the hell happened?"

Barry shook his head, looking depressed. "No idea, sir. It's our second stint on duty, last night went fine, tonight they went off to relieve the day sentries. Mr Hart rode up about an hour and a half ago to make sure they were all where they should be and couldn't find any of them. He searched, found them in here, and sent a message back to me."

Paul surveyed his junior thoughtfully. Nick Barry had joined the 110th as an ensign when Paul had first arrived in Portugal. From an army family, he was intelligent and conscientious, and Paul was fairly sure that he was guilty of nothing more than bad luck.

"Well, short of sitting on top of them constantly, I'm not sure what else you could have done, lad," he admitted. "Even I, with my highly suspicious mind, wouldn't have expected an entire company to suddenly decide that picket duty was overrated and go on a spree instead. What happened to the previous pickets - were they ours?"

"No, sir the 95th. They're in there with them."

"Jesus Christ, are you telling me that this section of the line has been unguarded for twelve hours? Thank God the French are so dopey, they could have cut through the line and slaughtered us. Jenson, are the 112th in position?"

"Yes, sir. Major Clevedon has given the order that all pickets are to be accompanied by an officer at all times."

"We'll make that general from now on. Which is going to interfere with the officers' social lives in town, but that can't be helped. Jenson, ride back to camp. My compliments to Captain Manson, will you get him to bring the rest of the light company out here. And get Sergeant-Major Carter if he's there."

"Yes, sir."

"While we're waiting for them, let's get them lined up, Captain - at least, those who can stand."

"Yes, sir. What about the riflemen?"

"Those too. Will you send one of your ensigns over to speak to Colonel Barnard - I think they're his."

"Yes, sir."

"Tell him he can collect them from our camp when he's ready," Paul said. "By the time he does, I rather imagine they'll have sobered up a fair bit. Get moving, Captain."

***

With his tent up and his bags unpacked, Nicholas Witham went in search of his friend and found Carlyon in his own tent, looking around in slight bewilderment.

"Organised, isn't it?" Witham said with a grin. "I feel a bit superfluous, to be honest. Have you met Captain Lewis, yet?"

"Yes, he just stopped by," Carlyon said. "Gave me the welcome speech and said he'd introduce us to the men in the morning. It's all very leisurely."

Witham shook his head. "It's an illusion," he said positively. "They didn't get this way by studying their manners; this is the result of a lot of hard work on somebody's part. Are you going up to supper with the 110th? I wondered…"

"Yes, we're invited, it'd be rude not to," Carlyon said quickly. He seemed to interpret Witham's look of enquiry and shook his head. "I don't know, Nick. I can't get my head straight yet. One day at a time. Come on, let's walk up."

There was a good deal of activity in the lines of the 110th as Witham and Carlyon arrived. A sentry made a token challenge, having seen them earlier, and Carlyon led the way towards the Colonel's tent. Cooking fires were being tended by the camp women and those on mess duty, but Witham's attention was drawn to the path down to the river, where a large number of men seemed to have congregated. Curiously, they followed the crowd and joined a group of officers.

"What's going on?" Carlyon asked.

One of the men turned and surveyed him with interest. "New?" he asked.

Witham nodded. "Witham and Carlyon, 115th second company," he said. "Just arrived."

"Welcome to Spain," the officer said. "Lieutenant Crispin, 110th fifth company. This is Lieutenant Steele who serves with me. As to the excitement, I'm not sure, but I've been told that the entire fourth company has just been found drunk in a wine cellar and dumped into the Duero by our esteemed commander, who has lost his sense of humour. I can't believe…"

"David, look," Steele interrupted. Witham followed his pointing finger. A mule cart was approaching, driven by a dark-haired sergeant and it appeared to be piled high with a collection of clothing and kit, including muskets, coats, shoes and a miscellany of other garments. The Sergeant was grinning and as he drove past, somebody raised a cheer. Others followed and the Sergeant laughed and saluted.

"What on earth is happening?" Carlyon said.

"I'm not sure," Steele said. "But I suspect the fourth company have

32

just been ordered into the river to sober up. It must be freezing at this time of day."

"But what is all this?" Witham said, bewildered.

His answer came immediately with a bellow which must have reached the French on the far bank of the river.

"Fourth company, MARCH. Quick time, stand up straight and if any one of you falls out, you are spending the night on watch, wearing exactly what you are now."

They were approaching up the path in marching order, although Witham thought that some of their movements resembled a stagger rather than a march. He blinked, finding it hard to believe what he was seeing, and there was a whoop from behind him, followed by a loud huzzah and then there was cheering on all sides as the officers and men of the third brigade of the light division applauded the spectacle of the fourth company of the 110th returning to camp stark naked and frozen from their unexpected dousing in the river.

The evening air was cold, and darkness was fast approaching. Some of the men were shivering already; all of them had goosebumps and many looked as though they had either just vomited or were about to do so. As Witham had the thought, a lanky private of around forty stepped out of formation and cast up accounts at the side of the road to the ironic cheers of the rest of the brigade. He had barely straightened when the impressive yell came again.

"Dransfield, get your skinny Lancashire arse back into line, before I throw you back in the river. Sergeant-Major Carter, march them into camp and get them lined up. I want a word with them before I have my supper."

They lined up in neat formation on the edge of the camp and the rest of the brigade formed a wide circle around them. Witham looked around. Officers and men mixed freely in the crowd and he could see Portuguese and King's German Legion uniforms as well as British regiments. They were all laughing, some of them with tears running down their face. Colonel van Daan stepped out in front of the hapless fourth company and his Sergeant-major rapped out orders at a volume which rivalled his commanding officer. The men stood to attention, dripping and shivering in the gathering dusk. The Colonel surveyed them.

"Jenson, do you know where my wife is?" he asked.

"Back at the tent, sir, waiting for you. Major Swanson suggested she might want to stay there for a while."

"Thank you, Jenson. I wouldn't want to put her off her supper."

There was another ripple of laughter, quickly stilled, and Van Daan surveyed the men. Then he pointed:

"Over there, on the far bank. They're called the French. Sometimes referred to as the enemy. You were sent out there this evening to guard our army, our guns and Lord Wellington and his staff. You were also guarding your own women and children and my wife.

"Do you have any idea what might have happened if they'd launched a surprise attack? We'd have been caught unprepared. Some of us would have got to arms, because we're the best bloody brigade in this army, and we'd have made a fight of it, probably held them off long enough to get warning to the rest of the Light Division and then on to the rest of the army, but most of us would have died to buy them that time. They'd have gone through our camp and our supplies and they'd have got to our women."

The laughter had died away and there was suddenly total silence around the camp. Witham looked around at the faces of the men around him in the last vestiges of daylight and saw their expressions and he felt, suddenly, as though he had stepped into a different world. He realised that there were images in the heads of every man here and they were images that neither he nor Carlyon yet understood.

"Enough of you have been with me long enough to know what that means," the Colonel went on, relentlessly. "You risked all that, for a drink and a laugh with the arseholes from the Rifles. They might not know what they've done tonight, or they might not care - Colonel Barnard will deal with them. But you - you know. You understand. And the fact that you thought so little of your brigade, your regiment, your comrades, your families and your honour has shocked me to the core. I thought I knew every one of you better than that. I've never been more disappointed in my life."

There was a choking sound from one of the men, what sounded like a sob, turned quickly into a cough. Paul van Daan let the silence lengthen before he spoke again.

"You have disgraced your company, your officers and the 110th light infantry. But mostly, you've disgraced yourselves as men. I could let you stand there until you freeze to death, but I won't. You are a pack of useless, drunken, disreputable gobshites, but you're my drunken gobshites and in the 110th we look after our own. Sergeant-Major Carter, stand them down and get them to sort out their kit and get dressed, then get them fed. Take their names, every one of them, and make a separate list of the riflemen to give to Colonel Barnard when he sends an officer up to collect them. No grog for any one of them for two weeks and they're to be separated from the rest of the battalion and kept under guard until we march again. Now get them out of my sight, they sicken me."

Carter yelled an order and the men saluted, managing it with surprising dignity, given their nudity. There was a very long moment and then Colonel van Daan returned the salute. He turned to walk away, and the crowd began to disperse, talking quietly with no sign of the hilarity of earlier. The speech had sobered every man among them, and Witham wondered what memories had been conjured up by the Colonel's words.

Witham felt slightly awkward approaching the officers' tents of the 110th but as they arrived, Major Swanson detached himself from a group around one of the fires and came forward.

"Welcome," he said cheerfully. "Come and get a drink. It's local wine, very good. Our fourth company recommends it."

There was a general laugh and Witham went forward. He had been expecting some form of mess table, either in a tent or under an awning, but the officers had simply pulled out a collection of camp chairs, chests and boxes and food was being handed out in mess bowls with wine in pewter cups. The informality surprised Witham. He would have expected it among a mess of impecunious junior officers and had been part of such arrangements since he joined, but on the rare occasions he had been invited to dine with his seniors there had been at least an attempt at formality even in the field.

There were several women present and one of them rose as they approached and came forward with her hands outstretched. "Simon," she said warmly. "Welcome to the 110th. Come and sit down. And you must be Mr Witham; I'm so glad to meet you."

Witham was not sure what he had expected of the scandalous young wife of the Colonel of the 110th, but Anne van Daan was a surprise. She appeared to be little more than a girl, dressed informally in green velvet and she was startlingly lovely with almond shaped dark eyes and a smile which melted his heart.

"Ma'am - thank you for inviting us," Carlyon stammered. "It's good of you."

"Nonsense, you're family and part of the brigade. Come and sit down, I've saved seats near me."

Witham saw his friend glancing around and could sense his unease. Anne van Daan put her hand on his arm. "Simon, listen. If you're worried about Colonel Wheeler, don't be, he isn't here. He's dining with Lord Wellington over at headquarters. You'll meet him tomorrow and he wants to speak to you privately to make sure there's no awkwardness, but you can relax this evening and get to know your brigade officers."

Afterwards, Witham would always remember that evening as something of an oasis, a moment of calm before the storm. At the time he was just conscious of how much he enjoyed it. They sat late into the darkness, the camp lit by the cooking fires and some oil lanterns which the servants brought out from the tents. The officers of the various companies tended to group together but there was movement between the groups and Witham was introduced to a bewildering number of people. There were two other women in the group, Miss Trenlow, a young Englishwoman with dusky curls and a shy smile who appeared to be some kind of companion to Mrs van Daan and a Spanish woman with a young baby in her arms who was introduced as the wife of Sergeant-Major Carter. Witham was astonished when Carter himself joined the group later, seating himself beside his wife and accepting food with a familiarity which suggested that it was not unusual for him to eat with the officers.

The conversation ranged over a wide variety of subjects and Witham and Carlyon listened with interest to men who had fought in this army for four years and had a good deal to say about Lord Wellington's probable strategy. When the party finally broke up, they rose to say their goodnights and thank their hostess and Anne van Daan summoned Carter.

"Sergeant-Major Carter will walk you back to your tents with a lantern; it's easy to get lost in the lines until you're used to it and I don't want you wandering around in the dark, you must be tired. Goodnight, I hope we don't have any alarms to disturb you."

"Goodnight, ma'am, and thank you. You've been so welcoming, and I hadn't expected it," Carlyon said.

Anne van Daan stood on tiptoe and kissed her former brother-in-law on the cheek. "Dinna be daft, lad," she said, assuming a broad Yorkshire accent. "Get thee to bed, now, and sleep fast."

***

The Light Division spent two weeks at Rueda and the men of both armies quickly established an informal truce. Both sides bathed in the river at the same spots and Paul saw them exchanging smiles and a word and eventually sharing rations and wine and tobacco. There continued to be incidents of drunkenness. It was impossible for the officers of the division to watch all of the men, all of the time and the wine caves and cellars were too vast and too easily accessible. His own men were very careful, and although Paul knew that their grog ration was being well supplemented with the local wine, there were no further incidents of dereliction of duty because of drink, and his officers and NCOs turned a blind eye when they could and stepped in only when the drinking looked as though it might get out of hand.

An army in camp for more than a few days was always likely to get bored and Paul knew from long experience that it increased the risk of disciplinary problems. He tried hard to keep his men busy, taking the opportunity to do kit inspections and to replace threadbare clothing. The French had left vast stores in Salamanca when they fled, and he sent his quartermasters with lists of requirements. He also found time to work with the 115th on skirmish training, using the hills and defiles which ran down to the river although he was careful to keep them out of sight of the French, not wanting to give the impression that an action was imminent.

The storming of Badajoz had left Wellington's army seriously depleted. Of the three brigades of the Light Division, Paul's brigade had suffered the least during the battle. He had not been engaged in the main breaches which had experienced the worst of the slaughter and although the escalade over the western wall had been costly, both the 110th and 112th had done surprisingly well. There were more wounded than dead, and although some of these would need to be repatriated to England, the medical services were beginning to set up a series of convalescent hospitals through Portugal which meant that many men could recover without need to go home.

The worst casualties in Paul's brigade had occurred from the explosion of a mine. The 115th North Yorkshire foot, were new to the division and very inexperienced, and during his successful escalade they had made their attempt too far south, on a stretch of wall known to be mined. Of their six companies, only half remained able to fight, and most of their officers had been lost. The explosion had also caused deaths and injuries among his Portuguese and German battalions and Paul was still trying to work out how to staff the remaining companies from his current officers. He had received a hundred reinforcements from the 110th second battalion and had been furious when a third of them arrived in no condition to fight, still suffering from the recurring fever picked up in Walcheren three years earlier. Lord Wellington had sent him new Portuguese troops which he had detached from the fourth division to replace those lost but Paul was missing Captain Peso who had served under him for several years and had died at Badajoz. He had not realised how close he had become to some of his young Portuguese officers who had trained under him and taught him their language and a love of their country.

With time to spare awaiting Wellington's orders, Paul's officers divided their forces and their time and began patiently to bring the new recruits up to scratch along with the remaining men of the 115th. The men of the King's German Legion who served under him had been close to the mine but had been luckier than the other battalions although a number of their officers had been lost to death or injury. Paul had promoted one of his longer serving officers from the 110th to brevet major commanding them and brought up a number of promising young NCOs from their ranks including his wife's particular favourite, the former Private Theo Kuhn, a trained doctor from Halle who refused stubbornly to join the medical staff as he did not choose to treat the French who had killed his father and brothers in Germany. The new Captain Kuhn's opinion of his enemy had not been improved by Anne's recent ordeal, but he would make a good officer and Paul was glad to have him.

The amount of administration involved in managing the promotions, assimilation of new recruits and ensuring adequate supplies of food, drink, uniforms and equipment was appalling, but by now Paul's brigade had been operational for more than a year and he was beginning to feel confident in the system. He took the opportunity to promote Captain Breakspear, who had been with the 110th for several years, to major in charge of the quartermasters of the brigade, and his assistant took over as quartermaster for the 110th. Both men were accustomed to working alongside his wife who had acted as unofficial quartermaster for many years, and Paul was ruefully aware that when it came to bullying local merchants and arranging transport for his brigade, she was more effective than anybody. The daughter of a prosperous Yorkshire cloth manufacturer, Anne had a hard-headed practicality when it came to money which meant that the third brigade of the Light Division had the best-balanced books in the army. Paul knew that other regiments sneered at what they saw as the privileged position of the 110th and their associated regiments, in terms of equipment and supplies, but he understood better than anybody that Anne's work in reducing waste and inefficiency meant that he had more ready money to spend, which given the current shortage of cash in Wellington's army, was vitally important.

Working with the 115th brought Paul into daily and regular contact with the two new officers of the second company. He had read the service records sent by their previous commanding officers and he was not surprised to find both Witham and Carlyon intelligent and hard-working officers who were keen to learn new skills. Both were quick to develop a good relationship with

Captain Lewis as well as the two ensigns and both seemed very comfortable with the men. The only difficulty appeared to be Simon Carlyon's intransigent loathing for the Colonel of the 112<sup>th</sup>.

There was no real need for the officers of the 115<sup>th</sup> to have much to do with Johnny Wheeler, who acted as Paul's second-in-command, but the brigade was accustomed to mingling very freely on social occasions and during the evenings, Paul had given permission for all officers not on duty to ride into Rueda to attend the evening dances organised by the other two brigades. Paul attended several himself and was pleased to see Johnny there, dancing with some of the local girls. His friend was still struggling with the end of his love affair with Caroline Longford, the wife of another officer, who had returned to England with her husband and although Johnny was very good at hiding it, his taut grief saddened Paul. But it had not escaped Paul's attention that Lieutenant Carlyon, generally a very lively addition to any social occasion, left the dance as soon as Colonel Wheeler arrived. Paul knew that Johnny was very aware of it and was choosing to stay away to avoid awkwardness.

Awkwardness was impossible to avoid. Riding back from a meeting with General Alten one afternoon, Paul turned the knotty problem over in his head. It was difficult to find good young officers and he was very impressed with both Witham and Carlyon, but he was reluctantly beginning to wonder if it might be best to arrange an exchange with a lieutenant from one of the other divisions for Anne's former brother-in-law. Paul knew that Johnny had spoken to Carlyon on arrival about the death of his brother. He had asked Johnny about the meeting and Johnny had shaken his head.

"I don't know, Paul. He's angry and he's also bloody confused and I understand both. You and I remember Robert Carlyon as a man who beat his wife regularly for two years and ended by trying to shoot her to death when she tried to leave him. Simon Carlyon saw none of that. He remembers his big brother as a hero in a scarlet coat who inspired him to go into the army."

"He also remembers Nan as his childhood friend."

"I know. And he doesn't seem to have any problem with her. Or you. But he looks at me and sees the man who pulled the trigger and blew his brother's head off and I don't think he can get past that. He can barely bring himself to speak to me and I'm doing my best to stay out of his way. But if we ever find ourselves in a position where I have to give him orders in battle, God knows how he'd react."

Paul sighed. "Poor bastard. I wish we could just tell him the truth," he said.

"We can't. It might solve his problem with me, but we can't rely on a man we don't know, not to spread that story through the army. I'd probably be cashiered for lying on oath when I told the provost marshal I shot Carlyon, and Sergeant Hammond, who actually did shoot him, would be hanged. Which is why I told that lie in the first place."

Paul shook his head. "I know, Johnny. But his attitude is so bloody obvious, it's causing talk throughout the division. Even Charles Alten has heard about it and he's usually worse at hearing the gossip than I am. Every ancient piece of scandal about my wife and her first husband is being gleefully passed down to any new officers, and if just one of them says anything in her hearing or so much as looks at her the wrong way because bloody Carlyon can't control himself, I am going to send him the same way as his brother."

Johnny shook his head, laughing. "You don't mean that, Paul, you like him."

"I do. But if I have to choose between him and my lass, Johnny, he is history."

"Give it some time," Johnny said. "I've a very thick skin, I can put up with it."

Paul was not sure that he could. He was accustomed to the various minor quarrels between officers and men and tended to ignore anything which did not interfere with discipline or the running of his brigade, but Carlyon's silent resentment of Colonel Wheeler bordered on open disrespect and Paul was not prepared to ignore it.

He found his wife in their tent with Keren Trenlow. Anne had apparently been sorting through her clothing and a variety of garments were strewn about the tent, draped over every surface. Paul paused in the entrance, watching in some surprise as Anne stood with unusual patience while Keren made adjustments to a gown she was wearing.

"What's all this? I'm glad I didn't bring Lord Wellington back with me to supper, this looks like a Calcutta bazaar, bonny lass."

His wife looked over her shoulder at him regally. "If you walked into the tent unannounced with Lord Wellington, Colonel, he would be likely to get the shock of his life."

"Or a treat, depending on how you look at it," Paul said, admiring the honey gold of Anne's shoulders as the gown slipped down. "Do I recognise that gown?"

"No, because it is new. Keren had the material, Carl bought it for her months ago, but she did not make it up because she didn't think the colour suited her. She has been working on it for weeks in secret for me, she borrowed one of my gowns for the size. And she has done an astonishing job, it fits almost perfectly, just a few adjustments. Look at it, Paul, it's beautiful."

She turned to face him, and Paul smiled. The gown was a vivid jonquil yellow muslin, with short sleeves and a neckline that flattered Anne's admirable figure without raising a blush. Bodice, hem and sleeves were decorated with tiny blue hand embroidered flowers. Paul had seen Keren's talent with a needle on the linen and clothing she had made for their small son the previous year, but she must have spent an enormous amount of time on this and the sheer joy on Anne's face made him want to embrace the girl.

"Love, it's beautiful," he said. "Keren…"

"It's a gift, sir," Keren said quickly, looking up from pinning the hem. "I was never going to wear this, and I wanted…you've both been so good to me."

Paul could not speak for a moment, his throat unexpectedly tight. Keren Trenlow had been a frightened girl when she arrived in Portugal with her young sweetheart and by the time she met Anne, he was dead of fever and she had taken up with a brutal drunk. Anne had employed her as a maidservant and Keren had quickly become a valued part of their household. Paul had expected her find a husband in the regiment and it had been something of a shock to discover that instead, she was sharing the bed of Major Carl Swanson.

Paul had assumed that the affair would be short lived, but he had been mistaken. Keren had moved by gradual stages from a casual bed mate to a valued companion and Paul's unconventional wife, far from shunning the girl, had become closer and closer to her maid. Another woman in Anne's position might have been insulted by her former attendant's presumption in making a gift for her, but it was clear that Anne was delighted by the gesture, probably more so than if Paul had paid for an expensive evening gown.

"Lass, thank you," Paul said. "You don't need me to tell you how much it means to her; you can see by the look on her face. Will it be ready for this evening?"

"Easily, sir."

"Why don't we go up to Rueda; you can show it off dancing with General Vandeleur? And I'd like to dance with Miss Trenlow; next to you, she's the prettiest girl in the Light Division."

Keren blushed but she was laughing. "Unless Major Swanson is on duty..."

"I'll make sure he isn't. We'll eat early and go up together. I'll leave you to finish. Keren, thank you."

\*\*\*

The Light Division had made Rueda its own during the two weeks it had been quartered there, and Paul and Anne arrived to find the dance in full swing. The officers of the first and second brigades had spent their time well, collecting as many pretty girls from the district as they could manage to join them in their festivities. There had been a few social mishaps, since some of the better born ladies of the district had retired in high dudgeon when they realised that they were expected to dance alongside the daughters of farmers and artisans, but not all were so particular, and there was an interesting mix of social classes which made Paul's arrival with his wife and her former maidservant seem far less singular than it might have been.

The party this evening, was being held in an enormous hay barn and the officers of the Light Division had provided handsomely in terms of wine and food for their guests. Music was the province of the bandsmen of the 52$^{nd}$ and Paul led his wife onto the dance floor. He saw her smile across the set and realised too late that he had been inveigled into a social situation he would have preferred to avoid.

Paul had always liked Captain Harry Smith of the Rifles, a talented young officer in his mid-twenties but since his precipitate marriage to the very young Spanish girl who had sought his protection from the horrors of the sacking of Badajoz, his previously good relationship with Paul had vanished.

Paul had been horrified when he had become aware that far from helping the girl to find safety with relatives or older friends, Smith had moved her into his tent. He had asked very quickly for permission to marry her, and Wellington had granted it with grim resignation. Smith was one of his favourite young officers along with Manson and one or two others and if the boy was set on the marriage, Wellington wanted to ease his path and had arranged and attended the wedding for very much the same reasons as he had attended Paul's two years ago. Paul had not attended. Anne had been twenty when he married her, newly widowed and considerably more experienced than the bright-eyed fourteen-year-old that Smith had taken on and Paul was appalled at the idea of a child of her age being married at all, let alone following the army. He had spoken furiously to Smith and Harry had taken the reproof in thin-lipped silence since he was not in a position to be equally rude to a senior officer.

Juana Smith was opposite Paul in the set, and he wondered if his wife had engineered the situation. He was irritated; he was not yet ready to forgive Smith's behaviour, but it was hardly the child's fault, so he summoned a pleasant smile for her. Juana looked back at him with huge dark eyes and managed a nervous response.

She was dancing with Lieutenant Kincaid, a friend of Smith's, who was evidently on excellent terms with her. Paul watched his wife as they danced and decided that the situation had been engineered by the rifleman rather than Anne. It made him feel slightly less annoyed. As the dance progressed, Paul felt himself relax. It suddenly struck him as exquisitely funny that he, of all people, should be feeling so censorious about a young officer's behaviour towards women when his own past had been such a rich source of army gossip over the years. It made him feel unexpectedly old and staid and he wanted to laugh aloud. Catching Anne's eye, he saw a spark of amusement there and he wondered if she was thinking the same thing.

The music ended with a slightly off-key flourish which brought a barrage of cheerful abuse from the dancers. Kincaid bowed to his partner, taking her hand and Paul put his arm about Anne.

"Am I being an arsehole about Harry Smith?" he enquired, and she laughed and shook her head.

"No, Paul. I do understand, she is ridiculously young. But she doesn't seem it, somehow, and she is very sweet. More to the point, they're married now, and you can't accuse him of not being good to her, he clearly adores her."

Paul eyed her thoughtfully. "I still can't decide if you have just set this up, girl of my heart. But we're here now. Go and find Captain Manson, he's standing over there, trying to catch your eye for a dance."

He kissed her hand and turned to find that Captain Smith had reclaimed his wife. Paul put a hand on his shoulder and steered him firmly to one side.

"Go away," he said. "It is high time I made the acquaintance of Lord Wellington's latest flirt. Mrs Smith, will you honour me?"

Juana blushed. She was a pretty child, Paul thought, not with Anne's classic beauty, but with a winsome charm that appealed to him. There was a good deal of character in the big brown eyes. She was regarding him somewhat nervously, but she put her hand into his without hesitation and made a very graceful curtsey. "It is I who am honoured, Colonel," she said gravely.

Paul led her into the dance, conscious of a number of surprised looks. He had not attempted to hide his disapproval of Smith's behaviour, but his wife was right, the marriage was a fact and he realised that he disliked the fact that Juana might be made to feel uncomfortable. She had already had to deal with a frosty reception from one or two ladies who had visited headquarters, not because of her youth but because of the undeniable fact that she had been sharing Smith's tent before their hasty marriage had taken place. Paul's concern had been for the girl and he was still angry that Smith had seduced her, but it was probably time to move on.

"You are a very good dancer, Mrs Smith."

Juana cocked her head to look up at him. "So are you, Colonel. Me, I have watched you dancing with your lady many times. It is good to watch. So many of the officers dance like bears, but not you."

Paul was surprised into a splutter of laughter. "Bears?"

"Si. You know, like this." She pantomimed a sudden loss of grace, heavy footed and clumsy, and then returned to her usual light-footedness in the next turn without missing a step. Paul took her hand again and swung her across, still laughing.

"Was that an impersonation of your husband, lass? I thought I recognised the style."

The girl laughed with him. "He is getting better," she said. "I have told him, if I must learn to ride a horse, he must learn to dance without treading on my feet. Thus far, my riding is better than his dancing."

"I know, I've been watching you improve. When is he going to let you ride a decent horse?"

"Soon. He is afraid that I will fall and break my neck, but I think no. Perhaps you should tell him this, Colonel? He will listen to you."

"I have a very good scheme, ma'am. Why don't you come up to camp and go riding with my wife one morning; she has a spare horse that will carry you very well and she's the best horsewoman in the army. If she is sure that you are ready, we will simply inform Captain Smith that your days on that dopey animal are over."

Juana gave a broad smile, her nerves all gone. "Really? May I? Will she mind?"

"No, she'll be delighted. She's been wanting to get to know you better."

"But you have not," Juana said, surprising him again.

"No," Paul admitted. "But that had nothing to do with you, lass. I thought your husband should have waited until you were older, and I've been worrying about you. But I don't think I need to, do I?"

The girl's smile was dazzling, and Paul suddenly began to understand how Harry Smith had managed to forget himself so thoroughly with this engaging child. "No," she said warmly. "But it is very kind that you should

42

care. Enrique has been very sad that you are so angry with him; he says you are one of the best commanders in the army and a very good fellow."

Paul managed not to laugh too obviously at Juana's naive sharing of her husband's remarks. The music came to a slightly more tuneful end and he bowed.

"Thank you, ma'am. Let me escort you back to your husband."

Juana put her hand on his arm and Paul led her across the room to where Smith was waiting, his expression a comical mixture of apprehension and defensive belligerence. Paul took Juana's hand and kissed it before giving it to Smith.

"I thought you might want your wife back, Harry."

"Thank you, sir."

"We've been discussing your irrational refusal to let her ride a proper horse. That groom of yours, what's his name, I can't remember?"

"West, sir?"

"That's him. Get him to bring her up tomorrow, she can try out Pierrot, my wife's spare horse. If Nan is satisfied that she's comfortable on him, she'll do well enough on that pretty Spanish mare you've bought for her."

Paul saw Smith's eyes widen. "Sir, she'd be happy to."

Captain O'Reilly of the 112th appeared beside them, bowing to Juana. As he led her away to dance, Smith said:

"Thank you, sir. That's very good of you. Especially given that I know how much you disapprove of her."

"Don't be an arse, Smith, I don't disapprove of her at all, I don't know the girl, but actually I rather like what I've seen of her. She's very intrepid, and as you are probably aware, I like that in a woman. You are never going to convince me that marrying a fourteen-year-old is a good idea, but you've done it now. How old are you?"

"I'm twenty-five, sir."

"Only two years more between you than between Nan and I." Paul studied him. "You should have bloody waited," he said quietly. "But she isn't your typical fourteen-year-old, I'll give you that. And given that you'd taken her to bed about twenty-four hours after you set eyes on her I'll accept you didn't have much choice other than to marry her."

"Sir, I swear to you…"

"Don't swear to me, Harry, I'm not a bloody idiot. I've heard you rewriting this touching romance to half the army and I'm impressed at how well it's going, but you forget that I spend my time with my enlisted men, I know bloody well what happened, your lads gossiped. And I also know that you did not have to hold her down, which is why the ladies in winter quarters are going to look down their nose at her in the same way as they look down their noses at my wife. The notion of a female with red blood in her veins horrifies them. But I've been watching you both for the past month and it's very clear to me that you might have got yourself into this because your dick was in charge of your brain, but you're in it for something else now. You're in love with her, aren't you?"

43

Smith met his eyes steadily. "Yes, sir."

"And she follows you around like a devoted puppy. I still think you were an arse, but for what it's worth, you've got my support. Not that you really need it with Wellington on your side, but…"

"I value it, sir. More than you'd know."

Paul regarded him thoughtfully. "I'm told married life suits you. Your commanding officer informs me you're not neglecting your duty."

"My wife wouldn't let me if I wanted to, sir. And it's even more important now, I've a wife to support and my way to make."

"You'll do well. In fact, if I thought I could persuade you…"

Smith laughed aloud. "I'm a rifleman, sir. I don't look good in red."

"I know. And in this war, it's unlikely you'll need to change regiments for promotion any more than my lads do. But if you do ever get stuck, come to me, would you? I'd take you like a shot."

"Thank you, sir. And for allowing your wife to take care of Juana, she'll be good for her."

"Harry, you have known me for a number of years, you must know that it is never a matter of me allowing Nan to do anything; she pleases herself. Have you…?"

Paul broke off at the sound of an altercation across the room. He turned to look and was exasperated to see that it appeared to involve Lieutenant Carlyon and two officers of the Rifles. As Paul watched, their voices grew louder and he was furious to see Carlyon give one of the riflemen a provocative shove.

"I am going to send that young bastard for court martial before the end of this campaign," he said, moving forward. "There's always something, with him."

"It's not entirely his fault, sir," Smith said quietly, and Paul paused, looking back at him. Across the room, he saw that Captain Manson had forestalled him and was leading Carlyon towards the door with one hand firmly on his shoulder, so he turned to Smith.

"Not his fault?" he enquired frostily. "Do you have a view on my junior officers' attitude to their seniors, Captain Smith?"

"No, sir, that's not my business. But he is coming in for a lot of raillery from some of the others and it's not kind."

Paul frowned. "What kind of raillery?" he asked.

"On the subject of his brother, sir. I've heard more than one officer saying that a man with his background shouldn't be allowed to hold an officer's commission, and they're not saying it that quietly."

"Is that what you think, Harry?"

"Of course it isn't," Smith said, sounding irritated. "What a stupid idea, if you look back far enough most of us will have a dirty dish or two in the family tree and if you and Mrs van Daan don't care about it, I can't see that it's anybody else's business and I've said so very clearly if they open their mouths around me. It's this bloody place; too much wine and free time and not enough action. They should save it for the French. But it can't be easy for him."

"No. And the easiest person to blame is going to be Colonel Wheeler," Paul said slowly. "Poor bastard. Harry, thank you, I should have realised. The advantage of a mouth like yours is that you'll tell me things that nobody else has the nerve to, I appreciate it, although I'd like to know why none of my officers have raised it."

"They probably don't realise how bad it's getting, sir, most of it is coming from outside the brigade."

"Most?"

"Why don't you talk to Witham, sir, he's very well aware, he spends most of his life at the moment smoothing the waters."

"He spends a fair bit of it whisking Simon Carlyon out of the way whenever Colonel Wheeler comes past, I've seen him doing it. I wonder if he'd try to do the same in the middle of battle?"

Paul broke off at the sound of a bugle. It was eerily clear through the night air and tailed off into haunting silence, only to be picked up by a second and then a third. Paul looked at Smith.

"Looks like your party is over, Harry, general alert."

"Yes, sir. Might be nothing, we've had a couple of them that have come to naught, but I'd best call West and get Juana out of here…"

"Don't worry, I'll see to it, she can come up with Nan and the others. If it's a false alarm you can collect her on the way back to bed, if it's real, she can stay with them until it's over."

"Thank you, sir."

"You're welcome. Get moving, Captain." Paul turned and surveyed the room, watching his officers drifting towards the door. Paul raised his voice to a bellow.

"Officers of the third brigade, it's an alert, not the dinner gong, say goodnight to the ladies and move. Your men will have stood to arms and be tapping their feet by now."

As his officers scrambled to horse, Paul collected his wife and her companions and set off quickly into the darkness towards the camp and possible action.

# Chapter Four

After a little more than a fortnight at Rueda, it was a relief to Paul to get his brigade moving. Night marches could be difficult, depending on the terrain, but most of his men were very experienced and followed each other through the darkness, relying on the voices of NCOs and officers to guide them. The clink of horses and the thudding of hooves followed the progress of the cavalry who were advancing with the Light Division. Paul rode up the long column to find General Charles Alten in conversation with his big German orderly. Peering through the darkness he recognised Paul and waved him forward.

"Colonel van Daan, I am sorry to have interrupted your festivities this evening."

"It's a relief, sir, I've had enough of waiting. French on the move?"

"It seems so, although I know very little, just that we are to advance with the cavalry and await orders."

Paul pulled a face which Alten could probably not see in the dark. "When we get there, why don't we play a hand or two of 'let's all sit around and guess what the hell Lord Wellington is doing now', sir?" he said. "I should have gone up to see him instead of prancing about with the Rifles for the evening."

"Where is your wife, Colonel?"

"I left her in camp for the night with half a company of the KGL to guard the baggage and supplies. They'll pack up early and follow us up. Where are we going?"

"We will halt behind Castrejon and await Lord Wellington."

"That's always a treat," Paul said gloomily. "I hate marching around for no apparent reason, and I've got a feeling that's what we're doing."

Alten gave a soft laugh. "There is usually a reason, Colonel. It is simply that you hate not knowing what the reason is."

Paul acknowledged the truth of this over the next few days of monotonous, repetitive marching interspersed with several fierce skirmishes as Lord Wellington and Marshal Marmont began a cautious facing dance which each day failed to result in a battle. There was nothing urgent or frenetic about their movements. Facing each other across the river and the rolling plains around Salamanca, the two armies manoeuvred in perfect timing, attempting to outflank each other without forcing a pitched battle on any ground of which the two commanders were unsure.

"It's like a pavane," Anne said, on the third day. She had ridden up to join Paul and was looking over the lines of Wellington's army and then beyond to the distant columns of Frenchmen on the opposite bank. "I've never seen anything like this before."

"Nor have I," Paul said. "What the devil is a pavane?"

"It's a dance. A bit like the Allemande but slower and statelier; it's very old."

"What is an Allemande? No, don't tell me. How do you know all this?"

"There was an Italian dancing master," Anne said, and laughed aloud at his expression.

"Your stepmother should have locked you up," Paul said grimly.

"If she had, Colonel, we probably wouldn't be where we are now."

"True. But it's a lesson to me about keeping an eye on my daughters as they're growing up. I'm shocked at how young girls behave."

"You didn't say that to me in a shepherd's hut in Thorndale," Anne said serenely. "How long is he going to keep this up?"

"I don't know," Paul admitted, looking out over the lines. "He's not saying much even to me. I don't think he's sure."

Anne followed his gaze. The countryside was a vast plain with low rolling hills and the river snaking between the two armies. An occasional shot was fired when the two came too close but for the most part, the forces moved watchfully along, ready to fall into position at a moment's notice. They passed villages and small towns and the people came out to watch them sombrely. There was none of the excitement and joy of their entry into Salamanca. It was as if the locals knew that the generals were contemplating battle and dreaded the consequences for their crops, their homes and their families.

At night, Wellington's army bivouacked with no tents, the baggage kept to the rear, ready to retreat. Paul lay with Anne wrapped in his arms and thought back several years to the retreat from Talavera when they had slept like this for the first time. He had been astonished back then at how adaptable Anne was and at how well she coped with hardship. These days he knew he took her hardiness for granted.

Marmont's army remained nearby, growing larger by the day as reinforcements began to arrive. The two armies were marching ever closer together, separated only by the river, and Marmont moved several times to threaten to cut off Wellington's supply line back to Portugal. Paul understood his commander's sensitivity about these movements. Wellington had the reputation in London of being an over-cautious general at times, but Paul, who had known him since India, disagreed with the assessment. His chief was capable of flashes of sheer brilliance and had the best eye for terrain and surprise in battle that Paul had ever seen, but he had learned long ago of the importance of keeping his supply line open. Sir John Moore's disastrous retreat to Corunna four years earlier and Wellington's own difficult retreat after Talavera had taught him that he could not maintain a campaign with starving troops and that the Spanish, even the most well-meaning of them, could not be relied upon to provide for him.

Since his early days in Portugal and Spain Wellington had improved his supply train out of all recognition, aided by a commissariat often in disarray, a quartermasters' department frequently understaffed, and his own administrative brilliance. With the help of his quartermasters and his wife, Paul had set up a system for the third brigade which Wellington had begun to introduce to the rest of the army, organising the building of bullock carts and wagons, buying his own pack animals and employing teams of mainly Portuguese drivers who were paid for and responsible to the army rather than self-employed and open to corruption and inefficiency. The system was still in its infancy, but it was already beginning to pay off and Paul agreed with Wellington's determination not to risk a breakdown in supplies at this crucial juncture.

At the same time, Paul's nature rebelled against the sheer frustration of being within sight and sound of the French and not giving battle. He knew that Wellington was watching closely, receiving intelligence daily about the activities of the other French commanders around Spain. His intelligence service had always been better than Bonaparte's and he had continued to refine and improve it with the help of a team of exploring officers who spent lonely and dangerous lives beyond enemy lines gathering information and sketching and mapping the terrain. Major George Scovell and his Corps of Guides had done a brilliant job of co-ordinating his intelligence services with very few resources, and had broken open Bonaparte's codes several times so that letters intercepted by the partisans and local armies could add to Lord Wellington's knowledge of enemy intentions and troop movements.

Under carefully controlled conditions, the French had moved their army to the south bank of the Tormes and it was clear that they were attempting a flanking movement by marching south. Invited to a rare meeting at headquarters, along with General Alten and the other divisional commanders, Paul thought that Wellington seemed very unsure.

"It's possible we'll have to retreat," he said abruptly.

"To Salamanca, sir?" Major-General Pakenham asked. Paul glanced at him in some gratitude. He was so accustomed to the silence of the other generals at Wellington's pronouncements that it was a relief to hear another voice. Ned Pakenham, who had been given temporary command of the third division in Picton's absence, was the brother of Wellington's long absent wife Kitty. Paul was aware of his commander's extremely tepid regard for the mother of his two sons, but he liked Pakenham, who was not especially intelligent but was personable and likeable with immense courage in battle.

"To Portugal, Ned," Wellington said, somewhat gloomily. "If they've cut our supply lines their forces are going to be able to join up and we'll be very outnumbered. I'd hoped to be able to force a battle before that happened, but conditions have not been right."

"Sir, I think we can still do it," Paul said. "It only takes one wrong move by them. We're still well supplied…"

"It's a mistake," Sir Stapleton Cotton said forcefully. "We don't have their numbers and if they manage to join up, we'll be running for our lives. Better to make an orderly retreat now…"

"What makes you think it will be orderly, sir, once Marmont sees us running?" Paul said evenly. "The first thing he'll try to do is chase down our baggage and supplies and we then have the choice of fighting for them at a place of his choosing or abandoning them and retreating with our tails between our legs. Again."

"Colonel van Daan, are you suggesting that Lord Wellington retreats because he is afraid?" Marshal Beresford said.

"I do not think that the Colonel was suggesting anything of the kind, Marshal," Alten said calmly. "After all, this is just a conversation. His Lordship will make up his own mind."

"Lord Wellington knows I don't question his courage, sir. And I've been through a few retreats with his Lordship, we all have. They tend to lead to something fairly useful. I'm just not sure we're quite there yet, but to be fair I don't have access to his intelligence."

Wellington gave Paul a withering stare. "Thank you for your confidence, Colonel. General Alten, what is your opinion?"

"Like the Colonel, sir, I lack your knowledge of the enemy's movements, but I think that something has happened which causes you concern."

Paul shot the German a look of some surprise. He had been wondering himself what had happened to shake Wellington's confidence, and he was impressed at Alten's shrewdness. Wellington's expression suggested that he had also been taken by surprise.

"Very perceptive, General. The Mayor of Pollo has ridden in, to inform me that a large cavalry force has reached the area on its way to join up with Marmont."

Beresford shook his head. His expression was doleful. "We need to retreat, sir, I am in agreement with you."

Wellington looked around the tent at his various commanders, waiting for a dissenting opinion. None came. Eventually Wellington's gaze returned to Paul.

"You disagree, Colonel?"

"Yes, sir. But I'm trying to be tactful here, the last time I had this argument in your tent you threw me out."

Alten gave Paul a questioning look and Wellington gave a snort although it was one of his more cheerful ones. "It is true, General Alten, I did. On that occasion Colonel van Daan was preaching caution. But then we were about to storm Badajoz and the Colonel dislikes storming a citadel."

"Unless it's wearing skirts," Le Marchant murmured. Several of the men laughed and Paul lifted a hand to acknowledge the hit. Even Wellington was almost smiling.

"Not these days, Le Marchant, Mrs van Daan has him very much in hand, I am glad to say. I am not ready to order a full retreat, we will play a waiting game a while longer, I believe, but I am detaching the baggage and sending it on the first leg of the journey back to Portugal. Colonel van Daan, it will include my carriage, which is at your wife's disposal should she require it."

Paul had bitten back an instinctive protest and was glad he had done so. He fully understood Wellington's reasons, but he hated the idea of Anne travelling even a short distance without him. He realised that his chief understood very well.

"Thank you, sir."

"She may prefer to ride if the weather is fine, but I would recommend she make use of the carriage if there is the slightest concern about a French attack, it will make her status very clear. I am sending an escort of General D'Urban's cavalry to escort it."

"It's good of you to think of her, sir, she'll be very grateful. As am I."

Paul found himself beside Pakenham as they walked to their horses. Pakenham glanced at him. "What do you think, Colonel?"

"I think he wants to make a fight of it," Paul admitted. "Whether he'll find the opportunity or not, I don't know. How is it going with the third division, sir?"

"Well, I think. It's busy. I need to find myself a couple of extra ADCs, I'm spending all my time searching for a man to take a message and suchlike."

Paul felt a stir of interest. "Is that so, sir? Would you be interested in taking a young officer on temporary secondment for a few weeks?"

General Pakenham surveyed him in some surprise. "One of yours, Paul?"

"From the 115th. He's new out here but he's very good. He's bright and hard-working and the men like him. He'd be an asset."

"He sounds as though he'd be useful in one of my companies, we have far too many officers down with this illness. What's the catch?" Pakenham said suspiciously and Paul laughed.

"None, I swear. Not from your point of view. Look, sir - his name is Simon Carlyon and he's the brother of Nan's first husband. He's finding it difficult to settle, largely because a few arseholes from the rifles are giving him a hard time over his brother's reputation. I'm worried it's going to end in a duel or some such stupidity and then he's out. And I don't want that because he's actually a really promising officer, he just needs to shake off Robert's memory. I'll come up with a solution when I've got time, but in the meantime, if you can find a use for him, I'd be really grateful. An ADC post can't possibly be seen as a punishment."

"It might be seen as undue favour to a relative, Colonel, but if you don't mind that, I certainly don't care. Send him over and I'll find something for him to do.

With Simon Carlyon despatched to the third division, Paul breathed a sigh of relief and went to speak to his wife. He found Anne packing, her boxes and bags neatly lined up, the baggage wagon drawn up outside the tent and two of his men helping her.

"I see you've received your orders, girl of my heart."

Anne turned, smiling. "His Lordship sent a message," she said. "He has also provided me with my own personal escort, a dozen dragoons from the King's German Legion. I am not sure why, but it is very kind of him, so I intend to accept graciously."

"I'm glad to hear it. I'm hoping you won't get very far before we either join you or you're called back, bonny lass. Are you all right?"

Anne smiled a dismissal to her two assistants. When they had gone, she came into his arms. "It's not me who's struggling with this, Colonel."

"No, it isn't. It's the first time I've had to send you off on your own since..."

Paul broke off, not even wanting to refer to it, but his wife said calmly:

"Since I was taken by Colonel Dupres. It's all right, Paul, we can say his name."

"I've no wish to. I'm sorry, Nan, I'd rather you stayed here. But Wellington has made the point, that if I can't be with you, you're probably safer to the rear. Keren and Teresa will take care of you, and..."

"It is possibly going to be the other way around, but we'll be together," Anne said.

"What do you mean?"

"Keren's a little upset. There's been something going on for a few weeks, but I have finally bullied it out of her. It appears she is having some trouble with a major of the cavalry."

"Trouble?"

"He's pursuing her rather assiduously. He lays in wait for her every time she goes out alone, pestering her with advances she has no interest in. I think it's starting to get her down."

"Has he laid a hand on her?" Paul demanded. "Because if he has..."

"If he had, he would be history by now," Anne said, with calm ferocity. "He hasn't, but he is upsetting her. I have offered to speak to him about it but she does not want anybody else involved."

"Why doesn't she tell Carl?" Paul asked, bewildered, and saw from his wife's expression that he had been guilty of a piece of masculine stupidity.

"She cannot tell Carl without raising the whole question of her extremely awkward status, something she is not willing to do."

"Nan, if Carl knew some arsehole from the cavalry was annoying his girl, he would deal with it in a heartbeat, I promise you."

"Carl has absolutely no right to deal with anything, Paul, she is a camp follower, who has no actual status whatsoever in this army, other than that of a kept woman. If he ends up challenging or accepting a challenge from Major Clifton over her honour, he is going to be the laughing stock of every officer's mess in Spain and she knows it. She will not put him in that position."

Paul knew from Anne's clipped tone that she was angry and not knowing what to say, he bent and kissed her very gently. "I'm sorry, lass, I didn't think," he said.

"It isn't your job to think about it, Colonel, but it ought to be the job of your bacon-brained friend. He got her into this situation. While she was my maid, she had a position and if any of them spoke a word out of turn to her, I would have gutted him with a bone saw. Since Major Swanson took to parading her openly up and down the lines as his mistress, she is seen as a prostitute of the better kind and there are a number of wealthy officers who can easily outbid the son of a country parson who got his promotions without purchase."

"I have to confess some of this is my fault," Paul said ruefully. "I've encouraged Carl to be open about this; I thought it would keep some of the other officers of the 110th off her back."

"It has," Anne said. "To be honest, our own lads treat her as if she's Carl's wife, they're not the problem."

"But she isn't," Paul said quietly.

"No. Do you think she should be punished for that?"

"No," Paul admitted. "Look, love, this is not the time - and don't think I don't know that you've just neatly distracted me from worrying about you travelling without me. But I will come back to this, and I do take it seriously. Personally, I think a few well-chosen words from me will send Major Clifton scuttling back to whatever hole he crawled out of and I am not ruling that out. What I'm not going to do is ignore it; as far as I'm concerned, she's under my protection whoever the hell she's sleeping with and if he persists he's going to end up face down in the regimental dung heap, but I'll let you talk to Keren again before I do anything. I'm sorry, I can see you're furious."

"Yes, I am," Anne said and for once there was no laughter in the dark eyes. "I know that you will deal with it, Paul, and I do appreciate that, but you should not need to. We should not require the intervention of a man in order to live our lives without insult or assault. Keren has done nothing that Carl has not also done, yet his behaviour is so little thought of that he is able to continue his life without even being aware that there is a problem while she is unable to walk beyond our lines without at the very least facing a barrage of vulgar remarks. And I know that is the way of the world, and that you will tell me it is inevitable in an army camp. I am sure you are right. But I do not believe it is acceptable, any more than what was done to me by Robert Carlyon and Jean Dupres was acceptable. It is wrong and we should say so, very openly."

Paul looked at her for a long time. "Yes, it is," he said finally. "And I am sorry."

Unexpectedly, Anne smiled. "Paul - dear Paul - you have nothing to be sorry for. Of all the men catcalling and pestering an unaccompanied woman for sexual favours as though they were a right, I am well aware my husband is not going to be among them. I'm very fortunate."

"So am I, love. Get your packing finished and we'll eat, I've got the men putting up the big tent or we'll all drown over our supper, that rain is getting heavier, I don't envy any of them still crossing the river."

"With any luck, Major Clifton will be among them, and he will either drown or die of an inflammation of the lung," his wife said remorselessly. "I shall see you at supper. I hope we're not in for a storm."

*** 

The storm came quickly in the way that summer storms did in Spain, further soaking those troops already wet from crossing the Tormes. The night sky was lit up with jagged flashes of lightening and the army huddled miserably under huge crashes of thunder. High winds frightened the horses, some of which broke free from their tethers and ran amok, trampling everything in their path. Some of the cavalry had settled to sleep with their horses beside them, holding onto the reins, and there were a number of injuries to men kicked or trampled by their terrified animals.

It was the wholly unofficial duty of Corporal Jenson to supervise the safety of the officers' horses and Paul was not surprised, when he left the tent to check on them, to find Jenson already there, calmly giving orders to the grooms and sentries to check the tethers. He had found a relatively sheltered copse of trees away from the sleeping men and the horses were spooked but still firmly tied. Paul found a number of other officers out in the rain, checking on their mounts. Horses and baggage animals were both expensive and difficult to come by, and their loss would be a disaster for an impecunious young officer. They stood together for a while, watching the spectacular display in the sky and the somewhat more prosaic sight of some of the dragoons trying desperately to catch their terrified horses. A few of them had stampeded among some of the tents and there were yells of fright as the officers scrambled out, shouting at the men to get the horses under control.

"Do you think all that yelling is helping?" Johnny Wheeler asked, as a portly captain of dragoons, only half dressed, shouted abuse at three of his men who were trying to corner a black gelding.

"They're cavalry, they share a brain with their horses, and in most cases the horse has the bigger portion. Oh, for God's sake, has he no idea how to calm a frightened horse? Jenson, can we spread the pickets out in a line to grab any of the cavalry horses before they break through and trample us to death in our tents?"

"Yes, sir. Already caught a couple," Jenson said cheerfully. "Come and look."

"Give me a minute." Paul splashed through the puddles, wishing that he had taken the time to put his boots on rather than shoving his feet into shoes. "Captain, stop yelling."

The dragoon turned to glare at him. "What the bloody hell has it got to do with…oh - sorry, sir. Didn't realise…"

"I don't need a parade salute, Captain, I just need you to close your mouth for five minutes. You three, stand still and stop shrieking like a girls' school outing, you're making more noise than this storm. Here, boy, settle down a bit."

Paul reached into his pocket, where he generally kept a selection of treats, and withdrew a rather dried out nut. He moved very slowly towards the gelding, talking quietly to him, holding out his hand with the nut. Eventually he stood still and waited. After a moment, the horse came to take the nut. Paul took hold of the bridle, still talking, and ran his hand down the animal's wet, cold neck.

"It's a bloody cold night to be out in this, lad, isn't it?" Paul said, and then tightened his grip as another clap of thunder made the horse shy nervously. "Calm down, now, it'll pass over soon. Captain, is this your horse?"

"Yes, Colonel. My thanks."

"You're welcome. He's a good-looking lad, you'd not want to lose him. You can take him now, Trooper."

Paul rejoined Johnny who had taken shelter under one of the trees and was watching with apparent enjoyment. "Well done, sir," he said enthusiastically. "There are at least another dozen still roaming free. That should keep you busy until morning."

"Kiss my arse, Colonel Wheeler. If that tree gets struck by lightning while you're standing there laughing at me, it will be justice. I'm going to see what Jenson wanted me to look at and then I'm going back to bed."

Johnny fell in beside him and they walked along the horse lines. "Do you think we'll retreat in the morning?"

"We will if this keeps up. I wish he would, to be honest, I'm bored with dancing with the French all day. What's this, Jenson?"

"Over here, sir."

Paul followed his orderly to where one of the grooms was tying up a tall light-coloured horse with elaborate saddlery. A second horse stood beside it, already secured, pawing restlessly in distress. Paul put his hand on its neck.

"All right, boy, it'll be over soon," he said gently. "Where did these come from, Jenson, they're not...oh bloody hell, these are French, aren't they?"

"Yes, sir. They've obviously had the same problems as we have. But these aren't cavalry stock."

"No, they're not," Paul said, running his hand down the sleek, wet nose. "I can't see properly in this light, Freddie, but I'd say these belong to an officer, and one with money."

"Belonged, sir, I'd say."

Paul laughed aloud. "Put them with my horses, Jenson," he said. "It's good to know that even if we end up marching back to Portugal with our tails between our legs tomorrow, this trip wasn't wasted. Good night."

The baggage train was loaded up and ready to go at first light. The men had been up before dawn loading up the luggage and tents and as the wind died down it became clear that the storm had blown itself out and it was going

54

to be a fine day. Paul mounted up and rode out with Anne to join the long baggage train. He found a collection of his men already there, speaking to their wives or holding their children.

Paul stood holding Anne close, hating the fact that he would have to let her go. Along the column, the escort was mounted and shouting orders and Anne's Portuguese groom stood waiting with her horse. With a sigh, Anne drew back. "I need to go."

"All right, bonny lass. Take care of yourself and remember how much I love you. I'm hoping this is a false alarm and we'll be together in a day or so, but if you do make it back to Portugal ahead of me, get yourself back to the quinta we stayed in before and I'll come to you there."

Anne looked at him and gave a quizzical smile at his sombre expression. "Paul - you do know, don't you, that of the two of us, it is far more likely that it is you who will get yourself killed? Officers' wives seldom do."

Paul laughed. "I know. Keep up that tradition. I love you, girl of my heart."

"I love you too, Colonel. Look after our lads."

"I will." Paul kissed her for a long time. Raising his head, he saw Major Swanson further up the line, about the same business. He watched for a moment as Carl reached out and wiped tears from Keren's face with careful tenderness before lifting her onto her horse. Keren had been learning to ride, and during their brief time in Salamanca, Carl had bought her a horse, a pretty bay mare with white socks. She was looking down at Carl and as Paul watched he saw her bend to caress his face lovingly before turning her horse to join the convoy.

Paul rode up to meet Carl who had remounted, watching the long snaking train move out, throwing up a cloud of dust. "Best get back," he said. "I'm expecting orders immediately."

His friend turned his horse without speaking and Paul glanced at him. Carl's expression was unusually serious. "Are you all right?"

Carl fell in beside him. "Yes," he said. "I just hate saying goodbye to her and it's not getting any easier." He looked at Paul and gave a lopsided smile. "You must think I'm bloody mad."

"Why, because the girl you're saying goodbye to was born in a miner's cottage instead of a mansion?" Paul asked. "Did you know, by the way, that Nan's grandfather was a weaver, doing piecework in a two roomed cottage and then travelling with a pack horse to sell it? Or that my great great-grandfather apparently ran a print shop in Antwerp? Who was your grandfather, Carl?"

"He was a churchman; it's a bit of a family tradition. As a matter of fact, and you may not know this, but my great-grandfather came to England in the train of King George, chaplain to one of his retinue."

Paul gave a splutter of laughter. "No, I bloody didn't know that. No wonder my father was so generous with that living. A court chaplain will have impressed him no end. Should I curtsey or something?"

"I would pay to see you try."

"You can't afford it, the amount you've spent on that girl these past months. Do you even have enough left to pay your mess bill?"

"If I don't, my wealthy but low-born friend can afford to subsidise me. I don't eat as much as you anyway. I gather you've made it up with Harry Smith."

"Yes, although that's one love affair I really didn't approve of. Where on earth is she, by the way, I thought she'd be here?"

"Apparently she won't leave him," Carl said. "Keren tried to persuade her it would only be for a day or two but she's adamant."

"Poor Harry. It's one of the things that has always surprised me about Nan, she'll go when she needs to."

"Something's going on," Carl said. Paul followed his gaze and saw a flurry of activity around General Alten's command post. He urged Rufus into a trot.

"Let's go and find out what."

\*\*\*

Paul's hope of early action was quickly disappointed. Instead, the morning wore on with a series of frustrating manoeuvres and very little indication of the intentions of either commander. What action there was, did not involve the Light Division, and Paul sat his horse beside General Alten and Colonel Barnard, looking over the countryside and surveying the various troop movements that they could see from their position out on the left of Wellington's line.

The countryside to the south of Salamanca was open and largely bare, with several wooded areas towards the river and a number of corn and wheat fields. It was surprisingly dry; given the storm of the previous night, Paul had expected his men to be trudging through mud but as the sun rose, it dried the ground quickly and by mid-morning his men were sweating in the heat, and the various manoeuvres were marked by clouds of dust kicked up by horses and men. There were a number of low hills and ridges, none of them particularly high, but Paul marked them, knowing how well Wellington could use even the lowest of slopes in his management of troops.

The exception were the two isolated hills, rocky and bare, which the locals called the Greater and Lesser Arapile. They stood out in stark relief against the undulating countryside and it was obvious to Paul that possession of these was likely to be key if a battle were to take place. It was by no means certain that one would; most of the regiments had sent off their baggage and Lord Wellington's staff had been instructed to prepare for a general retreat.

"Do you think we will see action today, Colonel van Daan?" Alten asked. He was studying the field through his glass.

"I don't know," Paul said frankly. "I usually have some sense of what he's thinking, but I honestly don't this time. I think he'd like to fight them; we've been manoeuvring like chess pieces for so long, he's going to explode with frustration if he doesn't get a battle out of it. But I also think Badajoz is

56

very recent and he's not keen to send his army to be slaughtered again unless he's very sure he can win."

"It's good ground," Barnard commented. He had a soft Irish accent which Anne loved; she had informed Paul she could listen to Colonel Barnard all day. Paul reflected that his wife had not heard either the bellow or the language that Colonel Barnard was capable of in the heat of battle, or she might have changed her mind.

"It is," he said. "And now that we've taken the smaller of those two hills, he could do a lot with the high ground to the south of the village. Although I'd feel happier if we'd managed to keep them off the Greater Arapile as well."

"We were not fast enough," Alten said regretfully.

"The Portuguese weren't fast enough," Paul said shortly. "If somebody could explain to me why he used them instead of the Light Division for that particular job, I'd be grateful."

"We were not in the right position, Paul," Barnard said patiently.

"Well we should have been."

Nobody spoke. Paul knew that both Alten and Barnard shared his frustration about the French capture of the Greater Arapile. The two armies had begun skirmishing just after dawn with both infantry and cavalry involved but neither commander ordered a decisive move. Neither Wellington nor Marmont had a clear view of their opponent's entire army and it appeared that Marmont's intention was to continue his movement to extend his left in the hope of turning the right wing of the Allied army. He did so cautiously, constantly watching the Allies for signs of a sudden movement.

Strategically, the Lesser Arapile was more important for Wellington, as it was at the end of the string of low hills and ridges occupied by the Allied army. If the French had taken it, Wellington's position would have become impossible, and Paul approved his commander's early decision to send a detachment from the fourth division to occupy it at first light. He did not understand why Wellington had not also sent men to take the larger hill; possibly in the darkness he had not realised how close it was. By the time Major Lillie's Portuguese troops were sent to occupy it, they were too late and were swiftly driven back by the French.

Both sides appeared to have paused to consolidate their positions and Paul could see various troop movements around the field. The seventh division had been pulled slightly west behind the fourth and sixth and the Light Division had taken their place on the far left of Wellington's line. Since then they had done nothing but watch and wait.

Two horsemen approached from the lines to join them; General John Vandeleur of the first brigade and Colonel Johnny Wheeler. Behind them came the stocky form of Corporal Cooper with a collection of tin cups balanced on a piece of wooden plank. He held it up and Paul took one, gratefully.

"Do I remember giving permission for fires to be lit, Corporal?" he demanded, passing a cup to his commander and then to Barnard. "Here, Andrew."

"I don't remember you telling us we couldn't light fires, sir," Cooper said, innocently. "Did I not hear that order?"

"You keep that up and you'll get a thump on the ear that'll stop you hearing for a week," Paul informed him, watching as Cooper passed tea to Vandeleur and Johnny. "Thank you, Cooper, I don't give a damn what my orders were, this was a very good idea."

"You hungry, sir? We've got some chicken, I can get one of the lads to bring it up."

Paul stared at him over the steaming cup. "Chicken? What is this, a church picnic? Where the devil did you get chicken from, you unprincipled bastard? Have you been looting the locals? You'd better not have, they're pissed off enough with us for abandoning Salamanca."

"Only half of them, sir. The other half are dusting off their French flags and cheering Bonaparte. And we've not been looting, the French have. About a dozen of our lads were left in Salamanca, in the hospital. When Lord Wellington gave orders for the city to be cleared this morning, they decided they'd rather be back with us, than joining the baggage train so they took a different route, so to speak."

"Against orders?" Paul demanded. He was trying to inject a note of severity into his voice, very aware that his divisional commander and his two fellow brigade commanders were listening with great interest to the exchange.

"They didn't have an officer with them to give any orders. It was a bit chaotic, from what I hear. You probably don't want to order them arrested for desertion for coming back to join their regiment, sir," Cooper said reasonably. "It wasn't just our men, there was about ten riflemen from the 60th joined them. Good lads, sir, not had much to do with the 60th, but apparently, they're bonny fighters."

"Fighters?" Paul said, raising his voice a notch and completely forgetting his attempt to sound like a senior officer. "Cooper, stop prevaricating and bribing me with tea and tell me what the bloody hell happened before I punch you."

"Just a bit of a skirmish, sir," Cooper said, in the soothing tones he might have used to a five-year-old. "They came across a French patrol from Foy's brigade. Long way from their lines, mind, they shouldn't have been there."

"Scouting?" Alten said sharply.

"Looting, sir. Burned out a farmhouse and two cottages, spiteful bastards. The families got out, the men found them hiding in some woods. From what the French prisoners said, they were sent out for wood and water and decided to collect a bit extra. They'd cleared everything out of the houses and slaughtered a sheep and all the poultry. By the time our lads came on them, they'd cooked the meat on a fire they'd built from some of the furniture."

"Did they see our men coming?" Paul asked.

"No, sir. Not a bloody clue, they'd not even set sentries, the stupid bastards, they thought all our men would be busy up here. A couple were wounded and one dead, he tried to take on two rifles with a bayonet and lost.

58

They took the rest prisoner, I've sent an escort up to headquarters with them now. Seemed a shame to waste all that meat, though, sir, so our lads brought it with them."

Paul wondered what else the men had acquired from the Frenchmen, but he knew better than to ask.

"You should have been hanged years ago, Cooper. Bring it up, I've been listening to General Alten's stomach growling for fifteen minutes. Oh, and Ben - any to spare?"

"Plenty, sir. We can't carry it around with us in this heat."

"Do me a favour and send some up to Lord Wellington, will you? With my compliments."

Cooper gave a broad grin and saluted. "Certainly, sir," he said promptly. "Wonder if it'll put him in the right mood to fight the French?"

Paul grinned. The thought of food had made him feel immeasurably better. "With a leg of chicken in his hand, Cooper, who knows what he can achieve," he said cheerfully. "But bring ours first, will you? Just in case."

# Chapter Five

Lieutenant Simon Carlyon joined the staff of Major-General Edward Pakenham with a mix of furious resentment and sheer relief in his heart. He had been summoned to an interview with Colonel van Daan ready to receive, at the very least, the news of his transfer into another and less prestigious regiment and at worst, the news that he would be sent for court martial after the incident at the ball in Rueda. He found the Colonel with several mangled sheets of paper in his hand, glaring at the shaggy form of his wife's dog, who was regarding him with lifted eyebrows and an expression of considerable surprise.

"I should send you over to the French; they'd probably eat you during the next retreat, you mangey, demonic carpet on legs," Paul was saying severely. "I had just finished these and they need to be sent off with the courier tonight which means I will be rewriting them instead of eating supper with my officers and my wife. And if I have to sit here, so do you; you're not bloody going out there to dine on scraps like a lap dog while I suffer."

Craufurd tilted his head to one side and gave the Colonel a look which made Simon want to laugh aloud despite his apprehension. The Colonel did not appear in the least embarrassed at being caught in conversation with a dog, by his orderly and a junior officer in trouble.

"Mr Carlyon to see you, sir," Jenson said. "You want me to get one of the lads to take Craufurd for a run?"

"I want one of the lads to drown Craufurd," Paul said grimly. "Sadly, my wife would never forgive me."

"No, sir. Although I should point out, it wasn't Mrs van Daan who carried a puppy out of Badajoz tucked into his coat because he couldn't bear to leave him to starve. If he's just eaten a pile of paper, though, he probably ought to go outside for a…"

The dog coughed. All three men looked at him. Craufurd looked back innocently, then retched violently, spewing a revolting pile of vomit onto the floor of the tent. It contained, very obviously, the remains of three sheets of paper. Nobody spoke for a minute.

"You might want to take Mr Carlyon into Major Swanson's tent, sir, he's at drill with the 110th just now," Jenson said finally. "I'll get that cleaned up. Private Griffith can do it and then take Craufurd for a run, he's waiting outside Major Clevedon's tent for a chat about his drinking habits this week."

"An excellent idea, Jenson," Paul said. "This way, Mr Carlyon."

Inside Major Swanson's tent, Simon saluted and stood to attention. His Colonel sat down in a camp chair and surveyed him.

"You remind me of me," he said.

"Sir?"

"Five years ago, in a house in Denmark, waiting for Sir Arthur Wellesley to take my head off and send me for court martial. Sit down, for God's sake, and drink some of the Major's wine, I happen to know he's run out of brandy. Sorry about the dog but at least he didn't do it all over your shoes. He did it to Marshal Beresford last month on parade. Of all the people to choose; the Marshal is so conscious of his dignity. I thought Lord Wellington would actually explode with the effort of keeping a straight face."

Simon lowered himself cautiously into a chair and took the wine cup. "Thank you. Look, sir, I know…"

"No, you don't know. But to be fair, I didn't know either, until Harry Smith told me how much shit you're getting over your brother. Why didn't you tell me?"

"It's not your problem, sir."

"It is, if it causes my junior officers to get into scraps with the rest of the Light Division every five minutes. But it's not just that, is it, Lieutenant? It's the expression on your face every time Colonel Wheeler walks past. It's rude and it's disrespectful to a senior officer and if I can see it, the men can see it, which means it's bad for discipline. It either has to stop or you can't serve here, I'm sorry. I like you, Simon, and you're shaping up to be a bloody good officer but if you can't get over it, I'll have to find you a place somewhere else."

"Do you have a brother, sir?" Simon said, unable to stop himself.

"Yes," the Colonel said. "An older one, of whom I'm very fond. You can thank him for the fact that you're still here. But he didn't try to murder his wife. Your brother did. There's no doubt about it, nothing suspicious. If Johnny Wheeler hadn't walked in when he did, or if he'd not had enough courage to pull the trigger, a girl of twenty would have died that day and your blasted brother would have been publicly hanged for murder. Unless I'd got to him first, in which case he'd have died a lot more slowly. I'm sorry for you, Simon, but I can't make this decision for you. If you can get over your problem with Colonel Wheeler, I will deal with the rest of the Light Division and you won't hear a squeak out of the little bastards, I promise you. Otherwise, tell me and I'll arrange a transfer. In the meantime, we're marching out, possibly to fight. I don't have any further time to spend on this and I can't risk you in battle fighting under a man you can't speak to. I've found you a temporary posting in the third division. General Pakenham is a friend of mine and is in command while General Picton is recovering. He needs more staff members and is happy to take you on. It's a very good posting; frankly, under normal circumstances I'd have given the chance to one of my lads from the 110th. I'm giving it to you. It's a chance to show what you can do without this hanging over you. And a chance to clear your head a bit."

"Yes, sir."

"Unclench your jaw, you stubborn young idiot, I'm trying to help. Get your kit ready, I've a letter for General Pakenham, you can take it with you. Now get going, while I see if my tent is fit for human habitation yet and rewrite those bloody letters."

Despite his miserable uncertainty, Simon liked Major-General Edward Pakenham immediately. He was only a few years older than Colonel van Daan and Simon could easily imagine why they were friends. Pakenham struck him as an uncomplicated man with a cheerful manner and an ability to set people at their ease. He introduced Simon to the rest of his staff, half a dozen young officers all of whom were considerably better born and probably considerably wealthier but all of whom welcomed the newcomer with immense cordiality. None questioned his presence or seemed to know anything of him, apart from the fact that he had come with Paul van Daan's personal recommendation and that seemed to be enough.

Pakenham was abroad early after the storm, inspecting the men and ensuring that officers and NCOs had their orders and Simon rode with him. Pakenham did not have Paul van Daan's extraordinary gift of combining informality with iron discipline but his genuine concern for his men's welfare was obvious and Simon had the sense that he was very well liked.

The third division had remained on the north bank of the Tormes along with D'Urban's Portuguese dragoons but as the morning wore on, orders came and Pakenham's men, along with D'Urban's cavalry set off to cross the river, taking up a position near Aldea Tejada, to the north-west of the village of Los Arapiles. It was some way behind the Allied line and Simon wondered if they were intended to cover a retreat.

Simon was accustomed to the tedium of waiting for orders, but he could sense that both officers and men were unusually restive. None of them wanted to retreat without bringing the French to battle and all were frustrated after the long weeks of marching and manoeuvring.

The heat mounted as the sun rose higher. The crash of artillery was growing louder and more frequent and Simon wondered if, after all, battle would be joined today and if he would be part of it.

"Wonder if we'll fight?" Lieutenant Davis said, beside him.

"No idea. What does the General think?"

"Hasn't a clue although he's desperate to," Davis said. "Between you and I, he wasn't the obvious choice for this command, but Picton recommended him. In fact, I did hear a rumour that your Colonel was seriously considered."

"Colonel van Daan?"

"Yes. I don't think Picton liked that idea; he wants to come back and find his division the way he left it and you couldn't be sure of it with your man; he's a bit unpredictable."

The description struck Simon as a considerable understatement, but he was relieved to realise that he was not the only man in the army who thought Paul van Daan slightly mad. "Have you served with General Pakenham long?" he asked.

"No, I've been General Picton's ADC for over a year. Hope he recovers and comes back. I like Pakenham well enough, but I miss that grumpy old bastard."

As the day wore on, action seemed less and less likely and Pakenham, surveying the distant smoke of cannon fire and listening for any sound of pitched battle, finally gave orders for the men to cook their meal. It was a laborious process out here, with little wood immediately available and the men made the best of what they could find, using twigs and stubble. Pakenham's staff huddled around their own fire and drank brandy while waiting for water to boil for tea.

"Wish they'd not sent the baggage off," Davis grumbled. "Don't fancy another night without a tent and a camp bed. Bloody waste of time this, we're not going to see any fighting today. I reckon Hookey's lost his nerve, been listening to Cotton and that old woman Beresford."

"Colonel van Daan thinks he's going to fight," Simon said.

"Does he? He talks to Wellington a lot, doesn't he? Do you think...?"

"What's that?" Simon interrupted. He was looking out across the plain where two horsemen rode, their identities concealed by the cloud of dust kicked up by their horses. They were riding fast, leaving the lines far behind, and as Simon watched, the leading rider reined in, close to D'Urban's cavalry.

"By God, I think that's Wellington," Davis breathed.

Pakenham came forward to join them, his eyes on the two riders. Simon could sense his sudden tension and he felt a moment of kinship with his new commander who was hoping for a chance, like Simon, to prove himself. The third division, still struggling to cook its meal, largely ignored them, but those officers close enough to notice had all stopped to watch.

Lord Wellington had wheeled his horse away from D'Urban and was galloping flat out towards Pakenham, the horse sure-footed over the rough ground. Simon could feel his heart beating faster. Suddenly he was very sure and as he thought it, Pakenham said softly:

"We're going to fight."

Lord Wellington reined in, controlling the horse with the ease of a superb rider. Behind him was Colonel de Lancey and a third staff member, whom Simon did not recognise, was fast approaching. Simon had seen the commander-in-chief many times in the past weeks although he had not been introduced. The same was true of many young officers but Simon could not help wondering if Colonel van Daan had made a point of not doing so. Robert Carlyon had been a trusted member of the quartermaster-general's department until his passionate jealousy of his lovely young wife had set in train the events which led to his death. Robert had received a promotion to captain only months before his death which suggested that Wellington had valued him, and Simon imagined he must have felt a strong sense of betrayal.

"General Pakenham, I have your orders, sir," Wellington said. Simon was struck by the extraordinary calm of his tone. It was almost casual. "I have been watching their advance, they are marching to the left, extending their line. They're hoping to catch us out and outflank us, by God. They've advanced up onto the Monte de Azan and their line looks very stretched indeed."

"Sir?"

"I want you to attack, Ned, immediately." Wellington pointed. "Take those hills and drive them off. D'Urban's cavalry will support you and protect your flank."

Pakenham did not speak for a moment, but looking at them, Simon saw a flash in the blue-green eyes. Simon felt the same thing; the moment that battle became inevitable, mingled excitement, fear, and determination to succeed. Abruptly Pakenham nodded and put out his hand. Lord Wellington looked faintly surprised, but he shook it, and Pakenham turned his horse without another word and surveyed his assembled staff. His brother-in-law watched for a moment as Pakenham began to issue his orders and then rode off, his two ADCs at his heels.

The division, surprised in the middle of cooking, upended the camp kettles, muttering curses at the loss of their meal. They packed up swiftly and sent the baggage mules to the rear. Pakenham moved among them, speaking a word here and there, giving his orders to his senior commanders as the men checked their muskets and fixed bayonets. He paused to listen as Colonel Wallace who commanded the first brigade, addressed his officers, instructing them to lead from the front to prevent mistakes during the noise from the cannon.

"Mr Carlyon, will you go in with the first brigade, if you please?" Pakenham said unexpectedly. "Under Colonel Wallace, they're short of officers due to sickness, he'll tell you where he wants you."

"Yes, sir."

"Look after yourself, Mr Carlyon." Pakenham gave his ready smile. "I do not wish to have to tell Colonel van Daan that I have lost one of his officers, he'll shoot me."

"Try to, sir," Carlyon said and hesitated, then said impulsively. "Good luck."

"Thank you, Lieutenant."

Pakenham moved on and Simon saluted to Colonel Wallace, a slight man in his late thirties, some inches shorter than Simon. Wallace eyed him thoughtfully. "Carlyon, is it? 115th?"

Simon felt his heart sink slightly and he could sense himself stiffening. "Yes, sir. Temporary ADC to General Pakenham."

"Your sister-in-law mentioned you at dinner last week. Lovely women, ain't she?"

"Yes, sir," Simon said, somewhat surprised. "I've known her all my life, we were childhood friends."

"Welcome to the 88th, Mr Carlyon. Riding in, are you?"

Simon hesitated then shook his head. "Rather go with the other subalterns, sir."

"Good man. My groom will take your horse to the rear then, join the second company. Let's get them moving. What is it, Campbell?"

Captain Campbell, who was brigade-major, saluted. "Compliments of General Pakenham, sir, we're to move as quickly as possible without tiring the men too much."

Wallace snorted. "Thought that was fairly obvious, myself," he muttered, and turned to yell an order to his sergeant-major.

The brigade moved out at a fast but steady pace, descending into a hollow which would conceal all movement from the French. Looking over, Simon could see the left brigade, headed by the fifth, marching parallel to the right while the Portuguese brigade followed. A screen of skirmishers from the light companies and the riflemen of the 60th, distinctive in green jackets with scarlet facings, covered the left flank. The brigade advanced in a long, narrow open column, a single company wide and Wallace had left gaps between the companies to enable them to wheel into line easily.

Simon looked around. Apart from an occasional order, the men moved silently and swiftly over the ground. There was a sense of controlled purpose among them, as though they had been waiting for this moment over all the long weeks of marching and counter-marching. Under the blaze of the sun, with little breeze, the colours hung limply, fluttering a little with the movement of the bearers and despite the fact that they were not the colours of his regiment, Simon felt a sense of pride at being here with these men, on this ground, on this day. He was not sure he had felt quite the same during his years in India; the battles he had fought there had been local skirmishes with the occasional pitched battle and although Simon knew that it had taught him his trade and taught it well, he had often felt that he was fighting for the wealth and prestige of local rulers or East India Company merchants rather than for any sense of country or regimental loyalty. This felt very different and quite suddenly he knew, beyond any shadow of doubt, that he wanted to stay.

With the officers and NCOs carefully keeping their men in position, the brigade covered the distance quickly and the head of the column began gradually to ascend the hill. If Wellington were correct, the French would be found at the top, still moving to their left. Pakenham moved to the front, signalling to his officers and the division fell into line with a smoothness that impressed Simon, the light troops and rifles still covering.

There was a shot, sounding loud in the silence of the advance, followed by another, and then more. The light troops and rifles had encountered the French skirmishers and were exchanging fire, and there were sounds ahead, shouts and orders yelled in French as the enemy divisions realised, to their horror, that they were under attack. Further sounds erupted from the right as the Allied cavalry charged and met with a barrage of fire from the French infantry. Simon felt a familiar hollow sickness in his stomach as he drew his sword. He had never yet gone into battle without feeling that he was likely to vomit at any moment although the feeling passed quickly once battle was joined.

The smell of gun smoke was beginning to fill the air, and already part of the slope was obscured to the left by acrid black clouds, but it was still possible to see Pakenham at the head of his men. The brigade had paused for a moment and Simon saw the General riding from one battalion to another, speaking to officers and men. As he did so there was a new crash of gunfire from a rise to the north as the batteries of Douglas and Bull opened fire on the French.

The enemy were in considerable disarray with only four battalions in any kind of order after D'Urban's cavalry charge. With Pakenham's men on top of them and preparing for close combat, there was no possibility of a retreat; no option but to stand and fight. Simon listened to the rhythm of the drums and felt the sound deep within him like the beating of his heart. He stood balanced and waiting, his sword in his hand.

With the mounted officers at their head, the brigade reached the top of the hill. The French charged forward and there was a deafening crash of musket fire which blew away a section of Wallace's front rank and some of the second. Simon felt a blast of powder and was temporarily shaken to realise that the man to the side of him was down, covered in blood. Wallace turned, yelling and pointing towards the French and the brigade raced forward over their dead and injured comrades.

The French second volley was less successful. They were already wavering, unsettled both by the cavalry charge and artillery fire and the determined rush of the Allies and confused them further. Their firing was uncoordinated and poorly directed and did little damage to the Allies. Eventually it petered out entirely and there was almost silence for a few seconds, then somebody further down the line to Simon let out an ironic cheer.

The cheer was taken up quickly until all three of the front regiments were roaring to a man. It was a fearsome sound and Simon could see the front rank of the French beginning to panic, backing away almost without realising they were doing so. The men beside him were clearly impatient, straining against the invisible bonds of discipline to be let loose against the French and Simon shouted at them to hold and wait. In the ranks of the French he could see the officers trying to rally their men, urging them forward before the Allies made their charge.

One of the French officers, his face scarlet with both the heat and the exertion of screaming at his reluctant men, ran forward a few paces. He was holding a musket, probably snatched from one of his men, and Simon watched as he raised it and fired. There was a collective shout of dismay around Simon and he saw that the officer's bullet had struck home, probably more by luck than good aim, given the notoriously unreliable aim of a musket. Major Murphy, on horseback at the head of his men, fell with a strangled cry. Simon watched in horror as his panicked horse took off across the front of the line, dragging Murphy's bloody body with one foot caught in the stirrup.

Simon had no idea if the Major was still alive, but watching the body bouncing across the dry ground, he knew with sick certainty that he would be dead soon. There was a swell of sound from the men of the 88th, all the more menacing because this time it was quiet.

A movement from the left caught Simon's eye and he looked over to where a rifleman from the 60th stood poised, his rifle aimed. He was looking over towards his officer, his expression almost desperate, pleading, but the officer was looking elsewhere. Simon looked back at Murphy's battered body, soaked now in his own blood, and caught up in a wave of sheer fury, shouted:

"Rifleman, take that bastard down."

The rifleman fired once, and it was enough. The French officer threw up his arms as the shot hit him and fell forward. Unlike Murphy, Simon thought, it had been quick.

It would be impossible to hold the 88th any longer and Pakenham did not try. "Let them loose, Colonel Wallace," he called.

There was a surge of movement, an atavistic roar which deafened Simon and the British line rushed forward, hitting the French hard and breaking open their ranks in a wave of savage death.

Simon's attention was elsewhere. With no specific command responsibilities, his eyes were on the terrified horse which still dragged the body of Murphy, now engulfed in a wave of furious redcoats. Amidst the roar of musket fire and the screams of wounded and dying men, the horse reared up. Simon pushed through the ranks, sword drawn and wary of a French counter-attack and reached the horse which was plunging madly amidst the fighting, endangering both itself and the men around it.

Sheathing his sword, Simon reached for the bridle, keeping clear of the thrashing hooves, and managed to catch hold. He could do nothing with the frightened animal in this melee, so he dragged it towards the rear. He was horribly aware of the bloody mess which had once been a man who had sat beside him the previous evening at dinner and talked to him about his previous service and his hopes for the future. Simon had liked Murphy enormously and had no intention of letting his body be trampled any further.

He reached finally, the rear of the lines and there was suddenly space and air around him. Ahead he could see some of the regimental bandsmen from the 88th, waiting with the medical staff and he shouted for help. Two men approached, a middle-aged Irishman with a shiny bald head and a boy of half his age whose uniform looked too big for him.

"What the devil is this?"

"It's Major Murphy's horse," the boy said instantly, and then saw the horrible burden. "Oh no. Oh shit, no."

"Get him free, I'll hold the horse," Simon said. His voice came out as a croak, partly from the choking clouds of black smoke and partly from tears he had not realise he had shed until he spoke. Both men ran forward and Simon held the black gelding close to him, trying to shield its eyes from the sight of its master's ruined body as the men freed Murphy and lifted what was left of him onto a blanket, wrapping him up as if in a makeshift shroud.

"Take him to the rear," Simon said. "And get one of the grooms to come and take his horse, the poor thing's mad with fear, he'll kill somebody."

"I'll take him, sir."

Simon looked round to see his own groom coming forward and he was passionately glad of it. "Reynolds, what the devil are you doing here?"

"The horses are safe, sir, I left them with a couple of the officers' grooms. I thought I might help up here with the wounded."

"Well get this poor creature back with them for now. And stay back there, Reynolds, I'm not having you within range of a musket. I'm going back up. Take care of him."

"I will, sir. Keep safe."

Simon turned and made his way back up into the fray. He weaved his way through the mass of red coats, stepping over both dead and wounded, and found that the Allies initial charge had slowed, not so much because of French resistance but because the men were exhausted by their run uphill in the heat. Those who had water, were refreshing themselves from their water bottles but many were empty. The fighting was fierce, hand to hand combat with bayonets and the French had fallen back some distance from the first rush but were now making a desperate stand.

"Carlyon. Did you get him off the field?"

Simon turned to find Colonel Wallace beside him. "Yes, sir, the bandsmen will take care of him. Very sorry, sir."

"We all are, he was a fine officer, well-liked by the men. Bloody tragedy. Well done, I saw what you did. General Pakenham has ordered up the reserves."

"What's happening on the left?" Simon asked. He could hear it now, the crash of musketry volleys hitting the French from a new direction.

"He's sent in the fifth, I think. Not that we can see, it could be anybody out there." Wallace coughed. "Reserves are coming in now."

The French infantry was in total confusion, only the iron determination of some of their officers keeping them from fleeing incontinently. Even so, some of the men were pushing back, becoming entangled with the back of the columns which was still trying to press forward against the Allies.

As always in battle, Simon had no sense of time. With the Allied lines pushing through the French, communication became difficult, and he found himself, by default, taking charge of half a company of the 88th which seemed to have lost all its officers, either dead or wounded or possibly separated on the field. Pakenham's men had steadily pursued the French column out onto an open plain, dry grass dotted about with small copses of cork oak trees. They were making good progress, with Simon urging on his company, when he heard a shout which he recognised as coming from Colonel Williams of the 60th.

"Cavalry coming up and they've got reinforcements."

It was clearly true; the French were suddenly renewed, turning to fight where they had been fleeing, and there were fresh troops coming in to face Pakenham's exhausted men. The Sergeant of Simon's company went down with a cry of pain as a ball caught him in the shoulder and two infantrymen were on him in a second, stabbing down viciously with bayonets. Simon went in furiously, swinging his sword, almost decapitating the first man who fell on top of the Sergeant, blood shooting up in a high arc, splashing Simon's face and neck. He had the thick, metallic smell of it in his nostrils as he turned on the second Frenchman and cut him across the body. There was a flash of blue at his elbow and he turned quickly and found himself in a furious duel with a French officer, a stocky man with an elaborate dark moustache, his face scarlet with effort and his eyes black pools of fury. He was a good swordsman; better than Simon, and for two terrifying minutes Simon parried frantically, backing up, unable to reach through the other man's guard, and wondered if he was about to die.

Simon did not hear the shot, it was lost in the cacophony of the battle around him, but he saw suddenly, his opponent's body jerk violently. A red rose appeared on his breast, spreading quickly and an expression of sheer astonishment flickered across his face, then he fell forward to the ground, and beyond him Simon saw a rifleman from the 60th reloading. He lifted his bloody sword in a grateful gesture.

"Cavalry! Form square!"

The sounds of musket fire along the centre had continued throughout and Simon's ears were ringing with the noise. There was clearly a battle raging to the left, but it was invisible to him through the thick black smoke. A dozen men sporting the blue facings of the 4th infantry appeared ahead of him and Simon realised that Leith's fifth division was becoming entangled with Pakenham's men.

He could hear cheering coming from behind and around him, men turned, alarmed, thinking that French cavalry were attacking from the rear. Instead, orders were shouted through to open up, and in place of the French, Simon saw with relief that the Allied heavy cavalry brigade of Le Marchant was coming forward in line at a swift canter. Simon called to his men to part and the thudding of hooves and jingling of harness passed him, although the smoke was so thick, he could see very little of them. Around the battlefield, areas of dry grass had been set alight, probably by discarded cartridge papers. The rolling smoke was suffocating.

Simon felt a momentary pang of sympathy for the French, who had been doing well against superior numbers. Prepared to fight Pakenham and Leith's exhausted infantry, they were faced instead with three regiments of cavalry. Simon could see the sheer terror on their faces and hear their officers screaming at them to get into square, but it was too late. The cavalry thundered into the charge and the French column scrambled into the best formation they could manage and stood. An order was yelled, and a massive volley of fire hit the cavalry as it reached them, taking many men out of the saddle and down into the first rows of the French bayonets. The first line of troopers suffered heavy casualties but there was no time to reload as the dragoons thundered on, cutting down the French in swathes.

Simon watched in fascinated horror. He had never seen such a destructive cavalry charge. The French were being slaughtered in line, the horses jumping over piled dead and wounded on the ground to chase down those who were trying to flee, and the British sabres were red in the garish light of the flames.

The French were running, no longer making any attempt to stand, and many of them ran towards Pakenham's infantry lines, taking refuge among Simon's men. They were beyond fighting further, beyond even rational thought, both faces and uniforms black with smoke and powder, many bleeding and limping, all of them exhausted. Simon shouted an order, but it was unnecessary; none of the surrendering Frenchmen were attacked. The third division closed protectively around them, and prisoners, not slaughter, were suddenly the order of the day. Both the third and fifth division herded them close, divesting them on the way of colours, flags, and trophies, but individual prisoners were left unmolested. With the battle sweeping further over the plain, Simon stood, completely exhausted, looking around him. On this part of the field, for a time, at least, the fight was over.

# Chapter Six

The sounds of battle reached the commanders of the Light Division out on Wellington's right as they waited, with ill-concealed impatience, for further orders.

"We have our orders, Colonel," General Alten said, watching with some amusement as Paul moved restlessly on his horse, shifting position from time to time to find a better view of the battlefield. "We are to stay here in reserve and watch the troops of Foy and Ferey."

"I'm not finding watching them all that interesting." Paul looked over at his commander. "I'm not very good at waiting. Is that Leith in action?"

"Possibly. Also, General Pakenham, I think. And you are to remain here with your brigade."

Paul gave a slight smile. "You're getting to know me, sir," he said softly and the German grinned.

"Your frustration is visible for us all to see, Colonel, but we shall have to wait. We have a task."

Another half hour dragged on. The ground over to the south-west was covered in rolling smoke and the crash of muskets and cannon made it clear that battle was fully joined. For Paul's men there was little to do although there was an occasional exchange of fire between the skirmishers and the French tirailleurs of Foy and Ferey's divisions. It was almost a relief to see any action at all. Paul knew that his men hated the tension of waiting inactive, knowing that should things go wrong they might be called into battle at any moment.

When the smoke occasionally cleared, Paul could see the French column on the heights fighting for its life against the Allied advance. There was a flurry of movement early in the battle as a large body of French infantry and the majority of the cavalry moved from their position facing the Light Division towards the action, leaving only a small force facing Alten's men.

"We could go through them in about twenty minutes," Paul said wistfully.

"Orders, Colonel."

"Sometimes, General, you are so German."

"Sometimes, Colonel, I begin to see why many people believed that

71

you and I could not work together," Alten responded, and Paul looked over at him quickly, wondering if he had given offence. He had not; Alten's pleasant smile had not changed, and Paul relaxed. He realised, in some surprise, how much he was beginning to value the easy friendship he was developing with the Hanoverian.

"Robert Craufurd would have been climbing the walls by now," he said. "But just at the moment I'm glad we have you, you're very calming."

The German looked sideways at him.

"I am glad I have you also," he said.

It was not in Paul's nature to wait patiently while others fought. At twenty-two, during his first major battle as a newly gazetted captain at the battle of Assaye in India, he had taken his own decision to go in ahead of orders, risking the wrath of a general who even back then had a dislike of officers acting on their own initiative. Almost ten years later, the balance between Lord Wellington's need to control and Paul's readiness to use his own judgement on a battlefield had been tested many times. Paul was aware that much of the army was constantly astonished at Wellington's steady support of an officer whose tendency to act without orders was legendary.

Paul's easy, almost affectionate relationship with his commander-in-chief was unique in Wellington's life but there had been frequent arguments, some more serious than others. Paul knew that his wife's friendship with Wellington was a considerable advantage to him on these occasions, and he used it shamelessly, knowing that the mention of her name would always cause his chief to stop, take a breath and possibly rethink. Wellington's officers and some of his own staff considered him to be difficult, arrogant, and sarcastic, a man who could not admit a mistake, often rode roughshod over the feelings of his subordinates, and who would never apologise. Paul could not entirely disagree, but he shared Wellington's dry sense of humour and was very seldom offended by him although he was often exasperated with his controlling leadership style. His chief annoyed him, but did not upset him, and despite their frequent differences of opinion, Paul considered him a friend.

Watching Wellington's genius enacted around him, Paul did not feel the urge to order his men into the fray. They were simply not needed at this point, but he knew that things could suddenly change and that the light division were the perfect force to be sent in quickly should they be required. Wellington needed them to be where he had left them, so Paul curbed him impatience and waited for orders.

Beside him, Major Swanson said placidly:

"Nice day for it. We should have brought chairs."

Paul grinned, knowing that his friends were very well aware how difficult inactivity was for him. "I wonder if he's ordered the baggage train back yet? I probably would. Still, it's barely started - things could still go wrong."

"We have company, gentlemen," Alten said placidly, his glass to his eye. Paul, Barnard and Vandeleur all turned to look as three horsemen approached at a gallop.

Paul grinned at the sight of his commander-in-chief riding well ahead of his staff. If it were at all possible, Wellington liked to be able to ride around the battlefield delivering orders in person and the sight of his staff officers scrambling to keep up with him while not getting themselves killed was a familiar one. Wellington reined in before Alten who saluted.

"Orders, Lord Wellington?"

"Remain in place, General. We will need you when they start to retreat, to keep Foy occupied, he's the one with the most undamaged troops. You'll see some action then."

"Yes, my Lord."

Wellington glanced over at the brigade commanders. "Colonel Barnard, General Vandeleur, you will remain under General Alten in reserve until you're needed. Colonel van Daan, get your men to form up. I want you out on the road immediately to cut off their line of retreat."

"Sir?" Paul said in surprise.

"Espana has a force of 2000 Spanish garrisoning the castle and guarding the bridge at Alba de Tormes. Do you know where that is?"

"I do, sir."

"Get your brigade over there. I've had scouts out, there's a clear line to the river to the north of Foy's men, through those trees." Wellington indicated a slight, dark man, mounted on a mule. "This is Jorge Collado, he has fought with a guerrilla band close to Salamanca for two years, he knows the land. He will guide you to a small ford just above the town, you can cross there and join up with Espana's men."

Paul studied his chief. "You think they're going to run."

"Yes," Wellington said briefly. "Eventually. They might well make for the fords at Huerta, it depends on where they break first, but if they go through Alba de Tormes, I want you there to steady the Spanish. They're brave enough but they don't have the experience. I've orders here, giving you operational command."

"Yes, sir."

"Get moving, Colonel, it will take you a couple of hours to get into position."

"Possibly less, sir, given that we're well rested. Good luck."

Even allowing for the fact that Paul was moving away from the action. it felt good to be on the move with a purpose. He led the eighteen hundred men of his brigade at a fast march towards the river Tormes, skirting widely around the French troops through the woods. Paul kept his men on the alert in case Foy's remaining men became aware of their movement, but it was clear that the General's attention was fixed on the battlefield.

Paul's men were fresh and ready to fight, and Paul pushed them hard, wanting them in position well before any retreat began. As Wellington had said, the French might well make for the fords, but if they did head for the bridge at Alba de Tormes, it would be a good position to hold them off.

It was summer and despite yesterday's heavy rain the ford was low, reaching barely to their ankles as they splashed through. With the distance covered, Paul gave orders for the men to drink and fill water bottles and Jenson and the other orderlies and grooms watered the horses. Paul wandered among his men, stopping to talk here and there, and noticed that his NCOs were using the opportunity to check that all the men had their bottles. There was a thriving market in the sale of equipment, usually to fund drinking or women, and penalties were severe for a man caught without some vital article when it was needed. Paul was lenient in matters of uniform. Over their years of service, the men had acquired a variety of garments from the French or the locals to replace items grown threadbare or fallen apart and as long as they retained their recognisable coat, he did not care what they wore. But items such as blankets for the freezing nights, kettles and pans to cook food and water bottles to get them through a fast march in scorching weather were essential to the health of his men and the functioning of his brigade, and retribution for a man caught without them was swift and merciless. Looking over at the light company of the 110th Paul watched the men for a while, unobserved.

"Private Garrett," he called finally. "Where's your bottle?"

The boy looked up, wide eyed. "Sir. I...it's here somewhere, sir, it must be. I had it earlier, I swear."

Sergeant Hammond came forward. "Earlier is no use to me, lad. Not much I can do about it now, but I'm writing you up and when we're back in billets, we'll find you a nice little job to remind you about taking care of your equipment. And the replacement comes out of your pay."

"Good idea, Sergeant," Paul said walking forward. "But make it a short punishment, will you, he's only guilty of losing it for about eight minutes and he won't need to pay for it. Private Dobson, stop fiddling with yourself, you're taking the longest piss in history over there, get your arse over here before I come after you myself."

Dobson, a thin sharp featured Cheshire man who had been with the 110th since just after Talavera, turned. The expression of horror on his face was ludicrous. He pulled his clothing straight and jogged over, saluting smartly.

"Give it back you thieving bastard," Paul said softly.

"Sir?"

"Are you seriously asking me to repeat myself?"

Dobson dipped a hand into his pack and retrieved the bottle. He handed it to the startled Garrett. "I was going to give it back before inspection was over," he said, sounding faintly apologetic. "Lost mine on the march."

Hammond reached out and cuffed the man hard around the head. "No you bloody didn't, Dobson, you lying toe rag, you sold it to fund that plump little widow you were parading around with in Rueda. I've been wondering where your funds were coming from, you're not that rich and she didn't look cheap. Get over there, open your pack and let's see what else is missing and when we get to camp you are digging the shitholes single handed until they're nice and deep. Get moving."

Paul laughed, watching the hapless Dobson spreading the contents of his pack for Hammond's ruthless eye. "Go and fill it, Garrett, and keep an eye on your kit in future. They might be your mates but they're still a bunch of

74

thieving sods and you're new and young and they'll bleed you dry unless you watch them. If he does it again, punch him hard and he'll move on to somebody else. And if you need a lesson in how to do that properly, I'll teach you."

The boy looked up at him. "Yes, sir. Thank you, sir."

"You're very welcome." Paul raised his voice. "Sergeant-Major Carter, another fifteen minutes and I want them lined up and on the road. Let's get up to the town and into position and then if you're lucky you can all get a rest for a bit. Although the speed that battle was moving, it might not be as long as you'd think."

The small town of Alba de Tormes was located on the eastern bank of the river on the far side of a medieval bridge. It was a prosperous looking town with the usual collection of white and ochre coloured houses with tiled roofs and wrought iron balconies, the windows protected from sun and rain by weathered or painted wooden shutters. There was a selection of impressive churches and the surrounding area was dotted with fields and vineyards. In these lands, occupied by the French for some years, agriculture had managed to continue, although Paul found himself wondering how profitable it had been, given the French troops practice of pillaging the locals without payment. Lord Wellington was ruthless in his condemnation of looting and theft and Paul knew that in part, that was due to his need to differentiate his army of liberation from the French invaders. It explained his fury at the depredations after the siege of Ciudad Rodrigo at the beginning of the year and the complete breakdown of discipline, law and order in Badajoz after the bloody storming in May.

Alba de Tormes had been the scene of a disastrous defeat for the Spanish three years earlier and Paul could remember Wellington's anger at the news. The Anglo-Portuguese army was still recovering from the exhausting retreat after Talavera and Wellington had fumed at the apparent determination of the Spanish to give pitched battle when they had no possible hope of winning. The town did not seem to have suffered much from the aftermath of the combat; either that or it had made a good recovery.

The third brigade marched into a shuttered and barricaded town which told Paul that the inhabitants were well aware of the battle raging a few miles away. Whichever army was victorious there was always the risk of a breakdown in discipline and Paul had not expected a cheering crowd to greet him in the warmth of early evening, although he had rather expected to encounter Spanish pickets. He supposed that knowing the direction a French retreat must come, the Spanish commander had set all sentries down at the bridge. Having just demonstrated effectively how easily a force from either side could use one of the lesser known fords to enter the town away from the bridge, Paul thought the Spanish had been fortunate they were not about to be hit from behind by a brigade of French infantry.

Paul halted his brigade on the edge of the town and went to consult with his guide. His men waited at ease but not breaking ranks as he studied the sketch map and talked quietly in Spanish. Collado pointed out the main road down to the bridge, not visible from this point as it was hidden by the buildings of the town and a thick belt of trees further on.

"Which is the road to Madrid?"

"This way, Colonel. They will come up from the bridge and pass through the town, then up this way."

Paul looked around him. "Is that why there's not a living soul in sight, Collado?"

"They will know of the battle, Colonel. They can hear it."

"Yes." Paul heard footsteps and looked around to find a stocky Spaniard in dark clothing and an impressive hat approaching, flanked by several other men.

"English?" the man said. "You are English?"

Paul's lips twitched slightly, and he dismounted, handing the reins to Jenson, and came forward. "As you see, sir," he said, indicating the ranks of red coated infantrymen.

The man looked relieved to hear his easy Spanish. "They are still fighting?"

"I think so. Colonel Paul van Daan of the 110th, I command the third brigade of the Light Division. Lord Wellington has sent us up to guard against a French retreat through here."

"You think they will retreat?"

"Fairly sure of it, sir. Are you...?"

"Forgive me. I am Luis Bamonte, Mayor of this town. All day we have waited. We fear for our town and our people."

"I understand. Don't look so worried, Señor Bamonte, we don't require a big welcome. You're doing the right thing. Keep your people within doors for a while longer and I think they'll be safe. Certainly, they're safe from us."

"Thank you, Colonel."

Paul mounted and lifted his hand to bring his brigade after him. Behind him, riding at the head of the 110th light company, Leo Manson glanced over at his lieutenant.

"Get the feeling we're being watched, Mr Denny?"

"Yes, sir. A fair few twitching drapes. Not so many flowers or kisses here, mind."

"No. They'll be waiting to see if we win."

Denny laughed aloud. "Cynical, sir. The Colonel seems confident."

"Lord Wellington seemed confident. I trust their judgement. I'm not sure we'll see action at all out of this one. I think two thousand Spaniards at the bridge will hold them off long enough for Lord Wellington to catch up with them. We might pick up some stragglers. It will make a change to have a nice convincing victory."

"We won at Ciudad Rodrigo, sir. And at Badajoz."

"I suppose we did," Manson said. "I spent too much time digging bodies out of the breaches and trying to identify men I liked with their heads blown off to really appreciate it, I think. Earlier I was disappointed we'd been left in reserve, but you know what? I think I'm happy to sit this one out, we've done our share."

"More than our bloody share."

Manson watched his commander rein in at the end of the street. The bridge was still out of sight and the road led through an open square lined with shady trees. A fountain with a white statue stood in the centre although no water was playing, probably because the source was too dry in the summer heat. It looked peaceful and cool and so far removed from the bloody field they had recently left, that Manson felt a sense of unreality. Paul lifted his hand. The brigade stopped to a man before their officers even had time to pass back the order and Manson wanted to laugh aloud. He had occasionally suspected Paul of teaching his brigade these tricks simply to irritate other officers who did not have his level of discipline over their men, but he knew he was probably being unjust. He saw his commander look back over his shoulder and beckon to Manson and Michael O'Reilly to join him.

"We'll wait here and in a minute, I'll go in search of the Spanish. There's not a bloody sign of the dopey bastards, it's a good thing we're not the French. There will be a garrison up at the castle, that's probably where their commanding officer is. Keep them alert and to arms in case they have to move quickly and make sure nobody wanders off to shoot their supper, but they can relax for a bit now, I think. No fires, it's warm, they've no need of them and I don't want them distracted by cooking or making tea, but if they've rations left, they can eat. At ease – but cautiously."

"Yes, sir."

With his company settled under the watchful eyes of his junior officers and NCOs, Manson went up to join his commander's party who had seated themselves under a spreading oak tree. Michael had produced a bottle of brandy and was passing it around. Manson accepted a swig, impressed as always with the quality of the liquor that the Irishman managed to purloin from somewhere. As he had expected, Paul smiled and shook his head and the bottle was passed on.

"Jesus, sir, you're a miserable bastard, so you are," Michael said. "One of these days you'll forget yourself and take a drink before a fight, it's a mouthful, no more, and you've said yourself we'll probably see no action, it's getting dark."

"I do better without it, Michael."

The Irishman laughed and waved his hand to where the men waited, sprawled over the square and into the lanes, relaxed and talking. Pipe smoke floated up from their ranks, hanging in the cooling evening air. "Don't tell me they don't have their flasks and the odd bottle out over there, sir."

"You think so, Michael? Perhaps I'd better go and check – shall I start with your company?"

Michael did not move. "Go right ahead, sir, they'll offer you a drink. None of them will be drunk."

Paul gave a broad smile. "Good," he said. "I'm not that bad, Michael, I know I won't be leading any drunken men into a fight today – at least from the 110<sup>th</sup> or 112<sup>th</sup>. I just feel better myself if I don't. Offer it to me back in camp tomorrow and I'll finish it with you."

"Lord love you, sir, there'll be nothing of it left by then the way this lot are going," the Irishman said, laughing. "I'd offer you a cigarillo, but I know you don't."

"I'm well enough as I am. In fact, I'm so relaxed I'm going to doze off if I don't do something. Johnny, take over here, I'm going in search of the Spanish up at the castle."

"Would you call it a castle?" Carl said.

"Tower, then. It was a castle once."

"You won't see much over the buildings."

"I will from the tower; I might even be able to see the battlefield. Certainly, I'll be able to see if there's much movement this way. And I want to know, it'll be dark soon. No don't move, Leo, you look comfortable, I'll be back in ten minutes and you can come down to the bridge with me."

Paul turned and ran his eye over his troops. Manson moved to join him. Among the lounging form of the redcoats he could see a few townspeople who had cautiously emerged from their houses. Some of them had brought food which they were offering to the soldiers. A lot of them were women and some were young and pretty. Major Swanson came to join them.

"Doesn't take them long, does it?"

"No. And you can guarantee that the prettiest of them is likely to be found hanging around Sergeant Hammond," Paul said, watching.

"I think our Jamie has a rival," Carl said. "Look at the girl with the fruit basket over with Captain Kuhn."

"Well they deserve a break and a harmless flirtation. All the same, can you send the word around with the NCOs that nobody is to be disappearing off into the town with a pretty Spanish girl or I will personally find them and castrate them. This might feel like an afternoon off, but officially we're still halfway through a bloody battle."

"You think they'll run this way?" Manson asked.

"Some of them definitely will but I doubt we'll have much to do. They won't stand for long, they'll be a mess. We might need to take out the first few ranks but if they surrender, we accept. These boys will have had enough."

He moved to where the horses were grazing, and Manson settled back. Michael passed the bottle again.

"Jesus, he's a fidgety bastard. The only time he ever relaxes is when his wife is with him."

"I'm not sure it's relaxing he's doing then," Carl said with a grin. He had spoken to Sergeant-Major Carter with Paul's orders and returned to the group. "But she does calm him down."

"And there's a man who can talk," Michael said. "You've got almost as bad with that girl of yours, Major Swanson, do you know that half the new recruits think she's your wife?"

"Good, if it means they behave themselves around her. I must say your manners have improved, Michael."

"I've learned my lesson, sir, you're awful touchy when it comes to that lass, I'm becoming suspicious. Should I be asking you your intentions?"

"You're not her bloody father, Michael, you should be minding your own business. Anyway, my love life is so predictable these days that you must be bored with it. Let us instead ask Captain Manson for more information about the lady who writes to him every fortnight and sends him boxes of very expensive wine for his birthday."

Manson felt himself flush although he was laughing. "I bloody knew this was coming," he said.

"You ought to have, lad. Surprised it's not happened before, can't believe the Colonel has been this restrained about it. But he's buggered off now with itchy feet, so we have you at our mercy. Tell us all about that very delicious girl who threw you an apple as we left Elvas a few months back."

"As you said, it's nobody else's business, sir," Manson said, laughing.

"It bloody is, if you ever want time off to see her again," Carl said with a grin. "I can't tell you the number of imaginative duties I can come up with in the course of a week. Early drill, late drill, skirmish training, messages to be taken..."

They were laughing uproariously, and Manson held up his hands. "I hate you all," he said. "All right. She is, as you are well aware, a very pretty prostitute who runs a tavern with half a dozen girls working out of it. She is very lovely and not at all what one would expect. We're friends."

"Friends, is it now?" Michael hooted loudly. "That's definitely a new word for it. Is she charging you for it, Manson? And does she offer special rates for your friends?"

Manson felt himself flinch internally and weathered it as best he could. His relationship with Diana Periera was impossible, given what she did, and yet they had both agreed that it not only existed but that they wished it to continue to exist. Given that he had not the money to ask her to give up her means of support and that they did not know each other well enough for that anyway, he had made himself accept it, but hearing his friends laughing about it was as painful as he had thought it would be.

"You're not her type, Michael," he said, forcing a laugh, and as he did so, Colonel Wheeler picked up an old acorn and threw it hard and accurately so that it hit the Irishman between the eyes. Michael swore.

"That hurt."

"Good, you asked for it. Stop being an arsehole, Michael, or I'll throw something bigger next time. What's her name, Leo, she's very pretty?"

Manson met the steady grey eyes with gratitude. "Thank you, sir. Her name is Diana Pereira, her father was English, mother Portuguese and she's twenty. She was left a fifteen-year-old orphan in Oporto when the French first invaded which is how she ended up doing what she does, by the way, Michael."

Michael lay back on the ground and closed his eyes. "Shoot me now," he said. "I am sorry, lad. Sometimes my mouth opens, and shit comes out without my brain getting in the way at all."

"It's all right," Manson said, and then he laughed and shook his head, suddenly remembering that these were his friends. "No. It is so far from being all right, that I can't even begin to describe it. But this is the way it is, so it has to be all right. And I have to learn to put up with it."

Michael sat up. "Not from me, you don't. Do I take it, given his restraint on the subject, that our Colonel knows all about her?"

"About as much as you do. He noticed the letters. It's nice, having somebody to write to."

Michael gave a wry smile. "Aye, it would be," he said. "Well you're doing better than I am, laddie, so keep at it. If we go back to Elvas at some point perhaps you'll introduce us. I promise to behave."

"I will. You'll get the shock of your life, Michael. I did. She's not what you'd expect."

Wheeler laughed, reached over and removed the brandy from Michael's hand. "Well you're all doing better than I am, my love life is a shipwreck," he said. "So I intend to ignore my commander's good example and help you finish this. I doubt we'll need to worry about the French tonight."

***

Paul could hear their distant laughter as he rode back up the street towards the castle and it made him smile. He was restless, wishing that he knew for sure what was going on out on the battlefield. It was less than ten miles away and he could no longer hear the crash of guns, but he was not sure if that was because they were no longer firing or because the still evening air and the river between them was muffling the sound. The light was beginning to fade, and other than the few people supplying the soldiers, the streets were deserted.

At the top of the hill Paul turned and looked back. He could see some of the river, but the bridge was not visible. The River Tormes ran north from here into the wide plains of Leon over flat open farming land with the town nestled on this eastern bank. There was no good defensive position other than the river itself for miles around and any exhausted French stragglers who had survived the battle were likely to be easy prey for the men of the third brigade and Espana's two thousand Spanish troops.

The castle at Alba de Tormes was towards the top of the small town which sloped down towards the river and was largely in ruins although it must once have been a spectacular building, dominating the surrounding area. Only one complete tower remained, along with a selection of ruined buildings and outer walls, reminders of its former glory. Paul knew nothing of the dukes who had once ruled the area, but his eye automatically assessed the defences as he approached. He imagined that in times of war the whole town would have taken refuge within these enormous walls, now broken and fallen down in places.

There was an iron ring set into one of the outer walls and Paul dismounted, looping the reins around it. He patted Rufus' neck soothingly and went through a crumbling archway towards the tower. It rose ahead of him, formidable against the darkening sky. A huge oak door provided access and a series of broken walls around it showed where other buildings, once part of the castle, had crumbled away. Paul stopped and looked around him in some bewilderment. There was no sign of a sentry and Paul suddenly felt a frisson of alarm. He walked forward to the door, taking out his pistol and ensuring it was loaded and ready.

The door was locked, and Paul banged hard. There was no response and he could hear no sound from inside. He tried again, then studied the rusted metal fastening. Raising his pistol, he stood well back, considering. Before he could do more, however, there was a shout from above.

Paul stood back and looked up. A man was looking down from one of the small windows part way up the thick stone wall. He was middle aged with wispy grey hair and a bony face. Paul lifted his hand.

"I'm looking for the Spanish commander," he called, in Spanish. "Are they here, there are no sentries set? Colonel Paul van Daan, 110th light infantry, I…"

"English?"

"Yes. Who is in command here?"

The man gave a wheezy laugh. "Me," he said. "Just me. Hold."

Paul waited impatiently and eventually the huge door creaked open. The man stood framed in the doorway, silhouetted against the light of several candles within. There was no other sign of life.

"Alberto de Gea, Colonel. Caretaker for the castle. I…"

"The Spanish," Paul said, without preamble. "There were two thousand Spanish troops here to guard the retreat a few days ago; where the bloody hell are they, there's not a sentry in sight?"

De Gea shrugged his skinny shoulders expressively. "Gone," he said. "Two, perhaps three days ago. They left, Colonel, before the French came."

Paul froze. "The French are here?"

"Gone, also," De Gea said, sounding uninterested. "Earlier today, they were called to fight. Now only the ones at the bridge."

Paul felt his entire gut clench in horror. "The French are holding the bridge?" he said softly. "But where are the Spanish? Why did they leave? What…never mind. Can I see the bridge from up here?"

De Gea nodded and Paul ran past him and took the crumbling spiral stairway at a run. High up at the top of the tower, he paused, trying to catch his breath, his heart pounding both with the effort and with fear for his men. He could not begin to imagine how Espana's men had marched out without a message being sent to Wellington, but it was clear that they had gone, and Paul was beginning to suspect that he had marched his brigade into potential disaster.

Paul was pleased to see that the tower gave him the view he had hoped for down to the river and he put his glass to his eye. In the far distance he could see the battlefield, a residue of black smoke hanging over the fields and ridges although it was too far to be able to see any details. It looked as though part of the battlefield had caught fire, with swathes of flame moving across the dry grass and Paul thought back to Talavera and felt sick. He had been carried off the field earlier, wounded and close to death, but his men under Johnny Wheeler had been there, trying desperately to get as many wounded men off the field as they were able, before they burned to death and Johnny had once told him that for months, he had awoken at night hearing the screams of men they had been unable to reach.

The flames spilled a garish light over the darkening battlefield. The fighting was over; Paul was sure of it. There were no sounds of cannon fire, no large-scale troop movements which would have been visible from here. Paul imagined that all that was left was the inevitable litter of bodies across the field. He had often thought how untidy a battlefield always looked when the fighting was over. Bodies were strewn carelessly about, but there was other litter too, ammunition boxes, papers from pockets, discarded weapons and packs. Traditionally in the darkness the looting would begin, local villagers, camp followers and victorious soldiers going through the bodies of both sides for money and food and other loot, stripping the bodies of their possessions as the vultures stripped their flesh.

Paul had long ago ceased to be shocked or upset by it. At least two of his officers were wearing boots taken from the bodies of Frenchmen because the uniform orders had not come through and the dead men would hardly care. Loot from a battle was taken and prize money for officers and men calculated and divided by the quartermaster general's officers but away from official eyes, Paul had more than once pocketed a purse and distributed it himself to his officers and men. He came from a wealthy family and had no need of prizes or loot, but he was always conscious that most of his young officers lived off their pay or little more and that his men were poorly paid, poorly clothed and lived in appalling conditions. They were mostly from the lowest levels of society; thieves and pickpockets and poachers, pimps and housebreakers, some of them fleeing starvation in Ireland and others fleeing charges of murder or assault.

Few of them came into the army from a sense of patriotism or even from choice and many had abandoned families into poverty to be here. Paul was always faintly astonished given the lives they had been obliged to live, that they fought so well and behaved better, in many cases, than the French conscripts who were from all levels of society. Since his earliest days as a very young officer in India, he had found himself more comfortable around a campfire with his foul-mouthed enlisted men than in the mess with officers of his own class. It had informed all his decisions about how he ran his company, then his battalion and regiment and now his brigade.

Scanning the darkening view, looking for signs of movement, Paul thought of Alten, and wondered if his other brigades had been engaged at all today and then of Anne, very probably on her way back to Salamanca. And then he froze suddenly as his wandering mind focused, and he realised what he was seeing.

"Oh, Jesus bloody Christ."

Footsteps sounded on the stairs and the Spanish caretaker appeared beside him. "What is it?"

"The French. I think they're retreating this way."

"Señor?"

Paul pointed. "It's hard to see in this light, but though the trees there, on the far side of the river. I can see movement and those occasional shots aren't a full battle. If you're right, and the French already hold the bridge, they're barely a mile away from my men, who have no idea they're there."

De Gea was looking at him blankly. Paul took a deep breath. "Who else is here? In the castle?"

"To live. Nobody, Señor. I live with my wife and daughter there."

He pointed and Paul could see the small white cottage, built up against one of the surviving walls of the castle. He shook his head.

"You can't stay there, it'll be in the line of fire. Get them out and into the town - with friends or into one of the churches, as far away from here as you can manage. Leave me the keys, I am officially taking over the castle. Move."

De Gea removed the keys from his belt with hands that trembled slightly. Paul did not wait to see if his orders were obeyed. He took off down the stairs and out to Rufus. Galloping along the street he reined in quickly and found his officers and men already reaching for arms.

"Sir, what the bloody hell is going on? It sounds like half the French army approaching."

Paul met Johnny's eyes. "It is half the French army, Johnny, the Spanish have run. Or got it wrong. It doesn't matter which. Listen, we've little time."

He outlined his plans quickly and as he finished, they ran to horse, yelling orders to drummers and buglers and NCOs, calling their men into line. Paul wheeled his horse and trotted down the street a little then stopped. He could already hear them coming in the near darkness.

Paul had no way of knowing what was happening on the battlefield. The French were clearly in full retreat, but he wondered how easy it would be to pursue them through the trees on the far side of the Tormes in the gathering darkness. If the Anglo-Portuguese army were on their heels the defeated French army would flee through the town without stopping and his brigade would be safe. If Wellington had stopped pursuit for the night, they would be coming through in some disorder but with time, and perhaps inclination, to turn on an isolated brigade of the enemy who had so thoroughly defeated them.

He had thought briefly of telling his men to seek shelter with the townspeople but there were too many of them and no time. Many of them would be surprised banging on doors and if the French caught them disorganised and in small groups, they would be slaughtered. Back at the bridge, Paul's men might have held but it was too late for that. The castle was his best option, with walls and ruined outbuildings which might provide enough cover for his experienced light troops. The fleeing French would probably attack, there was no way to hide his entire brigade, but the crumbling walls would provide some cover for a while, and if the men were pushed back, he could pull those still alive into the tower for a final stand.

Paul felt, watching his men scrambling into position, a passionate gratitude to both officers and men. In the face of impending disaster there was no sign of panic and no loss of discipline. Even his raw troops in the 115th were in place, their young officers ready beside them. He had placed them in the middle, with the 110th to hold the first line with his Germans and the 112th to steady the back along with his Portuguese. Sandwiched between the two the 115th had support from both directions. His rifle company was despatched up into the tower to take aim from the small windows and the battlements at the top. It would soon be too dark to aim properly but once they had the range, Paul hoped they could do some damage, even firing blind.

Paul dismounted as the first of the French came into view and handed Rufus to Jenson.

"Get the lads with the officers' horses right up to the back of the castle, Corporal. Keep them out of sight and out of the firing line in case they're needed. If this goes badly wrong – if we don't get reinforced…"

"You planning on making a dash for it, sir?"

"No, Freddie, that's your job. Get back to my wife and tell her I love her."

"You know what, sir, I think she already knows that. Don't get killed, I do not want to have to tell her that."

"I'll try," Paul said. "Get going."

He patted Rufus and watched Jenson limping away then turned back and moved to the front with the 110th. Looking across the line he saw Carl, steady at their head, and Manson close by, his golden eyes watchful through the remains of the light, his hand half raised to signal the sharpshooters of his light company. There was quiet now in the lines, waiting for the French to come.

# Chapter Seven

The French came. Their officers, eager to make their escape, were yelling at them to come back, and it gave Paul some hope. This would be no coordinated attack, no planned assault. It came from tired and injured men, exhausted from battle, black with smoke and streaked with blood and sweat and tears. They had marched, like Wellington's men, for days in a complicated dance of retreat and advance and then their enemy had struck and swept them from the field in four short hours. They were bloodied and beaten and furious and the sight of English troops in a defensive position so far from the main force maddened them.

He could sense the shock and confusion of their officers. They had expected a clear run once they had made it across the river and they were faced, instead, with a brigade in a place where nobody had expected them to be. Paul wished he could tell them to keep running. He no longer cared about stopping the retreat, he cared about his men, about to face a defeated and desperate army.

The French were angry. Paul heard the roar as they sighted his men behind the castle walls, the yells of triumph as they perceived a battle they might be able to win. With thoughts of friends and comrades cut down beside them, blown apart by cannon and howitzer and musket fire, they broke ranks and charged, roaring, a pack of black faced demons, towards the broken walls where the men of the third brigade waited, rifles and muskets in sweating hands. Earlier they had complained about not being engaged in this battle. They were engaged now.

Paul waited until they were close. His men were hugely outnumbered, and their defences were meagre, they needed to make every shot count. Behind them the French officers were still trying to call their men into line, and he was hoping that a few sharp volleys and a lot of dead would put others off and persuade them to continue their retreat. He had no idea if the Allied army was in pursuit or if it was pursuing in the right direction. There were major fords up at Huerta and numerous smaller fords along the Tormes. Wellington had too many choices and Paul could not rely on help arriving. He waited and waited, sensing the tension of the men around him under the onrush of the French infantry. In his mind he could see his former commander, Black Bob Craufurd at Bussaco, holding his nerve until the last possible moment.

"Fire!" he roared, and the order was called across the lines. The front ranks of the 110th fired a tremendous volley directly into the front rank of the French and it blew the first lines apart. Beyond them the second rank rocked back, shocked at the carnage, and his men took time to reload, steady and confident, sacrificing speed for accuracy as he had taught them. Some of them, the old hands, boasted about being able to fire four rounds a minute and they were very capable of doing so in practice with no distractions. But in battle it was important not to make a mistake and jam the gun, so he had trained them ruthlessly to ignore the watch hands and get it right.

"Fire!"

The second rank of the French disintegrated. They were close now and Paul looked over at Carl and nodded, and the Major took up the orders in a clear confident voice. The bugles called and the skirmish line dropped into position, moving from wall to wall in pairs, one kneeling while the other stood, taking it in turns to load and fire, picking off the hapless Frenchmen individually while they could still see to do so in the gathering darkness and waiting for the bayonets to reach them.

They struck after two more volleys and by this time the French were scrambling over their fallen comrades. One or two officers had joined them, perhaps hoping for some glory to take with them, on their retreat back towards Madrid. They gave the French lines some structure and discipline and within minutes they were in among the crumbling walls and buildings of the castle and the steady line of fire had given way to desperate hand to hand combat with bayonet and sword in the end of the evening light.

The 110th fell back, giving ground slowly and reluctantly and leaving piles of French dead behind them. Paul moved with them, sword in hand, cutting down men already bloodied and injured with a painful sense that this battle should never have happened. He had no sense of losses or wounded and no sense of time although in the back of his mind was the agonised awareness that if the French launched another determined attack, his brigade might be slaughtered while scrambling into the tower.

The light was fading further. His riflemen could no longer aim reliably from the top windows without risk of hitting their own, and the fight had become bloody and personal, and Paul looked into the smoke blackened faces of the men he killed. There was no longer a shape to the exhausted men of the 110th and looking across, Paul yelled an order and his men fell back fast and efficiently behind the fresh lines of the 112th and 115th.

He heard Johnny's voice steady through the darkness, calling his men forward, and Paul drank from his canteen, summoned his resources, and ran to join the assault. The French, who had thought the allied forces spent, were shocked by the sudden onslaught of the 112th and the Portuguese who cut through their first ranks ruthlessly. Paul was with them, shouting encouragement, and behind him he could hear Major Swanson's voice organising the 110th into a further defensive line and silently blessed his fellow officers for their ability to think for themselves in a crisis. To his considerable surprise the French were falling back, falling over the dead and wounded of both sides to avoid the fierce fighting of the 112th. He was astonished at how well they were doing. They must have been fighting for almost an hour, and they had still barely given ground, although he shuddered to think of the men cut down behind the walls, bleeding and perhaps dying in the darkness. He had helped lift bodies from the streets of Fuentes de Oñoro the previous year and the memory had stayed with him.

Paul paused to wipe sweat from his eyes and surveyed his lines then heard a yell from Colonel Wheeler.

"They've guns! Take cover!"

Paul dived, as the others did, for the shelter of the walls, and hit the ground hard, jarring his body as the first gun fired, ripping apart one section of the outer wall. He heard the screams of some of his men as the gun tore them apart, and he felt a burst of illogical fury that in the defeat of Salamanca somebody had allowed the French to escape with artillery.

"Michael, to me!" he roared, scrambling to his feet. "Take that fucking gun out!"

Paul was already running, counting in his head the time it would take for the gunners to reload. He had first learned how to time it, from his Irish sergeant at the battle of Assaye nine years earlier, and he knew he could reach the gun crew before they got off another shot. He also knew that he was much too far ahead of the 112th light company but he was too enraged to care. He reached the gun just as they were about to light it and dived into its crew, his curved Indian tulwar swinging savagely, and the gunners fell and then fled before his height and his skill and his sheer fury. One of them tried to make a fight of it and Paul killed him with a brutal slash across the body and pushed him away. He dropped to the ground scrabbling for the man's bayonet and came up, fumbling for the touch hole on the gun. He shoved the spike in and bent the bayonet to break it off.

Behind him, Michael's light company hit the second gun crew before it got off a shot and the gunners died a bloody death at the points of their bayonets. Paul heard Michael shout an order to spike the gun and he could hear the French officers yelling at their men. As sanity returned, he knew that he had come too far out and that he needed to get back and fast.

The French had seen him and recognised his rank, and they were onto him with the fury of men who had seen their army destroyed around them. Paul leaped over the bodies of the gunners and began to run back towards the castle, but they were too close. Several of them attempted a shot, but the muskets were inaccurate at the best of times and they missed in the darkness. But they were armed with bayonets and were closing fast. He had moments only and then he would be dead, and knowing it, he thought of Anne and his children and he took a deep breath and swung around, dropping his sword and holding up his hands in surrender.

It was a risky gesture, but it surprised them, which bought him time. They pulled up, a dozen of them, battle stained infantry with a bucolic NCO at their head armed with a wicked looking sword. For a moment Paul thought he had got away with it and that they would try to capture him, but he saw the NCO look at the closing gap as Michael's men charged to his rescue and then the man swung the blade. He was clumsy with it and in a one to one fight, Paul could have disarmed him in seconds, but by then the others would have charged in and he would be cut to pieces. Instead, Paul dropped like a stone to the ground and the man's weight carried him forward. Paul felt his hand close on the hilt of his sword and he rolled onto his back and stabbed up and the NCO died on a high-pitched scream. It was impossible from this angle to withdraw the sword and Paul did not try. He rolled over and snatched up a discarded French bayonet, staggered to his feet and held it steady as they advanced on him slowly, lips curled back from bared teeth like a wolf pack closing in on a kill.

In their midst a young French officer appeared, running in from the rear his sword drawn. It distracted the men and Paul thought that the man had probably just saved his life. He met Paul's eyes steadily.

"Surrender or they will tear you apart," he said in English, but Paul, who by now could hear sounds close behind him shook his head.

"Not today, lad," he said, and thrust forward with the bayonet. The French were on him in seconds and he felt pain in his arm and through his shoulder and a sharp graze down his side as he twisted away. The weapon fell from his hand and he was falling forwards to avoid another thrust and then hands grabbed him and swung him around and out of danger with such force that he fell hard and winded to the ground and he was conscious of a rush of men crashing into the French.

There was a confusion of screams and cries in two languages in the darkness. Paul shifted cautiously and began to pull himself to his feet. He was in considerable pain and he could feel blood running down onto his hand but he was somewhat surprised to find himself both alive and mobile. Ahead of him a figure with a sword was ruthlessly cutting its way through the Frenchmen and he recognised Captain Manson of the 110th. Cautiously Paul moved forward and searched the ground for his sword. He found it, still buried in the body of the French NCO and withdrew it, conscious of pain searing through his right arm.

"Sir, can you move?"

"I can, Mr Witham. Let's get some cover, shall we, I feel a bit exposed out here."

He heard Michael to his left, utter an explosive oath and then they were backing up, fighting and then running, going over the low wall in a scramble of arms and legs. As he hit the ground, Paul heard Carl Swanson's voice.

"Fire!" he said and there was an explosion of sound so loud and so close that it made Paul's ears ring. He was lying at the feet of a solid row of men and as he looked up, the row dropped to its knees and behind them was a second row and the explosion came again. A hand grasped Paul's.

"You all right, sir? Bloody hell, that was a bit mad, didn't think you were going to make it."

"Fire!" Carl's voice called again, and the third rank of men fired. Paul allowed Ensign Raby of the 115th to pull him up, and he stared into a wall of black smoke where the French had been. There was no sound or movement apart from a faint whimpering and he knew that the men who had pursued the skirmishers back to the wall were dead or wounded, cut down by the solid wall of fire which Carl had set up from two companies of the 110th and one of the 115th. He turned at looked over at his friend whose smoke blackened face he could barely see through the dense fog.

"Thank you, Major, that was very neat."

"Paul, you are a fucking lunatic!" Carl said furiously.

Paul laughed aloud and hoisted his sword. "That's why I have you and Johnny to keep me alive, Major!" he called and the men around him cheered. He knew the sound would infuriate the Frenchmen still streaming up the road but he did not care. He rubbed smoke from his eyes and tested his arm to check he could still use it to wield the sword.

"We need to retreat," he said to Johnny, as quietly as he could. "Up into the tower. The rifles will give us cover as far as they can. Johnny, take the back lines, we'll keep them busy."

"Sir, they'll slaughter us."

"They'll slaughter us anyway," Paul said, trying to sound calm. "We're running out of ammunition. Get as many as you can into that tower, I'll hold them here with the 110th. It's an order, Colonel."

Johnny did not reply. Paul heard him moving away and blessed his second-in-command for his ability to take an order. He had no idea what was going to happen next. The French were filling the road up through the town and he could hear the creak of wagons and the rumble of wheels over the cobbled street. Officers shouted orders and there was the occasional groan of a wounded man. This was a retreat not an attack and the French officers needed to get their men out of here without further loss. What Paul could not assess, was whether they would call them off in time to save his brigade.

Without being sure, Paul could sense there were fewer French coming forward. The men of the 110th had formed up around him behind what was left of the broken walls and Paul hoisted his sword. His arm felt leaden and the wounds in his shoulder and upper arm burned with an agonising pain.

"Steady, lads," he called. "If you're shooting, make it count, now."

It counted. Twice the French came on and twice Carl called a solid volley and the French fell back. There was occasional fire back and one or two men fell, but the French were no longer organised enough for a volley and it was almost pitch black. The darkness gave the advantage to the defenders who remained in place. The French who tried to advance were stumbling, some of them falling over broken stones and rocks in the darkness. Paul leaned on the wall. He was beginning to feel dizzy and he supposed it was loss of blood.

"Carl." Paul kept his voice low.

"Sir?"

"I'm not so good. If I go down, get them back into the tower fast. Hold for as long as you can."

"Paul, get back inside," his friend said furiously. "One of the lads can help you. You need…"

"No. I need to be here. If I go, they'll overrun us. They…"

Paul broke off as a new sound filtered into his exhausted brain. Horsemen were riding up the road and Paul felt slightly sick. French cavalry could be the end of them. Only a madman would ride a horse into the broken stonework before the tower but in his experience, cavalry were often mad enough to do things that a sane man would not. He waited, hardly daring to breathe, and then he heard a voice, speaking French, clear and authoritative from the darkness.

"Halt. Captain, withdraw your men. We need to leave the town before daybreak. Call them back; there will be no more battle tonight. Call them back."

There were half a dozen men, officers on good horses, the saddlery jingling in the darkness. To Paul's astonishment the French officers began to shout orders without any hesitation, and he realised suddenly that the voice came from no regimental officer but from a general. Straining his eyes, Paul peered through the darkness, but he could see nothing but a figure on a horse and the dark shapes of the retreating French along the road.

"I think that's Marshal Foy," Paul breathed softly.

"I don't care if it's the Queen of Sheba as long as it gets them out of here," Carl said. "Are you all right?"

"Yes. I wish I could see him clearly."

"Thank God you can't, if it was light enough, he'd probably send in half a regiment to slaughter us. The darkness is keeping us safe."

Paul knew it was true. He stood silent with the 110th around him, hardly daring to breathe as the French pulled back and joined the flood of men marching up the road out of the town.

For the first time, Paul allowed himself to believe that they were going to make it. Through waves of pain he straightened and held his left hand over his right arm which was bleeding badly and felt as though it was on fire. He lifted his sword to sheath it and then stopped. As the troops streamed past him up the road, something caught his eye, gleaming in the darkness and he realised incredulously what he was seeing only ten feet away.

"Carter, Hammond, cover me!" he yelled and began to run. Behind him he heard the Sergeant of his light company utter an oath so revolting that he wanted to laugh.

"Get back here, sir," he heard Carter bellow, but they were both following him without any understanding why. Then he was up with the retreating French, the pain of his wound forgotten as he slashed his way through a tightly packed group with his sword, hearing his two NCOs behind him, fighting with bayonets to protect his flanks and rear. He cut down two men, then a third, and then he was facing the man clutching onto the pole, a terrified boy of twenty or so, and as Paul bore down on him he released his burden and ran. Paul let him go and he disappeared into the melee of retreating men and Paul stooped and lifted his prize and beside him Hammond and Carter

90

pulled up breathlessly as they saw what he held.

"Oh bloody hell!" Carter breathed, and Paul looked up and saw the golden eagle above his head on the pole, shining above the battle, utterly indifferent to the bloody retreat of the French troops. None turned to look at him or stop him. They had had enough finally, and Paul allowed Carter and Hammond to pull him back behind the walls where he stood, leaning slightly on the pole of the eagle, watching the shapes in the darkness run, catching his breath and letting himself finally admit how close he had come to death.

"You all right, sir?" Carter said. Paul turned to look at him and took the battered pewter flask his Sergeant-Major was holding out to him.

"I think so." Paul drank, feeling the rum burning down and warming his exhausted body. "Thanks Carter. You too, Hammond."

"You're welcome, sir. Very pretty bird, that."

"Isn't it?"

Carter surveyed their prize admiringly. "It is, sir. Wonder if it's going to hurt much when your wife hears about this and shoves it right up your backside without benefit of laudanum?"

Paul gave a choke of laughter. "Are you going to tell her, Carter?"

"I won't need to, sir, the entire third brigade is going to be telling this story and I'm not sure there is any way we can dress this up to make you look like anything other than a suicidal lunatic. Oh look, I think Major Swanson wants a word."

Paul turned to see his friend approaching. "You come to yell at me, Carl?"

"Not out here. Get into the tower, the rest of the lads are in there."

It was crowded inside the stone structure with men on every floor and many sitting or standing on the stone, spiral staircase. It was too dark to make out faces.

Carter led Paul to one wall and several men made space for him to sit down, gazing in astonishment at the eagle. Hammond stood it up against the wall and Paul leaned back with closed eyes.

"Are you alive, Colonel?"

"So far, Major Swanson."

"Paul, I have seen you do some stupid things on a battlefield but not usually quite so many in one hour. I've literally no idea how you're still alive, that charge on the guns was bloody suicide. What in God's name were you thinking to get yourself cut off like that?"

Paul smiled wearily. "Sorry, lad, did I worry you? I lost my temper a bit there, couldn't believe that all those lovely English divisions kicking their arses on that field couldn't stop them getting away with field guns. I did go a bit far out, though. Thank God for you and for my two light companies, that was a hell of a charge. Leo, are you all right, you're bleeding?"

"I'm bleeding? Sir, I've got a nick on my head about half an inch long and you're standing there dripping blood like a demon from hell." Captain Manson came closer and crouched down. "Are you sure you're all right?"

"No, he's bloody not, he is a madman and should be confined for his own safety!" Carl said furiously. "If you didn't already look half dead I would bloody punch you for that."

Johnny Wheeler joined them, and Paul studied him. "What have you done, you're limping?"

"It's nothing, bayonet caught me in the thigh but it's not bad. I think you're in a worse state, Colonel. Get tired of running the brigade, did you?"

"I don't know what makes you all think I was trying to get myself killed," Paul said mildly.

"Evidence of our own eyes," Manson said. "Sit still for a minute and let me tie that up, you're bleeding like a lamb with its throat cut."

"An attractive analogy, Captain, I shall remember it. Ouch."

"Serves you right," Manson said unsympathetically. He had removed his sash and was twisting it firmly about Paul's upper arm and shoulder. "From what I can see in the dark you've got about three bayonet wounds there and it's a mess. Ashford, give me your sash to make a sling, it's the only thing they're useful for."

"I don't want a sling," Paul said.

"If you don't do as I say, I am letting Major Swanson hit you, sir, and he really wants to."

"Don't waste your energy, Leo, he'll take it off within about three minutes," Carl said.

Paul laughed weakly, conscious of a feeling of slight hysteria. "Thank you, Leo. For the medical treatment and for helping to save my life which I know you just did. I'm sorry, it was a bit mad. I lost my temper."

"I know you did, sir, I watched you do it. It was terrifying."

"Have we set sentries?" Paul asked, and Carl made a noise which sounded like an angry boar.

"No. I thought I'd leave that to chance."

"Sorry," Paul said. He could think of nothing else to say.

Carl did not speak for a moment. Then he said:

"So am I. I'm a bit jumpy."

Paul reached out in the darkness and gripped his hand, unseen. "You're going to get back to her," he said positively.

"I'd bloody better. I'm worried about the wounded out there but there's nothing we can do. Michael's lads are at the upper windows watching. As soon as it starts to get light and we're sure they're gone, we'll be out there. In the meantime, Colonel, you need to rest."

\*\*\*

It was full dark when Anne reached their former billets in Salamanca after a long and exhausting day of advance and retreat, with the battle raging out of sight but well within earshot. A message had come late in the day to tell them that the field was won and Lieutenant Pope, in charge of the Portuguese escort, had read it and looked at her hesitantly.

"We could camp here, ma'am, and set off early tomorrow..."

"No," Anne said firmly. "If the battle has gone our way, and I doubt Lord Wellington would have sent the message if he were not sure, they'll be sending the wounded back into Salamanca, Mr Pope. I want to be there."

"Yes, ma'am."

"Can we send a message ahead to make sure our billets are ready?"

"I'll send Mr Nani and Corporal Raven, ma'am. They'll get it sorted."

There was no news of Paul or the Light Division when Anne arrived. She was tempted to go in search of Oliver Daniels and the regimental hospital, but she knew it was unfair on her escort and her companions. Reluctantly, Anne settled down in the room she had last shared with Paul some weeks ago. There was plenty of space in the enormous college which the French had converted to barracks and officers' quarters but both Keren and Teresa hesitated when Anne suggested they occupy their former rooms and Anne was relieved.

"Why don't we stay together tonight?" she said. "Teresa, bring little Ana, we'll get the men to drag a pallet into the room and Keren can share my bed. None of us wants to be alone."

None of them did. Food had not been arranged and Anne sent her groom in search of a scratch meal of bread, cheese and cold meat from a local tavern. Costa returned, grumbling about the price.

"In Portugal, we know not to cheat the army who fights for our country," he said.

Anne managed not to laugh, thinking of some of the arguments she had had with Portuguese merchants looking to make a huge profit out of the English army's desperate need for supplies. "Thank you, Isair. Take some and eat. Tomorrow I will go myself to arrange supplies for the hospital and I will see to food for us also."

"It is not work for a lady," Costa said stubbornly. "I will go."

"You shall come with me to be sure they do not cheat me," Anne said soothingly. "Good night."

She closed the door firmly and turned to Keren and Teresa. "I am not sure this is going to work," she said. "If he tells me one more time that everything I do is not fit for a lady, I will stab him eventually. Teresa, sit over here, she's fussing, you need to feed her. Keren and I will wait on you."

They set out the food on a shawl, spread like a picnic rug on the floorboards and passed food to Teresa while she settled on a straw mattress and fed her daughter. Ana, at just over three months old was beginning to show an interest in the world around her. She had a dazzling toothless smile which broke Anne's heart every time she saw it and a sociable nature which meant that she seemed to have no objection to being passed from one person to another; a useful attribute in an army baby.

Anne, who was her godmother, was completely devoted to her and trying hard not to show it to Paul, since she knew he felt immensely guilty that their son, William, had been sent back to England to be raised by his family with his older children. Anne did not regret her decision; more than half the children born in camp died of sickness and she had not been prepared to risk

Will. She had not been prepared either, for her attachment to Teresa's daughter and she tried not to worry too much about Ana's health, since she could hardly demand that her former maid send her own child away to spare Anne anxiety.

Despite the underlying worry about their menfolk, there was an enjoyable sense of camaraderie between the three women. Anne could remember nights like this in girlhood, sharing a room with her sister and cousins, often crammed into the same bed while spending the night at some relative's home. With the food eaten and Ana asleep in Teresa's arms, Anne opened a bottle of wine from Paul's supply and settled in the big bed.

"Teresa, up here, you'll be cold on the floor and there's acres of space. Here."

They squashed in, close together for warmth and drank the Spanish red, which warmed Anne and made her feel very slightly tipsy after the long day and meagre meal.

"You two," she said seriously, "are my dearest friends."

There was a silence. Eventually, Keren said:

"I do not think you should be saying that."

"I am the wife of the commander of the third brigade of the light division. I can say anything I like."

Keren and Teresa dissolved into giggles. "You are supposed to be friends with the officers' wives," Teresa choked.

"I am," Anne said indignantly. "Mrs Scovell is a very good friend."

"If Mrs Scovell were here, she would be in the other end of the bed warming her toes," Keren said, and all three were laughing.

"Mary Scovell is an excellent person," Anne said. "I am not sure some of the others would approve. Fortunately, none of them are mad enough to be here."

"One or two are," Teresa said. "There is Mrs Dalbiac. And Lady Waldegrave..."

Anne laughed. "And I love them both. Mrs Dalbiac on that mule, is without fear; I wouldn't ride the thing, it's vicious. And Lord Waldegrave's lady..."

"Who is not his lady at all, as they are not married," Keren interjected, giggling.

"Is a friend to us all, since her open congress with the major - sorry, the Earl - is so shocking, that it sets all of us in the shade."

Teresa was holding her daughter close, shielding her ears against their laughter. "Of you all, I am the most respectable," she said firmly. "I am married and have no scandal."

"You were a prostitute," Anne hooted, leaning against Keren, shaking with laughter.

"Nobody knows that," Teresa asserted. "Keren, do not shriek so much, you will wake Ana..."

They lay finally, curled up together, Ana snuffling happily between them. "Do you think they are all right?" Teresa said.

"Yes," Anne said definitely. "Tomorrow, early, I will go up to the hospital and I will find out where they are. Keren, Teresa - thank you. And I love you both."

***

Leo Manson sat beside his Colonel through the night. There was constant movement as men went outside to relieve themselves or at the change of sentries. Paul was quiet but restless, in what Manson feared was more unconsciousness than sleep. When he stirred, Manson tried to give him water, but Paul drank little. Manson was desperately afraid that his Colonel had lost too much blood and even more worried about the danger of infection. Outside it was quiet now, with no more sign of the French.

As the first thin slivers of light began to streak across the inky darkness of the sky, Colonel Wheeler was up and issuing orders. The men made their way outside and began the painful process of sifting through the dead and wounded. Johnny had set sentries the night before and made some attempt to find those obviously injured and conscious, bringing them in to the relative warmth of the castle. Several times during the night there had been activity, as the sentries had chased off would-be looters from the local population.

As daylight brightened the sky, the men of the third brigade began cautiously making their way outside to assess their losses. Colonel Wheeler ordered the dead laid out and the wounded brought inside the castle. Manson had lost six of his eighty-five men with another twelve wounded. It was a heavy toll and he suspected it was reflected across the brigade.

Gradually doors were opened, and the people of Alba de Tormes emerged. They came, to Manson's relief, with food and drink and blankets for the wounded men. Around him, the men were unusually subdued, and Manson knew why. Colonel van Daan lay still and quiet within the keep, stirring occasionally in restless discomfort, but not speaking or rousing, and his absence quelled any high spirits or joy at their survival.

The first English troops arrived early, cavalry in pursuit of the fleeing French army. Manson watched as Johnny went out to speak to them. He returned to join Manson.

"Has he been awake?"

"Not, much. Very restless, I'm worried about fever."

"I've sent two messengers back to find the rest of the division, we need orders. But it seems clear that Salamanca is ours and the cavalry seem convinced that's where the medical staff will set up."

"What about the baggage?"

"He doesn't know. But if Mrs van Daan has news of a victory she'll be back here as soon as she can. Will you stay with him, Leo? We're dealing with dead and wounded and getting them fed. I'll send someone through with food…"

"I'll stay," Manson said instantly. "In case he wakes."

"Thank you, I want one of his friends with him. I wish his wife was

95

here."

Manson ate, when food was brought, and remained beside his Colonel as the dawn turned into morning. There were clear sounds of troop movements outside and Manson leaned back against the stone wall and listened, wondering what was going on.

"Leo?"

Manson turned, startled at the sound of his Colonel's voice. "Sir? Thank God you're awake, I was starting to panic. Here, have some water."

Paul drank then lay back. In the golden light which filtered in through the narrow windows and open door, he looked white and drawn. Manson saw him turn his head to look around him at the supine bodies of the wounded men of his brigade.

"How many, Leo?"

"Not as bad as we first thought," Manson said. "I lost six and twelve wounded. Across the brigade we've lost sixty-eight dead and about a hundred wounded, but quite a few of those are walking, they should recover."

"Sixty-eight men." Paul lay quietly for a moment. Then he said: "Officers?"

Manson hesitated, knowing that he was going to have to tell Paul and hating it. The blue eyes were steadily watching him and Manson knew that his Colonel already guessed that he had lost a friend.

"Only two killed, about a dozen seriously wounded, sir. A fair few walking wounded."

"Who have I lost, Leo?"

"Marcus Vardy from the fourth, sir. And Captain Kent."

"No," Paul said. "Oh, Leo, no."

"I'm so sorry, sir."

Paul closed his eyes. Manson sat quietly, holding his hand. He had known and liked both of the dead officers and had considered Jack Kent a friend, but he knew that Kent had been with Paul for a long time. Paul had been present at his wedding to a very young Danish girl whom he had met in Copenhagen five years earlier and was godfather to their eldest child. The Colonel was crying silently, tears streaking his blackened face. Manson could feel his own eyes wet. He had been trying not to think about their losses but with nothing else to do he gave himself some time to grieve.

There was a commotion outside, the sound of horses and orders shouted. Paul opened his eyes. "Find out what's going on, will you, Leo? We need to do something about getting our wounded out of here. I'm guessing the hospitals are set up in Salamanca. Has anybody heard from my wife? Is she all right?"

"I'm sure she is, sir, but I'll go and find out…"

Manson was on his feet when the door was pushed further open and a tall figure came in, removing his hat. Even in silhouette against the light, the man was unmistakeable, and Manson came to attention and saluted.

"Captain Manson, I suspected I would find you in here. How is he?"

The voice was clipped and short, but Manson recognised anxiety rather than rudeness and said quickly:

"He's awake, sir. Over here."

Lord Wellington came forward and Manson moved to make space for him. The commander-in-chief knelt down.

"Colonel van Daan, the reports I had of you were not good. I see that they were exaggerated."

"Oh no, what did the fools tell you?" Paul said quickly. "I'm sorry, sir. I'll be all right. A bit weak, I bled rather a lot."

"You look terrible," Wellington snapped. "What in God's name are they about to leave you in here on the ground, you'll catch your death."

"In this heat? I don't think so. Stop snarling at people, sir, they've had no time to do anything and we're all just getting over the shock and counting our dead."

"It was a shock to me too," Wellington said. "What in God's name happened? Where were the Spanish?"

"Marched out a couple of days earlier apparently," Paul said. He was struggling to sit up and Manson came forward quickly.

"Stop it, you'll injure yourself," he said peremptorily. "Here, if you must, let me help you."

"Captain Manson, get some of your men to carry him outside; the air in here is foul," Wellington said. "And then send somebody to find a proper billet for him in town, I cannot think why it has not already been done."

"I don't need to be carried, I'm not dead," Paul said irritably. "Give me your arm, Captain Manson, I'll walk. I'm not having my brigade think I'm dying, they've been through enough."

"You are as obstinate as a two-year-old," Wellington snapped back. "If you injure yourself further, your wife will be furious."

\*\*\*

Outside in the sunlight, propped up against a crumbling wall on a thin army blanket, Paul felt slightly better. Somebody had produced a wooden stool from a nearby house for Lord Wellington and they sat watching the activity in a rare moment of shared quiet. Troops were making their way across the bridge and out in pursuit of the retreating French army while the men of the third brigade tended their wounded and laid out their dead.

"What happened, Colonel?" Wellington said finally.

"We had no idea they were so close," Paul said. "We'd had a clear march, followed the line you'd suggested, the guide knew where he was going. It was all very routine. I wasn't concerned. We arrived in the town and I noticed there were no sentries set, but I thought they'd not bothered since the French wouldn't be coming in from that direction. Sloppy, but not disastrous. I left the men at ease and went up to the castle to speak to the Spanish command and realised that they weren't there. Believe it or not, the custodian told me that the French were actually in the castle until yesterday morning when they were called to the battlefield. They marched out, but left a battalion to hold the bridge, to protect their line of retreat. They were about a mile away from us and neither of us knew it. If I'd had more time I'd have attacked them on the bridge, got rid of the rear-guard and tried to hold it, but it was too late, I could already see them coming. We'd nowhere to go."

"You could have been wiped out," Wellington said softly.

"We would have been," Paul said flatly. "My men fought so well, I've never been more proud of them, but we couldn't have held off their numbers, it felt as though most of the army retreated this way. We'd been fighting for about an hour, they were very disorganised and most of their officers were trying to get them to leave us alone and keep marching. Then one of the commanders came through with his staff and called a halt. I pulled them back into the castle and said a lot of prayers. I think it might have been Foy."

"Very probably. Most of the army did come this way and he organised it very well. I expected more of them to go for the fords at Huerta. Even so, if the Spanish had been here…"

"That's a lot of 'ifs', sir. You can't predict everything."

"I would never have sent you out here if I'd known," Wellington said bitterly.

Paul managed a smile. "I know," he said. "But what are you doing here, sir?"

"What I am supposed to be doing is chasing the French. And I shall have to leave soon, to catch up with the army. God knows what they will do if I'm not there. I had a message just after dawn, the cavalry who crossed the bridge early thought I should know. They told me you were dying. I left immediately."

Paul's throat felt unexpectedly tight. There were a number of things he would have liked to have said, but he knew it would not be fair; Wellington was always uncomfortable with any display of emotion. It was approximately eleven miles from Huerta to Alba de Tormes and his chief must have ridden flat out, with only Fitzroy Somerset for company, to arrive this quickly and at a moment when he desperately needed to be with his troops, organising the pursuit.

"I'm told it was a great victory, sir," Paul said finally. "Congratulations."

"It was. Once again, we've failed to stop them getting away, though. Colonel, I have to go. I've told them to find you a proper room…"

"No, sir, I want to get back to Salamanca with the rest of our wounded, Daniels and my wife can patch me up. I've got Captain Cartwright out there finding some transport, the ambulance wagons will be busy with the wounded from the battlefield. I'll be all right here."

"That was not a matter for discussion, Colonel. However long you need to remain here to recover, I will have you properly cared for. Do not oblige me to see to this matter myself, I have far too much to do and I need to get back before one of the fools does something unconscionably stupid." Wellington's blue grey eyes met his, and Paul recognised, with considerable surprise, something like a plea. "I have no time to worry about you," he said.

"I'll behave myself," Paul said. "At least until transport is arranged. I give you my word, sir. Where do you want the rest of the brigade? Johnny is mostly in one piece, he can…"

"Fitzroy Somerset has delivered my orders to Colonel Wheeler already," Wellington said, getting up. "For the time being I am leaving them as part of the Salamanca garrison; he'll march them up there when they are finished here. You look upset, Colonel. Did you lose somebody?"

"Yes," Paul said. "Two good officers. One of them has been with me for a while. Do you remember Jack Kent from Copenhagen?"

"Kent? Didn't he…?"

"He seduced the parson's daughter after an acquaintance of about three days," Paul said. "Harry Smith could have taken lessons from him. But they did better than I'd expected, they seemed very happy together, two children. I'll have to write to her."

"I'm sorry, Colonel, I know how hard it is. And on that subject, I have a confession to make. When I received the news of your injuries, I sent one of my ADCs back to Salamanca to apprise your wife of the situation. I thought she should know."

Paul felt a deep sense of foreboding. "What did you tell her, sir?"

"That she should try to get here as soon as possible."

"Oh shit," Paul said feelingly. "You might want to leave, sir, before she gets here."

"I was just thinking that, myself," Wellington said. "I have also sent orders for them to bring my carriage over here; you should not be thrown about in a farm cart. Write to me, I may not be absent more than a sennight, but I expect regular reports of your progress. If I have to come back because I have not heard…"

Paul smiled faintly. "I'll write," he said. "Now get out of here before she turns up. And sir - thank you. I feel considerably better."

Wellington regarded him with his head on one side. "You don't look it," he said. "Get well, I need you. Where's my damned hat?"

"Jenson has it," Paul said soothingly. "Good luck, sir."

Wellington regarded him with a gleam in his eyes. "When your wife arrives here and sees your condition, Colonel, it is not I who will need luck," he said, and turned away, calling for his horse.

# Chapter Eight

Lord Wellington's letter reached Anne while she was assisting Dr Oliver Daniels with an amputation on the leg of a sergeant from the 73$^{rd}$. The man was thankfully unconscious, and Daniels was quick and accurate. During the aftermath of a major battle, the regimental surgeon of the 110$^{th}$ had developed an excellent routine with Anne. Daniels was quicker at amputations, but Anne was very skilled at the delicate work of tying the blood vessels and sewing up wounds. Working together meant they could treat patients very quickly and lost fewer men.

Daniels finished his work with a nod of satisfaction and turned to the next patient who was being lifted on to the table beside him, while Anne began to suture. Her hands were slippery with blood and she worked quickly, glancing frequently at the white face of the man on the table. He had been brought in from the field some hours ago and should have been seen sooner, but the usual shortage of surgeons and equipment meant that he had waited far too long and Anne suspected he had lost a lot of blood.

"Ma'am. Mrs van Daan."

Anne looked up at the voice of Gibson, one of the medical orderlies. "There you are," she said. "Have we a bunk ready for him, he needs to be kept warm, he's far too cold. I don't like…"

"Ma'am, there's a letter from Lord Wellington. Mr Beaumaris brought it, he insisted I call you immediately."

Anne froze, staring at him. She could think of no reason why Lord Wellington would have written to her other than that something had happened to Paul. Anne had always made a conscious choice not to dwell on the possibility of Paul's death. Early in the year, they had spent time with Paul's family, putting financial and practical arrangements in place, and having done so, Anne had tried not to think about it. Working with the wounded, meant that she had little time during battle to worry about Paul's safety. Suddenly she was faced with the reality and for a moment Anne thought she might faint.

"Gibson get her a chair," Daniels yelled. "Nan, sit down. Dr Guthrie, I need help here."

Guthrie, who had just finished with a patient, turned. "What's going on?"

Daniels was looking at Anne. "I've a horrible feeling it's bad news," he said.

"Oh God, not the Colonel?"

"What else? Where the hell is Teresa? Or Keren? Or that useless bloody groom of hers. Look, take over from her, will you, Guthrie?"

It was Daniels himself, eventually, who led Anne outside and seated her on a wooden bench by the convent door. Lieutenant Beaumaris was waiting anxiously. Anne held out her hand and took the letter. She opened it with shaking hands and read, then got up.

"He's not dead, but it's serious. Lord Wellington thinks I should go immediately, which must mean that he thinks Paul could die."

"Where is he?" Daniels said. He was still surveying the crowd of wounded men in search of one of Anne's attendants.

"Alba de Tormes. It's about thirteen miles south-east of here, I'm leaving now."

Daniels turned to look at her. "Ma'am, you can't go alone."

"I'm going, Oliver. Don't ask me where Isair is, he's vanished again, and I'm not waiting."

Beaumaris saluted. "Ma'am, Lord Wellington had ordered me to place myself at your disposal for as long as you need me."

Anne shot him a look of pure gratitude. "Thank you, Lieutenant. I need to get my horse saddled, will you wait here for me? Oliver, I'm sorry."

"Go," Daniels said. "Take care of him. Bring him back alive."

Anne met his eyes. "If it's possible, I will," she said softly.

Anne had stabled Bella at a tavern opposite the convent. As she entered, a groom was rubbing down a big grey gelding. He turned, and seeing Anne, bowed slightly, then returned to his work. Anne looked around. Bella was at the far end, her saddle and tack hanging over the stall. Anne was very capable of saddling her own horse, but an experienced groom would be faster.

"Excuse me," Anne said. "I'm wondering if you've time to help me saddle up, my husband has been wounded, I need to go to him, and I've lost my groom somewhere."

The man turned. "If it's that pretty Portuguese lad you're after, lass, I think you'll find he's having breakfast with the widow Perez," he said, and Anne stared in astonishment, recognising the Yorkshire accent of her childhood. "Happen he'll be here in time, but if you're looking for someone to go with you, I'm here."

Anne realised that her mouth was hanging open in astonishment. She closed it. "Reynolds? That cannot be you."

The man grinned and touched his hat. "Taken you a while to work it out, Miss Anne."

"You're Simon's groom," Anne breathed. "I've seen you with him, but with the beard...I didn't recognise you. Oh, Reynolds it's so good to see you again, and I'm in so much trouble. It's my husband - he's badly hurt. I can't bear it, I need to get to him."

Reynolds set down his brush. "Well Mr Carlyon's up with General

Pakenham," he said in matter of fact tones. "But I'm pretty sure I know what he'd want me to do."

"He's safe then? I've been worrying about him, I heard how heavily engaged the third division was."

"Aye, he's well. Get what you need and get back here, I'll saddle up for two of us."

"I've an escort," Anne said. "One of Lord Wellington's aides, Lieutenant Beaumaris."

"If he can keep up," Reynolds said placidly.

They rode at a fast canter, slowing from time to time to prevent the horses from over-tiring themselves. Anne's stomach was churning with fear and she was passionately grateful to both her escorts. She could not believe that Joseph Reynolds was here, so many miles from where she had last seen him when she left her family home almost four years earlier. Reynolds had been head groom at Helton Ridge ever since she could remember.

Looking over at him as they slowed again to a walk, Anne asked:

"Why did you leave, Reynolds? How did you come to be working for the Carlyons?"

Reynolds looked over at her. He was a tall, broad shouldered Yorkshireman in his late thirties with a pair of twinkling brown eyes and thick curly dark hair, just showing a sprinkling of grey. Four years ago, he had been clean shaven and proud of his good looks but now he sported an impressive dark beard.

"Got turned off, miss," he said finally, having clearly considered his reply. "Master called me in after you left, told me I'd not done my job properly. Said it was my job to keep an eye on you, make sure you weren't riding off unescorted, and Master said if you'd been able to do what you were supposed to have done with Mr Carlyon, it was down to me."

"Oh, Reynolds, I'm so sorry," Anne said softly. "I'd no idea. If I'd known, I'd have murdered my father. How dare he?"

The groom's face broke into a grin. "Don't suppose he would have dared if you'd still been there, lass, it didn't get past me that he waited 'til you'd gone," he said. "Not that he was wrong, mind, I knew bloody well you'd been up to something you weren't supposed to, it's just that I'd got the wrong man in mind."

Despite her misery, Anne felt her face grow warm. "Oh," she said.

"And then I got out here with Mr Carlyon and saw who you'd married, and I thought maybe I didn't get it wrong after all. Wasn't he married back then?"

"Yes," Anne said. "Rowena was my friend. She died in childbirth."

"Friend, was it?"

"I didn't know her then, Reynolds. Or I wouldn't have…anyway, it was a long time ago. How did you come to be working for the Carlyons?"

"I approached them. Needed a job, thought I could play for sympathy, like. If I got dismissed because I couldn't stop their son seducing my young lady…"

"All right, you unprincipled rogue," Anne said severely, aware of Mr Beaumaris riding close behind. "However you got here, I'm glad you did. And thank you for today. Whatever I find, it's good to have an old friend with me."

"It's good to be here, miss. Can't be that much further."

They cantered over the bridge into Alba de Tormes just after noon, with the sun blazing down on them. Sentries in red coats guarded the bridge and as Anne reined in, she saw, to her relief, Sergeant Grisham from the 112th coming towards her. She waited, her heart hammering in her breast, her eyes on the sergeant's florid face.

"Ma'am, we've been expecting you. He's all right."

Relief left Anne speechless for a moment. Reynolds moved closer and took hold of Bella's bridle. "You all right, ma'am?"

"Yes. Sergeant Grisham, where is he?"

"Captain Cartwright has found a billet up in town, I'll get Private Everton here to show you the way."

Anne followed her guide up into the narrow winding streets of Alba de Tormes. She still had no idea what had happened to Paul; all accounts she had received of the battle had suggested that the Light Division were hardly engaged, but it was clear that there was a good deal she did not know.

Everton led her to a respectable looking house on one of the main squares of the town, a tall white edifice with elegant wrought iron railings and balconies and a red tiled roof. The door was opened by a maid in a dark dress and white apron who bobbed a curtsey.

"I think my husband is here?"

"This way, Señora."

Anne turned to Reynolds. "Never fret, lass, I'll see to the horses and come back to wait for you."

The girl led Anne upstairs and indicated a room to the right. Anne opened the door, unsure of what she would find within, and then paused, her hand still on the latch.

He was asleep, his fair hair dirty against the pillow and his face still smeared with the smoke of battle. They had removed his clothing, but a grubby silver-grey sash, stained with blood, was twisted around his shoulder and upper arm, and he had pushed the covers down to his waist. He looked, relaxed in slumber, not much older than his son, Francis, and Anne felt tears fill her eyes at the sheer relief of seeing the rise and fall of his chest as he breathed.

She stepped back very quietly out of the room and turned to the maid to give her instructions. The girl, a comely young woman of about her own age with thick red hair and a mass of freckles, went quickly to do her bidding and Anne went quietly downstairs to find Lieutenant Beaumaris.

"He's here. Mr Beaumaris, will you find Major Swanson and tell him where I am. And then, I think, you should return to his Lordship; he may have need of you and with the brigade here, I shall be well taken care of. Please thank Lord Wellington for his message and for lending you to me, I can never be grateful enough to both of you. Tell him I shall take care of the Colonel and instruct him - and make sure he understands it is an order - that he is to take care of himself."

Beaumaris kissed her hand. "I will, ma'am. Please give my best regards to the Colonel when he is well enough."

"Thank, you, Mr Beaumaris."

Upstairs, Anne crossed the room and drew up a chair beside the bed. Paul was stirring restlessly, and as she sat down, he seemed to feel pain suddenly and opened his eyes, wincing. For a moment he lay very still and then he said:

"Nan."

Anne shifted onto the bed and bent to kiss him. "Keep still," she said. "I've sent for water and clean linen. What on earth were they about, to leave that filthy makeshift bandage on, somebody is going to hear about that. Is it very painful; you're so pale? Oh love - you frightened me half to death."

Paul reached out with his good arm and took her hand. "I'm sorry," he said. "I didn't send that message, Wellington did. Some fool from the cavalry who came through early heard I was badly hurt but didn't stay for more information. Poor Wellington left the front and rode back himself expecting to find me dead or dying. He'd already sent to you before he found out."

"Is he still here?"

"No, he had to get back, they're chasing the French, he only stayed an hour. Did he send Beaumaris?"

"Yes." Anne rose as the maid entered, balancing a big jug of steaming water which she set on the washstand. "Let's get you clean and settled, and you may tell me everything while I look at that wound."

Anne found three wounds, still sluggishly bleeding but held surprisingly well by Manson's makeshift dressing. One was very deep, almost to the bone, and she could tell by Paul's rigid body how much it hurt as she carefully cleaned it. The other two were more superficial but ragged and it took a long time to stitch them. Anne had brought brandy with her medical kit and clean clothing for him. She had closed her mind as she packed, to the thought that she might be laying him out instead of treating him.

Anne encouraged him to tell his story as she worked, as a distraction from the pain. Finally, it was done, and he lay back looking exhausted but happier, the blue eyes on her face.

"Better?"

"Much. Thank you, Nan. And for not yelling at me."

"I'd never yell at you when you're this feeble, Paul, it's not a fair contest. And what's the point? I can see you're upset."

Paul did not speak for a while. Anne poured more brandy and tidied the room while he sipped it, his eyes still watching her. Finally, she came back to sit beside him and took his hand.

"What is it, Paul?"

"It was my fault," Paul said abruptly. "All of it. I think sixty-eight men died because I made mistakes that a junior lieutenant would be ashamed of. And then to make it worse I nearly got myself and Carter and Hammond killed over a bloody trophy. Nan, I think I did this."

Anne had known it was coming. Her husband usually had a remarkable ability to recover from the vicissitudes of battle; it was one of the things that marked out most of the best commanders, but something was clearly bothering him on this occasion and Anne knew he would not be helped by platitudes.

"Why?" she asked.

"When we reached the edge of town there were no sentries. Not a sight of a Spanish soldier anywhere. I should have realised right then that something was badly wrong. I should have kept them back, found cover out of sight of the road, put them on the alert and sent scouts to find out what was going on. If I'd done that, we wouldn't have had to fight at all."

Anne suspected he was probably right. "Why didn't you?" she asked.

"Because I got sloppy. I thought Wellington had sent me on a wild goose chase, I was pissed off that we'd been left sitting around in reserve. And because I made the assumption, like the rest of the British, that the Spanish were quite capable of not bothering to set sentries properly. What an arrogant piece of stupidity. I should have had skirmishers going through the town and instead I let them have a picnic while I went for a stroll."

Anne said nothing; she could think of nothing to say. Paul was lying back with his eyes open, looking at the ceiling. Eventually, Anne raised his hand to her lips and kissed it.

"Love, I'm so sorry, you must feel terrible."

Paul turned his head to look at her and managed a slightly lopsided smile which broke her heart. "I feel like shit," he said. "And it's nothing to do with my shoulder, although that bloody hurts as well. Jack Kent...you never met Christa. She's Danish and she was very young when they married. Like Harry Smith, he'd taken her to bed about twenty-four hours after they met. Her father was the local parson, a good man. He wanted them married, and it was a good thing, she gave birth almost nine months to the day. At the time I felt a bit sorry for Jack, I thought he'd been neatly trapped by a flighty girl who'd used him to escape from a boring life in a tiny village." Paul gave a little laugh. "I still think I was right about that part, Christa would have married any one of my officers who gave her the chance, she wanted out of there. But I grew to admire her over the years. She may have married for practical reasons, but once she'd done it, she entered into it wholeheartedly. She set out to be the best wife she could possibly be, and within a couple of years they were wholly devoted. They've two children, I'm godfather to the eldest. They named him after me. I need to write to her."

"You can do it when you've rested," Anne said gently. "I'm so sorry, Paul. What happened with Hammond and Carter?"

Paul looked at her and then laughed again, properly. Suddenly he looked better, as though telling her had lightened the burden. "I'm scared to tell you," he said.

"If you don't, I'll get it out of them."

"I know. All right, just don't hit me, I'm very fragile."

Anne listened in indignant silence. When he had finished, she said:

"Paul, what possessed you? You don't even care about such things. You must have gone mad."

"I think I did. God knows, Nan. I'd like to be able to tell you, but I can't. Bloody thing. The men are overjoyed, they see it as a triumph for the 110th. I see it as a piece of idiocy that is going to put me to the blush for a very long time. I am sorry, love."

"So you should be. If they'd come back and told me you'd got yourself killed chasing an eagle, I'd never have forgiven you." Anne leaned over and kissed him on the forehead and then on the mouth. "Don't do it again," she said severely.

"I promise."

"What can I do to help, Paul?"

Her husband laughed. "Bless you for not trying to offer me soothing platitudes, Nan. I want to talk to my officers - the senior ones anyway. They'll all know how badly I buggered this up although none of them will say it to me. I need to apologise."

"Is that wise?"

Paul smiled. "Well bloody Wellington wouldn't do it, that's for sure," he said. "Nan - it's the way I've always worked. I'm not going to sit down with the men and talk it through with them and I can't afford to speak to the junior officers. It'll frighten the life out of them to think their commander doesn't know what the hell he's doing. But I need to talk to the others. They'll understand."

"Paul, I know you'll do what's right," Anne said gently. "And the right thing for you is to take responsibility for this. It's your job. But here, in this room, I'm going to tell you that it is a responsibility that should be shared. You do not run your brigade like an autocrat, every one of your senior officers knows that if they tell you you're wrong, you'll listen to them. I'm guessing nobody did."

"No. But…"

"No buts, Paul. Remember, I'm not asking you to say this to them. But some of them are going to think it, and probably say it. Johnny, Carl, Gervase - even Leo. Especially Leo. Any one of them could have spoken up. None did. You made a mistake but so did they. Think about it and learn from it but don't let it make you miserable. It won't help."

Paul kissed her hand again. "I promise," he said.

"Good. Now lie down and sleep. What is happening to the brigade?"

"Wellington has ordered us back to Salamanca, I think - Johnny has the orders. But I don't want to leave our wounded. And I want to attend the burials, Nan."

"Well you'd better get some rest, then. As for the wounded, of course we will take them back."

"Transport is a problem, I think."

"Nonsense," Anne said robustly, because she knew it would make him laugh. "I shall deal with it immediately. What is wrong with Major Breakspear that he cannot find half a dozen wagons for hire? Honestly, this brigade falls apart when I am not present. Go to sleep, I'll wake you when I have arranged everything."

"Yes, ma'am," Paul said meekly, and Anne kissed him, and left to find Johnny.

***

Paul's brigade left Salamanca over a week later and caught up with Wellington's advancing army in Cuellar, an attractive little medieval town with a solid looking castle. The town's churches and public buildings had been thoroughly looted during the French invasion, but the buildings themselves were mostly intact, and for once the headquarters staff had enough accommodation, with the army spread out in camps nearby. Paul had been amused and somewhat touched to find that his chief had ruthlessly evicted the provost-marshals department to a nearby hamlet to provide a neat little house close by for Paul and his senior staff.

Paul's wounds were beginning to heal, although he still found moving his shoulder extremely difficult, a fact which he was trying hard to conceal from his wife. His decision to leave Salamanca had precipitated a furious quarrel, which Paul found more painful than three bayonet wounds.

He and Anne seldom had serious arguments, but when he had received Wellington's request that the third brigade join him on his progress towards the capital and had informed Anne that he felt well enough to accompany them, she had lost her temper very thoroughly. Paul knew that it was an indication of how worried she must have been about him, but he could also sense that his chief was struggling to decide on his next course of action and wanted Paul with him to discuss his various options.

Paul had overridden Anne, trying hard to be gentle about it. Anne had not been at all gentle about it and the ensuing argument had been a salutary reminder to Paul that his wife did not enjoy being patronised. Knowing that she was right had made him defensive, and the ensuing argument had probably been heard by every officer with rooms on the third floor of the university building and possibly those above and below as well. Anne had walked out eventually and had frozen him out for an entire day and half the night until she had ended his misery in the early hours by sliding in beside him.

"I'm cold," she said.

"I had noticed that, girl of my heart."

"I didn't mean that," Anne said loftily. "I meant that my feet are freezing, I don't know how the men sleep under those thin blankets."

"Practice. Where have you been?"

"There is a room at the end of the corridor. It smells of damp and the hangings are moth-eaten. And you knew perfectly well where I was, because you sent Teresa on a completely spurious errand to check that I was all right."

"I did," Paul said gravely. "She informed me that you were sleeping like a baby."

"I told her to tell you that. I haven't slept a wink."

107

"I know. I haven't either. It's a long time since I lay awake regretting what I've said to you in a quarrel."

He felt her snuggle into his undamaged side. "You called me an interfering, managing female."

"Well I did. But that's hardly likely to upset you, given that it's true. I also told you that if you couldn't keep from meddling you should pack your bags and go back to England. I have been lying here wondering how I would keep going if you decided to do just that, and recognising that I couldn't. I am sorry, Nan, I am such an arsehole when I lose my temper."

Paul felt her body shake with silent laughter then she shifted and leaned over to kiss him. "You really, really are, Colonel."

"I am. I know it. Thank God I don't do it very often with you."

"You had better not, Paul. But I was angry too."

"You called me stupid. More than once."

"It would be less infuriating if you actually were stupid, Paul, because then you would not be able to help it. But you're very intelligent. You know you ought to stay here, you're doing it because he wants you there. And I shouted at you because I can't shout at him."

"You can't exactly yell at the commander-in-chief, Nan."

His wife gave a sigh. "Of course, I can, Paul, it's simply that he isn't here. If he were, that argument wouldn't have happened, because he would have got it instead of you. Now kiss me properly and then go to sleep. If you insist on this madness, you need to rest as much as you can, while you can."

Paul kissed her for a long time. Eventually she drew back, and he could see her smiling through the darkness.

"Not a chance, Colonel. You're not fit enough yet, and you need your rest."

"I bet I could persuade you."

"I don't advise you to make the attempt, Paul, I've not forgotten what you called me yesterday and I know exactly how to hurt you just now. Settle down."

Paul obeyed. "Nan?"

"Mmm?"

"I really am sorry, love. You know how much I love you, don't you?"

He heard, to his relief, a familiar gurgle of mirth. "I love you too, Paul. Goodnight."

Wellington greeted Paul's arrival with such obvious pleasure, that Paul was glad he had risked Anne's wrath to join him. In between scouting the movements of the various French armies, writing dozens of letters and poring over maps, Wellington found time to bring Paul up to date with the full story of the battle and the pursuit of the French. Paul joined Wellington every day, leaving the daily business of his brigade to Johnny and Carl and spent time studying maps and listening to his chief considering and discarding plans.

Wellington had the choice of marching north, to drive Clausel's army further back beyond the fortress of Burgos or to head south over the Guadarrama to Madrid. It was tempting to push northwards to harry the already damaged Army of Portugal and possibly to take Burgos by surprise; this would have had the advantage of securing Wellington's northern flank. Paul knew, however, as did his chief, that sieges could be unpredictable, and Wellington could not afford a protracted investment of Burgos which would give Marshal Soult time to march north from Andalusia. There was also the political impact of taking Madrid and its effect on the morale of both armies, and Paul agreed with Wellington's final decision.

Wellington's army left Cuellar on August 5th and entered the Spanish capital on the afternoon of the twelfth, to a reception which put Salamanca in the shade. The French had taken the capital four years earlier and there was an explosion of exuberant joy at their departure. Riding through the city at the head of his brigade, Paul was surprised at how much it affected him. For four years he had fought and bled and suffered in this war, and he was honest enough to admit that it had not all been for the liberation of Portugal and Spain. He had felt on arrival in Lisbon, no especial affection or loyalty to either country. The army was his chosen career, one at which he had discovered he excelled, and he served where he was ordered.

The war had changed him. He had lived among the Portuguese and had learned their language and become genuinely interested in their art, their architecture, and their culture. He had ridden through villages and farms burned out and despoiled by the French and seen the corpses of men, women and children lying openly in the streets, the signs of the torments inflicted on them written plainly on their bodies. He had met women who had been raped and men who had lost their wives and children and at times he had gone quietly away to cry. He had commanded Portuguese troops, got to know their officers, and then watched them die beside him. They were his friends.

He did not yet have the same warm affection for the Spanish, but the jubilation of the crowds touched him, nonetheless. Looking over at his wife he was amused to see a sparkle of tears in the dark eyes, and he moved his horse closer to her.

"Heroes again," he mocked gently, and she looked up at him.

"You have to make a joke of it, Paul. But to these people, you actually are. And I find that makes me very proud."

"Then that makes me happy," he said and leaned out of the saddle to kiss her, well aware of the swell of delighted cheering around them. It was an emotional day, and a show of emotion was valued, especially among the English who had the reputation here of being a passionless race. Even Wellington seemed affected by the enthusiasm of the crowd and was smiling and waving more than was usual for him.

Paul looked around him, admiring the bedraggled spectacle of Wellington's army as it tramped up the main street into the city. The men were shabby and dusty from their days on the road. Without notice of a formal parade, even the vainest of the officers had not been given time to change into their dress uniform, and most of the men had nothing else to wear. Their jackets were dirty and faded and those who still had their shako hats no longer even bothered to try to beat them back into shape. Many wore tatty forage caps or went bareheaded. They wore a variety of trousers in shades of grey, blue and brown depending on where they had looted them from and an even wider variety of footwear. They were an army on the move, come straight from the field of battle, and they marched with unconscious authority.

There was a burning pain in Paul's injured shoulder, beginning to get worse. Paul moved it slightly, trying to find a more comfortable position and Anne made a small, irritated sound.

"I told you that you took that sling off too soon," she said.

"I'm fine, love. It's difficult to ride with a sling, anyway."

"You shouldn't be riding," Anne said shortly. "You shouldn't be here at all, you should have stayed in Salamanca until that healed properly."

"And missed the parade?" Paul teased. "You couldn't expect me to do that."

"You didn't do this for a parade," his wife said acerbically. "You did it because Lord Wellington wanted you here and you never say no."

"It's my job not to say no, bonny lass, he's my commanding officer."

"Charles Alten is your commanding officer and he wanted you to stay where you were until you were well enough. Don't talk to me about it, Paul, or we will quarrel again."

Paul wanted to point out that he had not raised the subject but seeing the expression on Anne's face he bit his tongue. They had not revisited their quarrel, but Paul knew that he had spent the journey up to join Wellington, trying to find ways of making it up to Anne. He could see that she was scanning his face now, trying to work out how much pain he was in, and he felt guilty at how much he must worry her at times.

"I hate it when we quarrel," he said.

Anne took his hand and squeezed it gently. "You are a baby when we quarrel," she said lovingly. "You spend weeks afterwards treating me as if I were made of china and would break at a cross word. Or leave you and go back to England. As if I ever would."

"Good, because without you, I would fall apart. And without me, I wonder sometimes if Wellington would fall apart. Which would mean the army would fall apart and Bonaparte would be in Lisbon within the year. You see, the entire fate of Europe rests in your very lovely hands."

Anne laughed aloud, shaking her head at his nonsense. They had come to a halt. In the narrower streets of the city, progress was slow and at times impossible. The balconies and windows of the tall, elegant buildings on both sides were hung with drapes and tapestries and many women were spreading cloaks and shawls for the army to march over. At their head Lord Wellington was dressed as always in a plain blue coat, standing out among the gaudier Spanish generals.

"Poor Hookey," Paul said, watching his chief. "Two parades in as many months, he'll be the one wanting to sail home to England. I wonder if they'll want him to make a speech as well?"

"They'll be out of luck if they do," Anne said. "It's lovely to see this, but I'm seeing a lot more than banners and ribbons. Some of the poorer people look half starved."

"Hardly surprising," Paul said. "They've been hosting the French for four years, I very much doubt they made a profit out of that."

"No. They're unlikely to make a huge profit out of our lads either, a lot of them will be short of funds by now."

"Especially the ones who had to use their last pay in order to fund the debts they'd already run up," Paul said. "Wellington tells me he can afford to issue two months back pay but is still waiting for funds from England for the rest. I rather imagine Harry Smith is going to be hanging around the 110th for a free dinner as usual, his pockets are always to let."

Anne laughed. "Paul, you like Harry. And I'm getting very fond of Juana; she's very mature for her age."

"I presume that's how she ended up where she did, bonny lass," her husband said grimly, and Anne shook her head.

"I never thought I'd hear you sounding so puritanical," she said, and Paul gave a splutter of laughter.

"I never thought I'd live long enough to be called puritanical. I'm honestly not, Nan. God knows I'd hate to be called to account for some of the things I did when I was younger. Including some of my behaviour with you. I think it was just the fact that she's so young."

"I was three years older, Paul."

"I know, girl of my heart. And I'm over it. They're married now and seem ridiculously devoted, so I hope they do as well as we have. We seem to have come to a complete standstill here. Anybody have any idea about the billeting situation? I'd rather like to be able to tell my lot what they're doing before they start wandering off of their own accord."

"We're putting the men in tents to start with," Anne said. "There's a good area up to the west about thirty minutes out of the centre of town. Breakspear and Davy Cartwright rode on ahead today and have sent directions back. It was a royal hunting estate, but a few of the nobility have also built country houses in the vicinity including the Marina family. They have just removed themselves very fast from Madrid owing to their enthusiastic cooperation with King Joseph and the French, so Captain Cartwright has commandeered the palace."

"I see."

"It's apparently enormous. I did suggest to Lord Wellington that he join us there, but he is to stay in the royal palace, although he is happy to have us up there, and General Alten may join us. As soon as we can escape, I'll ride up and see what there is." Anne caught his grin. "What?"

"You're amazing, bonny lass."

"The challenge is going to be restricting the men from poaching the royal deer."

"The men can poach the royal deer to their hearts content as far as I'm concerned, or anything else they find. They've shed blood trying to kick the French out of Spain this year, as have my Germans and Portuguese, his Majesty can spare a few deer. As a matter of fact, when we're settled in, I'm rather tempted to slaughter a few beasts and feed some of these poor children huddled at the back of the crowd in rags and if anyone comes bleating to me about royal hunting rights, they're going to get a kick in the arse."

Anne was laughing. "You're a revolutionary at heart, Paul van Daan. I wonder which side you'd have been on if you'd been in France during the revolutionary years?"

"Given the indecent size of my personal fortune I rather imagine my head would have been decorating a spike fairly quickly; I'm apt to defend what's mine. But I am a believer in taking responsibility, and it's clear looking around here, that nobody has. And I'm not sure if the arrival of the famous Spanish guerrillas is going to be much help given that when they arrived in Salamanca half of them started looting the local shops and demanding that the girls go to bed with them for nothing."

His wife reined in to avoid a plump woman who was reaching up to hand Paul a cup of wine. Paul took it and drank from it, then handed it to Anne with a formal gesture. His wife took it and drank, her eyes on his. He knew that for all her Yorkshire hard-headedness, there was a surprising streak of romance in his down-to-earth wife which she fondly imagined was visible only to him. At moments like this Paul was aware that it was clearly visible to the entire army and half the population of Madrid. He passed the cup back to the woman with a smile of thanks.

The crowd had shifted a little and they made their way through to a wide square, where Wellington was dismounting outside the town hall. Paul moved his horse to join General Alten.

"Do we need to be here just now?"

The German shook his head. "No. Your wife tells me you have found billets already."

"Yes, she's sent our baggage over there. If you don't need me, sir, I think I might…"

"Colonel van Daan. Ma'am."

Paul pulled a face at the sound of Colonel Campbell's voice. "Another ten minutes and I'd have been out of here," he said softly, and Alten laughed aloud. "Yes, Colonel, you want me?"

"Lord Wellington's compliments, Colonel van Daan." Colin Campbell, who was an old friend of Paul's was grinning from ear to ear. "You're invited to dine with him and the senior staff at the palace later."

"Just me, Colonel?"

"How likely does that sound, Paul?"

"Sometimes I wonder what he'd do if I decided to sell out and go home," Paul said with considerable restraint. "Do you think he'd offer her a formal position as his social secretary, deputy chief medical officer and assistant quartermaster general so that she'd stay?"

"He'd probably offer her my job," Campbell said mournfully. "Best get off and get yourself changed and ready to be social."

"I really hope this isn't going to be a repeat of Salamanca," Paul said grimly. "I observe that Don Julian has some friends with him this time. I am looking forward to the next few days."

"Cheer up, Colonel," Campbell said. "You might not be aware of it but there's still a French force occupying the Retiro, we may need to storm it to get them out."

"Another dinner watching Sanchez looking down my wife's dress, Colin, and I might find that quite appealing. Why don't we get the Spanish to kick the remaining French out? It'll give them something to do?"

Campbell laughed. "Get going, Colonel, he won't want you to be late."

"He wouldn't care if I didn't turn up at all. Come on, girl of my heart. Let's go and find something not too revealing for you to wear this evening."

He wheeled his horse and looked back as Anne smiled kindly at Campbell and Alten both of whom looked slightly nonplussed. "Please convey our thanks to Lord Wellington," she said. "Tell him we should be delighted to dine with him this evening. We'll be with you as soon as possible."

"Thank you, ma'am," Campbell said. Anne joined her husband.

"Your company manners get worse and worse," she said.

"I think they're fairly consistent," Paul said. "Are you sure I'm well enough to dine with his lordship? I'm in a lot of pain."

Anne gave him the full benefit of her most ferocious scowl. "It is a pity you didn't think of that before leaving Salamanca," she said frostily. "I believe it is this way."

# Chapter Nine

Joseph Bonaparte, Napoleon's elder brother, had been made King of Spain after the departure of the Spanish ruling family four years earlier. Both Napoleon and Joseph seemed to have underestimated the amount of opposition that the appointment would meet with. Bonaparte had successfully appointed Joseph King of Naples in 1806 and other family members as rulers in Holland in 1806 and Westphalia in 1807 and it seemed to have surprised him that his appointment in Spain had met with such fierce resistance.

The Spanish had risen up in rebellion in 1808, causing Joseph and the French high command to flee Madrid for Vitoria. Much of Spain was abandoned for a time and French policy in Spain hardened. Joseph reorganised the government and adopted a program of reform which included the abolition of the Inquisition, the end of feudal rights, the reduction of religious communities and the abolition of internal customs charges along with the introduction of measures to modernise trade, agriculture and finance. Paul, whose Spanish was fairly good by now, had read about the changes in several government sponsored news pamphlets. He found it ironic that on a personal level he actually approved of a lot of the changes that Joseph had introduced although he disagreed with Bonaparte's right to impose them by force.

As the popular revolt against Joseph Bonaparte spread, many who had initially co-operated with the French deserted them, but there were still many Spanish, known as afrancesados, who saw the arrival of Bonaparte as an opportunity to reform and modernise Spain and who supported his government. Most of these had fled with Joseph as Wellington's men marched into Madrid. Paul did not blame them. There was no danger of reprisals from the Anglo-Portuguese army, but he suspected that the temper of the citizens of Madrid after four years of French rule could not be trusted. The Marina family was one of these, leaving their graceful country palace to the mercy of the invading troops and Paul thought that should they return, they could be grateful that the 110th had commandeered it for his headquarters; it would have been wrecked in a day had the ordinary soldiers broken in.

Paul attempted to conceal his relief on arriving at the palace to find his room prepared and hot water ready, but he knew that Anne would realise how tired he was. The Marina Palace was enormous, a baroque masterpiece with tiled floors and more space than Paul's brigade had ever occupied before. Paul and Anne descended into chaos as the officers' baggage and boxes were unloaded into the vast marble hallway and the quartermasters stood at the centre with hastily scribbled plans of rooms to be allocated.

"It's like Bedlam," Anne said. "Thank heavens for Lord Wellington's invitation. I can leave it to everybody else, and by tomorrow it will be organised, George will be in charge of the kitchen and I will be left with nothing to do."

"I'm sure you'll find something," Paul said.

"As a matter of fact, I already have," Anne said. "Lord Wellington captured Marshal Marmont's main hospital in Valladolid two weeks ago, but there is a substantial hospital here, in one of the convents, and I am informed that the conditions are appalling. With our own wounded being very well cared for in Salamanca, I thought I might see if I can improve things."

Paul glanced at her with pride and amusement. His young wife's determination to play an active role in army affairs had long since ceased to surprise him, but every now and again it struck him anew how remarkable she was. He had no doubt that the French wounded would not be languishing in filthy wards with inadequate treatment for long once Anne became involved. She had a genius for getting the staff on her side, and although in the early days of her work on the wards, many of the elder surgeons had protested at her being allowed to continue, these days such protests were rare.

"We seem to have a carriage, bonny lass," he said, spotting Lord Wellington's coachman. "I'm surprisingly glad of it."

"He probably thought you would find an excuse not to go if he didn't send somebody for you," Anne said, serenely, lifting the skirt of her muslin gown out of the dust. "Are you sure you're well enough to do this, Paul? I could get one of the others to escort me."

"No, I'm fine. I feel better for a rest."

The drive through the streets of the Spanish capital was magical. As darkness began to fall, the streets were brilliantly lit and thronged with people. British officers were everywhere, many of them with Spanish ladies already on their arms and local businesses, including the numerous lemonade shops as well as the inns and taverns, were inviting the liberators inside, waving aside all thought of payment. Paul's brigade was occupying the palace in solitary splendour while the rest of the Light Division had the locals fighting over the privilege of providing accommodation for them.

There was music on every street, spilling out of well-lit houses and taverns or sometimes played openly on the roadside, with impromptu dance displays attracting small crowds of officers from both British and Portuguese regiments to the music of guitars and the clicking of castanets. Paul held his wife's hand, watching her face as much as the entertainment outside, as the carriage made slow progress between the glorious buildings of the Spanish capital.

"Oh, it's so lovely," Anne breathed.

"It is," Paul admitted. "I'm glad I was here for this."

Anne looked around with a quick smile. "So am I. And you seem very well, so perhaps I am not going to be cross with Lord Wellington anymore."

"Or me."

"Oh love, you know I'm not. Is this it? What a spectacular palace. Although I always find, when visiting a new city, that I have a crick in my neck for days, trying to take it all in. I hope it is not to be all politics this evening, I would rather like just to enjoy it."

"Let's do that then," Paul said, helping her down from the carriage. "I have decided to set aside my well-known dislike of these affairs and be charming to everybody. Do you think I can keep it up?"

"You can if you try," Anne said, taking his arm. "Goodness, look at some of these gowns; I am terribly under-dressed. I should have worn my black lace."

"You look like a queen," Paul said softly. "I love that mantilla on you. Come on, Wellington is waving at us."

The evening retained its enchanted quality, ending at midnight with a spectacular firework display which the guests watched from the balconies of the palace. Paul stood with Anne in front of him, his arms about her. She leaned back against him and Paul held her and allowed himself a moment of sheer enjoyment. When the last sparkling shower had fallen from the sky, Anne turned to smile at him, and Paul kissed her very gently and adjusted the lace about her shoulders.

"Let's go and find your cloak, bonny lass."

"Colonel van Daan."

Paul turned and saluted his chief. Wellington was looking unusually mellow. He kissed Anne's hand. "Did you enjoy yourself, ma'am?"

"Oh, so much. I know there is a lot of work to be done, sir, but it was lovely just to celebrate for an evening. And so beautifully. Thank you for inviting us."

"You are very welcome, ma'am. And I am sorry that I must allow business to intrude for a moment. Colonel, you will probably have heard that the French have not all left Madrid."

"Yes, sir, General Alten has been telling me about it. Around two thousand men in the Retiro, I understand."

"Indeed. My sources tell me that they have cannon. I cannot imagine they will turn them on the city, but after my recent experiences in Salamanca, I am not wasting time on them. You may have detachments from the third and seventh divisions and use whatever you wish of your own brigade. Get them out of there, preferably without too many casualties."

"Yes, sir," Paul said, saluting. It was a purely instinctive response but as soon as he had made it, he felt Anne's entire body stiffen at his side. He could feel himself flinching internally, having literally no idea what she was about to say to his chief. He did not even dare to turn and look at her.

There was a frozen moment of silence. Into it, his chief said hastily:

"Or Colonel Wheeler can lead them, of course, if your wound is not fully healed. I will leave that to your discretion, Colonel."

Paul gave a splutter of laughter; he could not help himself. The expression on Wellington's face told him that he had just been in receipt of one of Anne's most appalling glares. "It's all right, sir, I'm fit enough," he said, putting his arm about Anne. "It's not as if you're asking me to handle a forced march."

"No. But you may be sure that if it appeared convenient to his Lordship, he would not hesitate," Anne said frostily.

"Ma'am, I can assure you..."

"Oh, do not think of it again, my Lord. Look at his face, he is completely delighted. Men!" Anne said, in tones of disgust.

***

Marching out, King Joseph had taken his guard and the train of afrancesados with him but had left a garrison in the fortified Retiro palace. They had enough cannon to do Madrid considerable damage and Lord Wellington was determined to remove the danger as quickly as possible. Madrid was still going wild with celebrations on the following evening, as Paul assembled his men in one of the quieter squares. Even so, the columns of men were initially mobbed by the jubilant Spaniards, who seemed under the impression that this was a parade for their entertainment. Paul ordered the 110th light company to clear the square of spectators, and Sergeant Hammond's men cheerfully began to escort the civilians back behind makeshift barricades while Paul surveyed his troops. Wellington had given him six hundred men from the third and seventh divisions and Paul had added the light and second companies of the 110th, the light company of the 112th and the first and second companies of the 115th.

Paul wondered about Wellington's motives for giving him this command. He was not the obvious choice; he was recovering from a wound, and there were many capable commanders in both the third and the seventh divisions. He found himself wondering if Wellington was making a point. There had been no questions asked about the skirmish at Alba de Tormes; Wellington had made a good deal of the unexpected departure of the Spanish troops and Paul had not heard even a whisper of criticism of his own leadership but he was very conscious of what Wellington had not said. He knew, and Wellington knew, that he ought to have been aware of the retreat of the Spanish and got his men out of danger before the retreating French army reached them. He knew, because he was not especially modest, that his performance during the ensuing fight had been exemplary. He also knew they should not have been there.

Over the previous few years, Paul was aware that he had been seen as overly favoured by the commander-in-chief. It had become less of an issue recently; younger men were rising through the ranks and gossip had a short lifespan in the army, but Paul knew that a man's reputation was only as good as his last battle. He knew that his chief's affection for him was both real and lasting and if there had been any snide remarks about Paul's actions at Alba de

Tormes, Wellington was very capable of giving him this command to demonstrate his continuing faith in Paul's abilities. It was the reason Paul had not handed it on to Johnny. Like Wellington, he had a point to make.

Looking out over the assembled troops, Paul was surprised to see the willowy form of Lieutenant Simon Carlyon at the head of one of the companies from the seventh. He made his way through the men and Carlyon saluted at his approach.

"Mr Carlyon. It's very good to see you, although I'm confused."

"Sorry, sir. I thought General Pakenham had informed you. He asked me to take temporary command of the third company of the 94th while the captain is injured. We're hoping he'll be back soon."

"No, he didn't," Paul said. "Probably because he knows I could have done with you here. I'm told you distinguished yourself in the battle, lad."

"I'm told you captured an eagle, sir."

"Which my wife threatened to stab me with; she was not impressed. It's good to see you, Simon. We've no time now, but when this nonsense is over, come up for dinner tomorrow evening, we're missing you."

"Thank you, sir. I'd like to."

The French defences consisted of a fortified area on the Retiro heights to the east of the city. It was protected by two lines of defences, and a star fort. King Joseph had left General Lafon-Blaniac, the governor of La Mancha, to defend the city with 2000 men. Paul wondered if Joseph had thought that the fortress might be able to hold out as the forts at Salamanca had, in the hope that Soult might be able to reach the city in time. Studying the defences, Paul thought it had been an unrealistic hope. The Retiro had nothing like the defensive capability of the Salamanca forts.

The outer line consisted of the existing wall of the Retiro Park with loopholes cut into it and some supporting positions, the strongest of which were the Retiro Palace and the Prado museum. The inner defences were stronger, with ten bastions, but were more like field works than proper fortifications. The star fort, which was built around the old royal porcelain factory, was the strongest part of the entire works.

The French had left outposts at the Prado, the Botanical Gardens and the walls of the Retiro Park itself. Dividing his men into three sections, as soon as it was dark, Paul sent in half his force to attack from the north and the rest from the south-west.

They were met by a hail of musket fire which did no damage; it was impossible to aim in the dark, and the French outposts fell back quickly under his steady advance without serious resistance. Paul gained the strong impression that there was little conviction among the defenders. Having gained the Royal park, he halted his men behind a series of long walls close to the forts and sent the Chasseurs Brittanique from the seventh division to make a breach large enough to take his men through. The breaching attracted a steady fire from the French through the night. The rest of Paul's men settled to rest behind the walls and some even managed to sleep.

Paul did not sleep. His healing shoulder was painful, the muscles cramping in the cold and making him restless. He lay wakeful, deliberately not thinking about the pain. He had survived several worse injuries and he knew that the pain would ease eventually. Part of him, the logical part, mocked himself for his folly in putting himself through this when he could have handed the command to Johnny Wheeler. Wellington would not have thought ill of him and he could have been sleeping warmly at Anne's side.

A scream of pain broke through Paul's uneasy rest and he sat up, looking around. The sound had come from the lines of the 51$^{st}$. A barrage of insults rained down on the head of the offender. Paul got up, stretching his stiff limbs, cautiously keeping low behind the wall. Something about that scream sounded real.

"Are you all right, sir?" Captain Manson said, sitting up.

"Yes. I'm just going to see what that was, Leo."

"I'll go. You should rest."

"I'm not resting." Paul smiled at his junior through the darkness. "My shoulder feels as though it's being bayoneted all over again. And if you tell my wife that, Captain, your career is over."

He heard Manson laugh softly as he slipped silently through his resting men and over towards the 51$^{st}$ where there was a scuffle of sound.

"Hooker, what's wrong with you? You're bloody dreaming, pipe down."

"I'm not dreaming," a voice said. "I've been shot."

"You haven't been shot, you've got bloody cramp. Shift your arse and shut up, will you?"

"I've been shot, I tell you."

"Officer in the lines," a voice said, and there was a move to rise.

"Stay where you are," Paul said quickly. "Colonel van Daan and I don't need a parade, I need to know what the racket's about."

"It's Tom Hooker, sir. Got a cramp in his leg, and he thinks…"

"It's not a cramp," a new voice said urgently. "There's blood everywhere here, he's been hit."

There was a scuffle of movement as the men surrounding the hapless Private Hooker shifted to look. Paul scrambled over the men and crouched down to where a young soldier was bending over Hooker, his hand clamped to his leg.

"It's his thigh, sir. Bleeding badly."

Paul swore softly, feeling for the wound in the dark. It was hard to believe that in the sporadic and inaccurate musket fire, a stray shot had managed to hit a man, but it had clearly happened. "What's your name, Private?"

"Wheeler, sir."

"All right, Private Wheeler, I'm going to twist this scarf around his leg, and I need you to hold it for me. Keep it tight, it'll help stop the bleeding. Private Hooker, can you hear me?"

"Yes, sir."

"Hold on. I know it bloody hurts, I was hit there myself back at

119

Assaye, years ago. We'll get you out of here in a minute. Is there…?"

"Sir?"

Paul peered through the darkness. "Is that you, Smithy?"

"Yes, sir. Sergeant Hammond sent me over to see if you needed help."

"We need to get this lad out of here, he's hurt. Can you run up to the town and get some sort of transport for him? My wife is setting up the regimental hospital in a riding school next to the palace, Dr Daniels will probably be there."

"Give me ten minutes, sir."

Paul sat quietly beside Hooker, holding his hand. The man was silent now, although Paul could feel his pain in the tension of his hand. Within ten minutes there was a soft hail.

"Over here, sir. We've borrowed a handcart."

"Well done, Smithy. Private Wheeler, let's get him up."

With the wounded man removed, Paul went back to his companies. It was still full dark, and he settled down, the pain still there, although somehow it was easier now. He rested, without sleeping, until dawn began to send silvery streaks across the inky black sky.

Dawn, and then full daylight, brought a new problem. The early sun lit up the astonishing spectacle of an audience. The citizens of Madrid, some of whom had probably not been to sleep from the previous night's celebrations, began to throng the streets close to the Retiro, ready to watch the attack on the interior lines. Others appeared on the roofs and balconies of nearby houses. Paul, trying to call his men into order to storm the breach in the wall, surveyed the area in complete astonishment.

"Jesus bloody Christ, we need the Light Division amateur theatrical group over here, it'd be the biggest audience they ever got. And probably the most appreciative. Where's Lord Wellington, has he seen this sideshow? Can we get them cleared out? If the French decide to make a fight of this, people are going to get hurt. Major Swanson, we need to send a message down."

It took thirty minutes for the reply to come, a brief and clearly exasperated message from Wellington. Paul read it and looked up at Carl.

"Apparently he's made representations to the town council, but people aren't willing to leave," he said. "I feel my patience diminishing, which is never good."

An enormous cheer greeted the manoeuvring of three companies of the seventh division into position. The British soldiers echoed the cheers with a response of their own, drowning Sergeant-Major Carter's shouted orders to his men about their position. Carter took a deep breath and looked over at Paul.

"This is bloody chaos," he said. "They're dopey bastards in there, mind, I'd have opened fire by now."

"If they've got any sense they'll surrender and hope we can get them out of here alive," Paul said grimly. "They're not getting past our lads, but even if they did, these people will tear them to pieces. Why the hell did Joseph leave them here?"

"Making a point, sir," Captain Manson said. "He might have left his capital, but he didn't leave it undefended."

"Two thousand men against the entire army isn't a defence, it's a present."

Another enormous cheer swelled the crowd and Paul swore fluently. "Carter, get them moving over to the right. Use hand signals if you need to. Any trouble with them, I'll kick their arses personally. I don't...ah look, we've company."

Lord Wellington was approaching, making his way with some difficulty through the crowded streets, his two young ADCs trying hard to make a path for him with their horses. Paul waited several minutes to be very sure that Wellington had got the point about the difficulties of conducting operations with a crowd of civilian spectators. When he suspected that his chief was on the verge of laying about him with a riding whip, he called over to Sergeant Hammond.

"Sergeant, get over there and clear a path for his Lordship, will you?"

Hammond was wearing his most deadpan expression. He saluted. "Right away, sir."

Paul dropped his voice. "Don't make it look too easy, Sergeant."

"Wouldn't dream of it, sir."

Wellington's horse emerged finally from the throng which was being neatly held back by the 110th and Paul saluted his chief with a pleasant smile.

"Morning, sir, come to see the show? I think they can find you space over on that balcony, and I must say I like the look of the pretty dark-haired lass on the end, see if you can squeeze in next to her."

"I will remember to mention to your wife how observant you are when she's not around," Wellington said smoothly, reining in and dismounting. "Do not think that I am unaware of how long it took you to intervene there. Have you had a good night?"

"No," Paul said briefly. His attention had been caught by a movement up at the fort, and he shielded his eyes from the brilliant early sun. "Is that...?"

"A white flag? I think so," Wellington said. "I wonder if we might be able to avoid bloodshed after all. Signal that we will meet with them, Colonel. Let's see if we can put an end to this."

The messenger was a young officer in a dusty uniform who looked as though he had slept as badly as Paul had. He spoke fairly good English, which was presumably why he had been chosen, but Wellington chose to conduct the negotiations in French. There were the usual civilities. Wellington introduced both his ADCs and Paul and led Captain Girard to a small wooden table and chairs which Captain O'Reilly had managed to produce from a cafe opposite along with a jug of lemonade and cups. The Captain accepted the hospitality formally and then drank at a pace which gave Paul a piece of information that he should not have had. Having drained his cup, Girard put it down, caught Paul's eye and realised his error. Paul smiled faintly.

"Captain Girard, have some more," he said, reaching to pour. "You seem thirsty. It's very good. Captain O'Reilly?"

"Sir?"

"Will you go to the lemonade shop and get a bottle of this for the Captain to take back to General Lafon-Blaniac, when he goes. After all, we've plenty more, no need to go thirsty."

"Yes, sir," O'Reilly said easily. Paul could sense Wellington's amusement, but he said nothing. Instead he addressed the young officer.

"Have you been given terms, Captain Girard?"

"The Governor has asked me to inform you, my Lord, that should your men attack, he will regrettably have no option but to open fire on the city, with great loss of life."

"We all wish to avoid such desperate measures," Wellington said gravely. "Naturally, your General must do as he sees fit, but I hope we can come to a better arrangement. Should your General slaughter the citizens of Madrid, we will have to evacuate as quickly as possible. Eventually you will run out of ammunition and then we will take the citadel. My concern is that we will be unable to restrain the people of Madrid from taking their revenge on your men."

"We have a good deal of ammunition, my Lord."

Paul was studying the young officer. Girard could not have been more than twenty-four or five and Paul thought that in the Governor's place he would have sent an older man with more experience. Girard betrayed his thoughts too easily on his open countenance; he would never have made a card player.

"That's interesting," Paul said pleasantly. "How much powder do you have, Captain? And where is it stored?"

Girard flushed and Paul shook his head. "Nice try, lad," he said very gently. "You're a good soldier and I've got a feeling your General is too, which means he isn't going to fire a cannon which might blow up two thousand of his own men. Just now, my men are bringing up our own artillery. If I see you moving those guns into position, we'll fire first and you're going to go up like a November firework display. You've said your piece. Now drink some more, you've been on rationed water for a day or two, I'd say, and his Lordship will explain our terms. After that, my men will escort you back and you can put them before the Governor."

Paul stood beside Wellington, watching the young officer walk back to the fort. "Do you think they will accept, Colonel?" Wellington asked.

"You've offered surrender with the full honours of war, the officers can keep their swords, horses and baggage and the men their packs. He'll jump at it, he'd be mad not to, sir."

Wellington shot him a sideways glance. "You're a better negotiator than I had expected, Colonel," he said. "I shall remember that for the future."

"Always glad when you get the chance to add to my list of duties, sir," Paul said placidly. "That lemonade was good. I wonder if they do food, I've not had breakfast yet."

"I do not think that is likely to be a problem, Colonel," Wellington said. Paul looked and saw that some of the crowd were coming forward with baskets, offering food to his men. Captain Manson looked over at Paul enquiringly and Paul nodded.

"You can stand them down for a while, Captain," he said. "It will take some time before we get an answer, I imagine. Put sentries on the gates, mind, I don't want them wandering out of the gardens and finding a tavern just in case they're needed."

It took several hours and two more conversations with Captain Girard for the surrender to be agreed. Paul watched the garrison emerge. He had seen more than one garrison surrender. Some were relieved, others were desperate. Many of these men were angry. They had been instructed to leave their muskets and ammunition on the glacis outside the fort. Paul watched as they lined up and there was a sudden commotion as some of the men began to bang the weapons hard on the ground, trying to knock off the butt end to make them unusable. Paul saw Sergeant-Major Carter move forward swiftly, motioning to some of the 110th. The French troops resisted briefly, backing up the glacis and continuing their pointless attempt at sabotage. Carter ordered his men forward and the French were firmly but sympathetically disarmed.

Lord Wellington had ordered up a contingent of Spanish guerrillas to escort the French prisoners out of the city. Paul knew that it was intended as a compliment to the Spanish people and he understood the need to allow a nation whose pride had been trampled carelessly by Napoleon's troops to participate in their own liberation. At the same time, he felt a twist of discomfort, standing next to Wellington, watching the Spanish march the prisoners away. "Sir, General Lafon-Blaniac's request was fairly clear. He asked for English troops to escort his men to Bilbao, for the transports to England."

"I did not agree to that, Colonel. I require my troops here in case they are needed. Besides, the Spanish have a right to be involved."

Paul glanced over at his chief. "I don't trust them," he said bluntly. Wellington gave him a sideways look.

"Would that have anything to do with Alba de Tormes, Colonel?" he enquired, genially.

"No, sir. That was a military blunder and I was as much to blame as anybody else," Paul said, keeping his voice even. "This is a matter of humanity. I don't trust them."

"I have given my orders to the Spanish guards, Colonel. I expect them to be obeyed."

Paul studied his commander. "I hope they are, sir," he said, neutrally. "Permission to stand the men down?"

"Permission granted, Colonel." Wellington studied Paul with thoughtful eyes. "May I suggest you take tomorrow off?"

"Thank you, sir. And for the warning. If I look that bad, I should probably try to avoid my wife for a bit."

Paul found Anne in their room. She appeared to be halfway through dressing for dinner but had abandoned the task and was curled up on the enormous four poster bed reading a depressing looking volume in French, wearing nothing but her shift and with her hair loose around her shoulders.

Paul closed the door and stood watching her. After a moment she looked up, breaking into a smile.

"I didn't hear you. How long have you been standing there?"

"Long enough to appreciate the view," Paul said, coming forward to kiss her. "Are you supposed to be taking that garment on or off?"

He reached for the laces at the front of Anne's shift and his wife laughed and batted him away. "Not in the state you're in, Colonel, you look half dead. Come and sit down and I'll call Jenson to get some hot water. And a brandy might be an idea."

She moved towards the door and Paul scooped her back. "Not like that you don't. Half the regiment is wandering the corridors trying to remember which room they're in; this place is enormous. I'll call him."

"Will you ask him if Keren is around, to help with my hair?" Anne asked as he went to the door.

"I will. She will probably be found tucked up with the commander of my first battalion, but I expect she'll oblige. You need a new maid, Nan."

"Oh, not again," Anne said, picking up the book.

"We will discuss it another time. Put that down or you'll get distracted again. What is it anyway?"

"It's a book I've been wanting for a long time, written by a French surgeon, specifically about battle wounds. It's fascinating. I asked my brother to get me a copy; it's taken him forever, but it arrived today. I think the post has been chasing us around, there's a mountain of it, including about eight letters in the same handwriting for Captain Manson. I took those to him myself, just to watch him blush."

"You're a wicked woman, Anne van Daan. Put something on before Jenson gets here, would you? It's not fair on the man."

Anne laughed and went to retrieve her robe which was thrown across an elegant chair before the fireplace. "You're getting very respectable, Colonel. Is it over?"

"Yes, they surrendered, thank God. They're on their way to Bilbao, to prison transports. I'm just a bit worried about them getting there alive with a Spanish escort." Paul opened the door and raised his voice "Jenson! Where the devil are you, have you got lost?"

He turned back into the room and Anne removed her hands from her ears. "Bilbao, you say?" she said pleasantly. "I imagine the citizens there heard you as clearly as Jenson did."

\*\*\*

Simon Carlyon presented himself at the Marina Palace promptly, feeling ridiculously nervous, and was conducted through what seemed like acres of corridors to a spacious dining room. He was trying not to look around him like a country bumpkin at the annual fair, but it was impossible. Soaring painted ceilings and elegant plaster mouldings gazed down upon tall mirrors and enormous paintings in gilt frames. The furnishings looked in remarkably good condition. Simon had been billeted in a variety of palaces in India, but he was astonished to find this in a country so beset by war and poverty. It appeared that Bonaparte's supporters had done very well under his brother's rule and Simon was not surprised that they had fled the city.

He was greeted by his Colonel's wife, beautiful in a simple yellow gown with dainty blue embroidery which looked as though it had cost a fortune. Anne held out her hand.

"Simon, it's so good to see you - welcome. Have you got a crick in your neck looking upwards yet? We're all doing it; Captain Manson and Mr Ashford walked into each other this morning."

Simon laughed aloud. "I have," he admitted. "This place is astonishing. It's huge."

"It is. We usually struggle for accommodation, but we are able to house all the brigade officers here, since the rest of the Light Division are billeted elsewhere. We've separated the regimental messes though, it's too much work to cater for that many people, and it makes it too formal. We have this central wing, the 112th are in the east wing and the 115th are in the west, along with the Portuguese and the German officers. It is very worldly of me, I know, but I do hope we are here for some weeks, it is a long time since I lived anywhere this comfortable."

Simon bowed over her hand. He appreciated her artless way of informing him that he was unlikely to accidentally run into Colonel Johnny Wheeler.

"I hope so too," he said. "It is good of you to invite me, ma'am. I have a comfortable billet myself in the city with a very nice family who run a bookshop, but it is nothing to this."

"Come as often as you wish," Anne said. "We do have another guest whom I think you will be pleased to see. Mr Witham, will you see that Mr Carlyon has a drink?"

She moved on to speak to somebody else and Simon saw Nicholas Witham holding out a glass of wine. He smiled and took it.

"I'm not sure if I'm supposed to salute you," Nicholas said. "Company commander, I hear?"

Simon laughed and touched his glass to Nicholas'. "It's only temporary," he said. "Hewson will be back in a month or two. Although I have been asked if I want to stay on as his lieutenant."

"I'd a horrible feeling you were going to say that," Nicholas said. "Are you going to?"

"I honestly don't know, Nick. It's a good chance, and I like the 94th, some good lads. But it's not the same as this." Simon looked around the room. "I miss it," he said, abruptly. "Didn't think I would, but I do. You get used to it very quickly."

"I know. I have."

"I've got some time to think about it, General Pakenham is of the opinion that we'll be here for a month or so, at least. He's not all that well at the moment, some kind of recurring fever, apparently."

"I'm sorry to hear that; he did a fine job in the battle, by all accounts."

"He really did."

"You weren't injured?"

"No, but it was bloody on both sides. I'm glad to see you in one piece, Nicholas, I gather you had rather more excitement than expected?"

Nicholas pulled a face. "I think that's the closest I've come to dying," he said. "We were lucky that Marshal Foy arrived and ordered them back. They might have been beaten but there were more than enough to overrun our brigade. Come on, they're calling dinner and I'm starving."

Seated between Nicholas and Captain Manson, Simon found the officers of the 110th keen to hear his account of the battle. They bombarded him with intelligent questions and talked of their own action at Alba de Tormes. Manson, who had friends in several other regiments, described the French counterattack on the fourth and sixth divisions which had come dangerously close to succeeding. Almost half the Allied losses had come from those two divisions.

"They held on though," Donald Elliott said. "Cole and Leith were both wounded. And wasn't Cotton on the injured list as well?"

"Yes," Manson said.

"Bloody shame about Le Marchant," Captain Zouch said. "Did you see him go down, Carlyon?"

"No, although I saw his first attack. It was like something out of a training exercise, the French didn't stand a chance, his men just cut through them. Half of them ran to us to surrender, we were busy taking prisoners. I didn't even realise that he was dead until afterwards."

"The French didn't do that well either," Manson said. "Marmont and Bonet wounded, Ferey killed."

"I heard the Colonel was pretty bad," Simon said.

"He was," Manson said, and his tone told Simon more than his words. "I thought for a while…but he's recovered very well."

"He was in more danger from his wife than that wound," Zouch said, and there was a general laugh.

It was with some reluctance that Simon said his farewells and thanks at the end of the evening. He had forgotten how much he had begun to enjoy the peculiar informality of Paul van Daan's brigade. Out in the corridor he hesitated, trying to remember which direction would take him back to the main door.

"This way. They'll have stabled your horse, there's a side door which will be more direct."

Simon froze and turned. He realised with bitter understanding, that his Colonel's wife had betrayed him. Colonel Wheeler had been seated on an elegant chaise longue, upholstered in blue damask under a portrait of a formidable looking Spanish lady in black. He rose and came forward, regarding Simon with steady grey eyes. Simon saluted.

"Thank you, sir. I'll find my way, there's no need."

"Don't be stupid, Mr Carlyon, you know that I want to talk to you."

They walked through the dim halls in silence. Outside, there was a full moon spilling silver light over the path which led towards the substantial stable blocks. Simon was beginning to wonder if the Colonel had forgotten what he wanted to say when he spoke abruptly.

"Colonel van Daan has asked me to speak to you, Lieutenant, about coming back to your regiment."

"Yes, sir."

Colonel Wheeler stopped and turned to look at Simon. "Do you want to?" he asked.

Simon did not speak. He had been hoping to have this conversation with Colonel van Daan or even Major Corrigan. To either of them, he could have admitted at least some of his confusion. He was furious at being faced with this situation without any warning although he also understood why Colonel van Daan had chosen to do it this way.

"If the answer is no, the stables are there. You can ride back to the 94th and Major Corrigan will arrange a permanent transfer. You shouldn't come under my direct command again unless circumstances change."

"Sir."

"If you want to stay, we'll need to have a conversation about it. I suggest you think about it. I'll be in the library."

Wheeler turned and walked back towards the house. Simon stood, stranded and bewildered, and said the first thing that came into his head.

"Sir?"

Wheeler turned. "Yes?"

"I have no idea where the library is."

Wheeler looked at him for a moment. Then he jerked his head. "This way."

There was a fire burning in the grate and the litter of a day's work scattered over several large tables. Wheeler collected a bottle and two glasses and set them on a low table before the fire then sat down in a well-stuffed armchair and leaned back, crossing his legs.

"Sit down, Mr Carlyon."

Simon wanted to stand, but he was suddenly very clear that an order had been given. There was something different about Wheeler's manner this evening, as though the older man's attitude had hardened. After a moment's hesitation, Simon sat.

"This is the second time that you and I have had this conversation, Mr Carlyon, but it is going to be the last," Wheeler said without preamble. "On the previous occasion, I was very gentle with you. I had a lot of sympathy with how you must be feeling, and I wanted to make it easy for you to fit in to the brigade. I thought you would settle down in time."

"Yes, sir."

Wheeler set his glass down on the table. "You didn't settle down," he said flatly. "I've stood out on the parade ground and watched you practically turning somersaults to avoid having to salute me. You openly leave any social event that I'm present at, making no attempt to disguise your reason, and when you have no choice but to be in company with me, your lip curls every time you look my way. Your whole attitude has been enough for me to put you on a charge, and if you weren't Mrs van Daan's brother-in-law, I'd have done it by now."

Simon's stomach was churning. He had never seen the pleasant-mannered Colonel of the 112th wearing this particular expression before and he had never heard him use this tone of voice. It made Simon feel like a green ensign who had forgotten to salute his commander at the Sunday church parade. He could feel his face burning with embarrassment. He moved as if to get up.

"Stay right where you are, Mr Carlyon, you chose to have this meeting, you'll leave when I say you can," Wheeler rapped out. "In addition to your appalling manners towards me, you have repeatedly got into arguments, and on one or two occasions, undignified shoving matches with other officers. I realise they've given you a hard time in places, which is why Colonel van Daan has been as lenient as he has, but your free ticket to behave like an arsehole has just been formally cancelled. If I catch you putting one foot out of line again, I am putting you on a charge."

"Yes, sir."

"Ungrit your teeth and say that again, Carlyon. With some respect, this time, because I've fucking earned it. I was commissioned ensign twenty-one years ago, I've fought all over the world, I've been wounded four times, once seriously and I've achieved command of a regiment through sheer bloody hard work and merit. I expect complete respect from a junior officer, and if you can't do that, starting now, you can't serve anywhere near me. Stand up."

Simon got to his feet and stood to attention, feeling as though he was going to be sick. He saluted.

"Yes, sir."

"Better. There is one more thing we need to clear up. I killed your brother. I didn't kill him for a laugh, or because I couldn't stand him or because I wanted to free his wife to marry a better man. I killed him to save a woman's life, and I'd do the same again tomorrow without a second thought. I'm sorry you're related to a wife-beating bastard, my Colonel assures me that the rest of your family are very good people, so it's clearly not their fault, or yours. But I do not intend to apologise for what I did. Get over it or leave; there's nothing in-between. This is the army, you don't get to choose who you serve under or whether you like them. But you bloody well have to hold discipline and show some respect, I'm not coddling you any further."

"Yes, sir."

There was a long silence. Simon stared at the wall above the fireplace, wondering if the Colonel was going to let him stand there until he had finished his drink and was ready for bed. Unexpectedly, Wheeler said:

"Now sit down, pick up that wine glass and have a drink, you look as though you need it."

Simon obeyed. Thoughts were whirling about his head and it was difficult to know if he was expected to speak or not. He was clearly expected to drink, so he did so, gulping down the wine in relief.

"I'll speak to Major Corrigan in the morning," Wheeler said, in his usual pleasant tones. "He'll liaise with your current officer about when they can let you go. General Pakenham wrote to Colonel van Daan about you in very complimentary terms about your performance during the battle. You're going to be an asset to the brigade, Mr Carlyon. Make the most of your undoubted ability, and do not let that bastard you have the bad luck to be related to, bugger that up for you."

"Yes, sir."

"Do you think you can find your way to the stables again?"

"I think so, sir."

"Off you go, then. Goodnight."

"Goodnight, sir."

Outside in the cold, moonlit air, Simon paused to take several long breaths before beginning to walk briskly down the path to the stables. He was surprised to realise that he felt a good deal better. Colonel Wheeler's brutal simplicity had made his choices very clear and Simon realised he preferred that to kindness, which had only confused him.

Setting off into the cold night, with Reynolds riding at his heels, Simon thought about his brother. He felt guilty at having shared a glass of wine with the man who had openly admitted to killing him, but it was accompanied suddenly by a burst of anger that had nothing to do with Colonel Wheeler. He was furious at Robert, for the constant need to excuse and explain and apologise for him. He was furious at the crimes he had committed and the scandal that he had created. And he was completely incensed that he had treated a woman the way he had treated his young wife. Simon found himself wondering what he would personally have done if he had walked into a room and found his brother pointing a pistol at Anne's head and it occurred to him suddenly that it would probably have led to fratricide.

# Chapter Ten

The Marina Palace boasted an excellent library, with books in several languages, and Anne took possession of it immediately, setting aside an enormous reading table as a desk for Paul and a smaller one for herself. With the responsibilities of a brigade came extra administration and the various regiments each had their own quartermasters, paymasters, and clerks. Paul insisted on regular meetings with the officers of each battalion and when it was possible, a weekly quartermasters meeting, to identify any problems with food, weapons, uniform or other supplies. He had told Anne that he thought it pointless to ensure that the 110th, his own regiment, was ready to fight or march at a moment's notice if the rest of the brigade was not.

Paul slept late on the morning after the fall of the Retiro and Anne gave orders that he was not to be disturbed. She asked Jenson to call her when he awoke, but he appeared in the library as Anne was writing letters. Anne studied him critically.

"You look much better."

"I feel it. I really needed that sleep, thank you, love. Jenson organised a bath for me as well, I feel like a new man. Anything for me?"

"There was a mountain of post, I told you, but most of it has gone to Major Breakspear. There are a few personal letters, I've put them on your desk. And one that I don't recognise which has come from Santander, apparently."

"Really?" Paul asked, with interest. "I was talking to Wellington about that only the other day. It appears that Popham has taken the city with a combined naval blockade and land attacks from the guerrilla bands. Wellington's delighted, it's going to be a very useful supply base."

Anne went to get the letters. "I think it's very unlikely that Sir Home Popham is writing to you, Paul," she said.

Her husband laughed. "Not a chance. He'll save all his energies for writing endless letters to Wellington reminding him what a good job he's doing. Which he actually is, by the way, he's distracting the French brilliantly on that coast. But he's going to drive Wellington up the wall. No, this won't be from Popham, although…oh my God."

"What is it?" Anne could see the news was good; Paul looked delighted. He was reading the letter quickly, his smile broadening.

"It's from an old friend. Funny that we were talking about Popham because this is from Hugh Kelly whom I met during the Copenhagen campaign. He was involved in that almighty cock-up that was the Walcheren fiasco. God knows who thought it was a good idea to send Kelly to serve under Popham again, I'm surprised he's not murdered him. Although to be fair, he's always had a far better grip on his temper than I have. Apparently, my name came up in some correspondence, he heard I'd been wounded and has written to ask."

"He's a good correspondent," Anne said. "Didn't you know his wife as well?"

"I organised their wedding," Paul said with a grin. "I'm not sure if she's back at home on Mann now, he tells me their second child was born last year. When we finally get home I'm looking forward to introducing you to Roseen Kelly. You'll like her."

He finished the letter and passed it to Anne who read it while Paul skimmed through his other correspondence. The letter made Anne smile. There was a dry humour behind the brief description of Kelly's current duties which made it easy to understand why Paul liked the Manxman so much.

They turned to more practical matters. The French had left enormous amounts of stores in the Retiro. Wellington had been furious to discover that some of the troops left to guard the stores had turned instead to looting them and had arrived in person with a guard, arresting not only the looters but the officers who had failed to prevent the outbreak of pillage. Paul, who had been given the news by Jenson over his breakfast, thanked God he had not left any of his own men on sentry duty. He sincerely hoped they would have resisted temptation, but he was glad it had not been tested.

Wellington's new quartermaster-general, Colonel Willoughby Gordon had sent out a memorandum asking for lists of supplies needed by the various regiments to see what could be supplied from the stores. Anne had only just received it, but she knew that in the heady first days in the capital, most regiments would not respond straight away, and she had every intention of making sure that the 110th received their share. She penned and then copied a memo to the regimental quartermasters asking them to make an immediate kit inspection and to provide her with lists of items needed by the end of tomorrow. When she had finished, she passed them to Paul to sign. Paul read the memo and grinned.

"They'll have to catch them fast if they want them sober," he said. "I think the junior officers are spending all their time writing out leave passes for the men to go into the city. Which reminds me, I want to write an order about looting. They're going to run out of money very quickly here, and I want it to be very clear that if they start helping themselves off the locals, I am going to nail their balls to a doorframe."

He reached for a pen and Anne took it from him to trim it. "Are you actually going to write that in the order?"

"I'm going to use the phrase 'serious disciplinary measures' instead. If my lot don't know by now that will not involve the provost-marshal and will

131

definitely involve something really unpleasant, they're too stupid to live, and they have it coming. What is it, Jenson?"

"Lieutenant Browne, sir, from the adjutant-general's office, to see you."

"Show him in, Jenson."

Anne got up, ready to leave, but Paul motioned to her to remain. Browne, a fresh-faced young man in his mid-twenties, came into the room and saluted.

"Mr Browne, what can I do for you?" Paul enquired. "He cannot have known I spent the morning sleeping late."

Browne grinned and shook his head. "No, sir. Although he's been up since dawn. He doesn't know I'm here."

Something about his manner made Anne get up. "I need to speak to Sergeant Kelly about dinner," she said briskly. "Excuse me, Mr Browne."

\*\*\*

When Anne had gone, Paul looked at Browne. "You look as though you need a drink, Mr Browne."

"No, thank you, sir. I can only stay a short time, I have a commission from Lord Wellington, it is very urgent. I stopped here first." Browne took a deep breath. "Actually, I am not sure why I stopped here first, sir. It is just that you were so very concerned yesterday about the French prisoners. And the Spanish."

Paul felt a chill. "What's happened, Lieutenant?" he asked.

"The prisoners, sir. Lord Wellington has received a very disturbing report; a guide riding towards Madrid brought it. He says that they are murdering the prisoners, sir. Ill-using them and sometimes killing them."

Paul sat very still, mastering his anger. "And this was an enormous surprise to his Lordship?" he said savagely.

Browne met his eyes. "Well yes, sir. I honestly think it was."

Paul got up. "Sometimes, he is as naive as a child," he snapped. "So he's sent you to do what exactly?"

"I am commissioned to ride after them, sir, at full speed, to find out if the report is true. If it is, I am to remonstrate with the Spanish commander and try to ensure better treatment for the prisoners."

"If there are any left," Paul said, going to the door. "Jenson! Get in here."

"I'm here, sir."

"Get them to saddle up Rufus. Provisions for a day or so, no baggage, I need to ride fast."

Jenson regarded him sardonically. "What's your wife going to say about that, sir?"

"When she hears why, she'll tell me to get a move on."

His orderly saluted. Paul turned to Browne. "I'm sorry, Mr Browne, I ought to have asked."

132

"No, it's all right, sir. I think…I think perhaps that's why I stopped here first. I think I'm worried that if it's true, they won't listen to me."

Paul regarded him soberly. "They might not listen to me, lad. But if they don't, I'm going to blow their bloody heads off."

Anne met him on the carriage drive as he was checking his saddle and girth. "Jenson said you wanted me. What's wrong, Paul?"

Paul told her briefly. He knew from her expression that she shared his feelings. "I'm sorry," he said, finally. "I have to go."

"Of course you do," Anne said, not disappointing him. "But you shouldn't be going alone, Paul."

"I'm not. Browne is with me and I doubt I'll get out of here without Jenson, it's like having a nursemaid."

As Paul spoke, he saw his orderly limping around from the stables leading his horse. Jenson rode a black gelding which Paul had bought during the Copenhagen campaign five years earlier. As he mounted, surprisingly agile given his wooden leg, Paul could see Browne looking at his orderly's horse, which was considerably better than the young staff officer's mount. Paul studied the grey mare that Browne was riding and suddenly said:

"Jenson. Get back to the stables and saddle up the black mare with the white socks we took off the French at Salamanca for Mr Browne. His mare can stay here and have a rest, she's still tired after the march and we need to move fast."

"Yes, sir." Jenson turned his horse and trotted back to the stable. Browne was looking at Paul, surprised.

"Colonel, there's no need…"

"We need to move faster than your mare can manage today, Mr Browne," Paul said gently. "My grooms can look after her and feed her up a bit."

He stroked the mare's nose and reached into his pocket for a nut, smiling as she nosed his coat for more. "She's a nice animal."

"I've had her since I came out here. I used to have a spare, but he was elderly, and I lost him last year."

"Then you need to take care of this girl, they don't pay you enough. I saw you looking at Felix, Jenson's horse. He's mine, I bought him in Copenhagen as a youngster. I'm lucky enough to have several spares so if you find yourself at a stand, come and ask, I'm happy to lend you a mount if she's sick or lame at any time. Ah, Jenson, thank you."

Paul kissed Anne. Her dark eyes met his, looking troubled. "I hate this," she said. "Damien Cavel or Louis Bernard could be among those men."

"It's unlikely, bonny lass," Paul said.

"They could," Anne insisted. She sounded almost tearful. "I've been thinking about them both since the battle. Don't laugh at me but it's one of the reasons I want to be involved with the French wounded. Just in case."

Paul took her face in his hands and kissed her again. He knew how Anne felt about the two Frenchmen who had tried to protect her during the horror of her captivity. Sergeant Cavel in particular held a special place in his

133

wife's heart. "It's a big army, Nan, and we don't even know where they went after Badajoz," he said. "But I promise you, I'll check."

"Thank you. Take care."

The road north was wide, but in poor condition, rutted and cracked in the heat of summer. Paul set a steady pace, not wanting to exhaust the horses in territory where water was unpredictable at this time of year. Low hills and ridges rose around them, for the most part, brown and bare, although orchards and some farmland brought relief to the eye. There was little shade on the road, and Paul thought how difficult it must be to farm this area at any time, let alone with the depredations of war. He also thought, with a soldier's eye, that the countryside would a nightmare for cavalry during the summer months.

They found a stream after an hour and rested the horses, allowing them to drink. The water was low and stagnant in places, but the stream ran from a small rocky ridge, with a track that led up to a straggling village, and Paul scrambled up the rocks to fill their water bottles from a small rivulet which tumbled over the rocks into a little pool, giving them clear, cold water to drink. Jenson thanked him, watching the horses drink the less appealing water.

"They're not as fussy."

"Neither have I been at times, if I'm thirsty enough," Paul said. "Pass me that when you're done, Mr Browne, I'll refill it."

"I'll go, sir." Browne accepted Paul's bottle and Paul waited, wondering if the staff officer realised that he had walked into a problem of etiquette. He saw Browne recognise it, but it only took him a moment, then he held out his hand. "Pass me yours, Corporal, you can't climb up there with that leg."

Jenson passed him the bottle with a smile. "Thank you very much, sir."

They watched as Browne made the scramble. "Think he feels like a change, sir?" Jenson said softly. "I reckon you could work with this lad."

Paul choked back a laugh as Browne climbed back down. Mounted up, they set off north again. Somehow the company felt easier now, as though the little interlude had helped Lieutenant Browne relax. They cantered for a while, then slowed the horses as Paul saw something up ahead beside the road. Paul looked over at Browne and saw the younger man looking back at him, appalled. There was no question about what they were seeing. Birds were wheeling overhead, swooping down over the body.

Paul set Rufus to a canter and arrived at the body ahead of his companions. He swung down, staring at the man on the ground in horror. He was French, a stocky man of probably around forty, with thinning hair, his blue coat soaked in his own blood. The birds had already done gory damage to his face.

The other two men arrived, and Paul handed the reins to Jenson and knelt to look. Browne crouched beside him. "He's been stabbed."

"Lance, by the look of it. They'd cavalry with them, hadn't they - the Spanish?"

"Yes, sir." Browne's voice was sombre. "It's true, isn't it?"

134

Paul glanced at him. "Didn't you think it would be, lad?" he asked.

"Yes. No. I don't know. I hoped. But slaughtering unarmed prisoners..."

"I suppose the Spanish feel it's justice given what has been done to some of their people by the French all these years. But it makes me sick too. Come on. I've got a feeling there are going to be more bodies along the roadside, but I'm not stopping again. We need to reach them and stop this."

Browne looked up at him as they rose. "What if we can't?" he faltered. "Why would they listen to us? We can't travel two hundred miles to keep an eye on them."

"No, we can't. So you need to put those doubts to one side, Mr Browne, and focus on what you're here for. You're the representative of Lord Wellington, you need to make sure they know that. I'm sure he's given you authority to speak in his name."

"He has."

"Good. Let's find the bastards, then."

They came upon the prisoners around twenty miles out of Madrid, having passed at least another dozen dead men, beside the roadside. Despite his intention, Paul could not help slowing down to look at each one. He knew that it was unlikely that he would find either Bernard or Cavel among them, but it was not impossible. None of the faces looked familiar, but each of them remained burned into his memory.

The convoy of prisoners was spread out, marching at a fast pace in the heat, and at the rear Paul could see two mounted Spaniards. Three Frenchmen were at the back, one clearly stumbling, and there was already blood on his coat. As Paul approached, a horseman prodded him again with his lance, and the man gave a little cry.

Paul touched his heel to his horse and set Rufus to a gallop, yelling at the top of his voice in Spanish. The lancer wheeled around, an expression of shock on his face. Paul pulled up and slid to the ground, approaching the little group. He looped the reins about his arm and drew his sword.

"Put up those weapons, now, or I am going to cut your fucking hand off," he said.

The two Spaniards shifted back out of range as Paul's companions reached him. Paul passed his reins to Jenson. "Jenson, take him. Mr Browne, why don't you ride up to find their commanding officer. This column is so strung out, he might not even realise what they're doing, although he should learn to bloody keep discipline if he doesn't. I'm staying here with these lads."

"I will, sir. I'll get him to halt the column and I'll speak to him."

Browne set his horse to a canter and Paul turned to the three Frenchmen. "What's been happening?" he asked, in French. The two Spanish horsemen had withdrawn a little, looking uncertain.

"They are murdering our men," one of the three said. He was the youngest, probably around twenty, and looked in reasonable condition. The injured man was stumbling, a wound in his upper arm bleeding steadily. Paul reached for the canteen at his belt and found it empty. He unslung his own and gave the man water, then passed it to his two companions.

"You need water," he said. "Did you not stop?"

"We stopped. They drank." The young Frenchman's face was tight with fury, his words clipped. "And ate. We have had no food or water since we left the city. We are dying, and when we fall back, they kill us. None of us will make it to a prison camp."

"Yes, you will," Paul said grimly. "Take the rest of this, I'll be back."

He mounted and turned to Jenson, reaching into his coat and taking out his pistol. "Take this," he said, handing it to his orderly, but looking at the two Spaniards. "If either of those two even looks at these men the wrong way, blow his bloody head off."

"Yes, sir. My pleasure."

Paul cantered up the column. He found Lieutenant Browne with the Spanish commandant, a grey haired, bearded man of around fifty. Browne was speaking Spanish, fluently and with considerable passion and Paul went to join them. He did not interrupt but took up a position a little behind Browne, hoping his rank and his expression would lend weight to the younger man's words.

After listening for a few minutes, Paul was not sure he had been needed at all. Browne was very eloquent and spoke with unconscious authority which had little to do with his use of Lord Wellington's name.

The commandant made several attempts to protest, but Browne cut him off ruthlessly until he had finished. The Spaniard spread his hands wide.

"It may be true what you say, Lieutenant. All of it, I have heard and understood. But my men - they have seen homes burned and families slaughtered by these French animals. What can I do to stop them?"

"You can tell them what is going to happen to them if they kill one more prisoner," Paul said. "You can speak to them now, before we leave, in our hearing, explaining to them everything that Mr Browne has just told you. Lord Wellington is furious. I am furious. I can promise you, Señor, that if one more French prisoner dies in your care, you will be disgraced. Your corps will be disbanded, and you will no longer be part of the Spanish army. You and your officers will be held personally responsible for any life lost among these men from this moment. I will count the men and keep their number, and I intend to write to the British agent in Bilbao. He will check the numbers and he will ask each one of these prisoners how they have been treated for the rest of this march. Just one incident will be enough to bring the vengeance of Lord Wellington down upon your heads. Do you understand me?"

"Yes. Yes, of course."

"They must also be fed and given water and rest," Browne said. "You were given supplies for them and money to buy more on the journey. I will see them fed before I leave today. Now assemble your men."

Paul stood listening as the commandant harangued his troops. He did not believe for one moment that the man had not known what his soldiers were doing, but he agreed with Browne that it was politic to pretend to believe him. If the man thought he might get away without further censure he might well take steps to ensure their good behaviour.

136

"Sir."

Paul looked around at Jenson. "Freddie?"

"Just been having a chat with one of the Spanish lads. They've ridden this route a fair few times. There's a village about two miles on, got some shade and a well."

"Has it? Yes, I think I'd like to make sure this lot get fed properly before we ride back. I'll speak to Mr Browne and the commandant. It might mean we have to sleep here, but a night of our presence might help to keep these buggers honest. Thank you, Jenson."

The village was small, a huddle of houses around a central square, with the usual walled gardens and straggling vineyards and orchards close by. Paul rode ahead and chose a shady area in a copse of trees, then leaving Jenson to guide the column, he went in search of the well and to speak to some of the inhabitants. He found, as he had expected, very little enthusiasm for a convoy of French prisoners of war spending the night nearby, but the sight of ready money brought rather more interest, and Paul paid an over-inflated price for several sheep to roast and all the bread that the village baker could provide. He would get the money back from Wellington eventually. His chief was obsessive about procedures when it came to officers' claiming expenses, preferring all rations to be issued by the commissariat, and Paul understood why; the opportunities for abusing the system were endless. Paul was fairly sure that Wellington would approve of his actions in this case; he was going to be horrified at what had happened.

It was growing late, the shadows lengthening. Several of the prisoners were set to drawing water for both men and horses. They had been allowed to take their packs with them from the Retiro, and a few of them took out pipes, keeping a wary eye on their Spanish guards. Some of the villagers, losing their fear as it became obvious that the French were captive and harmless, came out of their homes and were hovering nearby, staring at the interlopers as they sat around several fires waiting for the meat to cook. Three children emerged from a white walled cottage with a large garden close to the trees. Paul smiled at their wide-eyed curiosity; a boy and girl who were probably around eight and ten and an older girl who was on the verge of young womanhood and who reminded Paul of his wife. It was she who turned suddenly, tugging at her siblings and whispering something. They disappeared around the back of the house and then reappeared some minutes later with two large baskets which proved to contain apples.

They hesitated on the edge of the trees and Paul motioned them forward. "How much, Señorita?" he asked, in Spanish.

The girl shook her head. "No payment," she said. "We have too many and not all the fruit is good. My mother used to make cider, but she is gone now."

"Your father?"

"I do not know. With the army, I think, we have not seen him for many years. He may be dead."

Paul studied the pretty face. "Are you living there on your own?"

"Three of us; I care for Lorenzo and Paulina. Now he has work for the blacksmith, so we have more money. I help Señora Correa sometimes, at the big house. We grow vegetables and have chickens."

"What's your name, lass?"

"Elena. I am fourteen. The blacksmith wishes me to marry him, but I have told him no."

Despite himself, Paul laughed. "Elena, you're a very determined young lady. Keep saying it, if he's not to your liking, you'll find a lad who will be. Thank you for the fruit, the soldiers will be very grateful, they're hungry."

"I like the French," the girl said, completely unexpectedly. "They came to our village many months ago and stayed for some weeks. Three men stayed in our house. They were kind to us. They taught me to speak some of their language."

Paul thought how fortunate she had been that the soldiers billeted on the little family had been decent men. "There are many good men on both sides," he said gravely.

He watched as the children moved among the soldiers, offering the apples. There were too few to feed all the prisoners, but the Frenchmen shared them about, trading bites, eating the core as well. Paul thought that the child's story explained the relatively good condition of the village. It was clear that a troop had been billeted there, and presumably had lived off the villagers as they were expected to do, but he suspected they had been well led, by officers who refused to turn a blind eye to rape and looting. Paul wondered if Bonaparte had ever realised that he might have had more success in winning over the Spanish and Portuguese if his army was better behaved.

Close to where Paul was standing, one of the Frenchmen was talking to the boy. As Paul watched, he took something from his pack, a small notebook and a pencil. Gesturing to the boy to sit, he rested the book on his pack and began to sketch, looking up at the child from time to time and then back to his work.

Paul walked over to stand behind him. He watched in complete fascination as the child's face came to life on the page, with swift, confident strokes. The boy tried to look, and the Frenchman laughed and sat him back down. When the drawing was finished, he tore the page out carefully and handed it to Lorenzo. The boy looked at in in astonishment, then ran shouting to his sisters.

They came clamouring and the artist obliged, sketching first Paulina and then Elena and handing them the drawings. Paul was particularly impressed with the drawing of the older girl; he had captured an elusive charm which reminded Paul once again of Anne.

"You're very talented," Paul said in French, as the children left with their empty baskets. The Spanish were beginning to cut up the meat under the watchful eye of Lieutenant Browne, serving their own men first but then calling the prisoners into line to receive a portion along with a morsel of bread and a tack biscuit. The artist put his tools back into his pack and took out a mess tin to collect his share.

"Thank you. I was an artist in Paris, I earned my living painting portraits of the plain wives of rich men. Many of them lost their heads, and I drew political cartoons and almost lost mine. Now I fight for the emperor and draw what I see."

"May I?" Paul asked. The man nodded and took another notebook from the pack then went to join the line of hungry prisoners. Paul sat with his back against a tree and turned the pages. He was enchanted by the sketches, each one a masterpiece in miniature. Portraits of fellow soldiers, studies of camp life and a beautiful drawing of an officer's horse were interspersed with drawings of Madrid, clearly recognisable. Paul looked up as the man returned, sitting down to eat.

"These are incredible, you're wasted as a soldier," he said, returning the book.

"I was given no choice, Colonel."

"That is a great shame. I wish you could paint my wife."

"Is she pretty?"

"She's beautiful," Paul said, smiling. "And they are not merely the words of a besotted husband, all men see it. But I've never been able to get a portrait painted, we married out here, there's been no opportunity. I thought perhaps I would try to find a local artist when we are in winter quarters, but I'd be hard put to find one as good as you are."

The Frenchman suddenly smiled, making him look considerably younger. "I do not generally find art lovers in the army," he said. "I also wish I could paint the wife of the man who has probably saved our lives. There would be no charge. Wait."

He dug into the pack and pulled out a package wrapped in oilskin. There were two more filled notebooks. "Take them," the artist said. "This one also. I will keep the one I have not filled. They will probably take them off me at some point anyway. I do not know why I carry them, they make the pack heavier, but it would sadden me to see them burned or thrown away."

Paul looked down at the books then up into steady blue eyes. "Thank you," he said. "I'll treasure them. Perhaps, if we both survive this war, I will have the chance to give them back to you one day. Will you give me your name and regiment? Where are you from?"

"I was born in Paris; my name is Yves Roche, you will see it on my drawings; it is an artist's vanity, I cannot help it."

Paul handed him one of the books. "Write it down anyway for me, please, along with your regiment and company; I'd like to get word of you from time to time."

Roche complied. "That is very good of you, Colonel. May I know…?"

"My name is Van Daan, I command the 110th, and currently the third brigade of the Light Division. Conditions in prison camps are not always good, but I will make it my business to enquire after your welfare with the transport board."

Roche handed the book back. "Thank you," he said. "I began the day thinking I would be dead within the week. It has been good to talk with a civilised man."

Two of the Spanish guards came to sit nearby, eating their rations and Jenson appeared with a mess tin for Paul. They ate in companionable silence for a while. Eventually, Roche said:

"That man has a face worthy of a portrait."

Paul looked and could see what the artist meant. The Spaniard was probably in his forties, olive skinned and moustached with dark curly hair and deep-set dark eyes. There was a hawk-like quality to his features and an idea struck him. "Why don't you draw him?" he asked softly. "Don't worry about using up your sketch tablet, I'll find out where you are and send you more. Draw a few of them and hand them out."

He saw understanding flare in the intelligent blue eyes. Roche nodded and set his empty mess tin down, reaching for his pencil. He worked silently and Paul watched the drawing take form. He had never possessed any artistic talent beyond sketching a rough map and he was surprised at how much enjoyment it gave him to watch Roche work. When the drawing was done, Roche hesitated and looked at Paul. Paul understood; many of the Spanish had pistols and might fire if they saw a French prisoner approach one of them, thinking he planned some kind of attack.

Paul raised his voice and called over in Spanish. The guards looked at him and Paul beckoned. The man rose and came forward, saluting. Paul indicated the drawing which Roche was holding out. The Spaniard took it and stared at it in complete astonishment then looked up at Roche, pantomiming a question. Roche smiled and indicated the empty mess tin.

"Gracias, Señor," he said.

Suddenly the Spaniard gave a broad grin. He called to his companion who approached to study the sketch. Several others joined them, and they were talking, laughing, gesturing. Paul picked up the empty mess tins and passed them to Jenson, moving away from the voluble group. Roche clearly spoke some Spanish, probably picked up from his time in Madrid. He was answering questions and then Paul saw him reach for his pencil and begin to draw another of the men.

"That was a very good idea, sir," Jenson said, quietly, returning with the clean tins.

"I hope so. It's a lot harder to slaughter men whose names you know," Paul said. "With this and young Browne's masterly speech, I think they'll get to the coast in one piece."

"Just hope the transport board doesn't kill them on some pest-ridden prison hulk after that; be a shame after all this," Jenson said. "I just spoke with the lassie with the apples, sir. She's happy for you to bed down in their cottage for the night."

"Thank you, Jenson. I think I might stay out here. But if the lass can find somewhere secure for the horses, I'll pay her for stabling."

Jenson laughed aloud. "You're just trying to find a way to give her some money for those children without making it look like charity," he said.

140

"I'll sort it out and I'll stay with them. Can't imagine a horse thief will come this close to a guerrilla corps and two British officers, but better to be sure. Maybe she can provide us with breakfast which you can pay too much for."

"Oh, piss off, you Liverpudlian know-it-all, you've been with me far too long," Paul said, and Jenson laughed and left.

\*\*\*

Lord Wellington remained in Madrid for three weeks, staying in the palace which had been recently vacated by Joseph Bonaparte, with the rest of headquarters billets close by. Wellington was frantically seeking intelligence about the movement of the various French armies as he made plans for his next move and supervised, in surprising detail, the re-equipping of his battered forces.

Wellington was taking the opportunity to get to know the Spanish generals and guerrilla commandants, and hosted enormous dinners on a regular basis, along with his staff and officers from some of the other regiments in rotation. He also gave several formal balls to the delight of the officers of the third brigade, who unhesitatingly took the opportunity to dance and flirt with the local beauties. The grandees of Madrid were keen to reciprocate this hospitality and Wellington's officers found themselves with a choice of several receptions, dinners and dances every evening. The wealthier people of the city had weathered the French occupation well enough and many of the shops and merchant houses seemed surprisingly prosperous although condition of the poorer people horrified Anne.

The markets seemed to have no shortage of fresh food and taverns and inns were open and welcoming although prices were very high, with no concessions given to the heroes of Wellington's army and both officers and men of Paul's brigade mostly chose to eat and drink in the mess unless they were invited to dinner.

Discipline was relaxed for a few weeks and the men were allowed to leave their camp or billet, with a pass, to sample the delights of the city. Brothels were doing a roaring trade and Dr Oliver Daniels had informed Anne gloomily that he was expecting an upsurge of men suffering from signs of the pox. He had made the remark at dinner, and it had inadvertently fallen into a stunned silence, leaving Daniels stammering his apologies and Anne with tears of laughter in her eyes.

When she was not at the hospital or busy with administrative work, Anne found herself in considerable demand as an unofficial headquarters hostess, as Wellington entertained the local Spanish dignitaries and officers. Anne accompanied Wellington's party to the theatre one evening, sitting beside him in his box although Paul had politely declined the invitation. Despite his complaints Anne knew that her husband enjoyed seeing her act as Wellington's hostess. She had begun to take Juana Smith out with her a good deal. Captain Smith's wife was good company, an odd combination of sharp wits and childlike enthusiasm.

141

Their billets in the Marina Palace afforded a level of luxury which Anne had not known for many years. Throughout Portugal and then Spain she had slept in every kind of accommodation including convents and abbeys, the university buildings in Salamanca, farmhouses and cottages and often in barns, sheds and tents if nothing else was available. Life in the army had given Anne the ability to adapt quickly to almost any surroundings and her cheerful acceptance of difficult conditions set the tone for the officers of the brigade, who took the view that if Mrs van Daan did not complain they had no right to do so.

Madrid was a beautiful city. The streets were wide and surprisingly clean, and the men of Wellington's army strolled along graceful avenues shaded by wide-spreading trees and cooled by elegant fountains. There were museums and galleries and theatres which seemed to have thrived under Joseph's rule and for a time the war felt very distant.

The officers were invited to a bullfight given in their honour, and Paul declined firmly but politely on behalf of Anne. Some of the officers attended and proclaimed themselves sickened by the spectacle and Anne was glad she had not been persuaded. She did attend several shooting parties in the local parks and countryside and enjoyed the surprise on the faces of both Spanish and English officers as Captain O'Reilly of the 112th brought down the highest number of birds without appearing to concentrate very much at all.

Standing with Lord Wellington's staff, Anne watched Michael lower his gun. The young Dutch prince William was applauding enthusiastically.

"Bravo, Captain. Very impressive."

"The Irish like their shooting," Ensign Beaumaris said. "Big country estates and not enough to do. Not sure what O'Reilly's background is, but he's very good, isn't he?"

"I think his men taught him," Major Swanson said pleasantly, and Anne suppressed a laugh. Two years ago, the promotion of Paul's Irish Sergeant from the ranks had been the source of gossip and some resentment in the army but it was so little talked of now, that newcomers like Prince William and Beaumaris did not even realise that he had not always held a commission.

"Where is Lord Wellington today?" she asked. "It is unlike him to miss a sporting event."

"I believe he is sitting for his portrait, ma'am," Prince William said. "The artist - Goya you know - wishes to have it finished before Lord Wellington marches out, and it is hard to persuade him…"

"I would have thought it impossible," Anne said with a laugh. "He's almost as fidgety as the Colonel."

"It is to be his last sitting I believe. I have spoken to your husband ma'am and suggested that he talk to Goya about painting you. A lady of your beauty…"

Anne smiled. "You're flirting with me, your Highness."

"I am speaking only the truth, ma'am."

O'Reilly and Manson were approaching, laughing. "Are you going to try a few shots yourself, ma'am?" O'Reilly asked. "I'd be happy to teach you."

"I don't think so, Michael, I'd be embarrassed beside your skill. Even Captain Manson cannot match you although he's very good."

"It makes up for all the times that he's humiliated me at swordplay," O'Reilly said, bowing to the prince. "You did very well yourself earlier, mind, sir."

"Nothing to you, Captain. Do you not shoot, ma'am?"

"I'm afraid not, sir."

"The Colonel doesn't encourage her, sir," Manson said. He was on good terms with Prince William who was a cheerful boy a year or so younger than him. "He says that for the morale of his officers there needs to be something in the army that they can do better than she can."

There was a shout of laughter. Their host was calling them, and Manson led the way over to the bearers. Anne watched them go, smiling.

"And where is the Colonel today, Señora?" a voice said beside her. "Do not tell me that he also sits for a portrait?"

"No," Anne said, turning to survey the elegant dark features of Don Carlos Santos. She had not met him until her arrival in Madrid. He was a compatriot of Julian Sanchez and Pablo Cuesta, leading a band of guerrillas who had made the lives of the French very miserable in the east for the past year. Anne's beauty along with her fluent command of their language made her very popular with the Spanish leaders and she knew that Lord Wellington liked her to charm them. She found them a picturesque collection from a variety of backgrounds, and she knew that Paul had been right when he had remarked that some of them were little more than brigands who would steal from their own people or the English if the French were no longer around. It was difficult to judge them. In the chaos of Spain during the past five years the rule of law had completely broken down in many places. Atrocities were committed on both sides and ordinary people were often trapped between the warring armies. The English were generally better behaved than the French but there were too many incidents of pillaging and looting and there had been one or two spectacular breakdowns in discipline of which the violence and sacking of Badajoz earlier in the year had been the worst.

"The Colonel is meeting with the town council to discuss billeting for our men," Anne said pleasantly. It was as good a way as any to describe Paul's fury when he had been told that his men's orderly camp site at the edge of the ancient hunting preserves was not acceptable to the Spanish authorities. Anne had offered to attend the meeting with him, and his curt refusal had warned her that he intended to be very specific about his requirements for alternative accommodation in a way that precluded her presence.

Anne had smiled and left him to it, hoping that he did not hit anybody. She was confident that he would prevail. Paul had a habit of intervening personally in the administration of his brigade. When Anne had first come to Portugal, he was newly in command of a full battalion and struggled to delegate to a quartermaster or clerk. He had allowed Anne to take over some of the administrative duties which were weighing him down, partly because her ability to do so fascinated him in a nineteen year old girl and partly, she knew, because it was an excuse to keep her beside him when they were both married to other people. Since then, he had learned to let go of some of the detail to people he trusted and Major Breakspear had been with him for several years, as had Captain Fallon. Despite that, he had an awareness of what was going on in his regiment and his brigade which was extraordinary in a man at his level of command and even Anne, who was used to him, was often surprised when he suddenly stepped in to deal with a problem or situation which nobody else had even been aware of.

His enlisted men, largely the products of poverty and vice and the criminal justice system, adored him for it, understanding that for him, their welfare was paramount. He had managed to provide tents for every man in his regiment and then his brigade, a practical necessity which Lord Wellington was now beginning to introduce to the rest of his army. He chased up their pay, their new uniforms and their equipment with ruthless thoroughness which kept his quartermasters permanently on their toes, and it was well known that occasionally, such as during the retreat from Talavera, he had used his personal fortune to pay for wagons and pack animals to transport the wounded from his battalion back to Lisbon rather than leave them to a French prison camp. His men were fiercely proud of their unconventional young Colonel and gave him in return a passionate loyalty which was unparalleled in Wellington's army.

"It is good that he trusts his officers to take care of you, Señora," Santos said. "Had I a wife as young and lovely as you I think I would be more careful with her around other men."

Anne blinked in astonishment and turned to stare at the man. "Would you, Señor? I rather imagine that would depend on your choice of either officers or wives. Fortunately, I am married to a man who trusts me implicitly. I hope that when you decide to marry you are equally fortunate in your choice."

Anne turned away and walked to join the other officers, a little shocked at the Spaniard's open rudeness. She supposed that he was a traditional man who disapproved of her easy friendship with her husband's officers, but she was surprised at his readiness to express it so freely.

As she joined the others, there was a hail and Anne shaded her eyes to see her husband riding through the coverts with Jenson beside him. She went to greet him, and he dismounted and bent to kiss her.

"Have you settled it?" she asked.

"Yes. I've sent orders over to Sergeant-Major Carter to get the camp packed up. We've been allocated space in the military college about a mile from the Marina Palace. It's enormous; quite a few purpose-built barracks blocks as well as the college itself. There are also a lot of stable blocks and staff quarters."

"And are they empty?"

"They are. Joseph was using them for his household guard, but they've gone with him. Sanchez had planned to use them for his guerrillas, but I've told him he'll never get them out of the town brothels anyway so no point."

"And how did Don Julian take this?"

"We didn't really have much of a conversation about it, girl of my heart. I got a bit cross to tell you the truth, I think Sanchez was just glad to get me out of there before I punched the town council representatives in the face. Stupid bastards."

"Well it sounds an improvement if the weather changes. Are you intending to stay and shoot? If not, I think I'll ride back with you, I'm a little tired."

"A rare admission, girl of my heart. Let's go back and take a siesta. I can't promise you'll sleep much but you will relax."

"I'd love to. This is the most comfortable bed I've slept in since we left the villa, it's tempting never to get out of it."

"As long as I'm invited to share it with you, I can see no objection to that," her husband said. "Wait, I'll grab Manson to make our apologies. He seems very tight with Slender Billy these days; I wonder if he knows his tendencies?"

Anne laughed aloud. "He does," she said. "As a matter of fact, he intervened on behalf of Ensign Johnson a few days ago. He'd received an invitation to dine from the Prince and was unsure what to do about it. It seemed like a very exclusive party. Captain Manson advised him to decline, citing an appointment with a lady as the reason."

Paul laughed. "Very diplomatic, I take my hat off to Manson."

"I like Prince William," Anne said. "He's charming."

"So do I. He's not that bright, but then neither are half the officers in our army. But he'll get a decent military training with Wellington and he's keen and willing to learn. And I don't honestly care what he chooses to do in bed, although somebody should tell him to be a bit more discreet about it, half the army is already gossiping."

"Well they will. Most of them aren't as tolerant as you, love."

"I'm just not interested," Paul said frankly. "Wait here. If you go back over there, they'll be on at you to stay for the picnic and now that you've suggested it, an afternoon in bed sounds like an excellent idea."

Anne watched as Paul went to speak to Manson and their host. She had discovered the gossip about the young Dutch prince quite recently and entirely by accident, having overheard two officers of the guards laughing about it during a hunting party. Anne had retreated before the officers had realised she was within earshot, her face very warm. She had understood the gist of their comments about Prince William's sexual preferences, but she realised that she had discovered a gap in her education and had taken her questions to Paul as they were lying in bed sharing a glass of wine one night after making love. Her husband had spluttered wine over the sheet.

"What a question to ask me at a time like this," he had said, as Anne mopped up the stains and refilled the glass.

"Well I couldn't really raise it over dinner," Anne pointed out.

"A fair point, I suppose."

"Did you know?" Anne asked. "About Prince William?"

"Yes," Paul admitted, studying her. "Most of the army knows the rumours. His Highness arrived last year with a very pretty valet, whom I understand Wellington quietly sent packing."

"I'm surprised," Anne said. "He's an accomplished flirt and it feels real."

"It probably is," Paul said. "I have heard that the prince is as likely to be chasing a pretty girl as a pretty boy."

"Goodness, how confusing." Anne reached for the wine glass and sipped. "Does it bother you, Paul?"

"You mean because of what happened to me when I was a boy in the navy?"

"I suppose I do."

"No. I might find His Highness's proclivities a little odd, but I can't imagine him attacking either a boy or a girl; whatever he gets up to is entirely consensual. I don't consider it his business what I do with you in bed so why should his love life concern me? Does it make you feel uncomfortable, Nan?"

Anne had thought about it. "No, you're right," she said. "It's ridiculous that people are such busybodies. I shall not think of it again."

Paul returned to join her with Captain O'Reilly beside him. "Michael is riding back with us, it appears he has an invitation to dine in the city."

"Do you, Michael? Who is she?" Anne said with immense cordiality. The Irishman pulled a hideous face.

"It wouldn't be suitable for me to be rude to the Colonel's lady, ma'am, or I would be. It's a gentleman by the name of Alonso, he's a wealthy wine merchant who lives in a very beautiful house near the cathedral with his two sons. I met him at a reception last week."

"No pretty daughter?" Paul said sceptically.

"No, sir. Not even a wife; he's a widower. What he does have is an impressive stable. We talked of horses and he promised me the tour. I like him."

"Michael, I have misjudged you," Anne said gravely. "You are beginning to sound like an officer and a gentleman. Enjoy your dinner."

"And don't steal any of the horses," Paul said, lifting her up into the saddle. "They're a little harder to hide than a bottle of French brandy."

# Chapter Eleven

It was full dark when Michael left the house of Señor Alonso. He had stayed later than expected, finding his host a cultured man with easy manners and a love of horses which matched Michael's own. They had spent several hours touring Alonso's extensive stables, had dined well, with excellent wines, and had parted on very good terms. Michael had promised to return on his next free morning to go riding with the two Alonso sons, both in their twenties, and to try out a young Arabian stallion who was Alonso's pride and joy.

The main streets of Madrid were fairly well lit, but the side streets and alleys were pitch black, with only an occasional lantern hanging outside a house. Michael kept his pistol in his pocket and rode with his sword within reach. Only folly or desperation would cause a man to attack one of Wellington's officers, but Michael had seen enough of the heartbreaking poverty behind the city's sophisticated veneer to know that desperation existed.

Despite the late hour he could hear sounds of revelry from some of the taverns. Michael smiled slightly, thinking that Wellington's men would be marching out of Madrid without a penny left in their pockets. The pay chest was months overdue again and the Spanish could not be expected to waive payment indefinitely. Michael's own pockets would have been wholly to let had it not been for a useful windfall at Badajoz, a well-stocked purse taken from a drunken British soldier, who had killed its owner. The prize, which ought to have been handed over to Wellington as prize money, had been quietly shared between those officers and men who had chosen to go back into the city to try to protect some of the inhabitants and it meant that Michael was not praying for the arrival of money from England quite as desperately as some of the officers.

Michael was halfway back to the palace, when his horse suddenly shied nervously, spooked by something in the shadows. Michael patted his neck soothingly, listening, his senses alert. What he heard made him relax, smiling inwardly. Some local prostitute was clearly using the alley to earn her lodging money for the night. He could hear scuffling and grunting, and a groan of release and he passed by, giving the anonymous couple a wide berth. Glancing back, he saw the man leaving, a bulky figure in a red coat. The woman remained in the shadows.

Michael was at the end of the street when he suddenly reined in. He had not been consciously thinking about it, but he realised he had heard no further sound from behind him. The buildings on either side were warehouses, dark and silent at this time of night, and the sound of the woman leaving should have been clearly audible, but he did not think she had moved.

Michael sat listening for a moment, then swore softly under his breath and turned his horse back into the street and walked back, peering into the darkness. He saw nothing at first and was beginning to think that he had missed the sound of the woman leaving, when he saw a huddled figure on the ground, still and silent.

Michael dismounted, feeling around. Most buildings had some means of tethering a horse and he found it eventually, an iron ring set into the stonework. He looped the reins, patted Sligo's neck reassuringly and went to kneel beside the immobile form. To his shock, it appeared to be a boy, a slight creature with a tangle of curly hair, wearing a thin ragged shirt and breeches, pulled down around painfully thin thighs. Michael, feeling very sick, rolled the boy over and saw that he had been wrong after all; it was a girl in boy's clothing. He could see nothing of her features in the darkness, but he had the impression that she was very young.

Michael searched for a pulse in her neck and found it beating steadily. He lifted her slightly, restoring her clothing. The movement seemed to reach her, and she pushed out suddenly, trying to shove his hands away, shouting in Spanish.

"No, get away from me. Leave me alone."

"Lass, it's all right," Michael said quickly in the same language, capturing the flailing hands. "Stop it, you'll hurt yourself. I'm not going to harm you."

The girl struggled for a moment longer and then went still. Michael peered through the darkness trying to see her face. "Good girl," he said gently. "I'm sorry, I did not understand what I was hearing back there, or I'd have blown his bloody head off. I'm going to let you go; please don't run off."

He released her hands. As he had half expected, she scrambled to her feet immediately and stood with her back pressed to the stone wall like a wild animal at bay. Michael could see very little, but he had the sickening impression that she was barely beyond childhood. He could sense her terror and he held up his hands and spoke slowly in his careful Spanish.

"My name is Captain O'Reilly of the 112th light company. I am billeted in the Marina Palace. We have a regimental hospital there and my Colonel's wife, who helps the doctor, can have a look at you to make sure you're not badly hurt. At the very least we can find you a bed for tonight and some food. Please, let me help you."

The girl remained very still for a long time, watching him. Finally, she said:

"What do you want?"

"Want?"

"What do I have to do for food?"

148

"Oh Christ, child, nothing. It's common decency. Come on, up with you."

She sat rigid before him on the horse and Michael set him at an easy walk back to the palace. The hospital had been set up in an indoor riding school in the grounds of the palace, but Michael found it oddly deserted as he approached. He located the nearest sentry post, manned by Private Kane of the 110th light company.

"Kane, where is everybody? I've a patient for Mrs van Daan."

"Moved out, sir. It turns out there was a really good infirmary in the military college, a whole block with proper bunks and everything, so Dr Daniels had us pack up and move the patients over there. It's not far, less than a mile down this track and through the trees. But Mrs van Daan isn't there, she's probably in bed by now."

"She probably is, which is going to make me the least popular man in Madrid with our Colonel. Ah well."

Michael rode over to the palace. Lights were kept burning and two men were on sentry duty at the front door as Michael lifted the girl down from his horse and called for a groom. He could see the men looking curiously at the grubby urchin as he led her inside and made his way through to the big kitchen at the back of the house. It was very warm, the fire banked for the night, the ovens still giving off heat. Michael led the girl to a chair close to the fire.

"Sit. Put this around you, I'll be back in a moment. Don't you dare run off."

He draped his coat about the skinny shoulders and went up into the house and up the stairs. His commanding officer and his wife occupied an elegant suite at the far end and Michael lifted his hand to knock and then stopped at a sound. It was Anne's voice and it left him in no doubt what was going on inside. Michael stood for a moment, breathing deeply, trying not to let images of his commander's wife intrude into his thoughts although it was difficult given what he was hearing. After a moment he banged on the door.

There was silence and then he heard Anne giggle.

"Oh for Christ's sake!" Paul bellowed. "What is wrong with you lot, can't I get an hour's peace? Who the bloody hell is that?"

"It's Captain O'Reilly, sir. Sorry."

"You bloody will be, Michael. What's the problem, Bonaparte sighted on the road?"

"Not you, sir. Medical problem, your wife is needed."

"My wife is needed in here as well, but I don't suppose there's a chance of that happening. All right, Michael, give me a minute."

The door opened within three minutes and Paul motioned him in. He had pulled on dark trousers and a shirt. "She's getting changed, come and have a drink," he said. "I hate you."

"Sorry, sir," Michael said, sympathetically. "I didn't know what to do with the girl."

"Girl?"

"I picked her up in town; she's hurt. Some bastard had her down in an

149

alleyway and she's little more than a child. I wouldn't have disturbed you…"

"It's all right." Paul handed him a glass of wine. "I am about to tell Lord Wellington that my wife is officially indisposed for a few days. Tomorrow we are dining in our own mess and going to bed early, and we are not interested, no matter how many strange females my officers bring back from town. Christ, I get more time with her on campaign."

"You're in a better mood on campaign, sir," Michael said with a grin and Paul laughed aloud.

"I am. I can do this for a short time, but so much civility is killing me. Especially to bloody Don Julian Sanchez."

"Has he not got the point yet?"

"I think it's actually starting to get on Nan's nerves, and that's saying something. I'm trying to make a joke of it, but if I see him touch her one more time, I swear to God I'm going to punch him."

"Serve him right. He's married, isn't he?"

"Yes, but his wife isn't here and mine is. I'm generally fairly tolerant of other men flirting with her, but he goes beyond the line. Who's this lass, Michael? Was it one of our lads?"

"He had a red coat on but that's all I can tell you, sir, he was gone before I realised she was there."

The inner door opened, and Anne emerged wearing one of the simple dark dresses she wore to work in the hospital. Her hair was still loose, and she was slightly flushed, with the rumpled air of a girl newly come from her lover's arms. She smiled at Paul and he returned it and Michael felt a piercing stab of envy for their open happiness in each other.

"Sorry, ma'am," he said.

"Can't be helped, Michael. What's happened?"

Michael explained as he escorted Anne down to the kitchen. He was relieved to find the girl still there, curled up under his coat. Anne had brought a candle and began lighting lamps and candles, keeping up an easy flow of reassuring conversation in Spanish. The girl sat watching her with wide eyes as Anne brought a warm blanket which she wrapped around her thin shoulders, passing Michael's red coat back to him.

"Go to bed, Captain O'Reilly. I'll take care of her now."

Michael studied the girl. There was a cut above her eye which was bleeding steadily and one of her eyes looked swollen and dark, which made Michael wonder if this was the first beating she had received recently. Her hair was short, a tangled mass of dirty curls and her eyes were a startling green gold. She was looking at Michael with something like a plea in her eyes and Michael said:

"I can stay with you, ma'am."

"No you can't," Anne said firmly. "I need to examine her properly, you can't be here. Go to bed."

\*\*\*

150

Paul was asleep when Anne returned, sometime after midnight, slipping into bed beside him. Paul drew her close to warm her. "Everything all right, bonny lass?" he asked sleepily.

"For now. I've made up a bed in the corner of the kitchen for her tonight, it's warm. Tomorrow we'll find something better."

"What happened to her?" Paul asked. "Was she raped?"

"I think she went with him because she was starving, but he just took what he wanted and gave her nothing apart from a beating when she resisted. She comes from a village about ten miles north of here; lost her family about two years ago. Her father fought with the partisans, the French caught his band in the village during the winter and slaughtered the entire village. Ariana managed to hide but I think she watched them die. Horrible. She was alone and starving so she made her way here to Madrid and has lived on the streets. Begging, stealing, getting work when she could. And selling herself to the army when she could do nothing else. French or English, I'm not sure it makes much difference to her."

"Oh no," Paul said softly. "Michael says she's just a child."

"Fifteen or sixteen I'd guess. It's hard to tell, she's so thin. God knows what she's been through, she's black and blue."

Anne broke off and Paul put his arms about her. It was unusual for his strong-minded wife to be so visibly upset by any of the horrors she encountered.

"Have you told her she can stay here?"

"I've told her that we'll find her work. George has recruited a few local women to work in the kitchen or cleaning the rooms. There's always something to do; I don't want her to run off before she's healed. She's very wary, but I'm hoping she'll settle."

Paul lay holding her, feeling her relax into sleep beside him. Two weeks without the need to march or fight had allowed his wounds to heal finally and he knew that the interlude in Madrid had been a blessing. He drifted into sleep easily and deeply but came awake in the darkness hours later, to a terrified cry, a familiar sound which brought him into full wakefulness in a second. He sat up and reached out for Anne who was sitting bolt upright beside him, her whole body shaking.

"Nan, it's all right. It's all right. You were dreaming - it's me."

Anne resisted him for a moment, then awoke properly. "Paul," she whispered, and turned towards him, burying her face into his chest. Paul smoothed her tousled dark hair, whispering her name, waiting until her shivering eased, as he knew it would. They had been through this routine many times since her return from captivity five months ago, but it had been four weeks since her last nightmare and Paul had hoped she would have no more.

Eventually she began to relax in his arms. Paul kissed the top of her head and Anne moved and turned her face up to kiss him properly. "I'm sorry," she said.

"What have I told you about that?"

The dark eyes shone wet through the darkness, but she was also smiling. "I'm sorry I said I was sorry. I'm disappointed; I thought it was over."

"It is over, Nan. Just the odd dream. I'm not surprised you had a nightmare after tending to that girl; I should have realised it would bring the whole thing back. Are you all right? Can I get you anything?"

Anne gave a little choke of laughter through her tears. "Yes," she said. "I'd really like some warm milk. I feel like such a baby."

"You're not a baby," Paul said, sliding out of bed. "Get back under the covers, it's cold."

"Oh, don't wake Jenson."

"I'm not going to, I'm quite capable of heating a pan of milk and I'm guessing the fire will still be hot enough. Stay there."

Paul had forgotten the girl in the kitchen, soundly asleep in a nest of blankets close to the fire. Paul built the fire up and brought milk from the cold pantry, pouring it into an iron pan which he set into a bracket in the wall. The small domestic duty was oddly soothing and reminded him of their time near Freineda when William was tiny, and he had often done this for Anne during the night when she was feeding their son. The memory made him smile.

He had married Anne in a hurried ceremony in Viseu, returning to duty immediately. Since then, it often seemed to him that they had spent all their time on the move, the routines of their life dictated by war. There had been no time, as he had had with Rowena, to watch their child grow together, no lengthy spells in barracks to develop a habit of domesticity. He was enormously grateful for Anne's adaptability which enabled her to appear equally at home in a tent as she did in this palace, but he would have loved to have some time just to be with her, raising his children and creating the small, insignificant memories that were the building blocks of a life together. Their short time the previous year in the pretty surroundings of the Quinta de Santo Antonio, a few miles from Wellington's headquarters in Freineda, where Anne had given birth to William, had been a very precious interlude.

There was a rustle of blankets and Paul turned to see the girl sitting up, a shawl wrapped around her, her eyes huge in the thin face. Paul smiled reassuringly but said nothing. He brought two cups from a shelf and divided the warm milk between them, turning back to the girl.

"My wife was thirsty," he said. "I'm guessing you are too. Here."

She took the cup, with an odd little nod of thanks, wrapping her cold hands around it. Paul put two more logs onto the fire, then returned to Anne. She drank the milk, wrapping her hands around the cup in exactly the same way as the Spanish girl and Paul looked at her thoughtfully. He was beginning to wonder.

"Nan?"

"Yes, love?"

"Is there any chance you might be with child again?"

His wife's expression told him that the thought was not new. "Why do you ask?"

"Well, I know you're not that regular, and I never keep track, but I suspect it's been a couple of months since you bled. But it's more than that.

You've slept in the afternoon three times this week, and even in this heat, that's not like you. And wanting warm milk in the middle of the night feels very familiar to me."

Anne set the cup down. "Thank you, Paul, you're very good to me. I wasn't trying to be mysterious, it's just that I'm not sure. It's not like last time - both times, actually. I've not felt sick at all and my appetite is as good as ever. But this tiredness feels very familiar, and I've been feeling so emotional. All that weeping over you being wounded is not like me. Only I've been scared to hope, since the miscarriage."

Paul studied his wife's fine boned face, pale in the darkness, and felt an odd combination of fear and happiness. He had shared Anne's anxiety that the brutal beating at the hands of Colonel Dupres which had brought about her miscarriage earlier in the year, might have done some internal damage which would make further pregnancies impossible, despite Dr Norris's reassurances that it was unlikely. The prospect of another child was both a joy and a worry; he had lost Rowena to childbirth.

Paul leaned forward and kissed her very gently. "Let's wait and see," he said. "I won't mention anything to anybody else yet. I love you, Anne van Daan. Settle down and get some sleep."

***

By the time Lord Wellington marched out of Madrid towards the fortress town of Burgos, Anne was in no further doubt about her pregnancy. Experience had taught her the value of planning ahead and she spent some time searching for a suitable travelling carriage for when she would be unable to ride. In the past, Lord Wellington had often put his own carriage at Anne's disposal, but she could not rely on it always being available. Anne had just made the purchase when her husband informed her it would not immediately be needed.

"We're staying here," he said. "Wellington is leaving the Light Division in Madrid and the third and fourth divisions close by under Hill. He's taking the rest of the army to invest Burgos."

Anne studied him, wondering how he felt. In the past, Lord Wellington had always chosen to have Paul with him. "Would you rather be going with him?" she asked.

"No," Paul said briefly. He had dined with Wellington and some of the other commanders on the previous evening. "Firstly, because remaining here during your pregnancy will suit me very well and secondly because I hate storming a town, and if he's decided the Light Division has done enough of that this year, you are not going to see me arguing. I think, to tell you the truth, that he's leaving his three best and most experienced divisions to recover because he expects another major engagement before the end of the year and he wants us fully fit for that."

"I think he has a point," Anne said. "The hospitals are full of sick men. It's infuriating; so many of the reinforcements they're sending out are already ill. Did you hear about the 43$^{rd}$?"

"No."

"Apparently, a draft of around two hundred reinforcements with sixteen officers landed in Lisbon recently. Most of them will get no further, they're either in hospital sick or have died on the march. Some kind of fever."

"Christ, that's worse than our last draft," Paul said.

Anne was watching him. She could sense that he was unhappy although she had no idea why. "So, what is it, Paul?"

Her husband smiled. "I'm not sure," he admitted. "I've just been talking to Andrew and John about it. Colonel Barnard informs me that I am like a nursemaid worrying about her charge going on an excursion without her. Cheeky bastard; he'll be lucky to make it to the next battle."

Anne dissolved into laughter. "I think Andrew Barnard might have a point, Paul. I'm surprised Lord Wellington hasn't asked you to go with him as an observer as he did at Badajoz the first time." Anne caught her husband's expression and stopped. "He has, hasn't he?"

Paul shook his head. "Not exactly. He admitted that he'd like me to be there, but he wants me in Madrid rather more."

"Discipline?" Anne guessed.

"Yes. He doesn't want whichever division he leaves in Madrid to disgrace the army with outbreaks of looting. Particularly since they've not been paid. He's trusting Charles Alten and I to make sure they behave. Which reminds me, we're invited to dinner this evening; Andrew wants to show off his new cook."

"Colonel Barnard has a new cook? I very much doubt he'll be as good as George Kelly."

"Andrew thinks he might. He's French, Andrew took him prisoner at Salamanca. Apparently before he was conscripted, he was a cook. I believe Andrew gave him the choice of an English prison camp or a new posting and he took it without a second thought; he didn't enjoy killing people. Or risking his own life, I'm guessing. It was an ingenious idea, I must say. I wish I'd thought of it when I was talking to Yves Roche, we could have had a brigade artist."

"A cook is probably more useful, but I appreciate that I've married a cultured man," Anne said, kissing him lightly. "You seem on very good terms with your fellow brigade commanders these days, love, I must say I approve. Do you think they'll make Colonel Barnard permanent?"

"I've no idea, but I hope so. He was a lieutenant-colonel before I was, and both Beckwith and Drummond were no higher when they commanded brigades. You're right, I get on well with both of them which is why I hope Andrew stays. As for Wellington and Burgos...I'm sure it will be fine. I just worry that there are so many things that could go wrong. It feels so safe here, so secure. Almost as if we were back in Lisbon. But..."

"But we are not," Anne said gently, and Paul shook his head.

"No, we're not. There are French armies all around us, Nan, some at a fair distance, I'll admit. But if they manage to combine, we could find ourselves in trouble. However, that's for the commander-in-chief to worry about, he's paid more than I am. If any of us ever get paid at all. In the meantime, since I am a man of private means and an unexpected amount of leisure time, I intend to take my beautiful wife shopping to ensure that she is better equipped for pregnancy than on the previous occasion. Come along."

***

Simon Carlyon rejoined his company before the end of August and was welcomed back with obvious pleasure by his fellow officers. Captain Lewis was unwell, laid up with the summer fever which had depleted Wellington's army for weeks, so Simon and Nicholas Witham shared company duties between them. After several weeks of idleness, Colonel van Daan had declared the holiday over, and had begun drilling and training in the huge park which surrounded the Marina Palace and the military school. With some of his doubts assuaged, Simon threw himself into the process with new enthusiasm. He was beginning to get to know his men and their capabilities, and it was a challenge to work with them on learning new skills.

While Simon had been absent with the 94th, Nicholas had struck up a friendship with several of the officers of the 110th, particularly Captain Leo Manson with his two lieutenants, Denny and Ashford, Captain Zouch of the seventh company and Kerr, Heron, and Lloyd from the eighth. Manson was one of the youngest of the group but tended to take the lead. He was not an exuberant personality, but he carried an unconscious authority that Simon rather envied. It was clear that he enjoyed a close relationship with Colonel van Daan and his wife, which meant that his friends were often invited to balls and receptions as part of the headquarters party.

None of the young officers with whom Simon was friendly were wealthy; some lived purely on their pay and since that was several months late, there was nothing extravagant about their lifestyle. It suited Simon very well to play cards for pennies, share a cheap bottle of wine outside a common tavern and accept dinner invitations from local families who seemed never to tire of entertaining Wellington's officers. Simon learned Spanish dances and ate paella on rough wooden tables outside cheerful inns. His Spanish improved, he grew lean and brown and fit from long days training in the late summer sun, and he found himself forgetting sometimes that war was a reality, that French armies might well converge on Madrid at any time and that he and his friends were by no means invincible.

Simon met Valentina at an impromptu dance in one of the city squares, following a religious parade to celebrate a saint that Simon had never heard of. She was slender and pretty, with a wealth of red-gold hair and a smile which lit up the night, and Simon had no idea that she was married; he had not troubled to ask during their passionate encounter in the darkness of a small park. When he discovered the existence of Valentina's middle-aged, gout-ridden husband, Simon felt a pang of guilt which was quickly forgotten in the joy of every stolen moment. He inveigled invitations to every ball or reception she was likely to attend, and when he could not do so, he became an expert at sneaking in, finding even a dance with her worth the risk. She wrote him love notes on scented paper and sent him gifts of local delicacies and expensive wine, which Simon's friends fell upon with enthusiasm.

"Is she paying you in wine, Carlyon?" Captain Zouch enquired, sampling the glass Simon had poured for him. "If so, I hope you're making it worth her while, this is not cheap."

"He's taking a leaf out of Captain Manson's book," Ashford said with a laugh. "His girlfriend is very generous. Mine always expect me to pay for it, I'm doing something wrong."

"Possibly being an arsehole, Ashford," Manson said, coming into the room. Simon masked a grin as Ashford coloured to the roots of his hair. "Have we had a conversation before about my love life being none of your business?"

"Yes, sir."

"I thought we had. Strive to remember it, I don't want to have to punch you." Manson took the glass from Ashford and drank. "It's bloody good, though, is she stealing it out of her husband's wine cellar?"

"I've not asked," Simon said.

Manson regarded him thoughtfully. "I'm not sure you've actually spoken to her much at all, have you, Mr Carlyon? Look - I do understand. It's very easy to get carried away. But I've been making some discreet enquiries. Old Cabrera is a mean bastard and as jealous as hell of that girl. If he gets wind of what you're up to with her, you're going to be in a lot of trouble."

"We're very careful," Simon said.

"You're not bloody careful, you irresponsible idiot, half the Light Division knows about it and the other half soon will. God help you when our Colonel finds out. He's trying hard to keep the Spanish happy and that doesn't include sleeping with their wives. If you've got any sense, you'll end it before he hears about it."

Simon knew that Manson was right. He was beginning to feel uncomfortable about Valentina. He had begun the affair light-heartedly, without giving much thought to anything other than Valentina's beauty and the pleasure she gave him, but he was beginning to feel guilty, not so much about her unpleasant husband but about the girl herself. She had clearly become very attached to him and although she must know that the relationship had no future, he did not want to hurt her.

Simon was still wrestling with his decision when he attended a ball, given by one of Madrid's leading merchant associations. It was a glittering affair, and no invitation had been extended to the junior officers of the Light Division, but by now, Simon and Nicholas had become experts at finding an unlocked door or window, and in the throng of British, Spanish and Portuguese uniforms they had never been challenged. The ball was crowded, and Simon went in search of Valentina and found her without her husband as usual. Valentina found a partner for Nicholas, a shy child barely out of the schoolroom, who seemed dazzled to be dancing with a British officer, and Simon led Valentina onto the floor.

She refused him a second dance as she always did in public, although the pressure of her hand told Simon that she was hoping for more than a dance before the evening ended. Simon waited for Nicholas to join him, his brain turning over possible opportunities for an assignation, when a voice poured icy water over his amorous intentions.

"Your pardon, sir, but I do not know you. Were you invited to this entertainment?"

Simon froze, staring at the tall, thin Spaniard, dressed in an elaborate military uniform dripping with gold braid and medals. Instinctively he saluted; he had no idea of the man's rank, but he was clearly senior. Behind the Spanish officer, Simon saw Nicholas, stopping dead in his tracks as he realised what was happening. Simon sought frantically for an intelligent response.

"Do you not speak Spanish?" the officer said pleasantly, switching to English. "Your pardon, Lieutenant. Will you tell me...?"

"Simon, there you are," a voice said warmly, and Simon turned his head. "And I see Mr Witham was able to make it too; I am so pleased. General Torres, forgive me, these gentlemen are with our party but were delayed by military duties. May I introduce my brother-in-law from my first marriage, Lieutenant Simon Carlyon and his good friend Lieutenant Nicholas Witham."

General Torres took Anne van Daan's extended hand and kissed it. "Your pardon, Señora, I had not realised. Welcome, gentlemen. I am so glad you have arrived in time for supper. This way."

Simon saluted again. He was determinedly not looking at the party to which he supposedly belonged, but he was painfully aware that it included not only Colonel van Daan and his wife, but every single senior officer of the Light Division, including General Charles Alten, its commander. Simon stood back to allow his seniors to pass ahead of him, and felt a hand descend upon his shoulder.

"This way, Mr Carlyon. You too, Mr Witham. I believe there are fireworks after supper, which you should try to enjoy as much as possible. Tomorrow may be less of a treat for you."

\*\*\*

It rained for the following three days, a miserable introduction to autumn. The brigade huddled within doors, staring out at the grey skies, grateful that their exacting commander had cancelled drill and training.

Colonel van Daan's leniency did not extend to Lieutenants Carlyon and Witham or the men of their company. Simon knew that the Colonel could not possibly have arranged the weather personally when he invited them into his office and genially gave them their orders, but he certainly gave the impression that the downpour delighted him.

"Night march," he said briefly. "Full kit, your whole company. I've sketched the route out for you, it's around ten miles."

Simon saluted and took the paper in glum silence. Nicholas said hesitantly:

"Permission to speak, sir?"

"Don't waste your breath on an apology, Mr Witham, I wasn't the person you insulted by turning up at a party you were not invited to. Thanks to my wife's peerless social skills, an embarrassing incident was avoided. I'm hoping a nice run in the fresh air with your company for the next two nights will remind you of your manners."

"Yes, sir, but I still wanted to apologise. Only - it doesn't seem fair on the men."

"No, it isn't," the Colonel said bluntly. "Having an imbecile for an officer gets men killed and that is bloody unfair, I've seen a fair few examples of it during my time in the army. What you do affects your men. They know that. You ought to know it, neither of you are greenhorns. If you've forgotten it, hopefully this will remind you."

"Yes, sir."

"Excellent. Mr Witham, you are dismissed, wait outside, please."

When the door had closed, Simon stood to attention, staring at a portrait on the wall behind the Colonel's desk. Eventually, the Colonel said:

"It's over, Mr Carlyon."

"Sir?"

"Your passionate idyll with Señora Cabrera. In future, you will attend the parties you are invited to, and no others and you will keep your dick in your breeches or save it for the brothel or you are going to find yourself confined to your quarters for the rest of our stay in Madrid. Please do not insult me by pretending that you don't know what I'm talking about."

"Sir." Simon could think of nothing to say. He was shocked to realise how relieved he was to have the decision taken out of his hands, and the thought made him feel immensely, guilty. "Yes, sir. Of course. But I ought to tell her myself."

"That isn't possible, Mr Carlyon. Dismissed."

Simon felt slightly sick but did not move. "Sir, please. I know it was wrong of me, but I'm fond of her and I know she feels the same way. I'll make sure we're chaperoned; Nick will do it. I just..."

"God give me strength, he is clearly about as much use as a chaperone as that bust of Bonaparte. Less, actually, since I'd find his ugly face fairly off-putting."

"But, sir..."

"You can't see her," the Colonel snapped. "You can't see her, because she has been removed under heavy escort to her husband's country house to the west of Madrid, and she probably wouldn't want to see you anyway. My wife tried to get in there this morning on pretext of a morning call and was turned away, but Mrs Carter, who accompanied her, was told quietly by the maids that she has two black eyes and a split lip, and those are probably only the injuries that show, so she won't be fit for company for a while."

Simon felt a wave of nausea. "No," he said. "Oh no. I'll bloody kill him."

"No, you won't. You'll do what you ought to have done in the first place and leave the poor girl alone, she's got enough problems. You can't challenge a Spanish civilian because he disciplined his wife; according to law he has every right to do so. He could, of course, challenge you for sleeping with her, but he won't because he wants to be on the right side of the British; he's a merchant with goods to sell. Also, he's a coward, so he'll ignore you and take it out on her. It's what they do."

Simon froze. He had forgotten temporarily that he was speaking to a very senior officer. "You're talking about my brother, aren't you?" he asked.

Paul van Daan looked at him for a long time from troubled blue eyes. Then he said:

"Yes. But I shouldn't be. It still makes me angry after all this time, but it's not your fault. I'm sorry, Mr Carlyon. Go on, get out of here."

Simon did not move. "Is that what he did to her?" he asked. His voice sounded odd in his own ears.

"Yes," the Colonel said quietly. "More than once. He also punched her in the stomach and throttled her so hard he left bruises that she used to cover up with a scarf. When he was really angry, he held her down and beat her with a riding whip. It left a couple of scars."

Simon closed his eyes. He had never wanted to think about Robert's reported abuse of his wife. He thought about it now, and he felt, to his horror, hot tears behind his closed eyelids. "I can't believe he did that to her," he whispered. "Why would he do that to her?"

Unexpectedly, Simon felt a hand gentle on his shoulder. "Sit," the Colonel said. "Here, drink this. I'm sorry, this was supposed to be a routine bollocking for getting yourself into the kind of scrape that most young officers get into at some point. I hadn't intended it to turn into a conversation about your brother."

Simon drank the brandy. He could think of nothing more to say and his Colonel did not seem to require it. They sat in oddly companionable silence for a while. Eventually, the Colonel set down his glass.

"Go and find Nicholas," he said gently. "Have a drink, go to dinner and forget about this. Take your punishment and remember it the next time you're tempted. It'll make you a better person. Trust me, I know."

Simon rose. "Why didn't you kill him?" he asked.

"Because I didn't know. She lied to me to protect my good name and my career. By the time I found out exactly how bad it had been, he was already dead. Simon, there is no way to make any of this any easier for you. But for God's sake don't agonise about it any more than you can help. You're not Robert, you're nothing like him. Señor Cabrera is. I would like to blow his fucking head off for what he's done to that girl, but I can't, I don't have the right. And nor do you. The kindest thing you can do for her is leave her alone."

Simon endured the two nights of marching through freezing rain listening to the quiet grumbling of his men and the slightly louder complaints of his ensigns, like a penance. He thought endlessly of Valentina Cabrera; more than he had probably thought about her ever before. For the first time he saw her, not just as an attractive and enthusiastic lover, but as a young woman trapped in a miserable marriage, who had been desperate to escape, if only for a short time, with a man who had seemed to care. Simon was bitterly ashamed and angry that he had not stopped to think about the possible consequences for Valentina of being discovered. He wondered how her husband had found out. Possibly his attendance at a ball he had not been invited to had alerted Cabrera or possibly somebody had dropped a word in his ear. However it had happened, Simon had no doubt that a thorough beating had elicited a full confession from Valentina. He would have loved to have administered an equally thorough beating to Cabrera in return, but he knew that his Colonel had been right; it would not only cost Simon his commission, it would probably lead to worse reprisals for Valentina.

It was impossible not to think also of his conversation with Colonel van Daan about Robert. Simon believed his Colonel when he said that he had not intended to raise the subject, it was simply that Paul van Daan's anger was impossible to hide and Simon understood, for the first time, how it might feel. He was honest enough with himself to admit that his feelings for Valentina had involved more lust than love and could not be compared to his Colonel's evident devotion to his young wife, but his own suppressed anger at Cabrera give Simon a painful insight into how Paul van Daan must feel about the man who had regularly brutalised the girl he loved for two years and had almost murdered her at the end.

The second company of the 115th arrived back at the palace on the second morning into a dreary dawn light. Simon and Nicholas marched them over to the barracks where the smell of frying bacon made Simon feel almost light-headed with hunger.

"What's this?" he asked, as Sergeant Barforth of the first company appeared at the door.

"Early breakfast and hot spiced rum," Barforth said. "Compliments of Colonel van Daan, he thought they'd earned it."

Simon gave a weary smile. "They bloody have, Sergeant."

The four officers trudged across the park towards the palace, finding signs of activity even this early. In the hallway, Private Browning, one of the orderlies from the 110th met them with a salute.

"Food's ready in one of the small salons, sir. Major Corrigan thought you might need something."

Browning led them through a maze of rooms into a small parlour with covered dishes set out on a polished table and two covered jugs of spiced rum. Simon stood dripping on the polished floor watching his two young ensigns piling their plates and filling their glasses with the eagerness of children. Nicholas came forward with a glass of hot rum.

"Here," he said. "I think it's his way of telling us the punishment is over."

Simon took the glass and drank. "Oddly enough I'm not sorry it happened," he said.

"Are you all right? You've been very quiet the past couple of days." Nicholas studied him. "Are you worried about her?"

"Yes," Simon admitted. "But it's not really that. It's just that there's so much to think about, Nick, I'm not sure I can put it into words. Not just Valentina. It's over and I can't change what I did. I just hope she'll be all right. She'll certainly be better off without my so-called help. But I can't stop thinking about Robert."

"I'm sorry, Simon. I can't imagine…"

"I can't imagine either," Simon interrupted. "But I don't want to imagine. Who knows what went on in his fucking head when he thought it was a good idea to hold that girl down and take a horsewhip to her? I don't give a shit anymore. I'm tired of giving myself a headache trying to force myself to remember all the good things about him. Who gives a damn if he was nice to me during my first weeks at school? All I can remember now was the time the blacksmith came up to complain to my father that Robert had seduced his daughter and my father had to pay him off. Do you know what I'm thinking now? Was it seduction or was it rape? Did he hit her? Did he…"

"Simon, stop it," Nicholas said, with a warning glance over at the two younger officers. "Not here and now."

"No, you're right." Simon set his half empty glass down. "Sorry, Nick, go and eat. I'm not hungry."

Simon walked through the echoing halls to the library in the main wing. He had not been sure if anybody would be around, but he found Colonel van Daan writing letters at his big desk, with Captain Fallon checking invoices into a big ledger. The Colonel looked up at his knock.

"Come in, Mr Carlyon." The Colonel surveyed him and frowned. "You're still soaked, you need to change. Have you eaten?"

"Not hungry, sir."

Paul glanced at Fallon, who saluted. "I'll finish these later, sir."

As the door closed behind him, Simon said:

"I'm sorry."

"Lieutenant, there's no need. It's over, you took your medicine…"

"Not for that. I'm sorry about Mrs van Daan. I'm apologising on behalf of myself and my family, since they can't be here, for everything that he did. I can't believe I ever tried to justify that in my head. I can't…"

"Simon, stop it."

"Will you tell her, sir? I can't, it would be embarrassing. But I really need her to know how bloody awful I'm feeling about what he did to her. If he were here right now, I'd kill him myself."

"You wouldn't get the chance, lad, I'm quicker than you are," the Colonel said, and rose, coming around the table. He put both hands on Simon's shoulders.

"Listen to me. We're not having this conversation again. It's over and he's gone. I've noted your apology and I promise I'll tell her about it, but I can't accept it because it's not yours - or your parents' - to make. There's nothing of him in you. Put it aside and forget about the bastard. Agreed?"

"Yes, sir."

"Good. Now get yourself back to your friends and enjoy your

161

breakfast. And that is an order, Lieutenant."

Simon stood back and saluted. Leaving the room, he felt unexpectedly lighter of heart. He did not try to analyse it, but quickened his steps in case Witham and the two ensigns had finished the smoked bacon and baked eggs, a problem which felt suddenly more significant than a two year old tragedy long-buried.

# Chapter Twelve

Paul was surprised at how much he enjoyed the Light Division's sojourn in Madrid. Although he was a sociable individual, he preferred spending time with people he knew and liked and the kind of formal reception which he was often expected to attend as one of Wellington's senior officers was agonisingly tedious. Madrid was different. Once Wellington had departed for Burgos, and General Rowland Hill had led his men into a series of complex manoeuvres to try to second guess the various French armies, Paul found himself, with his General and the rest of the Light Division, in the unusual position of having little to do other than drilling and training the men and keeping the Spanish happy.

Paul did not pride himself on his diplomatic skills, but his wife excelled in such matters. Anne threw open the reception rooms of the Marina Palace and hosted a series of entertainments; balls, dinners and receptions, where the officers of Wellington's army and their Spanish counterparts could meet and dance and get to know one another. General Alten acted as host and Paul watched with pleasure as a comfortable friendship was established between his lively wife and his reserved German commander.

Anne had always been on excellent terms with General Robert Craufurd, Alten's predecessor at the head of the Light Division and enjoyed good relations with both Paul's fellow brigade commanders, especially Andrew Barnard, whose lively manner and ready sense of humour touched a chord in Anne. She had liked Alten from the first, but the Hanoverian could appear slightly shy in company and it had taken several months for Anne to properly get to know him.

Watching his wife in this elegant setting, gave Paul an extraordinary sense of pride. His first wife, Rowena, had hated the social aspects of regimental life but Anne's stepmother had taught her well and she had excellent company manners. Like Paul, Anne came from a mercantile background but unlike Franz van Daan, who had married into the nobility, Anne's father had never moved out of his local sphere and Anne had married at seventeen having very little experience of society. She had grown into her role as the wife of a senior officer and had learned to curb her natural outspokenness extremely well. Paul was amused and a little touched to see

Juana Smith, who was constantly at his wife's side on social occasions, carefully watching Anne and copying her manner. He thought that Harry Smith's young wife was a quick learner and would be an asset to Harry in future years.

The delights of the Spanish capital were limited, for the junior officers of the Light Division, only by their purses. Prices were high in Madrid and Paul was vastly amused, taking his wife shopping for new clothing, at Anne's Yorkshire disgust at the cost of a length of muslin.

"It would need to be lined with gold before I'd pay that for it," she informed the surprised shopkeeper, in fluent Spanish. "It's pretty enough, but we can do better than that on the price I think."

Generally speaking, Anne did considerably better on the price and throughout the capital Alten's officers and men settled in and learned the painstaking skill of bartering for everything from basic foodstuffs to a night in a brothel. Most of the men were reduced to living on their rations, apart from the occasional dinner invitation from a local family, while the officers managed their mess charges as best they could. There was an advantage to being part of a regimental mess like the 110th, because George Kelly, Paul's Irish cook, was able to negotiate good prices and even with their money running low, the officers of the third brigade dined well.

There were often guests for dinner, some more frequent than others. Harry Smith and his young wife became an almost permanent fixture with the 110th, causing Paul to regard him with a pained expression as his wife greeted Anne on their arrival one afternoon.

"Good afternoon, Captain Smith. What the devil are you doing here again, don't you have a billet of your own?"

"We do, sir. Major Swanson invited us. It's very much appreciated, sir."

Paul studied Smith thoughtfully. "Are you struggling, Harry?"

His junior pulled a face. "We've still not been paid, sir, and it's more expensive now that I'm married. Can't really pool resources with the others, officers with wives dine separately."

"And it's a stupid custom, I've always said it," Paul said. "Come and have a drink. Look, I can only invite you as a guest so many times, it's not fair on my own junior officers who have to pay their way. But how do you feel about joining the 110th mess while we're in Madrid? If you can't pay immediately, I'll settle your bills and you can repay me in stages when you get paid; I trust you for it. It'll be a lot cheaper than what you're doing, and Juana can eat with you; wives are welcome in my mess."

Smith's face brightened. "Seriously, sir? I say, that's really good of you. I'd be so grateful. I hate feeling like a beggar."

"I'll get Fallon to let you have the bill along with the other officers. If you can't manage it, come to me."

"I'll manage it, sir."

"There's just one thing, Harry. When we don't have guests, Keren Trenlow joins us for dinner. I'm sure you know her situation; we wouldn't

164

generally introduce her to the officers' wives, but since the only officer's wife here is mine and she has no standards whatsoever, it doesn't cause a problem. I'm not sure how you feel about Juana being introduced to her…"

"Me, I have met her already," Juana said, turning from her conversation with Anne. Smith's young wife had rapidly lost all shyness with Paul. "At the horrid baker near the white church."

Paul lifted his eyebrows. "You're very harsh on the baker, Juana, what's he done?"

"He tried to sell me bread with mould on it," Juana said disgustedly. "I thought he was being helpful, wrapping it and placing it in my basket, but it was to hide the underneath, which was green. But Miss Trenlow was in the line behind me and she told him to take it out and give me a fresh loaf. I was very angry; he treats me like a fool because I am young. We walked back through the town together and she told me of a better baker, only one must get there earlier before all his bread is sold. So you cannot ask me not to know her, Enrique, because I already know her. She is nice."

Paul met Smith's eyes, keeping his expression carefully neutral. "It's up to you, Captain," he said.

Smith shook his head. "It's really not, sir. If I told Juana not to acknowledge Miss Trenlow, she would probably seek out her company on a daily basis, just to teach me a lesson. Anyway, I'm not such a coxcomb as to turn up my nose at a female if Mrs van Daan don't."

Paul was beginning to laugh. "You married a sensible woman, Harry, I take my hat off to you. Juana, may I take you in to dinner?"

***

Long summer days shortened, and the nights grew longer and colder with autumn bringing more rain. Lord Wellington's troops fought and died on the slopes outside the fortress town of Burgos, while General Rowland Hill kept his troops in readiness to protect Madrid, and the French armies circled at a distance, looking for an opportunity to strike. In Madrid, the war felt strangely distant to the officers and men of the Light Division, who were accustomed to being at the forefront of every campaign.

Captain Leo Manson was at skirmish training with the 110th and 115th in the palace grounds when a hail from an approaching horseman caused him to turn. He saw Johnny Wheeler, scanning the well-laid out gardens, where Manson's men were using shrubs and hedges as cover. Manson stood upright from his position behind a bush which sported a mass of pink flowers and waved to Johnny. There was a bellow of warning from Sergeant-Major Carter who was acting as Manson's skirmish partner for the exercise and then an ominous click from behind him and Manson turned and found Private Cretney with his rifle at his shoulder, grinning broadly.

"Just blew your head off, sir."

Manson laughed and held up his hands in acknowledgement. "You did. But don't get smart about it, Cretney, while you're standing there looking pleased with yourself like a bloody amateur, I think you'll find Corporal Cooper just shot you in the back. Mr Denny?"

"Yes, sir."

"Take over, will you?"

"Yes, sir."

Manson walked across the lawn to where Wheeler was waiting and saluted. "Morning, sir."

"Good morning, Mr Manson. Get your horse, will you? I've had a message from the Colonel, he's just got back from seeing Lieutenant-General Alten. He asked if I'd bring you along."

Manson saluted, and turned to find Private Charlton, his new orderly, coming forward with his horse. Manson had never employed an orderly or a groom. His rank did not entitle him to any staff paid for by the army and Manson, who lived on his pay, had no money to employ either servants or grooms and had always managed for himself. He had been surprised when Charlton had waylaid him after training one morning and offered his services as an informal arrangement.

"I'd like to, Charlton, but I can't really afford it."

"Not looking to be paid, sir. Not like that." Charlton took a deep breath as if he had been steeling himself. "Learning to read, sir," he said, speaking quickly as though he might lose his nerve. "Have to read and write to get promotion. The Corporal's helping me a bit, but he's got no books to practice from apart from the Bible. It's awful dull, sir."

Manson studied Charlton slightly reddened face and understood. "You want to borrow a book or two."

"Just to practice, sir. I'd take real good care of them, bring them back."

Manson was unexpectedly touched. "All right," he said. "We'll give it a try, see how it goes. But borrowing a book isn't payment enough for dealing with the mess my tent gets into. How about I help you?"

Charlton looked astonished. "You, sir? Teach me?"

"Why not? You'll be around anyway. I've no idea if I'll be any good as a teacher, I've never tried, but we'll say half an hour a day before dinner. See how it goes."

Manson had been surprised and impressed with Charlton's enthusiasm for the lessons. He was also immensely pleased with the borderer's dedication to his interests and felt an almost childish pleasure when he returned to his room to find it clean and tidy with hot water provided and Charlton ready to take his boots for cleaning. He was careful to make sure that Charlton did not neglect his duties; Lord Wellington had forbidden the well-known practice of officers using private soldiers as their servants, taking them away from regular duty. Manson agreed with Wellington and insisted that Charlton be present for all training and drills.

Manson smiled his thanks at Charlton and rode to join Wheeler. They walked the horses through the gardens and up the sweeping carriage drive to the palace. It was a beautiful building, mellow stone looking almost pink in the

166

bright morning light. Hundreds of windows reflected sunlight back over the gardens, and as Manson watched, one of them opened and a maid leaned out, shaking out a blanket to air it. Manson recognised her as Constanza, a plumply pretty twenty-year-old who had worked for the Marina family and had remained to work for the army. Manson knew from listening to his fellow officers, laughing in the mess, that the girl was providing other services for several of them as well.

Manson's friends were beginning to tease him a little about his steadfast refusal to take up with any of the local girls or to visit the brothel with them. He had remained silent on his reasons although by now, all of them knew about Diana and he was fairly sure that behind his back there was a good deal of hilarity about his choice to remain faithful to a prostitute. Manson chose not to discuss it with any but his close friends. He had not made a reasoned decision about it, but he knew that it would have felt wrong to get up from another woman's bed and go back to write to Diana about the events of his week. He was enjoying their correspondence enormously and it was not difficult to resist temptation; Manson had never been particularly promiscuous. He had also recognised that getting to know Diana had changed his feelings about using prostitutes, possibly forever. Knowing what she had needed to do to survive during the years of the French occupation had given him a distaste for expecting any woman to service him for money; he would have spent his time wondering what had driven her to sell herself and whether she was hating having to do it.

Manson glanced at Colonel Wheeler, who appeared lost in thought. "Any idea what this is about, sir?" he asked.

"Not really, although I'm wondering if we have orders, finally," Wheeler said. "All the Colonel said in his note was that he'd been for a meeting with General Alten, and that he'd heard from both Wellington and Hill."

"I wonder if the siege is going any better?" Manson said, and Wheeler pulled an expressive face.

"The Colonel isn't optimistic," he said, and grinned at Manson's expression. "And I know how much he complains about any kind of siege warfare, but I think it's more than that."

Leaving their horses at the stables, Wheeler and Manson went up the steps and into the house. Corporal Jenson appeared and saluted.

"They're in the library, Colonel. Morning, Captain."

The company was already assembled as Manson and Wheeler walked in. Looking around him, Manson knew immediately that this was more than one of the Colonel's routine meetings. The senior officers of every battalion in the brigade was present, including Lt-Colonel Frasco and Lt-Colonel Huber, who had recently been appointed to command the Portuguese and KGL battalions. Manson was by far the most junior officer present and he could see Huber looking over at him in some surprise. Jenson was pouring wine for them, and Paul indicated that Wheeler and Manson should sit. Manson accepted his glass wondering if Huber was about to say something, but before

167

he could do so, the door opened, and Anne came into the room. She bestowed a smile on the assembled officers and went to her desk, reaching for paper and her ink pot.

"Good morning, gentlemen. You've probably guessed that we've both orders and news and I'm going to share both with you; I like my senior officers to know what's going on and why."

Huber raised his hand slightly. "Your pardon, Colonel, but I do not think that Captain Manson is a senior officer."

Manson closed his eyes but not soon enough to miss the freezing look that his Colonel turned upon the unfortunate German. "Thank you, Colonel Huber, you're very perceptive, I would not have noticed. Captain Manson is here as my unofficial ADC since I can't be bothered to employ any actual ADCs. And also because I want him here. Before you take the trouble to point out that my wife is also present, I have asked her to make notes; since she'll be writing up the orders anyway."

Manson looked over at Anne. Her shining dark head was bent industriously over her work and Manson looked away, knowing that she was hiding laughter. Colonel Huber did not look comfortable. Manson hardly knew the new KGL commander, he was probably not quite thirty, and along with Frasco, had been given a brevet rank from another division because Paul had wanted his KGL and Portuguese troops to be commanded by one of their own. He had also promoted Captains Withers and March to brevet-major as second-in-command to the two new men.

Huber appeared to have fallen into a stunned silence. Paul ran his eyes over his assembled officers.

"I've just come back from a meeting with General Alten. He's received orders from General Hill that the Light Division is to march out to join him at first light; it appears the French may be about to march on Madrid, so Hill wants all his troops. He's leaving the Spanish to garrison Madrid and is not moving out the baggage train. Ideally, we'll all be back here and settled in for winter quarters if things go well."

Johnny Wheeler was studying his Colonel from shrewd grey eyes. "Is it going to go well, sir?"

"No," Paul said baldly. "Lord Wellington's siege is going badly wrong. I've been in regular correspondence, not only with him, but with several friends with his army. They've lost far too many men, they don't have enough guns and it has taken too long. General Hill is hoping to be able to defend the Tagus, but if the French have the numbers we think, he isn't going to be able to do it."

"Do you think we're going to have to retreat, sir?" Major Swanson asked.

"Yes. Although I could be wrong, I often am. But given one or two previous experiences of retreat, I have decided not to take any chances. We'll march tomorrow but I'm leaving Major Breakspear with a small staff. Along with my wife, he is going to spend his time sourcing supplies and transport for a retreat. If they're not needed, I'll be very happy. If they are, we will be ahead of the undignified scramble in search of mules, food and anything else we'll need for the march. They'll organise a baggage train as if we are going. If we're not, we can all settle down again."

"Have you had orders to do this, Colonel?" Huber enquired. Manson felt himself cringe internally. His Colonel looked at the German and Manson saw Paul considering verbal annihilation and then deciding against it.

"You'll all receive detailed written orders within a few hours. Any questions?"

There was silence. Paul stood up. "Best get them moving, gentlemen," he said soberly.

The following weeks reminded Manson of his first campaign in the army, chasing Marshal Massena out of Portugal. He remembered long exhausting marches, poor weather and the abiding sense that he had no idea what he was doing or why he was doing it. The feeling had faded during skirmishes and battle, where he had discovered, to his surprise, a genuine talent for both fighting and leadership.

Since then, he had occupied a privileged position as Paul van Daan's unofficial ADC which meant that he was often included in conversations and given information not available to other junior officers. Nothing had changed in his relationship with the Colonel; the problem was that the Colonel knew as little as he did.

There were a series of pointless marches; several days spent in the attractive city of Alcala, then a march to Arganda followed by a miserable night march back to Alcala. Colonel van Daan, who had never been ill in the entire time that Manson had known him, had developed a head cold, which left him in a foul temper. His men walked on tiptoe, and his officers accepted his snappiness with affectionate resignation.

Hill's army, falling back on Madrid and preparing for a general retreat, was joined by a force under Colonel Skerrett from Cadiz. Manson was in Colonel van Daan's tent one damp evening, drinking wine and listening to his commanding officer sneeze, when Corporal Jenson appeared at the tent flap.

"Sir, someone to see you."

"Do I look as though I wish to see anybody, Jenson?" Paul demanded thickly. "Tell them I have something fatal and send them away."

"I can't do that, sir," Jenson said in soothing tones. "It's a Major Mallory of the 95th, just arrived from Cadiz. He has orders for you."

Paul made a sound which was suspiciously like a growl. "If I'm being sent to Cadiz, I am selling out," he said with finality. "Send him in, Jenson."

Major Mallory was probably in his late twenties with brown hair, dressed in an old-fashioned queue, and a pair of bright blue eyes. He saluted and handed Paul a letter. Paul opened it and Manson got up and quietly brought wine for the Major, as well as filling his colonel's glass. He had thought that he was being inconspicuous, but Paul turned his head and gave him a look.

"Are you trying to make me pass out?" he demanded.

"No, sir, I doubt if it would work. But I did hope it would help you sleep better."

"I can't sleep if I can't breathe." Paul surveyed the letter and lifted surprised brows. "Major Mallory, it appears you are joining my brigade."

"Yes, sir. Five companies of the 95th. I understand you already command two."

"No, I have one. I had two, but we lost so many at Badajoz that I had to combine them. You're very welcome, Major. You clearly know who I am; let me introduce you. This is Colonel Wheeler of the 112th, Major Swanson of the 110th first battalion, Captain Manson of the 110th light company and Captain O'Reilly of the 112th light company. They're all here drinking with me because I have a cold and they feel sorry for me. Where are your lads now?"

"They're bivouacked about two miles east, sir."

"In the open?"

"Yes, sir."

"Sorry about that, it's bloody cold. They'd best stay there now though, and we'll send orders in the morning when we get them. It's an odd time to be joining us but you're very welcome to the brigade. Now take a seat and tell me what's been going on in Cadiz, it'll take my mind off my headache."

\*\*\*

The Allied army bid farewell to Madrid on the last day of October, having blown up the remaining stores in the Retiro. Thanks to the frantic efforts of a number of British officers, including Major Breakspear of the 110th, at least some of the stores were removed and distributed to the poor of Madrid before the old buildings were destroyed. Hill's army, having fought several skirmishes with the approaching French, moved out in two sections, towards the mountains of the Guadarrama. The Light Division remained to cover the final troops leaving the city, and Simon Carlyon marched out with a sense of failure that he was not sure he would ever be able to forget. He could remember with unhappy clarity the joyous scenes of the army's entry into the city. On their retreat, the citizens stood silent and miserable, shouting the occasional insult. Some were in tears, entreating the British officers as they mounted their horses, not to leave them to the mercies of the returning French.

Simon had not seen Valentina again, but she was in his mind as he rode away from the city. He was fairly sure that her husband had been as enthusiastic a collaborator with the French as he was with the English and he thought she would be safe from the invaders. Her safety from her husband was another matter and Simon awoke at night with her pleading eyes before him and wished he had never been to Madrid.

Wellington had signalled a general retreat, hoping to join up with Hill in the vicinity of Salamanca once more. The retreat was orderly and well organised although the weather was beginning to deteriorate into the gloomy rains of autumn. Simon attended to his duties and played cards with Witham and several other officers in the lamplight during the evenings. He saw little of his brigade commander, who had been taken firmly in hand by his wife and was on restricted duties until his persistent cough had eased.

General Hill led his depressed army north towards the mountains, with the cavalry covering his retreat. They bivouacked for two nights in the Escorial park, and a few of the officers rode out to look at the beautiful Renaissance buildings which included a monastery, a royal palace, a church, a college and a library, constructed around a huge quadrangle and surrounded by gardens, parkland and woodland. Some of the officers had ridden out to visit the Escorial during their time in Madrid. Simon had not and he wished now that he had made the time.

"It's beautiful, isn't it? Although very plain. Somehow I thought it would be more elaborate."

Simon turned to find Keren Trenlow bringing her horse to stand beside him. Despite his sense of depression, Simon could not help but smile. He had taken a great liking to Keren during their time in Madrid, although he had found it difficult at first to know how to behave towards her. Simon had had past dealings with members of the muslin company, but the social situation had always been very clear. Here the lines were very blurred, and Anne van Daan treated Keren as a companion, completely ignoring her irregular relationship with Carl Swanson. Initially, Simon had found it awkward, but he had grown used to it and admitted to himself that he had developed something of a tendre for Major Swanson's pretty young mistress. He found her voice particularly attractive; it was deep, for a woman, with a rich west country accent.

"I think I did as well," Simon responded. "Nothing like some of the palaces in Madrid. I suppose it's a religious building as well."

"Oh, I doubt that made a difference, you'll have seen how gaudy some of the churches are. In truth, I wonder that they can concentrate on God at all in them; I'd be too busy admiring the stained glass or staring up at the ceiling to remember my prayers."

Simon laughed aloud. "You're not an admirer of grand church architecture then, Miss Trenlow?"

Keren shot him a smile. "I wasn't much in the way of seeing it as I grew up, although there's a fine church in Truro. But my Da was a Methodist, so we met in local cottages and only went to church when we had to. I do love all the statues and paintings, but my favourite kind of church is small and quiet and smells of incense and dust and old age. There should be memories in a church, not gold plate."

Simon was taken aback and then ashamed of his surprise. There was no reason why a girl from a miner's cottage should be any less insightful than a woman raised in luxury and he wondered how many other women like Keren Trenlow existed in a world he knew little about.

"Are you flirting with my girl, Mr Carlyon?"

Major Swanson's tone was good-natured, but Simon flushed slightly, knowing himself guilty as charged. "We were talking about the architecture of the buildings," he said.

"Well that's an excuse I've not heard before. Are you getting cold, Keren? Apparently, the monks are offering spiced wine before we ride back to camp, Nan has already taken the Colonel over there. I hope he gets over this soon, it's not like him to be unwell."

They arrived back in camp to the smell of food cooking. When the army first took possession of a camp ground, it habitually disturbed the local wildlife, and the third brigade had been delighted to discover that the park was full of hares. There had been a flurry of activity as the animals started up in alarm, to catch as many as possible, often using their hats as improvised nets. It had clearly been an excellent hunt. Simon dismounted at the edge of the 115th lines and handed his horse to Reynolds. Nicholas Witham was coming towards him; he had visited the Escorial with Manson and some of the others while in Madrid and had chosen to stay in camp.

"That smells good," Simon said. "I hope there's enough for the officers."

"The officers are dining on roast boar tonight," Nicholas said grandly. "We had a bit of a windfall, although it was almost a disaster."

"Windfall?"

"We had the usual crop of hares this morning, and then we heard the most awful racket from up in the lines of the 52nd; I thought the French had caught up with us. Either that or the hares had turned feral and were fighting back. Turns out that the park is full of wild boars as well as hares, and several of them came thundering through the lines. It was bloody chaos; some poor bugger from the 52nd ended up flying through the air and then getting trampled on, he's black and blue."

"Jesus, he was luck it wasn't worse, they're nasty bastards when they're cornered, I've hunted them in India," Simon said. "So what happened, wasn't the 52nd quick enough?"

"They were; they speared two of them with bayonets, but the other two got past them and went straight through the Rifles, they must all have dozed off. Fortunately, our company hadn't put their muskets on stand properly, they were lying around in the grass, they were onto them in a minute and caught one, hence our supper. The other one made it as far as the lines of the 110th and no further."

"Well thank God, I'm starving. Did you speak to the men?"

"I've told them that roast boar is the only reason they're not up on a charge, the idle bastards, but next time I'm taking the kill and writing them up as well."

Simon grinned. He had been slightly surprised at how well Nicholas Witham managed discipline. Initially he had wondered if Witham's reserved manner and quiet voice would make it hard for him, but Nicholas had a natural authority and did not seem to struggle at all.

Simon was grateful for the excellent meal, as the army marched at dawn, up into the mountains. The ascent into the Guadarrama was a steep three hour climb, a distance of around four miles. It was slow going, although not as bad as it might have been, due to the excellence of the royal road, which was able to take not only men and horses, but the baggage wagons and cannon without any difficulties.

The southern side of the mountain range was rocky and bare, with little vegetation, but scaling the top and coming over to the north side, the countryside was green. Rocky outcrops were surrounded by lush grass and thick belts of fir trees. It was misty at the top, and very cold. Simon stopped to pull on his heavy army greatcoat, looking back over the long column of Hill's army and remembered how differently he had felt on the march towards Madrid.

"Are you all right, Mr Carlyon?"

Simon jumped visibly and then felt stupid. He turned to salute Colonel Wheeler, who had reined in beside him. "Yes, sir. Sorry, just a bit cold."

"I'm not surprised, I gave in and put mine on as soon as we reached the top, I think I'm getting old. General Hill has ordered a halt in three miles, our scouts tell us there's a stream and good shelter under the trees. Will you take the order through your battalion, please?"

"Yes, sir."

"There's an additional order from Colonel van Daan. He wants all horses and pack animals to be given the opportunity to graze as much as possible; nobody is to touch the feed we're transporting. Grazing is good up here, he wants to make the most of it and save the feed until it's really needed."

"Yes, sir."

Simon watched as Wheeler rode off. He was struck suddenly by the normality of the conversation. Several months ago, he would have been both upset and angry after even such a casual exchange with Wheeler, but his anger had gone. Simon thought that it was made easier by the older man's quiet manner; Wheeler did not have the kind of personality that stood out. Simon was reminded a little of Nicholas Witham, and he wished suddenly that he could have got to know Wheeler without the shadow of Robert's death hanging over them both.

As the long march continued, the first casualties began to appear beside the road. Several mules seemed to have collapsed, and their owners were struggling to unload baggage. Three women were stumbling along, unable to keep up with the baggage trains of the leading regiments. One had a small child clinging to her hand, a white faced, skinny boy of around eight or nine. As Simon watched, to his horror, the woman suddenly dropped to her knees and fell forward.

Simon slowed to a walk, silently pleading with the woman to get up, but she did not move. The boy was on his knees, sobbing, shaking her. He looked blue with cold in thin jacket and trousers.

"What the hell do we do?" Nicholas Witham asked, and Simon realised he was also watching the small drama. "We can't just leave them."

"You've no choice, Mr Witham. We can't march at the pace of the camp followers; she probably shouldn't be here anyway," Captain Lewis said shortly. "Keep your eyes ahead. I don't even think she's one of ours."

"She is ours, sir," Simon said. "I think she's from the third division."

"Then she's not ours, is she, Lieutenant? This is the Light Division. If they can't look after their own, it's not our job."

Simon glued his eyes miserably on the column ahead, trying to shut out the child's sobs. He noticed two infantrymen jogging back along the roadside from the lines of the 112th. One of them paused and saluted, the other ran onwards to the fallen woman and Simon felt a surge of relief.

"Do you have a ticket to fall out, Private?" Lewis demanded.

"Yes, sir, from Captain O'Reilly. We've permission to take them down to the baggage wagons, apparently there's space."

"Let me see that ticket," Lewis said.

The man handed him a piece of paper. Lewis surveyed it and then shrugged. "All right, get on with it then."

Simon watched with considerable anxiety as the two men turned the woman over, feeling for a pulse. "She's alive," one said. "Help me get her up, Fletch."

"Not sure she can walk. All right, lad, calm down, your Mam just needs a ride for a bit. What regiment?"

"Da's in the 60th. A Rifleman." There was a ring of pride in the child's voice. "He don't know she fell; she couldn't keep up. Lost a baby four days ago, she's not well. Normally she's as strong as an ox. He don't know…"

"Course he don't, lad, he's up there doing his duty. We'll take care of you until he can. We need to get her to the wagons now."

There was an abrupt movement beside Simon and Nicholas Witham rode out of the line and over to the little group. "Can you pass her up to me, it'll be quicker? I can take her and the boy for that short distance."

Private Fletcher looked up gratefully, saluting. "Be very grateful, sir, thank you. Stand back a bit, lad, let's get your Mam up to the officer."

Simon watched, proud of Witham. With the woman and child balanced carefully in front of him, Witham rode off. He returned in fifteen minutes and fell back into place, saluting.

"Mr Witham, did I give you permission to fall out?" Lewis said very quietly.

"No, sir. Sorry, sir."

"If you do anything like that again, you bloody will be sorry. You're lucky I don't write you up for deserting your post, you arrogant young bastard. When we stop for the night, you're on picket duty."

"It's my turn, sir," Simon said.

"You have the night off, Mr Carlyon. I…" Lewis broke off as a rider approached, coming back down the column. "Ensign Cropley, have you orders?"

"Yes, sir. Colonel van Daan's compliments, we're to pick up any stragglers who collapse and get them to the baggage wagons. Mrs van Daan, Mrs Carter and Miss Trenlow are there, organising space for them and getting them something to eat."

"Oh, for Christ's sake, is this a charity hospital?" Lewis exploded.

174

"I'm sure that woman means well, but she'll have every malingerer in the army pretending to fall over at this rate."

Simon glanced at Nicholas then back at Ensign Cropley, who was about twenty with fair curly hair, wide blue eyes and an expression of permanent amiability. Simon had never seen Cropley look even remotely put out and he was surprised by the ferocious glare he was giving Captain Lewis.

"When you say, 'that woman' would you be referring to Colonel van Daan's wife, sir?"

Lewis looked uncomfortable. "Don't be impertinent, Ensign, or I'll put you on a charge."

"Yes, sir."

"I wasn't trying to insult Mrs van Daan," Lewis said. "Lovely woman. But she's a female, they don't understand the need to keep discipline, especially among the camp followers."

"Is that the message you want me to take back to the Colonel, sir?"

"No, of course it bloody isn't. Message received and understood. Mr Witham, you are in charge of any rescues that are required. I hope you catch something from one of them."

Witham's bland expression almost overset Simon. "Yes, sir. Thank you, Mr Cropley. Will you let Mrs van Daan know that Mr Carlyon and I are at her disposal if she needs any extra help?"

Cropley gave a broad grin. "Certainly will, sir. She'll be delighted."

# Chapter Thirteen

It took Hill's men two days to cross the Sierra de Guadarrama, and by the time they reached the final descent, even the officers on horseback were beginning to feel tired. Paul had refused Anne's suggestion that he ride part of the way in the carriage. His cold had left him with an irritating cough, and he was far more tired than usual which made the offer tempting, but he wanted his men to see him at their head, where he should be; morale was low after leaving Madrid. He rode up and down the column, stopping to talk to some of the men in each battalion, and then riding down to his brigade baggage wagons where his wife was organising relief for those men, women and children who had fallen by the wayside. Some of them had been impossible to save, and Paul's men had dug a hasty grave on the first night, for two women, three men and a child. All of them had already been ill before the march.

One of them had been the woman that Witham had carried to the wagons. She had slipped away silently, and Paul found his wife comforting her distraught husband when he came in search of her.

"What am I going to do about my boy?" he was sobbing. "He can't march up with me, he's too young. Not even old enough for a drummer boy and I don't know if he even gets rations now. Bad enough that we lost the baby, but I never thought Agnes would die. I feel like I killed her."

Paul came forward and sat down on the wagon steps next to the man. "You didn't kill her, lad, this retreat did. Have you spoken to your officer yet?"

"He says when we get into winter quarters he'll try and get him on a transport home. But there's nowhere to go, I've no family. Into the poorhouse most likely or apprenticed to some bastard who can mistreat him." The rifleman appeared to have finally noticed Paul's rank. "Sorry, sir. I didn't..."

"Don't be a prat, Rifleman, I don't need a salute from a man in your state. Let's worry about winter quarters when we get there, shall we? For now, he can stay with us, Mrs Carter will take care of him and he can help her with the baby. What's your name?"

"Rifleman Bannan, sir. My boy is Charlie. He's eight." Bannan had stopped crying and was regarding Paul from reddened eyes. "Can he? Stay here? I'm afeared of what might happen on the march if he gets left behind and the French..."

"He won't," Anne said definitely. "Go and talk to him now, and then you'd best get back to your company. You can come and see him at any time you've got leave. We'll look after him."

General Hill's army descended from the mountains the following day. Hill was setting a faster pace, having been informed that the French were beginning to pursue in earnest. It was slightly warmer down towards the valley but with steady rainfall, and Paul coughed miserably for most of the march, snapped at his officers and men and almost precipitated another quarrel with his wife when he refused again to make use of her carriage.

"The intention was for you to use it, but I can see that's not happening," he said irritably. "If something happens to this child because you're too stubborn to admit you shouldn't be riding..."

"Are you about to issue a threat or an ultimatum, Colonel?" Anne said in ominous tones.

Paul capitulated. "No. I don't feel well enough to have a fight with you, Nan."

"Which tells me just how ill you're feeling."

"It's just a cold, bonny lass. And don't change the subject, I'm worried about you."

Anne shook her head, laughing. "Don't be. I promise I'll be sensible, but I'm fine to ride at the moment. Honestly, Paul, I'm actually feeling quite well. Tired, but we all are. If I need to, I will evict some of our patients; they'll be strong enough to walk for a bit after a rest."

Paul smiled tiredly. "I might join you at that point. What the hell is that?"

The quiet of the afternoon was rent by a yell of pure fury, followed by a flurry of shots. Paul swore and wheeled his horse around, taking off in the direction of the sounds which came from further up the column. He could hear his wife cantering behind him and wished he had told her to stay where she was.

Paul reined in as he came upon the source of the disturbance. Captain Manson was off his horse, the reins looped around his arm. He was holding a pistol in his right hand, very steadily, and it was pointed at a group of men who looked like Spanish irregular troops. Beyond them were bodies on the ground, wearing blue coats.

"Oh Christ," Paul said. He swung down from his horse and turned to find his wife and his orderly behind him. "Jenson, take the horses. Nan, stay back."

Paul approached Captain Manson. "Stand down, Captain," he said quietly. "Lower your weapon, I rather think these are our allies here."

"No, sir. These are a bunch of murdering bastards who have just shot ten French prisoners in cold blood right in front of a marching British army, and I am waiting for them to tell me why."

Paul could hear the taut fury in Manson's voice. He had always known that Manson had a temper, but generally he had it very well under control. He had clearly lost it now. Paul looked over at the bodies. The

Frenchmen were thin and emaciated, looking as though they had not been fed for days. Paul remembered the prisoners who had been killed on their way to Bilbao and felt the same impotent fury.

"Leo, don't," he said softly. "Put that away and go and see if any of them are still alive. If you don't, my wife will, and I'd rather she stayed back. Give your horse to Jenson."

Paul had known that the reference to Anne would work. After a long moment, Manson lowered the pistol and went to check the Frenchmen. Paul turned to the Spaniards.

"This will be reported to Lord Wellington," he said, in Spanish. "You will furnish me with your names and the unit you are attached to, I will write personally to your commanding officer, recommending that you are shot for murder. Certainly, you will never serve under any British commander again."

"For shooting mad dogs?" the Spaniard said. "They wanted to die. They begged us to shoot them."

"Because you'd beaten them and half-starved them. No…" Paul held up a hand as the Spaniard began to speak again. "I've no wish to hear it. Captain?"

"They're all dead, sir." Manson's voice was flat.

"All right. Will you send somebody up to the baggage wagons and retrieve some spades, please? Commandant…what did you say your name was?"

"Suarez."

"Commandant Suarez, you will give your names and unit to my orderly who will write them down. You will then dig a grave for these men and bury them properly. Captain Manson and I will remain with you to ensure it is done. I hope you can dig fast. If I feel that we are in danger of getting left too far behind, I will simply shoot you in the leg and leave you for the French to find alive. That might be justice."

***

Through days of cold, damp misery, Hill's troops marched north-west towards Salamanca. Once past the mountains, there were supplies available in some of the towns and villages. During his sojourn in Madrid, Paul had sent a request to his bankers in London for funds. Cash was in short supply until the army received its pay chest and Paul had wanted to ensure that he had enough to cover any shortage until Wellington badgered London into paying his wage bill. He was thankful that he had done so. The commissariat did its best, but Paul was able to send out his quartermasters in search of supplies with cash in their purses. He had told them to ask for receipts and hoped to recoup the money in time, but if he did not, it was still worth it. His men, trusting that he would see them fed, held discipline and refrained from looting when others did not.

Paul's men did not encounter the French, although letters from Wellington suggested that his troops had been harried for much of their retreat, fighting a series of rear-guard actions. A day's march from Salamanca, the third brigade had invaded a small village of twenty or so houses and a church plus a substantial farmhouse, with a number of outbuildings. The rest of the light division had marched on into a more substantial town, but Paul was conscious of the number of camp followers he had acquired and wanted the space. He was also keen to conceal, as far as possible, the number of women and children who were crammed into wagons along with his sick and wounded men. Army regulations were clear about the position of women and those who could not keep up were left behind. Paul thought it very unlikely that Alten would make a point of it, given that his brigade had held discipline throughout the depressing retreat, but he did not wish the Hanoverian to be placed in a difficult position.

The brigade quartermasters moved quickly through the village, politely but firmly allocating space in every house to Paul's officers. Most of the inhabitants were resigned; a few, when told that the occupation would last for one night only, were welcoming, providing what food and drink they could to the tired, cold men of the third brigade. Rations were distributed and pickets posted, and the brigade settled down for the night in more comfort than they had known for days.

The village priest had raised the most objections to seeing his church taken over. Paul had put the 110th in there, with their officers to ensure his men did not break up the wooden pews for firewood and had commandeered the priest's house for himself and his senior officers. He and Anne had a tiny room at the back, but it had a bed and although the fireplace smoked horribly, it was at least warm. They joined the men for supper in the church, eating a somewhat rubbery stew made from goat meat and turnips which George Kelly had bought from some of the villagers. Paul had barely eaten a mouthful when Jenson appeared.

"Colonel Barnard to see you, sir."

Paul grinned. "I'll just bet he is," he said. "Come in, Colonel Barnard. Take a seat. The floor or a pew, but I'm sure you're not fussy. Finished your supper, have you?"

Barnard bowed to Anne. "Not yet," he said genially. "I was just on my way back to town now, but I thought I'd call in…"

Paul raised his voice. "Corporal Dawson, get some food for Colonel Barnard, will you? His French cook has let him down. What's the matter with him, Andrew?"

"He has the ague," Barnard said ruefully, and Paul gave a shout of laughter.

"What did I tell you? They're too delicate by far, French cooks. Never mind, we can't have you starving. This is not one of Kelly's best, but he didn't have much to work with. Still, it's warm and it's filling and there's plenty of it. Do you want some more, Nan?"

Anne passed her mess tin to Dawson. "Thank you, Corporal, I'm starving," she said.

Dawson went to the cooking pot and returned with food for Barnard as well. "Eat up, ma'am," he said cheerfully. "You're going to need it."

Paul shot Dawson a sharp glance. He and Anne had not made a formal announcement of her pregnancy this time. The memory of her miscarriage earlier in the year was still raw and Paul thought that both of them were cautious in their joy, fearing that something would go wrong. Anne had calculated as well as she could that she must be around five months pregnant, but thanks to a clever dressmaker in Madrid, she was equipped with a number of loose-fitting gowns, including a riding habit, which made the swelling of her body hard to detect. It was obvious that Dawson had worked it out, which probably meant that the rest of the 110th knew, or soon would. Paul saw Anne smile serenely at his Corporal and decided that she did not care.

"Charlie, will you get some wine for Colonel Barnard?" Anne said, and Paul hooted.

"Don't leave the bottle within his reach though, Dawson, or he won't be able to sit on his horse the right way."

Barnard accepted the cup with an air of injured dignity. "Thank you, Corporal Dawson. Best move the bottle away from Colonel van Daan as well, he sounds as though he's already had too much."

There was the sound of activity outside and Paul looked around. "What's going on, Sergeant Hammond?"

Hammond, who had placed himself on informal door duty, went to look outside. "Not sure, sir. It sounds like the priest making a fuss again. Might be some late stragglers coming in."

Paul got up. "Well if they've made it this far in the dark, I am not letting that miserable, skinny bastard chase them away," he said. "No, stay there, Carter, I'm just in the mood for him."

The rain had stopped outside although a cold wind whipped across the churchyard and cut through Paul's greatcoat. The sound of shouting was coming from the main street beyond the church gate and Paul made his way carefully down the rough path and through the gate.

"Off with you, before I take a horse whip to you. Bad enough that we must endure these Englishmen, taking our homes and desecrating our church, we have no room for beggars. Get out and die on the road where you belong."

There was a movement in the darkness, a small figure turning away from the church. Paul could make out little, although it seemed too slight to be a man. As he walked forward, he saw the priest stoop and pick something up. He threw it overarm and his aim must have been accurate because his victim gave a little cry of pain. The voice confirmed Paul's suspicion that it was a woman.

"That's enough," he yelled, furious. "Get yourself back into that house and don't let me see you again before we march out, or I'll forget myself, and it's probably a sin to belt a man of God. If that's what you are, you uncharitable bastard."

Paul had spoken in English and he had no idea how much of his tirade the priest had understood, but he clearly understood the threat behind it, because he turned and ran, lifting up his cassock and stumbling a little in the darkness. The woman had begun to run back up the street, but she stopped at the sound of Paul's voice and turned. Paul could see some kind of dark dress and a white face.

"Are you English?" he called.

"I am Spanish."

Paul moved towards her. "Do you speak English?"

"I do."

"I'm guessing that means you were with the army and got left behind. It's all right, I'm not going to hurt you. We've got the women and children in the church barn. Let's get you over there and fed and we'll try to get you back with your man. Which regiment?"

Paul had reached her by now and could see her better. She was shivering visibly, her teeth chattering, wearing only a thin shawl over the gown. A mass of wet curls framed a white, woebegone face and Paul studied her.

"I know you, don't I? Didn't you work at the palace, in Madrid? What's your name again?"

"Ariana," the girl whispered.

"Ariana, what are you doing here? Did you take up with one of our lads?" Paul remembered her clearly now, the half-starved young woman that Michael O'Reilly had brought in, beaten bloody in an alley.

The girl shook her head. "No man," she said. "I followed the army."

Paul was startled. "On your own? Jesus, child, what possessed you?"

"I had nowhere else to go. The French were coming. I was afraid."

He could hear it in her voice, the desperate terror that a new army would use her as brutally as the old one had. "When did you last eat?"

"Two - no, three days. Some biscuit, a German gave me."

Paul did not ask what she had done to earn it, he did not want to know. "Come on," he said gently. "Food and warmth, we can provide, for tonight, at least. Up into the church."

"The priest..."

"If the priest shows his ugly face anywhere near me again tonight, I'm going to punch it," Paul said. He coughed, and found that he could not stop, pausing by the church gate, leaning on it with one hand while he fought to catch his breath.

"You are ill," the girl said.

Paul controlled his breathing with an effort. "Not serious," he croaked. "Just a cold. This way."

It was blissfully warm inside the church. Paul looked down at the girl. She was staring around, wide-eyed, taking in the sight of the 110th finishing their meals, drinking their grog ration or settling themselves where there was space, to try to sleep. Anne had brought out all the church candles, much to the fury of the priest, and the room was well lit. The wives and camp followers had joined their men, and little family groups huddled together for warmth, their wet clothing beginning to steam as it dried.

"This way," Paul said gently, and she followed him, stepping over and around men lying on the floor. Anne was talking to Barnard, but at the sight of Ariana she rose.

"Ariana. What on earth are you doing here?"

The girl did not reply, and Anne seemed to realise that the question was unimportant. "You need food," she said briskly. "Have you walked all the way from Madrid? Never mind. Dawson, get her something to eat, will you?"

There was no sign of Ariana the following morning as Paul's brigade began to assemble in the freezing half-light before dawn, ready for the march. Paul wondered if, after all, she had gone in search of some man.

He noticed her again at the end of the march, as Hill's tired men tramped across the bridge at Alba de Tormes. It felt strange to Paul, to revisit the scene of his desperate skirmish earlier in the year. The town looked very much the same in the dim light of early evening. Paul reined in to watch his brigade pass by and blinked in surprise at the sight of Captain Michael O'Reilly with his baggage mule in tow, and Ariana perched precariously on its back. Paul caught Michael's eye, and his friend's rueful expression reassured him.

Paul caught up with Michael as the Light Division settled down in the woods on the far side of the river. Michael was standing beside a fire while one of his men filled a tin mug with tea. At the sight of Paul approaching, Michael saluted then passed him the mug and took another.

"How are you, sir? Your wife is worried about that cough."

"I'm worried about the cough," Paul said. "It's all right, Michael. I just need a couple of weeks in a warm, dry billet and it will go."

"And how is the love of your life and the burden she carries? You kept that one quiet, I must say."

Paul sipped the hot tea. "We weren't sure at the start," he said. "And then I suppose we weren't sure how it would go, given what happened last time. We think around January, when I'm praying we'll be in winter quarters. Stop trying to distract me, Michael. Where's that child?"

"I've sent her off with Sally Stewart to find something dry to wear," Michael said. "I gather she turned up with you last night."

"She did. We fed her and got her settled down, but she must have disappeared during the night."

"She came to find me; I woke up and found her on the floor next to my baggage, she frightened the life out of me. Christ knows what I'm going to do with her, but she'll have to stay for now, I can't abandon her in the middle of a retreat; some bastard will get hold of her again, either French or English. Either that or she'll die of hunger or cold."

"Why did she leave Madrid?"

"Nowhere to go. When we marched out, they closed up the palace. The servants who'd worked for us went back to their homes. Some of them will probably go back to work for the family again, or the French, or whoever commandeers the place next. She might have got a job in the kitchen, but she's terrified, sir. Since she was thirteen, she's been starving and cold and desperate, and whichever army has come through has used her and thrown her aside."

"Until you came along," Paul said. He was beginning to understand.

"I've told her I'll get her to safety and find something for her. I wondered if one of the convents would take her."

"Probably. In the meantime, do you want me to take her back to Nan?"

"I don't think she'll stay, sir. She's terrified beyond reason. She's been marching at the back of the army all the way from Madrid, begging for scraps and selling herself for a space by the campfire. And trying to find me. Poor brat couldn't even remember the name of the regiment, but eventually somebody recognised my name, which is how she turned up in the village last night. Don't worry about it. She can stay until we're in winter quarters, when she's recovered, she can make herself useful."

"It's up to you, lad. You know some people are going to think the worst?"

"With that skinny brat? If that's what they think of me, sir, why would I care? Get back to your wife and get some rest, you look like death."

***

The Light Division marched into Salamanca to join up with Lord Wellington's forces from Burgos on 10th November, a little short of five months since they had made their first entry into the city. Anne was conscious of a very different atmosphere among both the troops and the townspeople. The French were very close, and the three armies of Soult, King Joseph and Souham were finally in a position to join up, which left Wellington's army facing vastly superior numbers.

With the practicality of several years with the army, Anne was simply glad to be warm and dry, with plenty of food. The Light Division was billeted in the university colleges, with the third brigade taking over several buildings which had already been converted into barracks by the French. As Wellington exchanged letters with Hill, who was still in Alba de Tormes, and sent out scouts to ascertain the exact position of the forces closing in on Salamanca, George Kelly took over the enormous kitchens and sent his mess orderlies out in search of supplies and Anne organised some of the women to heat water and bullied her husband into a hot bath.

Anne had found a huge wooden bathtub in the kitchens, far bigger than the washtub which they generally used. It took forever to fill, but the expression on Paul's face as he lay back in the hot water, made it worthwhile.

After a long time, Paul said:

"I think I am going to live."

Anne laughed. "I do hope so, Colonel, you've had me worried in places. Here, drink this, Keren made it. It looks rather like a witches' brew, although I think it involves lemons and honey and possibly brandy. It's supposed to be good for a cough."

Paul sipped the steaming cup. He was silent again for a while, then said drowsily:

"Do you think there is any way we could induce Carl to marry this girl? I seriously don't want to lose her."

Anne looked at him in considerable surprise. She had no idea if he was serious or not, although it was a thought that had more than once occurred to her.

"I take it it's good then?" she said.

"It's nectar. I can feel it soothing away the soreness. We are paying Miss Trenlow to concoct this every day while we're here. Which probably won't be long. I don't care, though. Just now, at this moment, I feel better."

There was a knock at the door. Paul's eyes opened. "Shoot them," he said simply. "I don't care who it is."

"Even if it's Lord Wellington?"

"Especially if it's Lord Wellington. He got me into this in the first place."

Anne went to the door and took the letter from Jenson. She came back into the room studying it. "It's from Lord Wellington," she said.

"Tell him to fuck off," her husband said, and then opened his eyes and looked at her. "Sorry. My language."

"I shall forgive you. This is the happiest I've seen you look in two weeks. Do you want me to open this?

"Would you?"

Anne opened the letter and scanned it. "Lord Wellington wants you to attend him at headquarters immediately," she said.

Paul did not speak. Anne looked over at him and saw, with a rush of compassion, that his expression had changed. There was a slight splashing sound as he shifted in the water.

"I knew it was too good to be true. Will you hand me that towel, girl of my heart?"

Anne stood looking at him for a long moment. She felt, not for the first time on this campaign, pure, uncomplicated fury at the commander-in-chief. Taking a deep breath, she shook her head.

"No," she said.

Paul turned his head to stare at her and she saw the spark of amusement in his blue eyes. Anne thought, somewhat sentimentally, that she had never met anybody else with eyes of quite that shade of deep blue. They had melted her heart in a shepherd's hut in a Yorkshire snowstorm four years earlier and she had never entirely got over the way it made her feel when he looked at her and she saw the smile creep into them. He was looking at her that way now, and Anne, who had lived with him now for two years, knew that behind the look of genuine adoration, he was considering how best to turn her up sweet.

"I can get it myself, bonny lass," he said.

Anne held up the letter. "Don't bother, Colonel. I am going downstairs to answer this myself. I'll send Jenson in to ensure that you get yourself into bed."

"Nan…"

"He can wait," Anne said, and she knew that she sounded furious and made no attempt to hide it. "He has a dozen ADCs, General Sir Edward Paget as his second-in-command, eight divisional commanders, twenty-four other brigade commanders and a chaplain in case he needs divine intervention. He can survive another twenty-four hours without you. I know you'd die for him, and on a battlefield, I accept that. But you're not dying of inflammation of the lung because he needs you to hold his hand because he's too difficult and too arrogant and too bloody terrified to let anybody else get close enough. He can wait."

Anne turned and left the room, careful not to slam the door. Outside, she stood for a long time, her eyes closed, holding her breath, listening for the sound of him getting out of the bath. It did not come. Anne opened her eyes. Incredulously, she realised she had won.

"Well done, ma'am."

Anne jumped. She had not seen Corporal Jenson. He was watching her, his eyes sparkling with amusement.

"Freddie, you frightened the life out of me."

"I don't believe you, Mrs van Daan," Jenson said, and there was respect in his voice. "I don't think there's anything can frighten you. Go and write that note, I'll get him settled."

Wellington's army spent five days in and around Salamanca, as the French converged upon the city. Skirmishes and cannonades were constant, as the remainder of Hill's divisions tried desperately to hang on to Alba de Tormes, and then made plans to defend or blow up the bridge when they needed to retreat. Both armies engaged in a frustrating series of manoeuvres and counter-manoeuvres, jostling for position as their commanders tried to decide if another battle across the fields of the Arapiles was worth the risk. The rain fell constantly and those troops within the city made the most of dry billets and enough food while those at the outposts waited for the commissariat wagons and cursed the weather, the French and the Almighty for putting them in this position.

Paul slept almost constantly for two and a half days, waking only to drink and eat a little. Anne was always beside him when he awoke, and he realised that she must have abandoned all other duties to take care of him. He awoke on the third day into a dim afternoon light and lay still for a while, realising that his breathing felt clear, his headache had gone, and the persistent raw throat appeared to have eased.

"Good afternoon, Colonel. Ready for some tea?"

Paul sat up to see his wife bringing a steaming cup. He drank gratefully. "I feel a lot better," he said. "But Christ, I've slept like the dead. How long…?"

"It's the third day. Don't panic, the army hasn't marched out without you. Are you ready for a visitor?"

Paul studied her. "Am I allowed to see him now?" he enquired. Anne laughed, a little pink-cheeked.

"I think so. He has been very patient, but I am beginning to feel a little sorry for him. Poor General Alava seems to have been getting the worst of it. I think you're well enough; you've not coughed for over twenty-four hours."

"I could do with a wash and a shave. I'm not seeing him like this."

"I'll send Jenson in. It's almost the dinner hour, but I thought you and Lord Wellington could dine privately in the small parlour, I'll arrange it. He looks as though he needs the food."

"Don't tell me you've not been bullying him too, bonny lass."

"I have when I can get hold of him. There's a lot going on, Paul, but I'll leave him to tell you." Anne took his empty cup and leaned over to kiss him. Paul caught her and held her close, kissing her for a long time.

"Thank you," he said, releasing her finally. "I am such an arsehole at times, Nan, I've no idea why you bear with me. Have you been worried?"

"Yes," Anne said. "But I'm not now. You have the constitution of an ox, Paul, another man would have been laid out for a month with that. I love you."

"I love you too, bonny lass."

Paul found Lord Wellington in a small parlour, lit brightly from several large candelabras and two side lamps. Paul saluted as Wellington got up. He looked tired and depressed and in need of a good meal.

"I am sorry, sir."

"Don't be. You hardly chose to be so ill. I am only relieved that your wife was sensible enough to take charge. Are you sure you are well enough…?"

"Yes, sir, I promise you." Paul was not sure that he had ever heard his chief sound so subdued and he wondered what Anne had actually said to him. "As a matter of fact, I'm starving, I think I've been subsisting on broth, gruel and Keren Trenlow's magic potions. I think she's a witch, you need to try them."

Wellington managed a more natural smile. "Every time I become irritated with the appalling number of wives, camp followers and hangers-on drifting behind your regiment like the tail of a monstrous serpent, you remind me that they are occasionally useful."

Paul, who had been pouring wine, almost spilled it. "Are you referring to my wife, sir?"

"Don't be an imbecile, Colonel, I would never refer to your wife in those terms; she terrifies me. Is this dinner? I believe I may be hungry."

"I believe that without supervision you may have forgotten to eat for a day or two." Paul lifted one of the covers which had been set down on the table and grinned. "Roast mutton, sir. My wife knows you far better than I'm comfortable with. Come and sit down. Are you happy if we serve ourselves, it's easier to talk?"

"Yes," Wellington said, moving to the table. "Colonel - it is very good to have you back. You are, without a shadow of a doubt, the most exasperating, insubordinate, infuriating officer in my entire army, but I have realised that I do not function as well without you to shout at. The next time I am obliged to divide my army, your brigade will be with me. Unless you would seriously consider accepting a post on my staff? You can invent your own post and I will force it past Horse Guards. After inflicting Willoughby Gordon onto me, I have no further trust in their judgement."

Paul studied his chief and realised in some surprise that he was serious. "Sir, I'm genuinely honoured," he said. "And I'm almost tempted. But my place isn't at headquarters and you and I both know it. It works because I'm on the outside, I'd be useless at the politics and we'd drive each other mad. I'm better at what I do."

"I know. And I expected your refusal. I just wanted to make the offer. Thank you, this looks very good. Is your wife not joining us?"

"Not this time, sir. She wanted to give us some time. What's going on?"

Wellington took a deep breath and began to speak. Paul ate, drank, listened and recognised, in his undemonstrative chief, a real sense of relief. When they had finished eating, Paul rang for Jenson to clear and bring more wine and more candles, as those in the room were burning low. Paul said little, other than to ask an occasional question. Some of it, he already knew from Wellington's letters and reports to General Alten, but Wellington's need to unburden himself was so obvious that Paul sat back and allowed him to talk.

Wellington had known from the start that he needed to keep the armies of King Joseph and Marshal Soult from combining. He had counted on the autumn rains keeping the River Tagus high, providing a barrier to stop Soult and Joseph from threatening from the south. He had also relied on the Spanish to delay a French move towards Madrid and had hoped that the capture of Burgos would prevent a French drive from the north.

"Clausel rallied that army faster than I thought possible," Wellington said. "And I know they always do. It's a weakness of mine. I look at what I could do, and I base my calculations on that. I was wrong. This time, it was disastrous. But I thought I could take Burgos quickly. That's why I left Hill to defend Madrid."

"I know, sir."

"We invested the castle halfway through September; there were about two thousand defenders. I lacked guns; we had three eighteen pounders, and eight twenty-four pounders, plus a few lighter captured guns. Ammunition was short as well. We didn't have enough engineers, as always. I miss Fletcher."

"So do I," Paul said. "Both as an engineer and a very good friend. But he's recovering well, sir, he'll be back soon. And Fletcher isn't a magician."

"No. It wasn't the fault of the engineers. I made decisions…I wrote to you about Popham at Santander, didn't I?"

"Yes, sir. He's done well."

"Very well," Wellington said with a grudging smile. "Although I wish he would stop writing me complaining letters; he cannot think I wish to hear of his squabbles with the Spanish commanders at this time. He offered to land more heavy guns and get them down to Burgos. He could probably have done it too; he's clever at logistics. But I didn't want another Badajoz. I should have said yes. I sent for them afterwards, but it was too late by then, they didn't arrive in time. Anyway, we took the hornwork on the nineteenth, about 420 dead and wounded. Started digging in batteries. Major Cocks did very well on that assault. I mentioned him in despatches. You heard about him, I'm assuming?"

"Yes, sir," Paul said, sympathetically. "One of his officers wrote to Major Swanson and Captain Manson."

"Yes. I'd forgotten that they were friends. I should have written to them."

"You can't write to everybody about everything, sir, although I'm well aware that you do try."

Wellington snorted. It was the first time he had done so and it made Paul feel better. "Whereas with you, Colonel, we feel honoured if you find the time to send a note mentioning that you have marched your entire brigade elsewhere because you felt like it."

"I have never done that, sir."

"Perhaps not. Although you cannot say the same of your battalion. And when you commanded the light company…"

"When I commanded the light company, you sat on me so hard, I could scarcely breathe."

"It was necessary."

"It was excessive. What happened to Cocks, can you tell me?"

It was a French sortie. We were surprised, but the major rallied the men and led a counter-attack. We lost two hundred, dead and wounded. I shall miss Cocks, he reminded me a good deal of you, when you were younger."

Paul could not refrain from smiling. "He was only five or six years younger than me, sir."

"You know what I mean. I liked him."

"I did too. Manson was very cut up about it."

"I imagine so. How is Captain Manson? I should like to see him at some point."

"He's well, sir."

"Good. Good. Anyway, it dragged on. One step forward and two back. We were losing more and more men, running out of supplies and ammunition. The weather was growing worse and worse so that the trenches flooded. And all the time, news was coming in that the French were rallying. Soult from Cadiz, Joseph towards Madrid, Souham in the north…"

"What about the Spanish?" Paul asked. He saw his chief's lips tighten.

"General Ballesteros failed to obey orders," Wellington said. "He made no attempt to move to block Soult."

"You mean he got the orders and just ignored them?" Paul was genuinely shocked. "That's mutiny."

"And he'll be tried for it," Wellington said flatly. "I shall deal with General Ballesteros when we are out of this safely. I have also been deeply disappointed by the failure of General Maitland to move from Alicante."

"Any idea why?"

"No, but I shall find out. My scouts reported that the Tagus was unusually low for the time of year and would be impossible to defend and Souham outnumbered me. I had no choice but to raise the siege and retreat." Wellington took a long drink. "Honestly, Colonel, I feel fortunate that he did not attack me immediately. He could have destroyed me."

Paul did not speak immediately. He knew that Wellington usually valued his opinions, but he could think of nothing to say, faced with his chief's obvious unhappiness. Eventually he said:

"What was the retreat like?"

"Unpleasant," Wellington said briefly, reaching for the wine bottle. It was empty and Paul got up and went to collect another from the sideboard. Neither he nor Wellington generally drank heavily, but he had a sense that his commander needed the relief this evening. "We got a full day's start on them; they did not realise we were gone, but after that they were on our heels the entire time. Skirmishes and small actions day after day. It reminded me of chasing Massena out of Portugal, only the other way around. I have some sympathy for that old fox, it is not pleasant to be in danger of being overrun on a daily basis. I suppose Talavera was difficult, but they were not so close then. And I was not at Corunna."

"Nor was I, thank God."

"My army fell apart," Wellington said suddenly, and Paul suspected he had reached the root of Wellington's depression. "Looting and drunkenness at every town and village. They marched as and when they felt like it and the officers seemed to have no control over them and no ability to keep them in line. We have lost hundreds of prisoners, simply because the divisions could not keep together."

"Sir, I'm sorry."

"So am I. It began so well. I should have marched sooner after Badajoz, but the troops were in poor condition. And then the Spanish seemed incapable of properly garrisoning and supplying Badajoz and Ciudad Rodrigo; I couldn't march until I was sure of my line of retreat."

"I know, sir."

Wellington looked at him over his glass. The distinctive blue eyes looked heavy and tired. "Why can I not work with the Spanish, Colonel?" he asked. "I have managed to get the Portuguese on my side. I have worked with Danes, Indians, Germans…what is it that I do wrong with the Spanish?"

Paul felt a huge rush of sympathy. He had seldom seen Wellington so depressed or heard him so close to despair. "You can, sir. You work very well with D'Espana, Morillo, Sanchez…it's not the Spanish leaders, it's the system. Bonaparte has destroyed their infrastructure and broken their leadership; they're all over the place. Nobody could work with that. The Spanish can't work with each other."

Wellington set down the glass. "I should not drink this, it is making me maudlin," he said.

"It's making me tired, and I'm sick of sleeping," Paul said. "What now? Can we fight them, or do we run?"

"We may have to run," Wellington said bitterly. "My army wants to fight. Back here, on the Salamanca battlefield, they feel invincible. I understand that. But we are heavily outnumbered, with the possibility of more French troops on the way. I am not risking this army." Wellington studied Paul for a moment. "Will you be well enough to march?"

"Oh Jesus, yes, I'm much better. It was just a cold, sir, that got worse because of the weather. And Nan thinks the injury had weakened me, made me more susceptible. I don't even know if that's possible, but I'm not arguing with her, she's so often right. But I made it back from Talavera with a hole in my chest, you can't think I'm going to take to my bed and wait for the French?"

Wellington got up. "Unlikely," he agreed. "I am going to my bed. Thank you, Colonel. Expect orders tomorrow or the following day."

"Yes, sir."

They were met at the door by Anne, lighting the dark hallway with a candle. "Jenson has brought your horse round, sir, I'll walk you to the door."

Paul watched them go. At the front door, his commander bowed and spoke a few words. Paul saw Anne laugh and reply. Wellington's countenance lightened considerably. He took Anne's hand and kissed it and in response, Anne stood on tiptoe and kissed him lightly on the cheek. Paul remained where he was until the door closed behind Wellington. Whatever had passed between his wife and his commander, he suspected that Wellington had needed to mend bridges and he could sense that Anne was happier too as he put his arm around her.

"Time for bed," he said. "I've an odd feeling this might be the last night we're sleeping in one for a while, I want to make the most of it."

Anne shot him a sideways look from under long lashes. "My goodness, you are feeling better, Colonel," she teased.

"I am. So I really hope you're well rested too, bonny lass. I was hoping to stay awake rather later tonight."

190

# Chapter Fourteen

The army began its retreat from Salamanca on the afternoon of 15$^{th}$ November. Earlier in the day, Wellington had realised that the French were moving troops to cut off his route back to Ciudad Rodrigo. Outnumbered, and potentially outflanked, he made his decision and by two in the afternoon, he had put his army into three marching columns and was heading out to cross the Zurguen River before camping for the night.

The heavy rain continued throughout the day and into the night, and the army found what shelter it could in woods close to the river, huddling in cloaks and blankets and eating the rations they had carried with them. Paul had allowed his men to take whatever they could carry from the stores but kept a very careful guard on his baggage wagons and mules, instructing the quartermasters to be strict about handing out further rations. After discussion with Breakspear and Anne, Paul had elected not to rely entirely on the commissariat keeping up with the army, and to carry a quantity of basic rations and fodder for the animals. Paul was hoping it would not be needed; it was a four or five day march back to Ciudad Rodrigo and safety, but his previous experience of retreats was that it could be difficult to keep the army together and having a basic supply of food within reach might make the difference between a disciplined march and an army running out of control.

Anne had elected to travel in the carriage, at least at the start of the march, along with Teresa Carter and her small daughter, Keren Trenlow and young Charlie Bannan. Anne had bought the child new clothing during their time in Salamanca, and he was warmly dressed in a woollen suit with a thick jacket and sturdy boots. Paul reflected, as he saw the boy clambering into the carriage, that Charlie was probably better dressed than he had ever been in his life. Charlie had fallen desperately in love with Anne's oversized young dog, who was also in the carriage, and settled himself in a corner with his feet on Craufurd's thick fur.

The women, children and sick men who had travelled for some of the retreat in Paul's baggage wagons had been sent back to their proper places, fed and tended and rested, although looking at the weather, Paul was fairly sure that others would take their place.

The exception was Ariana, who had nowhere to go and who refused the offer of a place in the carriage in favour of leading Captain O'Reilly's baggage mule. Like Charlie, she had acquired new clothing in Salamanca, and Paul observed that she was dressed as a boy again, similarly attired to young Bannan, with a woollen hat covering her unruly auburn curls and a second-hand greatcoat which was too big for her, keeping her warm. Paul watched her managing Michael's recalcitrant mule with surprising efficiency and thought that she looked just like any of the other officers' servants. He wondered if it had been her idea or Michael's to go dressed as a boy, but he thought it a good one, which might well keep her both warmer and safer.

Weeks of heavy rain had turned the roads and tracks into swamps, quickly churned up by boots, hooves and wagon wheels so that walking became difficult. Horses picked their way carefully through the mud. It clung to their hooves and to the boots, shoes and clothing of the men and women trudging through it, making the march heavy work.

Walking was made harder by little streams which criss-crossed the roads and which had swelled in the heavy rains, so that at times the men were wading up to their ankles. Paul felt even more sorry for the women who were weighed down by their soaked skirts. Many of them had tried to kilt up the garments, exposing more than was strictly decent of their ankles and legs, in order to stop them getting heavier with water and mud.

The commissariat wagons failed to arrive on the first night, as the Light Division bivouacked near Cillero in the freezing rain. Paul thanked God that Anne had bought the carriage. There was no possibility of putting up tents with the French so close and he could not have borne the thought of her sleeping on the soaking ground. His men ate some of the rations they carried and Breakspear distributed fodder for the animals under heavy guard. Without food, beasts were going to start dying, and although Paul felt desperately sorry for the officers and men of the other brigades, he was not going to sacrifice his own.

He was talking to Anne in the carriage when a horseman reined in and Colonel Andrew Barnard dismounted. Paul went to meet him, beckoning him under the trees where the rain was less.

"How are your lads?"

"Cold, wet and hungry. And pretty pissed off," Barnard said. "They didn't get to fight, which is what they wanted, and they've had no rations. Yours?"

"All of that apart from hungry; they've carried some."

"I guessed. Look, Paul…"

"I'll get you something from the carriage."

"It's not for me; I'm not that fucking selfish," Barnard said sharply, and Paul turned, startled.

"Andrew, I know you're not. What is it?"

"My orderly. He got ill on the march from Madrid and he's not getting better. He fell off my spare horse earlier. He's burning up. I know you'll think I'm mad, Colonel…"

"Andrew, have you met me? Where is he?"

192

"We're bivouacked about half a mile to the west."

"Can you get a couple of your lads to bring him over here? I'm not putting him in the carriage with Nan just in case it's contagious, although it's probably just a bad cold gone wrong. But we can put him in one of the baggage wagons, we've more space than you have, and we'll keep him warm and fed."

Barnard's expression lightened. "I knew you would. I should have realised how bad he was, I feel like an arsehole."

"You are an arsehole, Colonel, but you're one who cares. Get him over here, I'll get Jenson to find him space and a meal. How are you for fodder?"

"Good at the moment, I loaded up a few mules. Where is the fucking commissariat, though?"

"God knows," Paul said soberly. "We're going to start losing them if it doesn't catch up tomorrow. But I suspect this is the final nail in the coffin of Willoughby Gordon."

"Good, he's a useless bastard and we need Murray back," Colonel Barnard said, heartlessly, and left in search of his orderly.

Wellington's three columns were each allocated their own route to Ciudad Rodrigo, in a similar manner, Paul supposed, to Massena's retreat from Portugal, when he had split his army to confuse the pursuing enemy. The first column, consisting of the second, third and fourth divisions, took the Matilla road under General Rowland Hill while the centre column, comprising the first, fifth, sixth, seventh and Light Divisions under General Sir Edward Paget, took the road towards San Munoz. The Spanish army, which formed the third column, took the main road to Ciudad Rodrigo.

In terms of road condition, the Spanish had the best of it, although Paul suspected that they would be harder pressed by the French, who might well choose the easiest route to attack, especially with cavalry. Paul's own route was not easy, consisting of swampy tracks, with the rain falling so heavily that when men stopped to rest, they had no option but to sit or lie in two inches of water. He had a suspicion that their Spanish guide was lost, taking them a complicated and circuitous route. The column created its own roads, dragging wagons and gun carriages across stony ground or ploughed fields, lifting them sometimes by sheer strength and bloody-mindedness, out of small valleys which had turned into bogs.

Men lost boots and shoes in the mud and could not retrieve them. On the second day, Anne left the carriage and went on foot to rest the horses. Paul walked beside her, ignoring the protocol of marching order and leading Rufus and Bella to preserve their strength on very limited rations. Following his example, his officers did the same, only Jenson, with his wooden leg, continuing to ride. There was still no sign of the commissariat wagons. Beside them walked Teresa and Keren, taking turns to carry little Ana who was wailing with misery, swaddled in blankets to try to keep her warm. Charlie Bannan led Craufurd on his leash, appearing so happy to be with the dog that the cold, rain and exhaustion barely touched him. Paul thanked God for the child, whose irrepressible good spirits seemed to lift Anne.

"I'm not going to want him to go back to his father, Paul, he's such a joy."

"Well it's up to Bannan, bonny lass, but if the lad can make himself useful, perhaps it's a solution. Maybe Jenson could take him on and train him up. He seems a bright child and it might be better than some charity school or poor house in England."

The rain eased a little that evening, and Paul's brigade tore down trees in search of wood to make fires. They had little success with the damp wood but managed to set fire, eventually, to some of the larger trees which gave out a good heat. Officers, men, women and children huddled together close to the blaze, with scant regard to rank or position, happy to share lice along with warmth in the desperation of their situation.

Some of the men from the other divisions had collected acorns from the woods and were experimenting with roasting them over the fires. A few more had discovered some vegetables growing half wild in the gardens of a deserted village, and as the rumour went through the lines, Sergeant George Kelly marshalled his assistants and went in search of additional rations. They returned within the hour laden down with cabbages and turnips along with half a dozen hares, and cooking pots were suspended over the fires to cook a weak stew. There was scarcely enough for a few spoonfuls for each man, but it was hot and had some flavour and the third brigade devoured it gratefully.

As they settled to another miserable night, a horseman appeared through the mist, and Paul recognised Captain Richard Graham, one of Lord Wellington's ADCs. Paul went to greet him, wrapped in his greatcoat.

"Orders, Captain?"

"No, sir. A delivery from Lord Wellington. It's for your wife."

Paul took the rush bag and opened it. The smell of food made him feel slightly light-headed. "What on earth?"

"Roast chicken, sir. We managed to buy a few birds from a farmer. Also there's some bread, it's a bit damp, but edible. And a few apples. Compliments of his lordship. He was worried for your wife, given her delicate condition."

Paul felt warm, despite the freezing weather. "Richard, tell him thank you. We've some food left, but not much, and I'm worried we'll run out entirely tomorrow."

"We've not much left. But I'm more worried about the horses, this poor old girl needs her food."

Paul could hear the anxiety in Graham's voice. He hesitated, then said:

"Have you got five minutes?"

"Yes. Why, sir?"

"This way."

Paul led Graham through the trees to where his baggage wagons had been arranged in a circle, heavily guarded. Graham looked at him in surprise. "Why aren't they with the rest of the baggage, sir?"

"Because I don't trust anybody but my men to guard them. And

194

because I value the contents. Get off your horse, go over to the carriage and pay your respects to my wife. Jenson is a magician and is going to feed your mare. Not much, but enough to keep her going another day."

Graham's eyes widened. "You've got your own supplies?"

"We have, but they're very limited. I'm not feeding every nag in the army, but you're a friend. Go on, go and talk to Nan, take her her supper."

The following day was the worst yet. It was the job of the Light Division to act as rear guard to the centre column, which meant that they were the first under arms in the morning and the last to settle into bivouac at night. It also meant that the other divisions had more opportunity to forage for what limited food was available. There was an alarm during the night as a number of men, driven mad by hunger, shot down a selection of pigs, which the country people had left to graze in the forest. Paul sent Captain Manson in search of information and he returned over an hour later wearing a sober expression.

"Lord Wellington's furious. It seems that discipline is breaking down in some of the other divisions, there's been a lot of looting and some drunkenness. He's ordered two men to be executed, hoping to deter others. I've never seen him this angry."

"You didn't see him the day after the garrison escaped from Almeida, it was something special, I'm telling you. Although he was fairly pissed off the time I laid myself open to a court martial by upsetting the Royal Navy in Copenhagen."

Manson grinned. "I've never heard the full story of that."

"I will tell you over a nice bottle of red back at Ciudad Rodrigo. You'll enjoy it." Paul studied Manson's face, looking gaunt and tired in the dim light of a weak moon. "Are you all right, Captain?"

"Yes, sir. I'm just hoping you're not going to shoot me."

Paul understood. He grinned. "Hand it over," he said, and Manson opened his coat and removed a package wrapped in what looked like a spare shirt.

"Pork, sir. Bought it off a private from the guards. Not sure Lord Wellington caught all of them, sir."

Paul put his hand on Manson's shoulder. "Captain, you never disappoint me," he said. "Come and join us for supper."

The French began to press harder early the following day. Paul divided his men, sending the 110th and 112th up to the high ground on each side of the road, leaving the rest of his brigade to guard the baggage train. The roadside was littered with dead animals, some still attached to baggage wagons. Among the beasts were the corpses of men, the sick or ill or simply those unable to keep up, who had collapsed and died by the roadside, lying in the mud.

Paul had given orders for his men to fall out and check corpses for signs of life. A number were picked up, still living, and loaded onto the wagons, which were half empty as food supplies were used up. Most were already dead, the birds of prey descending through leaden skies to feast on the corpses. Paul held Anne's hand and watched her face as she looked straight ahead. Behind him he could hear Keren crying, with Carl's arm about her. The discipline of the march had relaxed into necessity and men helped their wives and children along where they could. Paul made no complaint and hoped that Lord Wellington did not decide to join them; Wellington was unenthusiastic about the train of women and children who followed the army and was strict about their position during campaigns. Paul half expected a reprimand when General Alten rode back to consult with his brigade commanders, but to his surprise, Alten gave no more than a thoughtful look over the column and said nothing.

Up on the raised hillside on both sides of the road, shots were exchanged with the French, who circled like the vultures, hoping to swoop down on the weak. Stragglers were captured. As the road became a little easier, Paul decided the horses could take the strain for a while and sent Anne back into the carriage to rest, while he mounted Rufus and rode along the column, checking that his men were holding their shape, despite the struggle of the march. He stopped here and there to speak to them. The remains of the previous night's pork dinner were wrapped in cloth in his pocket, and he stopped beside some of the children and fed them scraps, wishing he had more.

The quiet of the morning was torn apart suddenly by shots from further up the line and it was clear that the column ahead of Paul was in action. Paul turned his horse and scanned his lines.

"Colonel Frasco, double the guards on the carriage and wagons, I'm going to see what's going on."

"Yes, sir."

Paul reined in and looked in at his wife. Anne put her arm about Charlie Bannan and stroked her dog.

"Get going, Colonel," she said gently. "I'll be all right."

Paul met her eyes. Every part of him was screaming at how wrong it felt to leave her, knowing that the French were so close, knowing of her ordeal at their hands less than a year earlier. He wondered, not for the first time, if it was worth abandoning his duty and remaining beside her to defend her, accepting the court martial and cashiering in favour of keeping her safe.

"Go," Anne said, and her voice was firm. "I have Charlie here to keep me safe. And there are more men like Damien Cavel than like Jean Dupres in the French army, love - same as in ours. Get moving."

Paul met Captain Smith on his way up the column. "Harry, what news?"

"Bit of trouble, sir. French made a dash on our baggage. We had it in the charge of Colour Sergeant Baller."

"From what I know of Colour Sergeant Baller, he may have made it out of there."

"Not this time, sir, as far as I know. But there's worse news. General Sir Edward Paget."

Paul felt a chill. He had been on excellent terms with Paget back at Oporto, and he had been present at the amputation of Paget's arm. After a lengthy convalescence, Paget had only recently returned to the field and been placed as Wellington's second-in-command. Paul had been glad to see him back, and he knew Wellington valued him.

"What happened?" he asked. "He's not dead?"

"Taken, sir. French cavalry. They're attacking up and down the column. Not in force, but small troops."

"They've not been near us yet."

"Neither would I, sir, they're not bloody stupid. They're looking for weak spots. Sir Edward realised that a gap had opened up between the fifth and seventh divisions and he rode back to find out why. Only took a couple of hussars with him. He can't have seen them coming."

"He can't have fought them off either, with one arm," Paul said soberly. Another burst of firing caused Rufus to shift restlessly. It was closer at hand.

"French skirmishers, sir," Smith said.

"Yes. I'm getting back, Harry, I want to make sure they're ready. Take care."

"I will. I'm not enjoying this. Sir..."

"If anything happens, we'll take care of her," Paul said, understanding. "Make sure your lads know where to bring her. But make sure it isn't necessary, will you?"

"I will. Good luck, sir."

French cavalry made their first attack on Paul's brigade at noon, searching for gaps in the woods. There was an undignified scramble among the Portuguese troops and Kings German Legion to defend the baggage wagons as twenty French hussars came thundering out of the trees, and half a dozen men were cut down before Paul's muskets managed to get the range and drove them off with a fierce volley of shots. None of the men were dead, but there were a variety of cuts and slashes. Paul, who had been up on the higher ground and had seen the attack from a distance, rode down at a canter. By the time he arrived, the troops had formed a rough defensive square about the baggage wagons. Paul could see Colonel Frasco in what appeared to be a furious exchange with Colonel Huber and he rode forward.

"What happened?"

"It was not the fault of my men," Frasco said angrily. "The Germans should have been watching our flanks, we had no warning..."

"Your men were too slow and did not form up as they should have," Huber said precisely. "My men were in position as they were ordered, but..."

"Your men did not give the alert, we might have been slaughtered..."

"Enough!" Paul roared. "Major Withers, get over here."

Charles Withers had been examining a deep wound on the shoulder of one of the KGL skirmishers. He ran over, saluting. Paul looked at him. There was a graze on his temple which was bleeding sluggishly.

"How close did those bastards get to my wife and the other women?" Paul asked.

Withers looked back steadily. "Too close, sir."

"Thank you, Major." Paul looked back at the two commanders who had fallen silent. "I have no interest in who got it wrong. There is no time here, for getting it wrong. Put your men on the alert. We've cavalry on both flanks and it's our job to keep them away from the rest of the column, and preferably away from our baggage wagons. When we are safe, I will have a conversation with you about my expectations of my battalion commanders, but this is not the time. Jenson."

"Yes, sir."

"Orders to Major Corrigan. Get the 115th down here, they are to exchange positions with the KGL and the Portuguese. Perhaps if you are out on the flank, gentlemen, you will have a better incentive to get your men moving faster. You will march in column at quarters distance and form square at the first sight of cavalry. Move."

The day was misty, with frequent, heavy rain showers. The light division marched on, fighting off attacks from the French cavalry, and coming under sporadic fire from their tirailleurs. Rifles and muskets were of limited use given the damp condition, although the rain began to ease off later in the day, and Paul set his rifles and light companies on each flank to hold off the musket fire from the French.

During the afternoon, the Light Division was joined by the commander-in-chief, who rode up with several of his staff on the left flank. Wellington looked chilled and miserable, but even the sight of him cheered the men, who regarded him as something of a talisman against bad luck. French cavalry continued to probe the lines and there was no sign of the English cavalry.

The Light Division approached the Huebra River at almost four o'clock, by which time the French had infantry and artillery, as well as cavalry in place. There was a lively musket and rifle duel already going on, and the shots sounded extraordinarily loud in the forest, reverberating strangely in the heavy atmosphere.

Lord Wellington reined in beside Paul. "Skirmishers out, Colonel van Daan. Rifles and light companies, keep their cavalry back, while I decide where best to stand, in order to get our men across."

"Yes, sir." Paul turned to call orders and watched as his officers and NCOs led out their men. Lord Wellington surveyed the ground and gave orders for several troops of horse artillery to get into position, as the Allied column began to cross the river.

It was a gruelling fight. The French had brought up almost twenty guns to the heights opposite the river, close to the village of Buena Madre, and began to fire both on the infantry and baggage crossing the river and the British artillery trying to defend them. Paul's brigade was under constant, heavy fire, taking shelter where they could among the trees and behind rocks, keeping up a steady fire to deter French cavalry and infantry from making a rush on the troops.

Paul made the decision to detach his baggage wagons and send them on ahead. He could no longer spare the men to guard them and he wanted Anne and his supplies safely across and out of harm's way as he directed his skirmishers back into the trees to take out French tirailleurs who were trying to creep through to reach the river further up.

The Allied cavalry was crossing the river, and Paul, keeping his men steady and under cover as far as possible from the punishing artillery fire, was bewildered to see Vandeleur's brigade formed up in a highly exposed position, covering the cavalry retreat. He was in no position to see what was happening, and he watched from the heights with growing anxiety, as the first brigade came under heavy fire, perilously in line. Paul felt slightly sick, watching the trees for sign of cavalry, and wondered what maggot had entered Vandeleur's brain to leave them so exposed.

"Jenson."

"Sir?"

"Get over to Colonel Wheeler and tell him he has command for a bit, I'm riding down there to find out what's going on. I can't see General Vandeleur, I'm worried something's happened. They're going to get slaughtered like that."

"Yes, sir. Be careful."

"I always am."

Jenson uttered a snort of disgust and turned his horse and Paul made his way cautiously through the trees, arriving on the flank of the first brigade. He was approaching the central column, his eyes searching the officers for Vandeleur, when a small group of horsemen appeared, riding fast from the direction of the second brigade. Paul recognised General Alten, with three of his staff members.

Alten bypassed the brigade, heading directly towards the advancing cavalry. As Paul rode down, two of Alten's staff broke away and rode to the brigade officers, which Paul could now see included John Vandeleur. To Paul's considerable relief, the troops halted, and then changed position, ready to form square. Paul rode past them and went to join Alten who had reined in alongside the officer commanding the cavalry and his staff. As Paul came closer, he recognised the man, seated on an exhausted looking grey.

Alten's generally pink cheeks were scarlet, and the mild blue eyes held an expression that Paul had never seen before. "General Sir William Erskine," he said formally. "I have ordered my first brigade into formation so that they may defend themselves as well as covering the retreat of this army. In future, I expect you to refrain from giving orders to my men which counteract those I have already given them. You command cavalry, not infantry, and you cannot be expected to manage men who are not under your command. I am angry that you should have considered it your right to do so."

Alten's precise, German accent was heavy with a menace which Paul had not thought him capable of. Paul reined in and hung back. His own relationship with Sir William Erskine was not good and he had no wish to make Alten's task more difficult. During the period of Massena's retreat from Portugal, Paul and his battalion had been under Erskine's command. Erskine was known to suffer from periods of madness, was short-sighted, arrogant and easy to offend. He had been removed from the command of two divisions and now held a cavalry command under General Hill, but Paul was of the opinion that he was not safe to be in charge of a church picnic, let alone a cavalry brigade.

Erskine visibly bristled. "Your division, sir, which was once mine, is under orders to form a rear guard. I merely..."

"My division, sir, is no longer yours, and are under orders to do exactly what I tell them to do. No more, no less. I suggest you turn your attention to your men before they find themselves under heavy fire. Good day."

Erskine's face was scarlet. "How dare you speak to me that way, you German upstart? I have..."

"General Erskine."

Paul turned, startled, and both Alten and Erskine did the same. Lord Wellington had reined in. He was dressed in a dark, oilskin cape, with water dripping from his hat, and his expression warned Paul that speech was unwise.

"Lord Wellington," Erskine said. "Sir, I have a complaint. I..."

"Get your men across that river, General, before I remove you from command and tip you off that horse," Wellington said, in a tone Paul had seldom heard. "General Alten, are your men in position?"

"All but Colonel van Daan, sir, but he is on his way," Alten said, without turning. Paul wheeled his horse smartly and set Rufus back up the hill at a gentle trot. On the way back to join his men, Paul remembered Alten telling him at dinner one evening, that he missed Christmas at home in Hanover, with a wealth of tradition unknown to the English. Paul rejoined his brigade, promising himself that if they survived this retreat into winter quarters, he would find out as much as he could about German Christmas traditions and recreate them for Alten. His commanding officer deserved it.

\*\*\*

The 115th were positioned out on the far-left wing of the brigade, huddled in sodden misery in a wooded area, while the French guns pounded them. There was nothing they could do to retaliate; muskets would be useless at such a distance. Simon Carlyon knew that their job was to keep watch for French infantry or cavalry, to avoid them sweeping down on the long column of the Allied army which was carefully negotiating the fords. The Huebra at this point was split into several branches, which meant that the men, horses and baggage train had to cross two and in some places three rivers. There were a number of fords, some deeper than others, and only one in this part of the river was suitable for wagons and gun carriages, and it was clear that the French knew it and were targeting many of their attacks onto the baggage wagons, hoping to scoop up prizes as well as prisoners.

Given the cannonade which had been pounding down on the Light Division since the morning, Simon was astonished that his company had not suffered more casualties. There had been some minor wounds, mainly from splinters as the trees were struck by shells, but the heavy rain, which had caused so much misery during the past few days, had worked in their favour during the French attack, as shells which fell into the soft, heavy ground died a harmless death. Judging from an occasional cry of pain further along the line, not all the Light Division was doing quite as well. Simon wished he knew more about what was happening elsewhere.

He was on foot, along with most of the other officers. As the French attack became more concentrated, the Colonel had sent word along the line that he was sending horses on ahead under an escort of the KGL, to ensure their safety. Few of the younger officers could easily afford to replace expensive horses, and the animals were already in poor condition, having survived on very limited rations for several days. Simon had been happy to send Reynolds with his horses out of danger; they were of no use here, other than to serve as a target for French gunners.

"Mr Carlyon, Mr Witham."

Simon shifted cautiously beyond the tree to see his captain coming through the mist. "Sir?"

"Orders from Major Corrigan. They've tirailleurs coming down over the top, through those pine woods, first and second company to cut through these woods and stop them. Five companies of the 112th are cutting round from the other direction to join up with us."

"Yes, sir." Simon turned to give orders to his ensigns and NCOs. It was a relief to have something to do other than listening to the crashing of the guns and wait for a shell to hit. Moving through the trees gave a sense of security which was probably false but felt reassuring. Captain Lewis threw his men out into skirmish formation, with Simon taking the left flank and Nicholas Witham the right. Simon kept a wary eye on his men, but they were keeping steady, remembering their training and covering their partners well.

They encountered French infantry in about half a mile, startled into action by a flurry of musket fire. There were shouts in French as the tirailleurs realised that they were under attack, and without further warning, the French were in among them. Simon moved in, his sword drawn, yelling to his men to use bayonets. In this kind of skirmish, with poor visibility, a musket shot was just as likely to hit one of their own, as a Frenchman.

It was a short, brutal encounter, with no quarter asked or given. The men of the 115th had no way of taking prisoners on their retreat and the French obviously realised that trying to guard captives over this terrain would be impossible. For fifteen bloody minutes, the two companies pushed forward, leaving blue-coated men dead or wounded on the forest floor and then they were out the other side of the belt of trees and a yell of warning told Simon that they had encountered the 112th fighting their way from the opposite direction. The French, neatly caught between two forces, retreated at speed over the top of the rise, and Simon paused to catch his breath.

"Sergeant May, what losses?"

"Only Barlow, sir. A few wounded, but they can all walk."

"Good, because I'm not carrying them," Simon said, and raised a weary cheer from his men. Beyond the tree line there was a fine view down over the Huebra and Simon could see the army making its way slowly over three fords. On the far bank the various divisions were forming up in watchful columns.

It was good to be out of the woods and temporarily out of range of the French guns. They were still firing, the sound echoing off the rocky hillside and through the trees. Simon found that it was easier to ignore them when they were not trained on his men and he stood for a while watching the activity on the various fords below.

Directly at the foot of the slope, a collection of baggage wagons and mules were making their ponderous way across. It was clearly heavy going; beside them splashed women and children, lifting up skirts and carrying bundles while the muleteers urged their exhausted beasts across to the other side.

A carriage was crossing, a big lumbering vehicle pulled by four horses. A number of women entered the river beside it and Simon, watching, realised suddenly that the carriage must be the one belonging to his Colonel's wife. She was there, dressed in a dark blue cloak, striding out into the water strongly and Simon wondered irrelevantly if any of the men guarding the column realised that she was pregnant and might need help.

Some kind of activity to the east caught Simon's eye and he turned and peered at the heavily wooded slopes. There was movement where he would not have expected to see it, masked by the trees. Simon peered, suddenly anxious, trying to catch a proper glimpse. He was still peering when he heard an enormous roar from the lines of the 112th.

"French cavalry in the trees. They're going for the baggage wagons, the Colonel's wife is down there. 112th, to me!"

There was a scramble and a blur of movement and Simon realised the voice had come from Colonel Wheeler who had been watching, as he had, the crossing of the Huebra. The men of the 112th who had made the climb with their Colonel were hurling themselves down the further slope at breakneck speed, leaping over fallen trees and sliding through muddy patches, bayonets and muskets in their hands.

Simon was moving almost before he had thought about it, yelling to his men to follow. He did not stop to find out if they had or wait for orders from his Captain. His only thought was for the woman in the river, who had survived too much to be cut down like this.

The cavalry swooped down on the wagons and carriage crossing the river, yelling in triumph at the same time as the men of the 112th and 115th took the final descent of the hill at a slide. The horses splashed into the river, the horsemen with drawn sabres, making for the straggling line of drivers, muleteers, women and children. Further across the ford, a company of infantry from the fifth division were guarding the far bank, but at the sight of the thundering hussars, they turned and ran, scrambling back up the steep bank to safety.

Simon charged towards the river, sword in hand, hearing the wet splashing of the men around him, some of them sliding in the mud. Several of them were barefooted, either having lost their shoes in the swampy ground during the march or having had to cut their boots off their swollen, bleeding feet. Up ahead, the leading horsemen had reached the column, and there was a scream as three Portuguese muleteers went down under their swinging sabres. The mules panicked, charging around and crashing into the cavalry horses and into each other, slowing the attack down and winning the fleeing women a few precious extra moments.

They used them well. Simon heard a woman's voice cut through the chaos, of braying mules and screaming women and children.

"Run. Drop everything and run. This way."

She stood, almost up to her knees in the water, dark hair straggling down around her face, guiding the terrified people past her. "Keren, take Teresa and Ana, get them out of here. Charlie, help them. Go. That side, it's shallower."

Simon, sliding into the water, realised she was right. Leaving the melee of abandoned wagons and mules, the camp followers, servants and wagon drivers splashed through the shallows. Some were reaching the far side. The infantry company was returning to its position, driven by its furious officers and possibly by a sense of shame, and the men were reaching out to help the terrified people up the bank.

The cavalry realised that they were under attack and many were turning to face the Light Division men. In normal conditions, the cavalry would have cut through such a disorganised infantry charge within minutes, leaving no survivors, but the French were having trouble controlling their horses. The animals were confused by the cacophony of sound coming from the abandoned pack animals and their riders were too close together in the river with no way to manage a proper charge. They had lost their momentum, and the furious men of the 112th and 115th were upon them, dodging their swinging sabres and stabbing up with bayonets, bringing several of them down.

The water was showing red with blood in the last of the afternoon light. Simon found himself engaged in a fierce one to one combat with a hussar who had been unhorsed but was on his feet, slashing about him with lethal intent. It was difficult to keep balance in the water, and twice Simon almost lost his footing. In the end it was his opponent who slipped, and Simon moved in to finish him quickly.

He heard a yell and recognised it as Captain O'Reilly of the 112th. Simon spun around and saw the Irishman running frantically, his sword in his hand, slowed by the deeper water on the far side of the stranded carriage. Another shout came from Colonel Wheeler who had been directing his men to line up on the banks, hoping to deliver a musket volley which would drive off the cavalry.

Simon turned to see what had caused the two men to panic and saw immediately. Anne van Daan had waited until the last of her retinue had gone past her and was now fighting her way through the water to the opposite bank, lifting her waterlogged skirts high, but two cavalrymen had broken away from the skirmish with the Light Division and had followed her. One had inserted himself between the woman and the opposite bank and waited, his sabre ready, his expression almost avid. The other was approaching from behind her to cut off any hope of retreat back that way.

Anne twisted her head to look back at the second horseman and Simon caught a glimpse of her white, terrified face. He could see her trying to decide which way to run, but she was going to be cut down in either direction, and he saw her realise it. She seemed to straighten her back, letting go of her skirts, and drew herself up to her full height, placing her hands on her rounded stomach as if to protect the child within. Simon did not know if it was a deliberate and intelligent attempt to appeal to the hussars or a purely instinctive gesture, but he saw the expression on the face of the hussar change as he realised that she was pregnant.

Simon did not know if the Frenchman would have withdrawn from the attack, allowing the girl to reach safety; he was given no opportunity to do so. A shot rang out from the opposite bank, and the hussar jerked and then tumbled forward into the river. His demise seemed to goad the other horseman into action. Raising his sabre, he urged his horse forward, advancing on Anne.

Anne did not attempt to turn or run. She stood facing the hussar, looking directly at him, as if she knew that her youth and her condition were her only defence. The Frenchman did not pause, and Simon heard a roar of sheer rage as O'Reilly scrambled through the water to try to reach her in time. Simon began to move as well, but he knew, with horrified certainty, that they were too far away and that they were never going to reach her before the horseman did. The hussar could not easily gallop through the water, but he was moving as fast as he could, and as he drew close to Anne and lifted his sabre high, he was smiling, and Simon heard himself give a sob of pure horror. At the last moment he closed his eyes, unable to watch her die.

# Chapter Fifteen

With the bulk of the army across the river, Paul stood watching the last of the troops making their way across the upper fords. It was impossible to see down river to where Anne would be crossing with the baggage wagons; the slopes were heavily wooded. Despite the heavy cannonade from the French artillery, none of his men from the 110th, the Portuguese and KGL had been killed, and only a few had suffered minor injuries. The guns had done some damage here and there, but the soft ground was absorbing most of the shells and only a direct hit was likely to cause casualties.

The light was beginning to fade, and the intensive skirmishing of the late afternoon was dying out with only occasional shots being fired. Most of the seventh division had crossed and were formed up on the opposite bank. The sound of hooves in the soft mud of the riverbank made Paul turn, and he saluted, recognising the caped figure of Lord Wellington.

"Not much longer," Wellington said. "I'm told that most of the baggage and hospital wagons are across. I have given orders to form up on the far bank and be ready to defend the position in case they try to cross. I doubt they will do so tonight, there should be a chance to rest and eat."

"Most of them don't have anything to eat, sir."

"I know, Colonel. When we are safe, I will make enquiries into the state of the commissariat on this march, it has been an appalling blunder. But once we are across, it is no more than a day or so to Ciudad Rodrigo."

"They're going to come after us again tomorrow, sir."

Wellington met his eyes. "I know. But if we can hold them at the river until most of the army is underway, I do not think they will follow us much further. And that is going to be your job, Colonel, I've given General Alten my orders."

"Yes, sir." Paul hesitated. "Sir, given that, may I have permission to make my way down to the lower fords. I'd like to be sure that my wife is safely across. Major Swanson can take over here and I'll rejoin them on the other side."

Wellington studied him for a moment and then shook his head. "I would say no to anybody else, Colonel."

"You can say no to me if it's necessary, sir, I can take an order."

"Go," Wellington said briefly. "Take a small escort. By now the other half of your brigade should be abandoning the heights and preparing to cross. If they haven't, call them in. I am told that Colonel Wheeler has done an excellent job of defending those slopes all afternoon; he is to be commended. I will speak to him personally in time, but you may tell him he will be mentioned in my report to London."

"Thank you, sir." Paul saluted and went to find Captain Manson. He had sent Jenson over with the officers' horses earlier, trusting his orderly to make sure they were taken safely to the rear. Jenson's wooden leg made it difficult for him to manage on foot during a skirmish and Paul was not prepared to risk him.

Collecting Manson, Sergeant Hammond and half a dozen of the 110th light company, Paul left Carl in charge of the final withdrawal and made his way up through the trees and down river. The thick belt of trees made it impossible to see anything of the Huebra. As they came closer, he could hear sounds up ahead and he paused, holding up his hand for silence. There was a jumble of noise; horses whinnying, mules braying and oxen bellowing and over it, the shouts of men and what sounded like a woman's scream.

"Christ, they're attacking the baggage wagons," Manson said softly.

Paul began to run. His common sense told him that there was no reason to assume that Anne was involved; she might well have been over the river and completely safe by now. He had been nowhere near the lower fords, leaving their defence to Wheeler, in command of the 112th and 115th while Paul joined Alten in covering the upper fords where most of the column was crossing with the 110th and his rifles, KGL and Portuguese battalions. Using two of his young ensigns as runners, Paul had kept in touch with Johnny through the day until Ensign Jones had been badly hit by a stray musket ball from tirailleurs in the woods. Paul had sent Sergeant O'Keeffe, his bandmaster, with three men to help carry Jones to safety and had told Ensign Loftus to discontinue his messages unless it was urgent.

Paul had been trying hard to get his wounded down and across the river, but he knew with miserably certainty, that men who had fallen and could not easily be reached would be left behind. This was not a battlefield with a victor and a loser it was a desperate scramble for survival, and once the Allied army were across the river, there would be no going back to bury the dead or retrieve the wounded. Paul had been told that Captain Dawson of the 52nd, one of the few officers killed, had been given a hasty burial where he had fallen, but many would not.

Paul led his men at full speed through the trees, risking a broken ankle in the fading light. Cutting down towards the ford, he followed the sounds of battle and came to a skidding halt as he emerged from the woods, his heart stopping for a moment at the tableau below in the river.

A line of stranded wagons and baggage animals were strung out across the river. Horses and oxen were thrashing about in terror, threatening to upset the big carriage which Paul recognised in horror as belonging to his wife. On the opposite bank, drivers, muleteers, servants and camp followers were scrambling to safety, dragged up the steep bank by the men of the seventh division, but a lone woman stood stranded in the ford. There was a fighting melee of French cavalry and British infantry in the river and one French hussar was walking his horse towards the girl, his sabre raised.

Paul heard himself call her name. He could do nothing; he was too far away although he could see several of the men in the river splashing frantically towards her. The opposite bank was closer, and Paul could not believe that none of the men of the seventh were going in to try to help her.

As he had the thought, several things happened all at the same time in a confused blur of movement. A fallen cavalry horse, which had been thrashing about in the water, suddenly struggled to its feet and stood shaking itself. Anne had turned her head at the sound of Paul shouting her name and seemed to be scanning the far bank searching for him, but now she spun around with surprising speed, given her condition, and grasped the bridle of the horse. The animal reared in fright, almost knocking the girl off her feet, but she hung on grimly. Paul knew she could not possibly mount the horse without help, especially in her condition, but she managed to get herself behind it, using it as a barrier. It would buy her seconds only, but it gave Paul, racing down to the water's edge, illogical hope.

At the same time, three men tumbled into the river from the opposite bank. Paul recognised them as Dr Oliver Daniels and two of his hospital mates, Gibson and Garrett. None of the three would be armed; they must have seen what was happening from the safety of the hospital wagons which had already crossed and were running to try to help Anne. The hussar was urging his horse forward, edging round the riderless horse, and Anne was pressing herself closer to the animal, but the sight of the Frenchman unnerved the horse and it reared up again, throwing Anne back into the water. She fell heavily, with a cry of pain, and the horseman was above her, cutting down with his sabre. Paul heard himself say her name again, this time as a whisper.

There was a blur of movement and the cavalryman gave a scream. Something hit him hard as he stooped for the kill, ripping into his arm with a snarl and dragging him from his horse. Paul could see nothing more; both horses were stampeding in terror and Paul felt a new fear, that his wife would be trampled where she lay. He was more than halfway across the river before both horses, mad with terror, galloped past him. The cavalry was retreating, driven back now by a steady volley of musket fire which Johnny Wheeler had managed to set up on the edge of the bank, and Paul could see that both Michael O'Reilly and Simon Carlyon had reached his wife. Seconds later, the three medical men joined them, and Paul felt his legs, running through the water, go weak with sheer relief as he saw her on her feet, soaked and dripping but able to stand.

"Nan, stand still, for God's sake, and let me look at you," Daniels was saying, as Paul reached them. "Are you hurt anywhere?"

"No," Anne said. Her eyes were looking past Paul into the water, and as Daniels let her go, thinking she was about to move into Paul's arms, she moved instead to a shape in the water and Paul understood suddenly what had happened to the French hussar. The hussar lay dead; either Simon or Michael had killed him before he regained his feet, and beside him, in a sodden mass, lay Anne's shaggy grey dog.

"Craufurd. Come on boy, don't you dare die on me, not after this," Anne was saying. She was lifting the dog's head out of the water into her lap, frantically searching through the thick fur for a pulse. Paul turned and scanned the opposite bank, then swore.

"Bloody hell, they've infantry coming down. As though this day could get any fucking worse. Captain O'Reilly."

"Sir."

"You are a hero. Get your men over here and get all these wagons and that carriage across the river. If possible, round up the mules, none of them have gone far. We need those bloody supplies or we're all going to die of starvation before we get to safety; I don't agree with Wellington's habit of abandoning all our stores every five minutes, it's fucking madness in these conditions. Get them over, up that bank, and to a safe place, I don't care where. And then you can start collecting our people together and feed them, if you can. And if any of those wagons aren't ours, take them anyway, it serves the stupid bastards right for not looking after them."

"Right away, sir." Michael turned, calling orders to his men and Paul turned to Simon Carlyon.

"Mr Carlyon, you are also a hero. Get back over to Colonel Wheeler, thank him for saving my wife's life with his muskets, and tell him to hold them off until the rest of the baggage wagons are over. He'll have to make a fighting retreat over the ford when it's clear. Tell him he's at liberty to kick those cowardly bastards from the seventh in the river if they get in his way."

"Yes, sir." Carlyon took off, splashing through the shallows, and Paul turned to Anne. Craufurd had revived and was choking violently, coughing muddy water into Anne's lap.

"I see he's alive, bonny lass."

"Yes, but he's struggling to get up." Anne raised a white face to his, and the misery in her eyes broke Paul's heart. "I think the horse kicked him. Paul, please."

Paul hesitated for a moment. He knew that it was madness, and that he should to get back to his men, to be sure they had made it over the upper fords, but he could not, at this moment, add to Anne's suffering. General Alten was in command and Carl had his men and he trusted both of them.

"Oliver, will you and Gibbons and Garrett help her over and up the bank. As soon as Michael gets that carriage up, I want you inside it, Nan, well out of firing range."

Anne met his eyes and he saw tears overflow, running down her already wet cheeks. "Thank you," she whispered. "You promise?"

"If I can, Nan. Get moving. I love you."

Paul watched her go, then looked over at the other bank where Johnny was marshalling his men to face the oncoming French infantry. Then he looked down at Craufurd.

The dog looked back up at him with huge brown eyes. As Paul bent, he struggled in the water, managing to pull himself up, but when he tried to move, his back legs gave way. Paul had no idea if a leg was broken and if the dog could survive the injury, but he was not prepared to break his word to Anne. Bending, he lifted the dog up and onto his shoulder.

Craufurd yelped in pain and struggled for a moment. Paul held him, as if carrying a young child, hoping his body would soothe the animal. To his relief, after a moment, the dog seemed to relax in his arms. He was heavier because of the weight of water in his shaggy fur, but he did not fight as Paul splashed his way over to the bank. It was difficult to climb out and he was thankful when hands reached to help him, and several officers and men from the seventh division hauled him up to more level ground.

"Sir - is that a dog you're carrying?"

Paul turned to glare at the young lieutenant. "No, it's a fucking elephant, lieutenant. And yes, I'm carrying him because he can't walk, because he picked up an injury saving the life of my wife, with more courage and a lot more brain than your bunch of lily-livered cowards. Our people are all across, get your men down there to help haul those wagons and animals up this bank, or your name is going to be on Lord Wellington's desk in a few days' time, with a recommendation that you be court-martialled for dereliction of duty. Where did they go?"

Paul found his wife at the centre of a group of crying women. Daniels had found an area of raised ground beneath a few cork oak trees and the earth was damp but not as boggy as some of the lower ground. All around them the men of the army were settling into sodden misery. He could still hear the booming of the French guns as they searched for the range to do some damage to the final retreat and to the men waiting for daylight on the far bank.

Paul lowered Craufurd very carefully to the grass and the dog lay still, not moving, but still breathing and alert. Paul straightened and looked for his wife, and Anne broke away from Teresa's embrace and came into his arms. She was soaked and cold and shivering and Paul kissed her for a long time.

"Oh love, what a bloody nightmare," he murmured. "I hope you'll be all right, you're freezing, and I've not a dry blanket to give you."

"I know. It's all right, Paul. Look, they're bringing up the carriage. And some of the men are trying to get a fire going. At least it's not raining."

Paul kissed her again. "I want to stay with you," he said. "But I can't, I need to get back to my men. Oliver, thank you for what you did back there. You too Garrett and Gibson. You weren't even armed, that was incredibly brave. I'm leaving her in your care; I'll rejoin you later, once the crossing is complete."

"We'll look after her, sir."

Craufurd barked suddenly. Anne turned to look at him, and Paul realised, in considerable surprise, that the dog was sitting up. He barked again, and Anne dropped to her knees in the mud and put her arms around him, kissing his soaked, shaggy head.

"You're going to be all right," she whispered. "You saved my life, and that of my baby, you silly, oversized hound. We will get you settled by the fire and in the morning, Oliver will help me get you into that carriage. You are going to make it. I am determined that you will."

Paul could feel himself smiling, tears behind his eyes. He stooped and kissed Anne's wet cheek, running his hand over Craufurd's ears. "Best listen to her, lad," he said. "She's never wrong. Try and get some rest, bonny lass. I'll be back as soon as I can."

***

There was little sleep to be had that night. At approximately one in the morning, Wellington circulated orders throughout the central column that the march was to resume before dawn. Most of Paul's brigade had come in during the night, often straggling in small groups, searching through the mass of the army for the rest of their comrades. It was impossible to do a full head count or check for losses. There had been heavy fighting for the Light Division on both the upper and lower fords, but surprisingly few deaths.

Paul had been astonished, when he joined his men well after dark, to find that several blazing fires were giving off a good heat, and a smell of slightly burned meat filled the air. He searched for his wife and found her seated beside one of the fires, feeding scraps to Craufurd, who was curled up beside her. The fire was drying her clothing and one of the women had constructed a makeshift clotheshorse out of branches, which had Anne's blue cloak and Teresa's grey one spread out to dry.

Paul bent to kiss Anne and lowered himself to the damp grass beside her. "Where did the feast come from?" he enquired, bewildered.

"Bullocks, sir," Sergeant-Major Carter informed him, passing a mess tin. "Several wagons went over in the fords and the beasts didn't get up. They belonged to the fifth division, I think, but they just cut the traces and salvaged what they could from the wagons. Sergeant Kelly got some of the 112th down there to haul them up here. It's a bit tough, but very tasty, and we've fed the brigade with them."

Paul began to eat, forcing himself not to bolt the food down. "Where's Jenson?" he asked, suddenly realising that there was no sign of his orderly."

"He'll be back soon, sir," Sergeant Hammond said. "He's just taken some of the grooms for a bit of a midnight stroll."

Paul stared at him, the food halfway to his mouth. "Grazing?" he breathed.

"Yes, sir. Captain Fallon and Lieutenant Wynne-Smythe went exploring as soon as we were settled. This area is too muddy and churned up to be of much use, but they found a couple of fields with some grass. It means we can hold on to the last of our fodder for the march tomorrow. It got a bit wet in the river, could do with drying out."

"At least the rain has stopped," Paul said. He passed his empty tin to Hammond and reached for Anne's hand, raising it to his lips. "How are you feeling, girl of my heart? I've been worried sick about you."

"I'm fine, Paul. Better for some food. Jenson tells me we'll be able to use the carriage tomorrow, with the horses properly grazed tonight. I'm going to pretend to be a lady and rest as much as I can. I'll have good company."

She scratched Craufurd's ear and the big dog shifted with a sigh of contentment, stretching his paws out towards the blaze. Paul laughed and eased the dog back a little.

"Don't you dare set fire to yourself, you daft animal, after I abandoned my duty and put my back out carrying you to safety."

Craufurd turned his head and licked Paul's hand and Paul ruffled his ears. "You lie there and enjoy it, lad," he said. "It's going to be a while before I start threatening you again."

"He was so brave," Anne said. "Michael said that he literally took that hussar out of the saddle."

"He did," Paul said, running his fingers through Craufurd's tangled fur. "He grabbed him by the arm. Once he was off the horse, there was no way he was getting up again. Leo tells me that Simon Carlyon well-nigh took his head off. Good day's work, as well, going after a woman like that."

"It wasn't the first time," Captain Manson said, settling down on the other side of Paul. Like Anne he was beginning to dry out in the heat of the fire and Paul was amused to see that his hair was drying in odd, spiky clumps, making him look like a slightly menacing hedgehog. Paul had noticed that recently, Manson had abandoned the army tradition of long hair, tied back, in favour of a short style similar to his own. Paul wondered if he currently looked equally as demented and was glad he had no mirror to tell him.

"What do you mean?" Paul asked.

Manson reached into his coat for his flask and passed it to Paul. "I was talking to Cadell from the 28th and he tells me that the Polish lancers cut down a few of the women who had fallen behind at Matilla. And when they captured part of a baggage train on its way from Madrid, they took a number of women with it, got drunk and raped several of them. A couple of the men got away afterwards and reported that the only way the French commander could stop it was to set up a false alarm of an attack."

Paul glanced over at Anne, knowing that Manson's story would bring back painful memories of her own ordeal. Anne's lovely face was pensive in the firelight as she stroked Craufurd's nose. "War can turn men into brutes," she said quietly. "Look at our own men, in Badajoz. And that girl that Michael seems to have adopted was abused by English soldiers. I don't excuse any of it, Paul. But I'm telling you that the second hussar, who was shot down, was not going to attack when he saw me properly and realised I was pregnant. It's a pity the seventh shot the wrong one."

"It's a pity the seventh didn't do their job from the start," Paul said caustically. "Where in God's name is Johnny? They should have been back hours ago."

"The firing only stopped about thirty minutes ago, sir," Manson said. Craufurd had wriggled his way closer to the fire again and was idly chewing on the sleeve of Anne's pelisse. "It'll be slow going, making the crossing in the dark, you can't see a thing and there's no moon."

"I think I'll walk down there, see if I can see them."

"Don't," Anne said.

Paul looked round at her in surprise. She had seemed completely calm after her ordeal in the river; more concerned about her dog than herself and the child she carried. He realised suddenly that he might well have got that wrong, and he shifted closer to her and drew her into his arms.

"I'm going nowhere unless I have to, Nan. You are so brave, sometimes; I take it for granted. You must have been terrified out there."

He felt her snuggle into him with a little sound of happiness. "There wasn't time to think about it, Paul. I just reacted."

"I'm often the same in battle," Paul admitted. "But Christ, Nan, you were quick with that horse, it was a stroke of genius. It bought some time for the men to reach you."

"It bought time for Craufurd to reach me," Anne said. "Charlie had him on the leash on the bank, but he broke away."

Craufurd appeared to hear his name. He turned his head and then sat up, looking around.

"Down, boy," Paul said. "You need the rest."

Craufurd looked at him and twitched his eyebrows meaningfully. Then to Paul's surprise he stood up and walked a few careful steps before settling back down against Anne's other side.

"He walked," Anne said in delight, reaching out to caress the dog's ears. "Well done, Craufurd. Clever boy."

"I don't think he's broken anything," Paul said reaching over her to run his hand over the dog's injured leg. "Keep him in the carriage anyway, though, I..."

"Men coming up, sir," Carter called. "I think it's the 112th and the rest of the 115th."

"Thank God for that," Paul said, getting to his feet. "What in God's name have they been doing down there, having a midnight swim? I..."

He broke off as the men climbing the steep rise came into view. They were not marching in line. They came in groups, some helping injured comrades along. All were dripping and walked with the leaden steps of exhausted men, driven beyond their endurance. Around the fires, men were getting up to make room for them, helping them to sit down and in some cases to lie on the damp grass. Paul was scanning their ranks frantically for Johnny or Gervase Clevedon or Pat Corrigan.

"Sir."

Paul ran forward. Major Clevedon was soaked to the skin, covered in mud and bleeding from a savage gash down his left cheek. He looked as though he could barely put one foot in front of the other, but it was the expression in his eyes in the firelight that chilled Paul.

"Major, what happened?"

"Gervase, come and sit down, and have something to drink," Anne interrupted him. "You can talk at the same time."

212

"Ma'am, I can't. I need to tell you." Clevedon's voice told Paul that it was going to be bad. He put a hand on his friend's arm.

"Gervase, breathe. She's right, come and sit. We've managed tea although there's no milk or sugar. Sergeant-Major, make sure the rest of the men are fed, as far as we can."

"Yes, sir."

Paul looked at Major Clevedon, who lowered himself wearily to sit beside the fire. Manson passed him a cup without speaking and Gervase drank.

"Is this all of them, Gervase?"

"Probably not," Gervase said. "They're still coming in, will be for a while, I hope. I've brought about three quarters of them back, but we couldn't search any more for the rest, it was too dark up there, and it was alerting their infantry to where we were. So I don't know. We lost about ten dead from the 112th, they were cut down by the cavalry. And about another twenty were taken prisoner. Not sure about the 115th. I know Captain Lewis was taken, about half a dozen of his men and I think one of his officers - it might have been Carlyon."

"Oh no," Anne said.

"I'm sorry, ma'am. Witham says he didn't see him fall, but he's not here. He might still make it back."

"Major, what happened? You were supposed to be covering the last of the baggage wagons coming over and then retreating."

"We did," Clevedon said, bitterly. "But the rest of the divisions who crossed at the other fords must have made it over ahead of us. We were holding off the infantry coming from the woods and Colonel Wheeler had called them in ready to make a fighting retreat over the ford. All of a sudden there were hussars, coming up the bank, I think they'd cut down from the other ford. Then they began shelling us; they'd shifted some of the guns to the top of the slope above us. They can't have been able to see much in the end, but it didn't matter, they'd got the range. We were trapped between the infantry, the cavalry and the artillery.

"Oh fuck," Paul breathed. He was afraid to ask the question, but he knew he needed to. "Gervase, where's Johnny?"

"I don't know," Clevedon said honestly. "Paul, I'm hoping to God he's been taken prisoner. Like Carlyon, nobody saw him go down, but he stayed to the end, trying to make sure they all got out."

"How did you get out?" Paul asked. He was trying to visualise the lay of the land, but it was difficult, he could only really imagine the section of the river that his own men had defended. "Is there another ford?"

"Do I look like I crossed by a ford?" Clevedon said with some asperity, accepting a mess tin from Corporal Cooper. "Thanks, Coops. I suppose it was a ford, or we wouldn't have made it, but I doubt it shows on a map as one. Johnny took us back up into the trees, which got us out of the firing line of the guns, at least. We made our way upwards, skirmishing the whole way, and eventually reached the river where it falls down into a deepish gorge. You couldn't get horses across it. Reminded me a bit of the Coa, to be

213

honest. But without the bridge, and a bit deeper."

"You went across that? In the dark?"

"Not much choice. The Colonel gave the order to make their own way across and get back here as we could. It was a bastard of a climb in the dark, we had to feel our way. A few men fell. Not sure if they made it. Most of the lads abandoned their packs and muskets at that point."

"Those can be replaced." Paul was studying his friend's face. "There's something else," he said, and suddenly knew what it was. "Gervase, where's Pat Corrigan?"

"He's dead, Paul," Clevedon said, and Paul understood now, the ragged grief in Clevedon's voice. He and Corrigan had been close friends. "He didn't make it out of the woods. Cavalry sabre, I think. Young Witham went back in to look for him. I called him back, I was pretty sure Pat was dead, but Witham was having none of it. He came out in tears. Poor bastard, what with that, and losing Carlyon. I hope he and Johnny made it. I hope they're prisoners. Or that they took another route and will show up by morning."

Behind Paul, somebody moved, getting up and walking away into the darkness. Paul knew who it was. He looked over and saw Keren Trenlow hand the sleeping baby back to Teresa and get up to follow Carl. Of all of them, Carl had been closest to Major Patrick Corrigan. Paul let her go. He had faith in Keren's ability to comfort Carl and he needed to stay with Clevedon, who was crying quietly now.

Paul put his arm about his friend and sat in silence. He had a sudden clear memory of the jovial, round faced Irishman emerging into a freezing dawn on a parade ground in Dublin six years earlier.

*"Morning, Lieutenant Corrigan. Jenson, get Mr Corrigan some coffee."*

*"You have to be all about in your heads. You don't even have a senior officer with you, and you're out here freezing your arses off. And you're crazier than the rest of them, sir. Don't you have a rather pretty wife tucked up in bed?"* Corrigan had regarded the four companies of the 110th moving across the parade ground. *"Mary mother of God, I'm not putting my lot out here at the same time as these, even I'd be embarrassed. You've practiced this, haven't you, sir?"*

It had set the tone for Paul's relationship with Patrick Corrigan for the next six years. He had found the Irishman immensely likeable, and a good soldier in the field, but infuriatingly lazy in barracks. It had not stopped him asking for Corrigan to be transferred to the 112th when Paul had been desperately short of officers, and he had enjoyed a good relationship with Corrigan, interspersed with occasional moments of frustration at Corrigan's carefree attitude to his duties. Paul wanted to say something, but was finding it difficult to speak, as though he had been punched hard in the gut. Anne moved closer and put her arms around him and he leaned his head against her. He could feel by the quiver of her body that she was crying, and he wondered why he was not. He was too shocked for tears.

Through the night, waiting for orders, Paul sat quietly, thinking about

Johnny Wheeler. Memories crowded in on him, the taciturn young lieutenant teaching him about drills and tactics for long hours aboard their first ship to India. Johnny laughing outside the walls of Ahmednaggur and then lying injured almost to death after the battle of Assaye. Johnny dancing with Anne in Lisbon. Johnny thanking him with muted joy after his first promotion to captain and then major. Johnny, helping to save all of them on the day that Anne had almost been murdered by her deranged first husband. It was impossible to imagine life without his steady, competent presence. Silently, Paul prayed for his friend. Captivity would probably last the rest of the war; the French did not often exchange prisoners. But unless he had been badly wounded, Johnny would probably survive it and come home eventually. Paul was trying to focus on that possibility; he could not bear to contemplate that Johnny might be dead, or even worse, dying out in the forest, knowing that nobody could come for him.

Men continued to straggle in through the night, starving and exhausted, telling tales of wandering lost in the forest for hours. Paul thanked God that he had insisted on salvaging the supply wagons and that his quartermaster had found a source of grazing. By the time the wagons were hitched, and the men stood to arms before daylight, both men and horses had been fed; not enough, but at least something, and considerably more than some of the other divisions. Marching out into the darkness, Paul wondered how the other two columns of Wellington's army had fared.

\*\*\*

Simon Carlyon regained consciousness slowly. Coming back to the world was an assault on all of his senses. He was wet through and shivering with cold. Although the rain seemed finally to have stopped, water still dripped from the trees. There was a heavy scent of rotting vegetation which made him feel slightly sick, and shifting his head, Simon realised that his face was half buried in the forest floor. He could almost taste the decay in his mouth, along with the metallic flavour of blood. Around him was darkness, with no sign of movement and no sounds apart from the rustling noises of forest creatures and a slight wind through the trees.

It was that which forced him to move. He had no idea what lived in woodland in this part of Spain, but he was fairly sure that whatever it was, would be willing to feed off a dead body, and he had no desire to slip into unconsciousness again and wake up to find a rat gnawing at his arm. It had happened to somebody he had known in India once, after a drunken spree and a bad fall, and the man had seemed more shocked by the rat than the broken arm he had suffered.

With an effort, Simon pushed himself into a sitting position. Cautiously he took stock of his injuries and discovered that they were not that serious. The blood seemed to have come from a cut over his right eye. It was deep and painful and was probably the reason for his banging headache, but once he had managed to scrub away the dried blood which gummed up his eye,

215

he could see perfectly well, and he was completely mobile.

Carefully, Simon got to his feet. He could see nothing in the darkness at first, but very gradually his eyes became accustomed to the dark, and he was able to make out his sword, lying a foot away from him. Simon picked it up, sheathed it, and checked his pockets. Nothing was missing although everything was soaked through, which suggested that the French had either been driven off or had withdrawn of their own accord. Even his water bottle was still hanging from its strap and Simon drank gratefully then used a little to wash some of the blood away. He did not expect to be short of water in his present situation.

Memory came back to him slowly. He had been making his way through the trees, conducting a running retreat after the French attack had killed Major Corrigan. Simon remembered seeing two of his men go down under the cavalry sabres, and then one of the horses had stumbled on the uneven forest floor. It was poor terrain for a cavalry attack, and the hussar had fallen heavily, almost at Simon's feet. Before he had had time to rise, the terrified horse had come down on top of both of them, and Simon could remember no more.

Simon looked around. Knowing what he was looking for, he found the body of the hussar only a few feet away. The man's head was a bloody pulp, smashed by the hooves of his panicking mount, and Simon felt slightly sick at what might so easily have happened to him. He felt the head wound again gently, and then made himself kneel and go through the hussar's pockets. He found little that was useful; the French were probably as short of food as the Allies by now, but he removed a wicked looking knife in a leather sheath and put it into his inner coat pocket.

Simon guessed that by now, Wellington's army would be across the river. He had no idea how many of his own battalion had made it through the difficult fight in the forest area, but he knew that they could not come back for him. There was no sign of the French here, but he knew they would be nearby, probably still guarding the main fords, possibly planning to launch an attack across them when daylight came. If Simon wanted to find a way across the river and back to the army, he was on his own.

Warmth and some shelter were his immediate needs. Simon remembered that the skirmishers of the 112th had run back with the news that there was another way across the river, via a difficult climb down a steep gorge. Simon had a vague sense of the direction and he wanted to keep moving. It would be slow going through the woods in darkness, but it was very cold, and he was concerned that if he lay down to rest, he would freeze to death. Feeling his way from tree to tree was tedious, and progress was agonisingly slow, but at least he was moving.

It was a relief when Simon became aware of an almost imperceptible lightening of the sky. He could see the shapes of trees properly now, and there were fewer stubbed toes and grazed shins. He could see other things as well, as dawn stretched lazily across the sky, with a surprising hint of sunlight. Here and there on the forest floor were the corpses of dead men, both French and

British.

When the sun was fully up, Simon stopped for the first time. He filled his water bottle from a small stream and ate his last two hard biscuits from his pocket. There was also a shrivelled apple, which Anne had given him, and after a moment's debate, he ate that too. He might well need his strength for the day's march.

When he started again, he came across two more corpses, both skirmishers from the 112th. The bodies looked untouched as yet, apart from some damage to the faces, probably by rodents. Simon gritted his teeth and set aside his revulsion. One of the men was wearing an army greatcoat and both had muskets and packs. Clearly the French had not stopped to loot in the dark and had not been back this way since, which gave him hope. Methodically, Simon went through both packs, sorting out anything that might be useful for a long march. He discarded unnecessary heavy objects, but he equipped himself with a musket and ammunition and took the coat. Despite the bright morning sunlight, it was still very cold.

He came upon the gorge more quickly than he had expected. Coming out of the edge of the woods, he found his way blocked by a mossy fallen tree trunk. Simon had heard no sign of troops of either side, but he felt slightly exposed beyond the trees. Simon put his foot on to the trunk and stepped up, his whole body tense, scanning the surrounding area quickly. His momentum almost carried him forward but at the last minute he realised what was happening and threw himself backwards, landing hard behind the tree, his heart pounding in fright. He lay there for a moment, recovering from the shock of what he had almost done, then he got to his feet and climbed very cautiously over the tree. There was a short stretch of long grass and then nothing.

Simon stepped forward and looked down into the gorge. It was difficult to estimate how deep it was, but he could hear the rush of the river below, running fast after the last days of rain, and he could not see it, could see nothing but thick shrubs and bushes and a few warped trees clinging to the steep sides. Another step would have taken him over the edge and although he might have been lucky enough to be caught on a bush, he might equally have tumbled to his death at the bottom.

Thoughtfully Simon surveyed the climb ahead of him. The opposite side of the ravine looked much shallower, and he could see more woods on the far side. If he made it across, he should be able to follow the river round and find his way back to the fords where the rest of the army had crossed. If he was lucky, the French would have withdrawn, he could find some food, and make his way on towards Ciudad Rodrigo, possibly catching up with the main force, since he should be able to travel faster. If he was unlucky, he might be picked up by the French, killed or captured, or he might die of cold or hunger.

Simon was a natural optimist and refused to dwell on the possibility of failure. Settling his looted pack and musket more comfortably, he studied the edge of the ravine again and very slowly and cautiously began his climb, using rocks, bushes and trees as hand and footholds, testing each one to make sure it was solid.

After climbing for a few minutes, he stopped and twisted his head to look down. To his surprise he could see the river already. The steep sides had been deceptive at the top, the gorge was not particularly deep and already the slopes were becoming shallower, running down to the river which was fast flowing and looked fordable. There were huge boulders lining the banks and the vegetation was sparser down there.

Simon shifted his position and continued to climb. He was cold but not unbearably so, although he suspected that during the night it would be worse. At some point he might be obliged to try to find shelter, but away from the river and the threat of the French, there might be a village or a lone farm which would give him space by the fire for the night, and possibly even some food.

He was probably only a few feet from the bottom when he heard a new sound, unconnected to the rush of the water and the rustle of the breeze through the trees. Simon froze, listening carefully. It came from below him, down by the river, and at first Simon thought it was an animal or a bird. As it moved closer, he listened intently and realised that it was neither. It was the sound of breathing, a man moving slowly and with difficulty along the bank of the river.

Simon remained very still. Impossible to tell anything about the man, but his effort to keep quiet suggested he was trying to avoid detection, which probably meant that he was more likely to be British than French. Simon did not move and after a few minutes the sounds stopped as if the other man too was listening.

Simon began to climb again, very cautiously. Below him, the movement stilled, the breath held, and Simon imagined a man holding himself immobile, flinching at every sound. He did not dare to call out. He thought it was probably an ally but it might possibly be a Frenchman with a loaded musket. At the bottom, Simon made his way slowly towards the place where he had last heard the movement.

He could see the man immediately, sitting with his back against a large rock, trying to keep as still as possible. This close, he could see the blood soaking the man's left leg, the grey regulation trousers stained red. It looked like a bad wound and Simon wondered if the man had stopped because he wanted to, or because he had to. The sight reassured him though; the uniform was undoubtedly British. Simon wondered if he was armed and he stopped, not wanted to get himself shot by a man looking for French infantry.

"Don't fear, I'm English. Lieutenant Carlyon, 115th. Did you come over in the dark last night?" he called.

There was a brief pause and then the other man stirred. "I did," he said. "Somewhat faster than that very careful descent I just heard you make, I must say, but then I rather think I fell half of it. Good morning, Mr Carlyon."

Simon felt a frisson of shock at the voice which he knew very well. He thought, confusedly, that of all the men he wanted to be in this position with, Colonel John Wheeler was probably the last, but it could not be helped. He slid down the last short distance and joined Wheeler behind the rocks.

"Sir," he said, saluting. "I didn't know it was you. I got knocked out during the skirmish, woke up on my own and made my way here, hoping to find my way across. How are you?"

Wheeler attempted a smile. "Not that good," he said. "Hit in the thigh, it's bleeding still. Hard to walk."

Simon knelt down beside him and looked an enquiry. Wheeler nodded. Simon bent to examine the wound and probed very carefully. He felt the other man flinch under his hands. The wound was deep and ragged and was bleeding profusely.

"I don't know much about surgery," Simon said awkwardly. "But it doesn't look as though it's gone through; the gash goes right down your leg. It's a very deep wound though."

"I think you're right," the Colonel said. Simon glanced at him and saw that his eyes were closed and there were beads of sweat on his forehead and his upper lip. "Look, lad, you need to get yourself out of here. Sooner or later the French are going to find me, I'll be all right."

Simon looked at him and recognised the lie. "The French have gone, sir. So have our troops. Any poor bugger lying wounded in those woods is going to die that way if they can't get themselves moving, and I think you know it. Are you hurt anywhere else?"

"I'm covered in bruises from my somewhat rapid descent down that cliff, but otherwise, no."

"That's good," Simon said. "The scouts said there's a place you can get across down here."

"There is, just up there. It's deep, but it's fordable. For you, at least."

Simon looked at him. He felt a deep and abiding misery that he was going to have to take responsibility for this man, when he had thought he could catch up with the army in a day, and he also wished that it had not been this particular man with whom he felt so uncomfortable. Wheeler had closed his eyes against the pain.

"I can help you," Simon said.

Wheeler opened his eyes and studied him with the grey eyes which lent distinction to his otherwise pleasant face. "Get going," he said quietly. "It's an order, Mr Carlyon. Once you're across, you can follow the line of the river until you reach the other fords. From there it shouldn't be hard to follow the tracks of the army. You might even catch up with them before they reach Ciudad Rodrigo. If you don't, you'll find them there. Tell Colonel van Daan I was taken prisoner."

"You mean tell him you might be, sir. Or you might be dead. Or lying here dying of cold and hunger."

"If you don't get moving, we might both die of cold and hunger."

Simon looked at the older man for a long time. Finally, he shook his head, pushing unworthy thoughts to one side. "I need to bind up that wound," he said. "Crossing the river and getting you up the other side is going to be the hardest part. After that, we'll just take it slowly and rest often. We'll get there, sir."

The grey eyes hardened slightly. "It's an order, Lieutenant. Get moving."

"I'm not going to obey it, sir. I'm going to get you out of here."

Unexpectedly, Wheeler smiled, and it transformed his face. "Lad, thank you. But I'm not going to make it."

"Maybe not. Maybe you'll die on the way. In which case I'll bury you and I'll take your message back to the Colonel. But I'm not leaving you out here to die alone. I wouldn't do that to any man."

Simon realised, even as he said it, how it had sounded, but he could do nothing to retrieve it. He saw Wheeler's expression and then the Colonel said:

"Even the man who killed your brother?"

Simon took a deep steadying breath. "Especially him," he said. "Because if I let you die, even if it was by your order, I'd always wonder. I mean…"

"You'd always wonder if you'd have tried harder to save another man," Wheeler finished for him. "You don't need to wonder that, Mr Carlyon. I can already tell you that you're not that person. Come on then, let's get this blasted leg tied up and we'll see if you can get me across that river."

# Chapter Sixteen

Wellington led off the central column of his army before dawn. Paul's brigade had spent a better night than many, and with most of the horses and pack animals fed, at least a little, they were able to make slightly better progress than many of the other divisions. Progress was still very slow; the country did not make marching easy. The landscape was covered with shrubs and dwarf oaks and the tracks were narrow and still very muddy, although for the first time in what seemed like weeks, a cold, bright sun lit the sky.

Surprisingly there was no sign of the French. Wellington had expected pursuit to continue at dawn and the Light Division had stood in grim readiness to defend the rest of the army as it set off on the last leg of the journey. The attack did not come, and apart from a few pickets and some distant cavalry, keeping watch, the enemy made no attempt to engage. Paul thought it was just as well, given that the rest of his column were desperately slow to move off, making Paul long to ride up to the first division and explain to General Sir William Stewart how to manage his troops.

Paul had quickly lost faith in his Spanish guide and with the horses a little recovered after a night's rest and some grazing, he sent out scouts of his own. He had been delighted to discover, during the previous day's skirmishing and endless waiting on the riverbanks, that one of his former officers and now a member of the corps of guides, Captain Giles Fenwick, had joined Wellington's army and was marching with the headquarters staff. Fenwick had been acting as an exploring officer for eighteen months now and knew the Spanish countryside as well as many of the locals. He joined Paul on the march and spent his time in the saddle scouting ahead along with his Spanish guide, Antonio, returning with a wealth of useful information.

"You can't take horses and pack animals that way, sir," Fenwick said, bringing his horse to a walk beside Paul's. "Christ knows what this guide has been drinking, but he should cut back. There's a stream about a mile ahead which is very deep. The first brigade is using a fallen tree to get across, to avoid leaving too big a gap, but they're searching for another path for the horses. I've sent Antonio ahead, he'll find the best route."

"Captain Fenwick, you're invaluable. I'll slow them all down and wait for more information. Have you informed General Alten?"

"He was there, sir, I've spoken to him and told him I'll let him know the best route for the baggage. How is Mrs van Daan; I heard what happened yesterday?"

"She seems surprisingly well, although very tired today. We're keeping the horses fed and trusting you to find us the best route to Ciudad Rodrigo before the fodder runs out; she's promised she'll stay in the carriage."

"With her dog, sir?" Fenwick said innocently.

Paul rolled his eyes. "Winter quarters is going to dine out on the story of me carrying my wife's dog out of the line of fire, isn't it?"

"Personally, I enjoyed the part where you compared the stalwarts of the 68th unfavourably to that carpet on legs. Will he be all right?"

"I think he will. One of the horses kicked him, but he's able to walk now although it clearly hurts. He'd better be because I can't separate him from Nan at the moment."

Fenwick studied him. "I'm sorry about Colonel Wheeler, sir. I hope he's all right. And Major Corrigan. It was bloody awful; most of the other divisions got off pretty lightly."

"Most of my brigade did; I only lost one man from the 110th," Paul said. "I've heard nothing yet about the Colonel, I'm hoping he's a prisoner, in which case we'll hear. Young Simon Carlyon, Nan's brother-in-law is missing as well. It's the oddest thing, I've never had an officer taken prisoner before, I don't know much about the procedure for getting information, but Lord Wellington has already heard from Paget, so I'm hoping we'll have news in a day or two. Giles, thank you for today, you've been a huge help."

The long day dragged on for Wellington's exhausted army. The cavalry was suffering badly, their horses dying or having to be shot when they could go no further. In some regiments there were more men without horses than with. Three of the officers' horses in Paul's brigade had collapsed during the march, all older animals, and several mules had also had to be shot.

Worse than the animals, were the men. Following behind the other divisions, Paul became accustomed to the sight of men lying dead of hunger, cold or sickness by the roadside. His men no longer stopped to check each one, unless it was obvious that a man still lived. Paul was agonisingly aware that he could not save every fallen man and he chose to hoard the small amount of supplies he still carried for his own men and horses. There was still no sign of the missing commissariat wagons, but Wellington had been informed that they had apparently taken the wrong route.

Wellington rode with the Light Division for some time, and Anne emerged from the carriage for an hour to ride beside him. Paul thought that his commander-in-chief looked white and drawn, but Anne's presence seemed to cheer him up. Paul rode on his other side as Anne told him what had happened during the crossing of the river. She kept it light-hearted, dwelling on the heroic conduct of her dog and failing to mention the unheroic conduct of the seventh division. Wellington heard the story to the end and turned a severe eye onto Paul.

"In future, Colonel, I think it would be best if your wife's carriage travelled with mine. She should not be travelling with the baggage wagons and the camp followers; it is completely unsuitable."

Paul suppressed a number of remarks along with a grin. "Thank you, sir, that is good of you. I am hoping not to find ourselves in this particular situation again."

"As am I, Colonel. What is it, March?"

"My apologies, sir, it appears there is a problem."

Wellington regarded his ADC glumly. "You astonish me, March. Pray, elucidate."

"It's the first division, sir."

"What of it?"

"Also, the seventh. And the fifth."

"March, I am aware of the existence of these divisions," Wellington said in glacial tones. "As yet, I am ignorant of the problem."

"They are missing, sir. Gone astray."

Wellington reined in, and Paul and Anne did the same. "Missing?" Wellington said. "Are you telling me, we have lost three divisions of my army, March?"

Lord March wilted under his chief's glare. "Not exactly, sir. It's just that they've gone a different way. Not this way. And it appears they are being followed by French cavalry."

"This is the way they were instructed to travel," Wellington said. He sounded like a man who had reached the end of his tether, and Paul, who generally rather enjoyed his commander's explosions, felt a tug of sympathy. Wellington both looked and sounded completely exhausted.

"Look, sir, things are going well here. Do you want me to go and find out…?"

"No!" Wellington shouted, and both Paul and Anne jumped; it was unheard of for the commander to raise his voice to such a degree. "You will remain here with your brigade, Colonel, and take care of your wife. March, have we any idea where they have gone?"

"Up towards the Yeltes, I believe, sir."

"That road is impassable," Wellington said. "There is a reason why I instructed this column to take a particular route. It is impossible for me to trust my generals, when they persist in disobeying the simplest order."

Anne looked over to where Corporal Jenson was riding. "Jenson, Lord Wellington must leave us, I am afraid. Before he goes, will you bring the last of the cold beef from last night; it will not keep. And there is half a bottle of the wine left."

Wellington looked at her. "Ma'am, you will not give your food away to me."

"I am well supplied, my lord." Anne met his gaze, and Paul recognised steel clashing against steel. "You would make me happy by eating and drinking before you leave. Otherwise, I will spend the day worrying about you which is not at all good for me."

Wellington visibly melted and took the food and wine from Jenson. He ate, while March waited with obvious impatience, then drank some wine and handed the flask to Anne. "I insist," he said. "It will do you good."

Anne drank. "Take care, sir," she said.

Paul watched as his chief cantered away and reached for the flask to finish the wine. "Well done, bonny lass, I'd never have got food into him, and he bloody needs it," he said. "All the same, I would not be in the shoes of Generals Stewart, Dalhousie and Oswald for all the riches of the East. Of course, I could have pointed out that if he had told them the reason for that order, they'd be more likely to have obeyed it. But it didn't seem like the right moment."

His wife gave him a sidelong look. "I'm glad you realised that," she said. "I'm feeling unaccountably fragile today, I don't think I would have been able to stand listening to you two yelling at each other."

"I suspect it would have moved very quickly from yelling to court martial this week, girl of my heart. Come on, it's time you went back into the carriage. Craufurd will be missing you."

*** 

Crossing the Huebra was agony. The water was high, and although Johnny had crossed many fords higher than this during his career, he had never done so with a serious leg wound and a mass of bruises from half falling down the ravine. He wondered, dragging himself through the freezing rushing water, if he was getting old. At thirty-seven, he had always considered himself physically very fit, but he currently felt closer to eighty than forty.

He would not have made it without Simon Carlyon. The younger man made the crossing twice, firstly on his own to test the ford and to carry his looted pack and musket over. Johnny approved the thought; it would be difficult enough, without trying to keep the weapon dry. He had also insisted on taking Johnny's army great coat and had left it spread out over a bush in the hope that it would dry a little. Johnny, perched uncomfortably on a rock, watched him wade waist high through the icy torrent and dreaded moving.

It was as bad as he had expected, possible worse. His arm about Simon's shoulders, Johnny limped painfully into the river, gasping at the cold. Initially, the shock of the freezing water took away the pain, then as he tried to move, he felt the pull of the water dragging at his weak leg, and he would have overbalanced and been swept away had Simon not held onto him grimly with both arms about him.

"Stand still for a minute, sir, catch your breath."

Johnny realised he had actually been holding his breath and he let it out slowly, not surprised to see it clouding in the cold air. He had not thought he could feel colder than he had during his miserable night at the foot of the cliff, huddled in his wet coat, wondering if he was going to die of exposure before morning, but he suspected he had been wrong. It was difficult to move his leg, but he did so, gritting his teeth and trying not to yell with pain. Slowly, step by step, he made his way out into the water. The stones under his boots were slippery, but Simon held him steady and did not try to rush him, although Johnny thought he must have been desperately cold, moving so slowly.

At its deepest, the water was almost chest high before the ground rose again and finally, after what seemed hours, they were staggering through the shallows. Johnny could feel his leg giving way, but Simon grabbed him and hauled him upright.

"Not here," he gasped. "Too close to the water. Just a few more yards, sir, up here."

He half dragged Johnny to the bottom of the slope, and Johnny understood why. An enormous rock formation, probably created by a cliff fall many years ago, had constructed a natural cave, its opening pointing down river, out of the biting wind. Simon had placed his pack and musket in the sheltered spot, and he eased Johnny to sit down with his back against the rocks. Going to the pack, he shook out two thin army blankets and tucked them around Johnny, rather as if he had been a child.

"Stay there and rest for a bit, sir. It's a fairly good breeze, I'm hoping your coat will dry a little."

"We need to get moving."

"You need to recover, or you won't be able to move at all. I'm going to try to find some food."

"Here?" Johnny said, somewhat scathingly.

"Up there," Simon said, pointing up the slope. "Rock rabbits. I saw them hopping about the first time I crossed. When we were children, my brother and I used to catch rabbits sometimes, using our hats, and I've seen the men do it over here. I'm hoping I've not lost the knack."

Simon broke off abruptly, realising what he had just said. The stricken expression on his face flooded Johnny with guilt. He was suddenly furious that this boy should have been placed in such a miserable position because of an accident of birth that left him related to a man like Robert Carlyon.

"I'll be back as soon..."

"Mr Carlyon stop a minute. We can't leave it there," Johnny said. His leg felt as though it was being ripped apart, and he was conscious too of a soreness in his ribs which might have been due to the fall. "If we do make it out of here, it could take days, with me in this state. I really do appreciate what you're doing for me, even if I doubt the wisdom of it. You're a stubborn young bastard. But you shouldn't have to tiptoe around my feelings about your brother on top of that. He was your brother. What happened later in life doesn't affect your childhood memories, and you are not to feel guilty about saying his name. And that is, by the way, an order, from a very senior officer."

"Yes, sir."

"Do you have a tinderbox in that pack of yours?"

"Two, sir, my own and one I found. Not sure which is drier."

"Hand them both over and get some wood before you go hunting. There are enough fallen trees around here, and it's quite sheltered. I might not be much use, but I can get a fire going. In fact, I'm known for the skill, I spent

225

a fair bit of my army career taking the tinderbox out of the hands of Colonel van Daan in his younger days, before he threw it at somebody; he has no patience with it. Thank God he's got Jenson, or he'd have starved."

The little anecdote surprised a laugh out of Simon. "I can't imagine the Colonel as a young subaltern," he admitted.

"It was an experience for all of us, believe me. Happy hunting, Mr Carlyon."

Both the fire and the hunting were successful. Simon returned with two rabbits and a pigeon, and they burned their fingers trying to eat the meat quickly.

"When did you last eat?" Johnny asked.

"Yesterday, I'd a couple of biscuits left. You?"

"Yesterday morning, I think. I'm rather losing track. This is good, Lieutenant. You keep this up, we might actually make it."

"We're going to make it, sir," Simon said, and Johnny laughed at the determination in his voice.

"Do you have something to do when you get back, then, lad? What's her name?"

Simon grinned. "I wish," he said. "I've not had much time for romance these last few years, apart from Valentina, which didn't end well. And besides…"

He broke off, and Johnny made a guess.

"Don't let Robert's experience of married life put you off, Lieutenant," he said gently. "I've seen some very happy marriages in the army."

"So have I, sir," Simon said. "It rather made me think, you know. Because it can't have been her doing, can it? That they were so unhappy. I always used to wonder if she was difficult. It was hard to imagine, because when I knew her as a child, I liked her best of all the girls. Not because she was pretty, although she was, of course. But because she was so natural, so friendly. Talking to her on the hunting field or at some awful party, was like talking to another boy. At thirteen, you don't want a girl simpering at you, pretending to know how to flirt. Christ, I'd no idea what to do with a girl at that age. But you could just talk to Anne Howard. When I first heard Robert had married her, do you know what my first thought was? I was jealous. I think, somewhere in my mind, I always thought that when we both grew up, I'd quite like to be married to her myself."

Johnny did not speak for a while. He was a little taken aback at the younger man's confidences, but as he had specifically given him permission to speak openly of his brother only an hour earlier, he could hardly complain. It occurred to Johnny that it must be a relief to the boy to be able to do so freely, and at this point, Johnny's gratitude was such that he was very willing to set his own discomfort to one side and listen.

"You're different to me then," he said, finally, gnawing the last scraps of meat from a bone. "One of my first impressions of Nan was that I couldn't be married to her if she was the last woman on earth." He saw the boy's expression and laughed aloud. "Oh, don't get me wrong, I liked her from the start. And I found her very attractive. Uncomfortably so, given that she was another man's wife. I was a bit of a prude in my younger days, to tell you the truth. But I found that free and easy manner too much for me. I couldn't imagine being married to a girl who behaved that way around other men."

Simon was frowning. "Do you think she…no, I'm sorry."

"At ease, lad. We're speaking freely here, we're not on the parade ground. No, I'm absolutely sure she didn't. She was the same with all of us, from Wellesley down to the Portuguese grooms, but it was just Nan being Nan. I'd be very surprised if she was ever actually unfaithful to your brother."

Simon was looking at him and Johnny knew what was coming. In different circumstances, he would have issued a sharp reminder to a junior officer to mind his own business and not be impertinent, and sent him about his business, but Simon Carlyon was risking his life to preserve Johnny's; the rules had changed.

"Ask," he said abruptly.

"All right. Not even with the Colonel?"

"He wasn't a colonel back then. Major Paul van Daan, and he had the reputation of being the worst womaniser in the army. I used to get so angry with him; he had no bloody self-control. If a lassie looked at him the right way, his marriage vows went straight out of the window. But that was in the first couple of years of his marriage. I think he'd already begun to change when he met Nan." Johnny tossed the last bone into the fire. "I wasn't there that summer, in Yorkshire. I've heard a few versions of their relationship, and I don't believe any of them. All I know was that he came back with something different about him, and then she arrived married to your brother. They don't talk much about it, and there's no reason why they should, it's their own affair. But the Colonel once told me that they both cared too much about his wife to betray her that way; Nan was her best friend. And for what it's worth, I believed him."

Simon was staring into the fire. He looked up. "Thank you," he said. "I think that's the most honest conversation I've ever had about it."

"You're welcome. To tell you the truth, I'm comfortable here and I've no wish to move, it's going to hurt like hell. But we need to. Come on, let's get going."

\*\*\*

French cavalry dogged the steps of most of Wellington's army for the whole of the day, although Paul's men, and the men of Barnard's brigade saw nothing of them, a fact which Paul attributed to the scouting abilities of Captain Fenwick and Antonio. Wellington had departed to deal with his insubordinate generals and General Alten, having listened intelligently to Fenwick's report on the best route, and on the movements of the French, made his decision.

"We will follow this road, I think," he said, studying the sketch map that Fenwick had drawn on the back of a letter. "It seems that the French are following the main part of the column. General Vandeleur has already crossed the stream, and will join up with us here, if he remains on that path, but I have seen it and it is ridiculous to take a road that narrow and muddy with no need. Can you guide us, Captain?"

"Yes, sir. Antonio is going to keep an eye on the French for me, in case they decide to change direction."

"You say they have only cavalry?"

"Yes, sir. Around two hundred at a guess, hussars and Polish lancers."

"Those bastards," Paul put in. "I'd rather they didn't catch up with us."

"I doubt they will, sir. They're picking up stragglers, taking prisoners. But they're slowing down. Their commander isn't going to want to wander behind our lines by accident."

"I believe Captain Fenwick is correct," Alten said. "We will follow his route."

Paul met his General's eyes. "It's not the route Lord Wellington is expecting us to take, sir," he said. "Are you sure...?"

Alten looked around him, his mild blue eyes scanning the surrounding forest. He turned and looked over his shoulder. Then to Paul's amusement, he gazed up into the trees, before returning his eyes to Paul and Barnard.

"I do not see Lord Wellington anywhere, do you, Colonel? Unless he is now invisible. And even then, given how enraged he must be by now, I think we would hear him."

"I should think you'd hear him two miles away, sir," Paul admitted.

"Then we will have plenty of warning of his approach. The guide, the one Colonel Vandeleur is following - what was his name? I have forgotten it."

"Luis, sir."

"Ja, Luis. If one followed Luis, which Lord Wellington gave orders that we should do, one could end up anywhere. Possibly even upon this road. And who is to say how we came to be here, after all? Give the orders, if you please."

Paul looked at him with something like awe. "Do you know, sir, I think you're worse than Craufurd. It's just you're so polite about it, nobody notices."

The road, although not easy, was considerably better than any that they had recently travelled on. There was no sign of the French cavalry and no sign of the litter of dead men and animals and abandoned wagons which Paul had grown accustomed to seeing, which made him suspect that Fenwick's route had not been used by either army.

"I wonder if this is the route that Luis was supposed to bring us?" Carl Swanson said, as he and Paul walked beside each other, leading their horses to rest them for a while.

"Very probably. I feel sorry for John's brigade, but at least we're taking care of their baggage."

"I'm told Dalhousie lost all of his to the French," Carl said, not without malice. "They must have been very happy, there was a lot of it."

"He's an Earl, Major," Paul said gravely. "He requires a great deal of baggage. Were you there in Salamanca when he asked my wife where the rest of her baggage was, along with a little jest about ladies needing their fripperies and fineries?"

"No," Carl said in tones of awe. "What did she say?"

"She smiled very sweetly and told him that her medical bag was in the carriage and the rest was before him," Keren said. "You could see him counting the bags and observing how small they were. Teresa and I had to pretend to have urgent business somewhere else, we couldn't hide that we were laughing. I hope the Earl didn't lose anything too valuable, poor man."

Carl was studying her. "You're limping," he said. "Have you hurt yourself?"

"Not really," Keren said. "I think I may have a blister. I've been trying to walk as much as possible to save poor Lily, she's exhausted."

Carl paused. "Let me see."

Keren hesitated, then put her hand on his arm to steady herself and took off her shoe. Glancing at it, Paul could already see the problem; the shoe had been worn through on the march. He heard Carl catch his breath and moved closer to look at the sole of Keren's foot.

"Oh lass, you can't carry on walking on that," he said quickly. "Is it just that one?"

"The other one isn't as bad."

"Into the carriage," Paul said firmly, observing the expression on Carl's face. Since the news of Pat Corrigan's death and Johnny's probable capture, his friend had been very quiet. Paul had watched him through the long day's march. He was upset himself, but Carl had taken it very badly. Paul suspected that he was worrying about the possibility that Johnny was not a prisoner but was dead or dying back in the woods. Carl was generally an optimistic soul, but he looked exhausted and depressed and Paul was concerned about him. He had many friends in the army, but other than Anne, Carl, Johnny, Michael and Leo Manson were his family, and with Johnny gone, Paul suddenly felt irrationally protective about Carl's tired misery. His slightly panicked reaction to Keren's relatively minor injury probably had more to do with Pat and Johnny than the girl herself, but Paul understood.

"Major, go with her. We've less than two miles to our bivouac, the horses can take it. Get some rest."

"I'm all right, sir."

"No, you're not." Paul put his hand on Carl's shoulder. "I'm not either, Carl. I won't settle until we know about Johnny for sure."

"What if we don't know?" Carl said, turning unhappy green eyes towards him. "I've no idea how long it will take to find out."

"Nor have I. I believe the French authorities will send lists to the transport board who will then notify the men's regiments and their families. But I'm not waiting for that, the minute I can, I'm going to get Wellington to write to them."

"I know you will, sir. But it's haunting me, I can't help it. I can stand the thought of him being a prisoner, although I hate it. And even if he's dead - I can't imagine life without Johnny, he's been there from the day we joined. But if he's dead, like Pat, I can cry, and I'll get over it. But we'll never know if he died quickly or if he's lying out there, dying slowly. Perhaps he's even still alive now…"

"Don't," Paul said sharply, and then caught himself and moderated his tone. "Please don't, Carl. I'm spending all my time trying not to think about that, because there's not a damned thing I can do about it right now."

"I know. I'm sorry."

"Get yourself into that carriage with your lass, Major. Your battalion can walk a mile or so without you."

"Yes, sir."

The Light Division came to a weary halt for the night close to the village of Sancti Spiritus. Despite the freezing weather, there was a different atmosphere among the men. All were aware that they were very close to Ciudad Rodrigo and Paul gave orders for any remaining provisions to be distributed. There was very little, but the simple act of abandoning the need for rationing lifted the mood, making his brigade feel that their ordeal was almost over.

The army marched early the following morning, along good roads, still boggy and churned up by the heavy traffic, but completely passable. For the first time in several days, Paul rode up and down the column speaking to his officers and NCOs, giving orders to keep the men in proper marching order. He had relaxed discipline in favour of common sense during the long retreat, caring only that his men stayed together, helped the sick and wounded and refrained from looting the local population. As they approached the city, however, Paul was aware of the desperation of some of the regiments. Supplies would be readily available, but Paul wanted them distributed in an orderly manner.

An hour from the city, Colonel Barnard rode back to join him, running his eyes over the neat lines of his men. "You too?"

"It makes sense," Paul said. "Look, it sounds mad, Andrew, but this lot have been amazing. We've had half the army running wild, discipline breaking down, looting and getting drunk. This lot? We had the worst fight on the Huebra, we've lost a battalion commander and several officers, and Johnny Wheeler and Simon Carlyon are either dead or prisoners. I hope. But as far as I'm aware, we've not had a single serious incident. They've been dumped all over the place, but they've held. I'm not naive, it's not because they're a choir of angels, it's because my officers and NCOs haven't slacked off once. And from what I've seen, neither have yours and John's."

"They haven't." Barnard gave a crooked smile. "Mostly. You're right, Paul, they've been bloody amazing. What is it about the Light Division?"

"Possibly its commanding officer?" Paul asked.

Barnard gave him a sideways look. "Yes," he said. "Both John and I agree. I'm glad you think so too. We thought you might struggle, you were so close to Craufurd."

"We were friends. And he was a bloody good commanding officer. But honestly, Andrew, I think Alten's better. And that's one of the reasons I want my men marching in like soldiers, not straggling in like starving beggars. Charles Alten deserves it. I don't know how all the divisions did, we've been too widely separated. But out of those in this column, the Light Division is the one that held."

Paul felt suddenly slightly embarrassed, feeling that he had allowed himself to show a sentimentality that he usually reserved for Anne and for close friends. He liked Barnard enormously, but their friendship was relatively new. He said nothing more. After a short silence, Barnard cleared his throat.

"Aye," he said, sounding more Irish than usual. "Let's get them in then, Colonel."

Paul glanced at him and saw that he had got it right after all. Barnard was looking directly ahead, but there was a suspicious sheen to his eyes.

"Trust the bloody Irish to get maudlin," he said.

Barnard looked around at him, and his smile was warm and unaffected. "You are such a bastard, Van Daan, I don't know why I bear with you."

"Because I feed you regularly and share my wine cellar. And lend you money when your pockets are to let."

"I'm glad you've mentioned that," Barnard said seriously, and Paul laughed aloud.

"You're never going to starve while my wife is around, Andrew. She loves your accent."

"Your wife is a queen among women, Colonel."

"My wife is a lot more than that." Paul scanned the horizon and pointed. "And if I'm not mistaken, those are supply wagons coming out from the city. Best get back to your brigade before they run riot and spoil our pretty display."

"On my way, Colonel," Barnard said, and set his horse to a canter.

\*\*\*

For three agonising hours, Johnny Wheeler dragged himself along the riverbank. He had no sense of the distance covered although he knew it was not enough. The banks were a tangle of weeds and bushes, dotted with huge boulders. Even on a flat path with no obstacles it would have been difficult for him to walk, but on uneven ground with the wound on his leg burning with pain and his whole body wracked with chills, he moved at a snail's pace.

Simon trod patiently beside him, helping him as far as possible. He had bound the leg wound before they set off with makeshift bandages torn from a spare shirt and stockings from his looted pack. It was already soaked through and stained red. Johnny wondered if the blood was all fresh or if it was just the rain making it look worse than it was. He could put very little weight on it and he felt nauseous and light-headed. They made their way painfully through the tangled undergrowth and more than once Simon caught Johnny as he stumbled, made clumsy by pain and weakness.

The weather continued to be unpleasant. Rain was followed by bright cold sunlight. Towards evening it was misty, with a miserable chill in the air. As darkness fell, Johnny stopped finally, resting on a rock, too exhausted to move any further. His companion looked around. The rain had eased finally but the night air was cold, and Johnny closed his eyes and wondered, in sudden despair, if he was going to survive this.

"Wait there, sir. Don't try to move, you'll fall over. I'll be back."

Johnny nodded. He wanted to tell Simon that there was no point in this. Already he was so weak that he doubted that he would be able to walk at all the following day and he was determined that Simon should not die in his attempt to save him.

Johnny thought about Caroline Longford. It had been more than a year since he had last seen her, riding away from him back to her husband. At his age, it was foolish, he supposed, to take the view that he would not fall in love again, but he was not sure that he wanted to. He wondered how Caroline was, and if she still thought of him. She had been determined to work at her marriage to her worthless husband and to raise the child, which might well be Johnny's, in a loving family. Johnny had doubted that it was possible with Vincent Longford, but he could offer her nothing but disgrace, and had encouraged her to leave, hoping that against all odds she might be happy. He hoped Anne would write to her, to tell her of his death. He wished, with sudden bitter sadness, that he might have spoken to her just once more, to tell her how much he still loved and missed her.

"Sir. Sir, wake up."

There was panic in Simon's voice and Johnny opened his eyes. "It's all right, Lieutenant, I've not died."

"You look as though you might," Simon said. "I've found shelter. It's not much, a ruined building. But it's dry and out of this wind. And more to the point, it's at the edge of a very good road. I think that's the road we need to take tomorrow. If I can get you up there, we can light a fire and you'll be warm. Let me help you."

Johnny winced as the younger man almost lifted him to his feet. He shuffled forward, feeling pain shooting through his thigh and into his hip with every step. Looking up the steep slope which led away from the river made him want to cry, but there was something about Simon Carlyon's dogged determination, that made it impossible to give in. Gritting his teeth once again, he began to drag himself up the slope, with Simon shoving him from behind.

The building was musty and smelled faintly of the animals which must have made their homes in it from time to time, but it was, as Simon had said, definitely dry and the open door faced away from the biting wind. Simon helped Johnny to sit down with his back against the wall and then began to move around, feeling his way. Eventually there was a shuffling noise and then the sound of flint being struck. Patiently Simon wielded his tinder box until a small flame burned. He set fire to a pile of dry leaves that he had scooped together and for a short time the ruin was lit with a flickering glow. It illuminated grey and white streaked walls. The floor was littered with debris blown in, over the years, leaves and twigs. Simon scuttled around collecting what he could before the feeble fire went out. When it burned more steadily, he disappeared outside and came back with armfuls of wood. Some of it was dry and burned well. Some was green and smoked horribly, but the warmth was so welcome that neither man cared.

When the fire was burning brightly, with a pile of wood beside it, to feed it, Simon finally sat down, stretching out his legs and holding his cold hands to the blaze.

"I'm sorry we've no food, sir. In the morning, I'll see what I can find. How are you doing?"

"I'm well enough, thanks to you. If I get out of this alive, Mr Carlyon, I owe you a debt I can't repay. Thank you."

"Just doing my duty, sir." The boy sounded suddenly awkward. "Do you think you could get some sleep? I'll keep watch."

"I'm not sure there's much to watch, other than this fire," Johnny said. "I don't think I'll sleep much, why don't you try? I'll yell if there's need."

Simon shook his head. "I doubt I'll sleep either," he admitted. "Perhaps in a while."

"Shift yourself around here, Lieutenant, next to me. It's out of the wind and we'll be warmer next to each other."

Simon hesitated then seemed to see the sense of it and moved to sit beside Johnny, his shoulder against him. He was rigid and uncomfortable, and Johnny sought for something to say to ease it. The thought that came into his head was so unsuitable that he almost laughed aloud.

"Sir?"

"Sorry, not really the time for a laugh."

"It might be," Simon said, and Johnny looked at him and grinned.

"All right. I was thinking that this is bloody typical of my luck. My esteemed commander met his wife when they both got stuck in a shepherd's hut in a snowstorm years ago. I, on the other hand, end up snuggling close with a man who hates my guts."

Simon gave a surprised splutter of laughter. "Bloody hell, sir, I hope you're not comparing me to Mrs van Daan?"

"Don't panic, Lieutenant, I do not find you that attractive."

It hurt to laugh but it was also a relief, and they laughed more than the silly joke really merited. Afterwards, Johnny reached inside his damp coat and took out his flask.

"Brandy," he said. "It's about half full, but it might help warm us up."

"You should keep it, sir, you might need it."

Johnny shook his head. "No point in thinking that way, lad. We'll either get help soon or I'm not going to make it, I'm not stupid. In fact, I don't know what tonight will bring. I'm feeling like hell, and if this wound gets infected or I get a fever, you're going to have to leave me."

Simon accepted the flask and took a pull, handing it back for Johnny to do the same. "I'm not leaving you, sir."

"You might have to. If I'm dying, I'm not taking you with me. Your parents have suffered enough. And besides, I need you to get back and tell the Colonel what happened. It will kill him not to know. I want your word, lad."

Simon looked at him in the firelight for a long time. Finally, he nodded grudgingly. "Only if it's bad," he said.

"If I'm dying, it will be pretty bad," Johnny said gravely, and Simon laughed again.

"You don't sound like you're going to die, sir."

"Well, I'm not going to sleep either, so talk to me. I realise I know nothing about you, Lieutenant."

"Other than who my brother was," Carlyon said.

Johnny smiled tiredly. "I'm not that interested in your brother. I didn't like him. Tell me about the rest of your family."

"My family?" Simon sounded tired, but curiously relaxed. "Only me left now, and my parents. My father has a small estate in Yorkshire, a few miles from Thorndale. He served as MP for the district for a long time. Retired a few years ago. He got sick of London, I think. He and my mother like to be at home. They entertain locally and go to church and he likes to ride out with the hunt, although I think these days he isn't at the front of the pack." Simon paused. "Robert broke their hearts. And then I broke them all over again when I refused to sell out and go home. I don't know how much you know about the Howards - Mrs van Daan's family. In Thorndale, they matter. Every year, twice a year, they give a ball for the entire neighbourhood. Summer and Christmas. It used to be the highlight of my mother's social calendar. They still invite her, but she won't go. Makes an excuse. She's so ashamed of Robert…"

Johnny felt his heart twist in sympathy. "Christ, I'm sorry, lad."

"It probably seems silly, that something like that should matter. When so many people are dying here."

"It's not silly. It's real life. Out here, what we do, isn't real to the people back home."

"No." Simon turned his head to look at Johnny. "What about your family?"

"I've none to speak of. My parents are dead. A respectable family but no money. My father was a lawyer. I'd an uncle in trade and he provided the money for my first commission and then my promotion to lieutenant. After that I was on my own."

Simon regarded him through the firelight with something like awe. "But you're a colonel."

"In charge of a regiment that nobody wanted. The 112th was in so much disgrace when the first battalion arrived out here, everybody expected it to be disbanded."

"Then how in God's name did it end up as part of the Light Division?"

"That was the Colonel's doing, not mine. But they've come a long way and I'm honoured to command them." Johnny studied the young face in the firelight and smiled. "Lieutenant, I've been very lucky. And I've also worked very hard. But sometimes it is genuinely about who you know. I was fortunate enough to serve alongside Paul van Daan, who was on his way up. But I hope you do as well. You deserve to. Now stop talking. I can see you need to sleep, and I do too. We're not going to get attacked here. Tomorrow we'll have a look at this road and see if we think I can make it any further. Good night."

# Chapter Seventeen

The arrival in Ciudad Rodrigo passed in a blur for Anne. The narrow streets of the old city were crammed with wagons and carts trying to get out to take supplies to the starving and exhausted soldiers who were bivouacking nearby and officers streaming into the city to try to find shelter and food and accommodation for their horses.

"This is bloody chaos," Paul said, after Anne's carriage had to pull off the street for the third time to allow a convoy of carts, pulled by mules and piled high with bread, barrels of beef and bags of tack biscuits, to make their way past. "We'll be here until midnight at this rate."

"Where are we going?" Anne asked. She had hardly spoken during the last few hours of the journey. It was as if, knowing herself so close to safety, her brain had quietly closed down, and speech was too difficult.

"We've billets by the eastern wall. Captain Cartwright rode on ahead and worked his magic. The men will stay outside the walls, but the minute we're reunited with the rest of the baggage, we'll have tents up and a full camp. I've left Carl in charge of it, he needs something to do. But I'm under strict instructions from the Commander-in-Chief to get you settled before I do anything else. Which I will do, if we can ever bloody get there. Oh for fuck's sake, now we have goats."

The extraordinary statement revived Anne's interest and she leaned further out of the carriage window to look. The street was blocked by jumble of supply wagons, a gun carriage, and a train of eight mules roped together and being led by a wiry Spaniard. The noise was unbelievable, a combination of creaking wheels, braying mules and yelling drivers. A herd of goats suddenly burst from a narrow side alley, bells jangling loudly from their necks. They launched themselves, with joyous enthusiasm, into the fray, weaving their way in and out of the stranded vehicles, bleating loudly enough to drown out all other sounds, while the goatherd, a skinny boy of around twelve, chased them in circles, calling their names in impotent fury. Craufurd, who had been dozing peacefully at Anne's feet in the carriage, was awoken by the noise and sat up, staring about him indignantly. He then shook himself, jumped up onto the seat beside Teresa Carter, stuck his shaggy head out of the window and began to bark loudly.

The goats bleated louder. One of the mules took fright at Craufurd's intervention, and bucked, kicking the mule behind him in the train, which in its turn, swivelled round and bit the mule at the back of the train. Little Ana, who had been sleeping in her mother's arms, woke in fright and began to yell. Anne started to laugh uncontrollably.

Paul surveyed the melee grimly, then moved Rufus forward and addressed the officer seated on the box of the first wagon beside the driver, a red-haired lanky ensign, who was watching the chaos with an expression of sheer enjoyment.

"You, on the box over there. What's your name?"

The officer saluted. "Ensign Dodd, sir. District quartermaster's department."

"Well, Mr Dodd, I can see how much you're enjoying this, and in your place I would be too. Glad to have provided entertainment, but my wife is in this carriage, she's pregnant and she's not well, so my sense of humour's not what it was. You've got about three minutes to get those wagons off this street before I come over there and rip your bloody head off. Are we clear?"

Anne saw Dodd's eyes widen slightly in surprise, but he saluted again, more smartly. "Yes, sir, very clear. Only it's a bit difficult, sir, with the mules and the goats…"

"I'm coming to that." Paul's voice raised a notch. "Mr Bell, if that's you making a pig's ear of moving that gun carriage over there, get it shifted if you have to carry it out of here, or I am going to insert it up your arse. What the bloody hell is it doing here anyway? It's not like the French are invading. No, don't answer that. Just move it." Paul switched to Spanish. "You, with the mules. Stop trying to force them through, there's no bloody room. Take them down that street over there and keep them out of the way until this is cleared, or I will feed them to my wife's dog, he's bloody hungry. As for these goats…"

Anne was crying with laughter. "There are a lot of goats, Colonel."

"An impressive number." Paul surveyed the goatherd, who had stopped running and was regarding him with wide, innocent brown eyes. "The only use I have for a herd of goats right now," Paul said, in Spanish and in matter-of-fact tones, "is to feed a thousand hungry men of the light division. They'd be very grateful. Stop chasing them around, stop making that noise, get them calmed down and get them out of here. Understand?"

"Si, Senor."

"Excellent." Paul turned to look at Anne and his lips twitched into a smile. "I see it's woken you up a bit. Let's see how long it takes them, shall we?"

The road was cleared surprisingly quickly. Anne called Craufurd down off the seat although she was pleased at how easily he had jumped up. Whatever had ailed his back leg was healing fast. Teresa had settled Ana to feed, to calm her down, and Keren was arranging a shawl about them both. Anne looked over at Charlie Bannan and smiled.

"Almost there, Charlie. I wonder what's for dinner?"

"Dinner, ma'am?" The child's eyes were wide. "You mean like real dinner?"

"I think so."

"I wonder if my Da will have dinner," Charlie said wistfully. "Shall I go and find him?"

"I've a feeling he might be a bit busy for a day or so, getting his men fed and settled," Anne said. "Do you think you could stay with me for a little longer? Craufurd would appreciate it."

Charlie stroked the dog with his feet. "Can I, ma'am?"

"I'm hoping you will. You look as though you need a good meal."

"So do you, ma'am." Charlie's eyes were scanning her face. "Ma'am, are you sad?"

Anne was startled. "Sad? Oh - yes, I suppose I am a little. One of our friends was killed and two more are missing and might be prisoners."

"I'm sad about Mam."

Anne stroked his head. "I know," she said gently. "Why don't you move closer and give me a cuddle? I think we both need it."

The boy shifted along the seat and snuggled into Anne's side and Anne put her arm about him. Opposite, she realised that Keren's eyes were on her face.

"What is it, ma'am?" she asked.

Anne shook her head. "Major Corrigan. Colonel Wheeler. Mr Carlyon."

"I know, ma'am, it's horrible. But I don't think it's just that. Something else is bothering you, you've been so quiet. You don't have to tell us, ma'am. But I wish you would. Because..."

"Because we are your friends," Teresa broke in. She too was watching Anne, and Anne blinked, feeling tears hovering just behind her eyes.

"I don't want Paul to know just yet," she said. "Please don't tell him."

"The baby?"

Anne nodded. "I've not felt it move for a couple of days now," she said. "Not since that day in the river. I've been trying to tell myself that it means nothing. That it could still be all right."

"It could be, ma'am," Teresa said quickly. "It happens many times. With rest and good food and..."

Anne wiped her eyes with both hands and tried to force a smile, although she suspected it was a poor effort. "I know," she said. "I've not lost all hope. But please don't tell the Colonel, not yet. He's so worried about his men, and about Johnny and Simon. And Lord Wellington, who hasn't been at all well these last few days. I don't want to add to that when there's nothing he can do."

The carriage was moving, bumping over the cobbles. It drew up outside a tall town house, and Paul dismounted, handing the reins to Jenson, and came to lift Anne down from the carriage. He did not set her down but carried her through a wrought iron gate and into the dim recesses of a panelled hallway.

238

"Up this way, sir," Captain Cartwright said, and Paul carried her up a wooden staircase and through into a bedroom. A late winter sun was shining through the panes and to Anne's complete astonishment, a bed was already made up and her boxes and bags, mud splashed and slightly battered, were neatly piled in the corner of the room. Paul set her down gently on the bed and Anne looked around her and unexpectedly burst into tears.

"I'll be downstairs, sir," Cartwright said quickly, and whisked himself out of the room. Paul sat down beside her and put his arms around her.

"It's all right, bonny lass," he said, kissing her very gently. "You're safe. We're all safe."

"We're not," Anne sobbed. "Pat will never be safe again."

"You know you don't believe that, love. Nor do I. He's safer than any of us. Probably getting a bollocking from Bob Craufurd for getting himself killed. I wonder if the afterlife has mellowed that grumpy bastard."

Anne gave a watery chuckle. "You are so irreverent, Paul. But I'm so worried about Johnny and Simon. I wish we knew for sure."

"So do I. As soon as I've got the brigade fed and settled, we'll do a proper roll call and then I'm going to start chasing, to find out how many of ours were taken prisoner."

The door opened, and there was a familiar tip-tap sound on the boards. Anne turned to smile as Craufurd advanced, sniffing interestedly at the faded counterpane on the bed. "At least I don't have to worry about him," she said.

"No, he's recovering very fast. I'm going to send Keren up to you, Nan. Kelly and Browning have gone out to buy food, we are going to eat properly tonight."

"Invite Lord Wellington, will you, Paul, or he will eat nothing sensible."

Paul laughed aloud. "My poor love, you're always worrying about somebody aren't you? Get some rest. I wish I could stay, but..."

"No, you have to go. Will you thank Davy for this, I have no idea how he did it, but I love him for it. Take Craufurd back to wherever Charlie is, will you?"

"I will. Sleep love."

\*\*\*

The road towards Ciudad Rodrigo resembled a reeking battlefield, with men and animals lying dead, in pools of stagnant water. The rain had stopped but there was no warmth from the sun. The smell rising from the corpses was horrible, but Simon Carlyon hardly noticed it as he half dragged, half carried Colonel Wheeler, step by agonising step.

The track was narrow and muddy, deeply rutted by those men, horses and wagons that had not fallen by the wayside, and the weeks of rain had created pools that reached as far as the knees in some places. There was no conversation along the route; Wheeler was in too much pain to speak and

Simon was too exhausted. He had abandoned the musket after the first day. There was no sign of the French, but if they did appear, the only option was surrender anyway. Simon had decided to keep the pack. He carried blankets against the cold and looted two more from dead men lying by the wayside. The spare shirts and stockings had all been ripped up to replace the bandages on Wheeler's leg, which were filthy by the end of each day's march.

They rested at night in the shelter of trees, lighting fires of green wood which smoked dreadfully but confirmed Simon's belief that all French pursuit had ended. They would have seen the smoke for miles. On the third morning he believed, for a horrible moment, that the Colonel had died in the night, and he shook him, relieved when Wheeler stirred and groaned.

"Sorry, sir. I thought…"

Wheeler opened grey eyes, dull with pain. "Not quite," he said. "But I don't think it'll be long now. Look, we need to talk."

"We should get moving, sir."

"I'm not going anywhere," Wheeler said quietly. "Simon, put your hand on my head."

Simon reached out and touched the older man's forehead. He almost jerked it away, feeling the burning heat.

"I've got fever," Wheeler croaked. "I'm burning up and I'm shivering, and my leg feels as though it's being run through with a hot iron. I don't need a doctor to tell me I'm in trouble. Either I've got an infection in the wound, or this is the result of being cold and wet and exhausted for days. It doesn't much matter. I can't walk another day, I'm sorry. It's time to leave me."

Simon felt physically sick. "Look, sir, you just need to rest for longer. Have some water. I'm going to see if I can find some food. I'll…"

"Stop it," Wheeler said, and there was a gentle finality to his voice that chilled Simon. "You're grasping at straws. If there was any wildlife in this area, the rest of the army cleared it out when they went through. You caught nothing yesterday, and you'll have no luck today. If you hang around here waiting for me to recover, you're just going to get weaker yourself while you watch me die. Mr Carlyon, it's time for you to take an order. Get out of here."

"Sir, I can't leave you."

"You need to get moving. A day's march and you'll reach the lines. If you stay here, you're going to starve to death. Or freeze. Or both. Go."

"No," Simon said stubbornly.

"Please," Wheeler said, and it came out a croak. "I don't need you to sit here and watch me die. I can do that without you."

"I don't want you to die alone," Simon said, and he realised suddenly he was crying. He reached for Wheeler's hand. Unlike his head, it was very cold. "I don't want you to die at all. Not now. Not just as I've got to know you."

Wheeler did not reply. Instead he covered Simon's hand with his other one. "I know," he said gently. "It's a bastard, isn't it?"

They sat without speaking for a long time. Wheeler had closed his eyes and Simon watched his face. It was white and waxy with pain and exhaustion and fever, the unremarkable brown hair plastered to his head, no longer neatly tied back as Simon had always seen it. Without the slate grey eyes, there was nothing distinctive about Colonel Johnny Wheeler's appearance, but Simon thought he was probably the most extraordinary man he had ever met.

Simon had watched, with growing admiration, as the Colonel had struggled through these past days. His agony was written in deep lines on his face, but during that time he had never complained, never snapped, never once expressed anything but appreciation for Simon's efforts. Simon knew himself to be capable of immense bravery in battle, but he was not sure that he had the quiet courage to endure this much pain and hardship with the dignity that this unassuming man had displayed.

"I'm so sorry," Simon whispered.

Wheeler opened his eyes and attempted a smile. "Oh, don't be, Simon. You've done everything a man could have done."

"I didn't mean that," Simon said. "I meant about before. About how I was with you when I first joined. I didn't know you then. And it's bloody obvious that I didn't know Robert either. I was an idiot, the evidence was very clear, but I just think I couldn't bear to accept that my brother was that bad. I'm glad you did what you did. I'm glad you saved her. She was worth saving. Whatever happens here, I'm going to put him to one side and focus on me. I don't need to live him down. Thank you for that."

Surprisingly, there was a gleam in the grey eyes. "Those are very wise words, Lieutenant Carlyon. You don't owe me an apology. It's possible I might owe you one. Look, before you go, there's something I'd like to tell you. It can't possibly make any difference to either of us, but I want you to know. It's about your brother."

"It's all right, sir, you did what you had to do to save her life. I understand."

"Simon, I arrived at the farm that day with a ball in my calf after that God-awful mess at the Coa. I'd left the rest of our wounded in the field hospital and I rode in to see Anne. The place was deserted, I thought she might have gone back to Lisbon after all, but then she appeared at the top of the steps which led up to her room - she'd a billet over the stables, I seem to remember - and she came towards me. She was black and blue, her lip was split and her face was bruised. One eye was almost closed where he'd hit her so hard. She was shaking."

"Sir, don't. Please."

"I'm sorry, but you need to know this. I asked her what was wrong, and she told me to go into the kitchen. When I did, I found Robert's body on the floor. He can't have been dead more than an hour."

Simon froze, staring at Wheeler in complete astonishment, his exhausted brain trying to process what he had just been told.

"You didn't kill him?"

"No. But the only people who know that, are the Colonel and his wife, Captain O'Reilly and Major Swanson. I went to the provost-marshal and told them that I'd walked in and found him with a pistol pointed at his wife and that I'd killed him to save her life. They believed me. The evidence of what he'd done to her was written all over her face and he was already charged as a deserter and a thief. It was a nice tidy ending, they took my evidence and practically thanked me. And it was over."

Simon scanned the older man's face. "So who killed him?" he asked. "Surely not Mrs van Daan?"

"No, although that was the story she told me. It was obvious it wasn't true. She didn't have a gun on the premises and besides it was a rifle shot not a pistol. I don't know the man's name, I never asked. A young deserter had stopped off at the farm to sleep in the barn and Mrs van Daan found him and fed him. Typical of her. He'd left with some extra food, but he saw your brother arriving and said he was worried about her, being there on her own. I suppose he was grateful. He doubled back to check she was all right and found your brother apparently about to kill her. He shot him dead."

"Oh, dear God," Simon breathed. "What happened to him? The man."

"I let him go," Wheeler said. "He was still there, had stayed with her to take care of her when he ought to have run. I couldn't send a man like that to the gallows."

Simon sat quietly for a while, thinking about what he had been told. Eventually he said:

"Did you tell me this because you're going to die, so it doesn't matter who knows?"

"No. I just wanted you to know. I was going to wait until we got back and tell you then, but we've run out of time."

Simon was suddenly furiously angry at the thought that this man was going to die. He also felt a deep and painful sense of grief and abiding loss. He could not bear the thought of saying goodbye, of getting up and walking away.

"Thank you for telling me," he said. "It's good to know the truth. I won't mention it to anybody else, not even Nicholas. But I should tell you, sir, that I don't give a damn."

Wheeler regarded him in some surprise. "You don't?"

"No, sir. Not just because of these last days with you, but because I've got to know people now. You, the Colonel, his wife, Major Swanson. And I realise that even without this, I couldn't bring myself to believe that any one of you would be part of a conspiracy to murder an innocent man so that his wife could marry a senior officer. I'm glad you didn't kill him because that makes it easier for you. But if you had, I'd have understood."

"Thank you, Simon, I appreciate that. Now stop finding reasons to delay this." Wheeler reached into his coat pocket and withdrew several folded notes. They were covered on both sides with small, neat writing in pencil. "I'd like you to take these. They're not sealed, I used my tablets and I'd not much paper left. I'm trusting you with them. One is to the Colonel, and there's one to Major Swanson and to Captain O'Reilly. The fourth is to be given to Mrs van Daan. It's not for her, it's to a lady, but Anne will see that she gets it. Promise me."

Simon could feel tears wet on his face as he took the letters and put them carefully into his coat. "I promise, sir," he said. "I didn't know…I mean, you're not married, are you? I'm sorry, it's none of my business."

Wheeler gave another painful smile. He looked, to Simon's distraught eyes, as though he was fading already. "I'm not married," he said. "Caroline…oh what, the hell, I can trust you. She isn't mine, Simon, she's wed to a fellow officer. They moved to Dublin. We were in love, but she left when she knew she was with child, and her son could well be mine. There's never been anybody else for me, I never expected to see her again. But I love her as much as I did the day she left, and I wanted to be able to say that one more time."

There were tears on Wheeler's cheeks, mirroring Simon's own. Simon scrubbed fiercely at his own eyes and got up.

"I'm going," he said decisively. "Before I do, I'm building a fire and making sure you've got enough water in case you get too weak to move. I'll leave you my bottle as well as yours. Ration it. I'll pile as much wood as I can within reach, and I'm leaving you my greatcoat, and all the blankets, I'll travel lighter without them."

"Simon, no."

"Listen to me. We can't be far. We're travelling like a couple of crippled snails at the moment, but on my own, I can move much faster. When we were back at the Huebra, before the battle, Major Corrigan told us we were only three days steady march away from Ciudad Rodrigo. I know we've not covered much ground during the past four days, but we've got some way. I can get help and come back for you."

"Simon, even if you do…"

"I can do it. We'll get you back and to a surgeon. You can survive this. You can tell your friends all this yourself. You can tear up that letter to Caroline and write a different one. Or not at all."

Wheeler was shaking his head, and Simon could sense his immense weariness. "Lad…"

"I know you've got a pistol in that coat and some ammunition," Simon said steadily. "I know that once I'm out of sight and earshot, you intend to use it on yourself."

"Do you blame me?"

"No. Christ, no, sir, I'd do the same. But please don't do it immediately. You can survive another day, with heat and water. Keep the pistol and use it if you have to. If I don't make it. But hang on for as long as you can."

Colonel Wheeler was silent for a long time. Finally he nodded. "All right," he said.

"You promise me, sir?"

"Yes," Wheeler said. "Just don't take too long, Simon. I'm really tired of this."

***

Lord Wellington had made plans to leave Ciudad Rodrigo on the morning of the 24th of November, to return to his headquarters of last winter in Freineda. Paul's quartermasters had brought the welcome news that his previous brigade headquarters at the Quinta de Santo Antonio were ready for him to reoccupy and on the evening of the 23rd, with baggage packed and ready, Paul lay in the darkness with Anne in his arms and wondered when she was going to tell him that she believed that their child was dead. He had guessed, eventually, the cause of her sadness, and he wondered if it would be better for him to wait until she was ready or if it would be more helpful for him to broach the subject with her.

She appeared to be sleeping finally, and he had no intention of waking her tonight to have a conversation which was going to be upsetting for them both. Time enough when they arrived back at the quinta. Paul was more worried about Anne's health than about the child, and he wanted to talk to Dr Daniels about her first.

He fell asleep finally, enjoying the sense of warmth and security of lying in her arms. He woke abruptly, several hours later to somebody hammering on the front door. The banging was so loud that Paul thought for a moment that they were under attack. He sat bolt upright, his heart pounding, disoriented in the unfamiliar room.

"Paul." Anne sat up beside him, huge dark eyes wide on his through the darkness. "What in God's name...?"

Paul's heart was beginning to slow. "I've no idea, love, but it had better be good, because I am going to...what is it?"

Anne had caught his hand suddenly, a completely different expression on her face. "Give me your hand," she said, ignoring the persistent hammering. Paul obeyed, letting her guide his hand to the swell of her belly under the linen shift she was wearing. He felt it immediately, a stirring, then a violent kicking against his hand.

"Oh Christ," he whispered. "Nan, he's alive."

"Or she is," Anne said. He could hear both joy and tears in her voice. "You knew? I couldn't find the words to tell you."

"I couldn't find the words to ask you."

The hammering had stopped and there was the sound of voices below, one of them Jenson's. Paul completely ignored them and took Anne into his arms, kissing her for a long time.

"I love you so much," he said, and she pulled him closer, running her hands through his hair. Paul felt, unexpectedly, the stirring of desire, and he read it in her eyes. They had not made love for weeks and in the misery of the retreat and their shared losses they had not thought of it, but he knew that she wanted to and he moved closer to her, hoping that whatever the crisis, Jenson could deal with it.

"Sir! Sir, you need to get out here, now!"

The urgency in Jenson's voice made them both turn. Paul got out of bed and went to open the door. His orderly stood there in shirt sleeves, his eyes bright with what looked suspiciously like tears.

"What is it…"

"Downstairs, sir."

Paul shoved his feet into shoes and reached for his greatcoat as the closest warm garment. "I'll be back in a moment, love. Stay here and keep warm."

Paul was halfway down the stairs before he realised who stood below in the panelled hallway. Lieutenant Simon Carlyon was covered in mud, even his hair looked plastered in it. He was thin and gaunt, his face dirty and white in the light of Jenson's lamp and his eyes looked sunken in their sockets. But he was very clearly alive, and not a prisoner.

"Simon," Paul said, coming forward. "Oh lad, it is very good to see you. Come in, you shouldn't be hanging around here, have you…"

"I can't," Simon interrupted forcefully. "There's no time. Sorry, sir, but we need to get out there with a wagon and some food. He needs a doctor, and it can't wait."

Paul's heart stopped. "He?"

"Colonel Wheeler, sir. I had to leave him, he walked for four days, but so slowly, he's hurt. I promised I'd bring help. But it needs to be soon, sir, or he'll be dead."

Hope surged through Paul, and he admitted to himself for the first time how terrified he had been that Johnny was lying in the forest, dead or dying.

"Simon, breathe. We'll get there, I promise. Let me go and get dressed. And you need a change of clothing and some food."

"No. We need to go now. I'm so frightened he'll give up. He's in so much pain and he's got a pistol. He promised he'd wait as long as he could, but I need to get back to him. I…"

Paul felt ice settle in the pit of his stomach. "He wouldn't," he said. "Not Johnny."

Simon Carlyon met his eyes and Paul saw tears. "Sir, he's in agony," he said. "You haven't seen him."

Paul turned to Jenson. "Get the grooms up. Saddle up Rufus and Nero. Fill the saddlebags with supplies and then send a message over to Dr Daniels - he's working in the hospital at the Casa Peron, it's only in the next street. We need a hospital wagon hitched up. Simon, you need to show me where he is on a map, I've one in my baggage, I'll bring it down."

"Simon."

Paul swung around to see Anne coming down the stairs. She was dressed in one of her velvet robes in dark green, her hair still loose and her face was alight with joy. She ran forward and into Simon's arms and he held her close, all awkwardness gone.

"Johnny's alive?"

"He was when I left him, ma'am."

Anne looked at Paul. "I'll feed him," she said. "We'll be in the kitchen, go and get dressed love. This way, Simon. I'm so glad you're safe."

***

Johnny slept, a fevered, restless sleep, coming awake late in the day to realise that the fire had almost died, and he was shivering. He forced himself to sit up and reach for the wood that Simon had left, building up the fire carefully. He had drunk most of the water. Slowly and painfully, he dragged himself to his feet and made his way down to the stream, holding on to trees to support him, and filled both bottles again, then made his way back to the sheltered spot between several huge shrubs that Simon had found for him, and settled down, lying on a blanket, covered with two coats and two more blankets, his head on Simon's abandoned pack.

The pain in his leg was unbearable now, but it was strangely comfortable lying there, compared to the previous days of hobbling along the rutted road. Johnny wondered if Simon Carlyon would make it back to him before he died. He felt curiously detached about it, as though it was an intellectual problem to be considered rather than a matter of life or death.

Johnny had been wounded several times during the twenty years he had served in the army, but the only other time he had been this close to death had been nine years ago on the field of Assaye, in India, where he had almost bled to death from a savage tulwar slash across the middle. He could still remember lying outside the surgeon's tent, waiting his turn among hundreds of other wounded men, feeling, along with the pain, the same peculiar detachment, knowing that it was very likely that he would die before a surgeon reached him and finding it hard to care as long as it stopped the pain. It would probably have happened then, if it had not been for the determined intervention of his young Captain, who had been promoted over him only a day earlier, who had limped into the tent, ignoring his own wounds, and demanded that Johnny be seen immediately.

As darkness came, Johnny fed the fire, careful with the wood, not wanting to run out and have to try to stumble around in the darkness trying to find more. His fever was getting worse and his clothes were soaked with sweat. Johnny drifted in and out of an uneasy sleep. He dreamed of battle and fire and blood and death. He dreamed of Caroline, lying beside him in bed, her fair hair falling about bare shoulders as she leaned over to kiss him. He dreamed of some unknown horror and awoke with a cry, hearing a scampering in the bushes and realising in sudden terror that some creature had thought him dead and come to feed on him.

The thought kept him awake through the rest of the night. Sunrise came with mist, a thick, cold miasma across the forest floor, which made Johnny cough. Coughing hurt his chest, which felt as though it was on fire.

Johnny managed one more trip for water, and then staggered about in the swirling mist to find more wood, feeding the fire until it burned brightly again. Collapsing back into his nest of blankets and coats, he thought for the first time about the pistol.

He had no idea if it would even fire, after the dampness of the past

246

days. He kept it as a security against the worst, against long hours of dying of thirst, his fever burning him and the pain intensifying, but he could not actually imagine ever using it.

When Johnny awoke again, he could not, for a long time, remember where he was or how he had got there. The blank part of his memory panicked him, and it was momentarily a relief when memory came flooding back. The fever had a grip of him now, and he could feel himself drifting in and out of unconsciousness. The fire died and the water was gone, and Johnny tried desperately to push himself up for one last effort, and fell back, too weak to stand. With the last of his strength, he drew the coats and blankets around him. Strangely, the pain was less now, more of a dull ache than a raging agony. He remembered Anne once saying that it was often the way with a man dying of his wounds, as though nature intervened to make the end kinder.

The pistol was in his coat pocket and well within reach, but Johnny did not search for it. He had thought it would feel like a release but instead it felt more like defeat, and Johnny discovered that he was not ready to surrender. He had never done so, in all those years of fighting, and he could not bring himself to do it now. He was certain that Simon Carlyon would come back for him, and it saddened him that the boy might well find him already dead, but he would not add to his unnecessary guilt by committing suicide. More than that, Johnny realised that he wanted Paul and Carl and Michael to know that he had held on for as long as he possibly could. They would expect no less of him.

Unconsciousness was another matter. Johnny yearned for it and then fought it, feeling suddenly that it would be for the last time. If he must go, he wanted the awareness of going, as though his life had meant something. Johnny was not particularly religious and had occasionally envied the steady faith of Carl Swanson, the parson's son or even the somewhat eccentric but nevertheless sincere beliefs of his commander. He was surprised to find that at this moment, prayer came easily to him, not for himself but for the people he was leaving behind. He prayed for Michael, whom he remembered as a hot-headed young private, permanently in trouble when he first joined, and for Carl Swanson, whom he had liked from the day he had first arrived in barracks and who was going to find it difficult to lose both Johnny and Pat Corrigan. He prayed for Anne, whose warm friendship had helped him through the difficult months after Caroline's departure, and for the child she carried. He prayed for Paul, with a sense of passionate gratitude for ten years of uncomplicated friendship and unwavering support in both his career and his personal life. He prayed for Simon Carlyon, who was beginning to find his way out of the misery created by his brother.

Johnny thought finally of Richard Longford, who might well be his son. The boy was a year old now, being raised by a man Johnny disliked and the woman he would never stop loving. Richard would never know about him and that was as it should be. No child needed to hear that he might be another man's son. Johnny had always hoped, nevertheless, that he would at least see the boy one day and it saddened him that he would not. He prayed for him and for Caroline and his last thought, feeling the darkness claim him again, was that he hoped that Richard was his, and that he was leaving some part of him behind.

Voices confused him. There had been no voices where Johnny had been, and the noise was an intrusion into the blessed darkness where he felt no pain. Coming slowly back to consciousness, the pain was bad, and he realised in some bewilderment, that it was because he was moving, being lifted by a collection of careful hands, into the back of a wagon. There was a thin, straw filled mattress under him, and somebody was tucking blankets around him like a devoted parent. Johnny's eyes seemed glued shut, but he made an enormous effort and forced them open. A pair of worried eyes studied his face.

"Sir. Sir, he's awake."

"Stop yelling," Johnny said, indignantly. "I've got a headache."

"All right, Colonel Wheeler," another voice said, soothingly. "By the look of you, I'd say that everything aches. Lie still, close your eyes, and rest. We've stolen one of Dr McGrigor's hospital wagons, so I'm hoping the journey isn't too bad, but it's going to hurt, that leg's a mess."

"Paul," Johnny croaked.

A hand took his. "I'm here. So is Simon. Don't try to move, we've got you well wrapped up."

Johnny turned his head and saw Simon Carlyon's young, anxious face on his other side. "You did it," he whispered. "You got back in time."

"I did. You'll be all right, sir. You just need to rest. I'm going to stay in the wagon with you. It's only seven miles and the horses are fresh. Settle back and try to rest."

Johnny could feel his eyes closing again. He reached out and felt the younger man's hand grasp his. All he could feel, drifting back into unconsciousness, was an overwhelming sense of relief and gratitude. He had worried, over the past days, if he might lose his leg, but at this moment it did not seem important compared to his life.

"Stay with me, Simon," he said drowsily.

"Right here, sir," the boy said, and Johnny slept, still holding his hand.

\*\*\*

Johnny had no sense of the passage of time when he woke finally with his head feeling clear. He lay still, listening to sounds of movement in the house around him; the creak of a floorboard and the clattering of pans in a kitchen somewhere. He did not recognise the room. It was a whitewashed bedchamber with plaster flaking off the walls and signs of damp in the upper corner of one wall. He had stayed in many similar rooms during his army career and been grateful for this much comfort, but he was not sure that he had ever felt quite such a sense of relief to be warm and dry and clean.

His leg hurt with a burning agony, but he had heard men who had lost limbs claim that they could still feel them long after they had gone, so he reached down with his hand to touch it. A hand covered his.

"It's all right, sir, they didn't amputate."

"Oh, thank God," Johnny breathed. He opened his eyes and studied the face of the boy sitting on a wooden chair beside his bed. "Simon, what in God's name are you still doing nursemaiding me, don't you have other duties?"

Simon laughed, a little shyly. "Relieved of them until you can be moved, sir. I asked the Colonel and he said if he'd managed without me while I was taking the long route back, he could manage a bit longer. Have some water."

Johnny drank. He felt, he realised, surprisingly well although he had no idea how long he had been here. "What day is it?" he asked.

"Saturday."

Johnny thought about it and laughed weakly. "Which Saturday?"

Simon grinned. "It's the twenty eighth, you've been here four days. Lord Wellington left for Freineda a few days ago and the brigade escorted him. The Colonel would have waited for you, but he was keen to get Mrs van Daan settled."

Johnny remembered suddenly. "Mrs van Daan...oh God, I'd forgotten. Simon, is she all right?"

Simon's smile had broadened. "She's very well, sir. Looking forward to the birth, she tells me she's bored with it now. I'm not sure if that's normal..."

"It's normal for her, trust me."

"They left me all kinds of messages for you and I promised to send word as soon as you awoke properly, you've been asleep for most of the past few days and there was some fever. You won't remember, but Mrs van Daan insisted on cleaning your wound and stitching it herself. It took forever, she was so careful."

"You've no idea how glad I am to hear that, she's very good."

"She wanted to stay and take care of you, but the Colonel said he'd trust you to me. She was quite cross about it."

Johnny knew that he was grinning from ear to ear and could not help himself. The sheer relief of hearing normal gossip from the brigade made his recovery real to him. He lay quietly for a while, thinking over the few days when he had begun to believe he was going to die and then turned his head to look at the young face of the boy sitting beside him.

"I owe you my life," he said. "Simon, thank you."

"Don't, sir. It was my duty."

"No, it bloody wasn't. It was your duty to get yourself back with your men and to keep yourself alive. You've a family waiting for you who care about you. If I catch you doing anything that mad again, I'm going to give you a bollocking you'll never forget. But I'm so glad you did."

"I'm glad I was with you," Simon said, somewhat abruptly. "I'm glad we talked and that I know...do you want something to eat and drink?"

"I do. I also want to sit up. Any chance of something stronger than water?"

Simon looked doubtful. "Do you think you should, sir?"

"If I can walk eight miles with only one leg and a half-baked greenhorn for company and survive it, I can sit up in bed and get a drink. And get one for yourself. That's an order from a senior officer, Lieutenant."

It took some time for Simon to locate the householder and slightly longer for him to bully the man into bringing food and wine. Johnny leaned back against the pillows which smelled fairly strongly of mould and listened to his junior haranguing the man in an appalling mixture of English, French and atrocious Spanish. He reflected that Simon could probably do with a few language lessons from Lieutenant Witham whose conscientiousness was already making him a target for other companies looking for transfers. Johnny liked Witham and admired his studious competence, but he already knew which of the two he would choose.

Eventually Simon returned, shepherding a middle-aged Spaniard with a round face and a sour expression, bearing a tray with bread and cheese and a dusty bottle of wine. Simon chased him out and closed the door firmly behind him then set about pouring wine and serving the food.

"He tells me he has nothing left because the English stole all he had when they stormed the citadel," he said. "It appears he forgot about this."

"He might have been telling the truth," Johnny said. "It was a bit of a shambles."

"He's had a year to recover, and he didn't get that fat on nothing," Simon said sagely. "I reckon he's been making a good profit selling to both sides, and hates having us billeted on him because it's harder to fleece us. I've told him if he gets you well quickly, he'll see the back of us sooner, so I think he'll be feeding you like a Christmas goose from now on. Here."

He passed the wine to Johnny who drank. It was not particularly good, but he did not really care at this moment. He ate the slightly stale bread and cheese and drank the coarse wine. Abruptly, Simon said:

"Sir, may I give you these back?"

Johnny took the letters, surprised. "Oh. Oh, lord, I'd forgotten. Thank you, lad. I don't think I'm going to need them now."

"I sincerely hope not, sir."

"Just as well, I wasn't at my best, I've a feeling they were a bit sentimental. Will you drop them in the fire for me?"

Simon took the letters and then hesitated. "All of them, sir?"

"Yes. Why not?"

"I just wondered if you might want to keep this one. To the lady."

Johnny took the folded letter and stared at it for a moment. "I can never send it to her, Mr Carlyon."

"I know, sir. You shouldn't. Perhaps you never will. But it just occurred to me...you don't really need the letters to your friends. Normally, they'd be there anyway. I hope nothing else bad ever happens to you. But if it ever did...wouldn't you like to know that she'd get that letter? She's bound to hear. Shouldn't she hear from you, how much you still cared? I don't mean send it now. But somebody could keep it for you. A friend. To be sent on just in case."

Johnny studied him, stopping himself from smiling. Carlyon was so earnest and so young, and it made him think back to his own early days with the 110th, broke and struggling even to pay his mess bills, hoping desperately for a way to earn promotion. It had taken him many years of hard work and patience and barely concealed resentment and when it had come, it had been at the hands of a younger man who had passed him on the way. He had learned a lot from the young Paul van Daan all those years ago but he was surprised and somewhat pleased to discover that he still had a fair bit to learn from the latest generation of young officers.

"Would you do it, Simon?" he asked.

"Yes, sir."

"Thank you. Keep it for now. When I'm back in winter quarters with some time, I'll rewrite it, rather better. But it was a good thought, I'm very grateful. Now get yourself out of here and let me sleep, I'm exhausted. You can spend your time working out how to beg borrow or steal a wagon to get me to Freineda because I'm not staying here longer than I need to, I want to get back to my men. Is my orderly about?"

"In the kitchen, I think, sir."

"Send him up later to give me a shave, would you? I feel like a sanding block."

"Yes, sir."

Carlyon got up and went to the door and as he opened it, Johnny said:

"Simon."

"Sir?"

"Thank you."

Two pairs of grey eyes met, and Carlyon smiled. "You're very welcome, Colonel."

# Chapter Eighteen

The Quinta de Santo Antonio was quiet, with both officers and men taking refuge from the appalling weather, as the creaking, ancient carriage pulled up beside the door to the main house. Gardens, pastures and barns were barely visible through torrential rain and Simon Carlyon scrambled down and helped Johnny out. They went directly into the main hall, dripping water onto the cracked tiled floor, and a familiar limping figure emerged from the kitchen region at the back.

"Colonel Wheeler. Good to see you back, sir. I'll get a couple of the lads to unload your baggage and take it up, you'll be in your old room."

"Thank you, Jenson. It's good to be back. Where have you put Mr Carlyon?"

"I'll show him; he's sharing with Mr Witham. Most of the officers of the 115th are in one of the estate cottages, but Mrs van Daan wanted Mr Carlyon in the main house. Come this way, sir. Colonel, why don't you go through to the office, Colonel van Daan is in there enjoying Lord Wellington's latest. If you're lucky, he'll read it to you. He's read it to everybody else he ever met, so it'll be nice for him to have a new audience."

Johnny grinned, allowing Jenson to take his wet coat. Walking was still painful but becoming easier with the use of a stick and he limped through an archway and found his way to the warm panelled room which had been used last winter as Paul's brigade office.

He found his commanding officer seated at the big table he used at his desk. Across the room, at a smaller table, was his wife, her dark head bent over a large book which appeared to contain medical notes. She was putting the finishing touches to a sketch of what looked like a spidery creature of some kind but what Johnny had a horrible suspicion might be some part of the human anatomy. He did not want to enquire which part. Anne sat back and surveyed her work with a critical eye, then nodded in satisfaction and added an annotation to the diagram.

Paul got up and came forward as Johnny saluted. "Come and sit down," he said, pulling out a chair as Anne got up and came to kiss Johnny. "You look a hell of a lot better than you did the last time I saw you."

"So do both of you," Johnny said, embracing Anne then lowering

252

himself into the chair. "Ma'am, you have the most incredible powers of recovery. Should you even be out of bed?"

"I would like to see somebody try to confine my lass to her chamber over something as trivial as childbirth," Paul said with obvious pride. "She does look better, doesn't she? Wait there."

He crossed the room and picked up a large wicker basket which had been beside Anne's desk and which Johnny had thought contained laundry. He was amused to see a tiny pink face, crowned by a few sparse tufts of fair hair, nestling among the linen.

"She is very pretty," he said, reaching out to touch the little fingers. "Georgiana, I understand? Wasn't she very early?"

"We think so," Anne said. "She gave us a bit of a fright to tell you the truth, I wasn't at all ready for this and I've never seen a child this small. But she seems very healthy. You may greet her properly once she's been fed; she's worse than her father for hunger, Will was nothing like it. How are you, Johnny, we've been so worried about you?"

"I'm very well now," Johnny said, watching as his commander returned the basket to its warm corner near the fire. "Glad it's winter quarters, though, there's no way I could fight like this, I'm limping like a greybeard."

"You'll recover quickly with rest and care," Anne said. "I'm going to take Her Ladyship upstairs for her feed and leave you two to talk. Is Simon with you?"

"Yes, I've sent him off with Jenson to unpack. Thank you for leaving him with me, he's been a blessing."

"I doubt I could have got him away, short of cashiering or shooting him," Paul said, going to bring brandy as Anne scooped up her child and left the room. "It's good to have you back, I've missed you."

"How's Lord Wellington?" Johnny asked innocently and Paul set the glass on the table with an unnecessary clink and looked at him suspiciously.

"Did Jenson tell you?" he asked, and Johnny laughed aloud.

"Not much, only that he'd managed to piss you off again."

His commander sat down at his desk and picked up his glass. "I am over it," he said with great dignity. "After a few hours of complete fury, I have begun to see the funny side. Sadly, I suspect that is not a view which is going to be shared by every other officer in this army."

"What's he done?" Johnny asked.

Paul reached across the table and picked up a letter. "Settle back and enjoy," he said. "This is a memorandum which has been circulated to the officers of this army. Needless to say, it is not going to stay within the officers of this army. I confidently predict it will be in every newspaper in London within the month and His Lordship's gallant officers are foaming at the mouth in sheer rage at the slur cast upon them. I won't read the first part. It concerns putting the army into cantonments for the winter and isn't that interesting. But it gets funnier." Paul drank some brandy, set the glass down, and began to read.

"I must draw your attention in a very particular manner to the state of discipline of the troops. The discipline of every army, after a long and active

253

campaign, becomes in some degree relaxed, and requires the utmost attention on the part of the general and other officers to bring it back to the state in which it ought to be for service; but I am concerned to have to observe that the army under my command has fallen off in this respect in the late campaign to a greater degree than any army with which I have ever served, or of which I have ever read."

"Oh Jesus," Johnny said, setting down his glass. "Doesn't he know what happened on the retreat to Corunna?"

"Well he wasn't there," Paul said fair-mindedly. "But I can't see how he could have missed Badajoz. But it goes on.

"Yet this army has met with no disaster; it has suffered no privations which but trifling attention on the part of the officers could not have prevented, and for which there existed no reason whatever in the nature of the service; nor has it suffered any hardships excepting those resulting from the necessity of being exposed to the inclemencies of the weather at a moment when they were most secure."

Johnny picked up his glass and drank, thinking about the bodies he had seen lying by the roadside, pulled apart by animals and birds, often naked after looting by both the locals and their own soldiers. "Should I hear the rest of this?"

"Actually, you're obliged to. As your brigade commander - this is addressed to me, by the way - I am requested to share it with you."

"You don't have to enjoy it this much. My leg is aching again."

"Put it up," Paul said, shoving a wooden bench towards him. "Here, take this cushion and sit in respectful silence while I share the rest.

"It must be obvious, however, to every officer, that from the moment the troops commenced their retreat from the neighbourhood of Burgos on the one hand, and from Madrid on the other, the officers lost all command over their men. Irregularities and outrages of all descriptions were committed with impunity, and losses have been sustained which ought never to have occurred. Yet the necessity for retreat existing, none was ever made on which the troops had such short marches; none on which they made such long and repeated halts' and none on which the retreating armies were so little pressed on their rear by the enemy."

Johnny looked down at his injured leg, now supported on the bench on an elaborately embroidered cushion and said nothing as eloquently as he could manage.

"We must look therefore for the existing evils, and for the situation in which we now find the army, to some cause besides those resulting from the operations in which we have been engaged. I have no hesitation in attributing these evils to the habitual inattention of the Officers of the regiments to their duty, as prescribed by the standing regulations of the Service, and by the order of this army."

Johnny felt an unexpected wave of sheer fury sweeping through him. He wanted to get up and leave but it was too difficult to stand. Instead, he said:

"Stop reading this fucking letter, Paul, before I thump you with this cane, I've heard enough. How dare he sit there pontificating about my officers? It's a good thing he's hiding behind his fucking desk in the village because I'd like to shoot the arrogant Irish bastard right through his thick skull."

Paul got up and went for more brandy. "You're really not right yet, lad, are you?" he said sympathetically. "I'm sorry, I should have waited. You can hear the rest another time. Have another drink."

"I don't want a drink. Do we get any right to respond to this bollocks? I lost five good officers in the almighty fuck up that he created because he was too lazy or too arrogant to make proper provisions for a siege and several good men besides. I lost Pat Corrigan, who was a friend. The fact that, to my knowledge, none of our men died of exposure or hunger on that hellish march is due entirely to the care and attention of my junior officers who kept discipline, kept the line, managed their men and shared their last morsel with the sick and wounded. As did, may I say, most of General Alten's Light Division. It's a bloody disgrace."

Paul put his hand gently on Johnny's shoulder and refilled his glass. "Johnny, calm down. I thought I was bad when I first read it, but this isn't like you. Don't take it personally, he isn't talking to you or me or any one of our officers and when I read this to them, because I'll have to, I'm going to make it very clear that they all understand that. He knows what we did. He wrote this in a temper without thinking it through and it's been sent to all of us because that's how it works. It's not aimed at you or me."

"It's still addressed to us though, isn't it?" Johnny said.

Paul nodded. "At some point, when he's calmed down, I'm going to point that out," he said. "He'll never back down or apologise, but he should at least be told the effect it's going to have on morale, the stiff-rumped, bad-tempered, long-nosed Irish bastard."

The tone of his commander's voice inexplicably calmed Johnny's fury. He drank more brandy and studied Paul. "Over it?" he queried, and Paul laughed aloud.

"Getting over it," he said. "Gradually. Nan forbade me to go over there until I could read it from start to finish without one single expletive. Clearly, I'm not quite there yet. Want to hear the rest or shall we leave it there?"

"You might as well finish it," Johnny said, and Paul picked up the letter again and struck an oratorial pose.

"I am far from questioning the zeal, still less the gallantry and spirit of the Officers of the army, and I am quite certain that if their minds can be convinced of the necessity of minute and constant attention to understand, recollect, and carry into execution the orders which have been issued for the performance of their duty, and that the strict performance of this duty is necessary to enable the army to serve the country as it ought to be served, they will in future give their attention to these points.

"Unfortunately the inexperience of the Officers of the army has induced many to consider that the period during which an army is on service is one of relaxation from all rule, instead of being, as it is, the period during which of all others every rule for the regulation and control of the conduct of the soldier, for the inspection and care of his arms, ammunition, accoutrements, necessaries and field equipments, and his horse and horse appointments, for the receipt and issue and care of his provisions' and the regulation of all that belongs to his food and forage for his horse, must be most strictly attended to by the officers of his company or troop, if it is intended that an army, a British army in particular, shall be brought into the field of battle in a state of efficiency to meet the enemy on the day of trial.

"These are the points then to which I most earnestly entreat you to turn your attention and the attention of the officers of the regiments under your command, Portuguese as well as English, during the period which it may be in my power to leave the troops in their cantonments. The commanding officers of regiments must enforce the orders of the army regarding the constant inspection and superintendence of the officers over the conduct of the men of their companies in their cantonments; and they must endeavour to inspire the non-commissioned officers with a sense of their situation and authority; and the non-commissioned officers must be forced to do their duty by being constantly under the view and superintendence of the officers."

"Where is Carter just now, by the way?" Johnny interrupted. Suddenly he was beginning to be amused.

"No idea. Taking a holiday with his wife, according to Lord Wellington," Paul said. "We're going to need to draw lots to decide who is going to undertake the duty of constantly superintending Sergeant-Major Carter, by the way, because I am telling you now, it's not going to be me. Maybe Manson could do it, he likes a challenge."

"Get Michael to do it," Johnny said. "He used to be an NCO, he'll know all the tricks."

"He taught Carter all the tricks," Paul said. "But there's more."

"Jesus, what is this, a memorandum or a three-volume autobiography? I'll be drunk by the end of it."

"You'll certainly wish you were," Paul said. "By these means the frequent and discreditable recourse to the authority of the provost and to punishment by the sentence of courts martial, will be prevented and the soldiers will not dare to commit the offences and outrages of which there are too many complaints when they well know their officers and non-commissioned officers have their eyes and attention turned towards them."

Suddenly Johnny was laughing. "Well that definitely wasn't aimed at us," he said. "The last court martial for any member of the 110th that I can remember attending was yours."

"Shut up, or I'll damage your other leg," Paul said cheerfully. "The commanding officers of regiments must likewise enforce the orders of the army regarding the constant, real inspection of the soldiers' arms, ammunition, accoutrements and necessaries, in order to prevent at all times the shameful waste of ammunition and the sale of that article and of the soldiers' necessaries. With this view both should be inspected daily.

"In regard to the food of the soldier, I have frequently observed and lamented in the late campaign, the facility and celerity with which the French soldiers cooked in comparison with those of our army." Paul had begun to laugh as well, now. "Mind, they use far too much garlic in it, you can smell them for miles when they're trying to skirmish unobtrusively."

Johnny was leaning back in his chair, tears of laughter running down his face. "George Kelly," he croaked. "Can I be there when you tell him he can't light a fire and get a meal cooked fast enough?"

"Once again, that duty is not mine. I'm delegating all of this to my officers and as my second-in-command, you get Kelly all to yourself. Stop it, you're going to choke yourself."

"I can't help it," Johnny said. "Is there much more?"

"Of course, there is. Given Hookey's attention to detail, you cannot think that he doesn't go on to explain exactly what the men are supposed to do to improve the speed of their cooking. He's an expert, you see him out there all the time with a mess kettle and a pound of beef in his hands. Do I need to read that part? He also explains how we should run field exercises and march ten to twelve miles a week to keep them fit."

"Is that all?" Johnny wheezed. "It's a holiday he's offering them."

"I'll skip to the end; I'm worried about your health, here," Paul said. "But I repeat that the great object of the attention of the General and Field Officers must be to get the Captains and Subalterns of the regiments to understand and perform the duties required from them as the only mode by which the discipline and efficiency of the army can be restored and maintained during the next campaign."

Paul put the letter down, picked up his brandy glass and raised it. "I give you the Commander-in-Chief, Colonel Wheeler, in all his wisdom."

Johnny drank the toast. "Thank God that's over," he said. "But seriously, Paul, this is going to send morale into the dust."

"Morale is already in the dust after Burgos. This is just going to trample on it a bit. But they'll get over it." Paul set his glass down. "And of course, he's right."

Johnny studied him, thinking about it for a long time. "Yes, he is," he said. "Just not in your brigade."

"Our brigade, Johnny. Which is why we train all the way through winter quarters, keep them fit and healthy and teach the new recruits to throw up a camp, light a fire and cook a meal in half an hour. And since Alten took over, the rest of the Light Division is fast catching up. He's an obsessive German perfectionist and he rides the lines as often as I do, which I love about him. Hill is very good. But a lot of the others don't do it and because they don't, it filters down. Wellington has been a complete arse about this, he should never have done it this way, especially after what they've just been through, but he is right about some of it."

"This wasn't the way to get them to listen," Johnny said.

"No. And I think by now he knows it, he'll have calmed down. He won't retract a word of it but he'll probably find some other poor bastard to do the pretty with them and jolly them along and try to get the officers to understand what he's really trying to say in the middle of all that scathing invective."

There was another silence. "So, when has he asked to see you about that, then, Colonel?" Johnny said.

"Thursday," Paul said in hollow tones. "He has written with orders for me to speak at a general meeting of divisional and brigade commanders to explain how we do what we do and what they should do to achieve the same. The letter came earlier."

"Oh, bloody hell," Johnny said. He was trying not to laugh. "You are about to be the least popular officer from here to South America. He's going to stand you up there, wave that letter and point and by the end of it they'll be thinking he wrote that with your enthusiastic support and encouragement."

Paul picked up his glass. "And once again they will be referring to me as Wellington's Mastiff and dreaming up ways to get the French to shoot me," he said. "Pass the brandy again, will you, Colonel?"

\*\*\*

Captain O'Reilly saw her immediately as he dismounted outside the substantial stables at the back of the quinta. She was huddled in the shelter of the stable door, out of sight of the grooms going about their work but close enough to keep at least some of the rain off her. Even so, the auburn curls were plastered to her head and the shirt and jacket clung wetly to the skinny body. Michael could see her shivering, even at a distance and he swore fluently and strode across the yard, handing the reins to a groom.

"Up," he said shortly.

She rose, lifting those arresting turquoise eyes to his face. "Captain. I am sorry."

Her English was getting better. Michael took her by one soggy shoulder and steered her across the muddy yard and into the main house. There was nobody about as he guided her up the stairs and into his room. Most of the junior officers shared quarters but Michael had been allocated a small room to himself overlooking the dried-out fountain on the terrace at the back. He closed the door and shoved the girl onto the single wooden chair. She was shivering violently, soaked to the skin.

"What happened to the gown that Mrs van Daan gave you?" Michael demanded, going to find a towel. He could only find one and he rubbed it quickly over his own hair, stripped off his wet coat and then handed her the towel. "Get yourself dry."

The girl looked at the towel uncertainly and then began to wipe it over herself. Michael went to his chest. There was a pile of neatly folded clothing on top which told him that Mrs Bennett had been in. He smiled a little, conscious as always of the sheer pleasure of winter quarters and having clean, dry clothing for most of the time. Billets were not always as comfortable as this one, but he always enjoyed the sense of remaining in one place even for a week or two. He picked up one of the shirts and carried it to her.

"Dry off and put this on then wrap the blanket around you, I want to talk to you."

He turned his back and sat on the edge of his bed to pull off his boots, then changed his own shirt, still not looking at her. Finally, when he was sure she had had enough time, he turned. She sat on the wooden chair, the thin grey army blanket around her legs and the shirt enormous on her.

Michael sat down on the bed again and studied the girl. He had last seen her in Ciudad Rodrigo at the convent, dressed in a dark woollen gown that Anne had bought for her. She had resisted any notion of taking the veil and Anne had not pushed the idea. Instead, she had paid the nuns to provide board and lodging for the girl until she could find work. Michael could not believe she was here again.

"You can't keep doing this, brat," he said as kindly as he could. "I left you with the nuns, they were going to take care of you."

"I followed you from the city," the girl said.

"Brat, that's a walk of twenty miles, what were you thinking?"

"I have walked much further."

"I thought you were going to look for work in the town?" Michael said.

"There is no work," the girl said simply. "Only selling myself to the soldiers. I could not bear it again, so I put these clothes on and followed you."

"The nuns would have..."

"The nuns cannot protect me," the girl said. "They cannot protect themselves. I did not feel safe there. I feel safe here, with you."

Michael's heart turned over. "Oh, brat," he said softly. "What the devil am I going to do with you?"

"You should have a servant."

"I can't afford a servant. And if I could, it would have to be a boy, not a girl."

"I can be a boy. I look like a boy. I can work hard. I can wash your clothes and clean your boots and brush your horse. I like horses; my father had a horse and two donkeys before the French stole them and killed him."

Michael regarded her. "Who was your father?"

"He was Juan Ibanez. A good farmer with a house and fields and cattle. He could read and write; he learned with the priests, and he taught me."

"Had you brothers or sisters?"

She shook her head. "My mother died with my baby brother and then there was just we two until they came."

Michael did not want to know more. He looked at the skinny little frame. "I've no money to pay a servant," he said again, but he heard the wavering in his own voice, and she was on to it instantly.

"I need no money. Just food. I can sleep in the kitchen or by the campfire. I will be a boy. Nobody will know." The huge eyes fixed on his face. "I feel safe with you."

The words pierced Michael's heart. "You are the most stubborn brat I have ever encountered," he said.

"I was a good servant," Ariana said. "On the march. When the French attacked, I stayed with your mule and your horse, I did not run away."

Michael got up. As he passed her, he reached out and ruffled the auburn curls. "I know you did," he said. "I was frantic, I thought you were going to get yourself killed."

"I got them across the river."

Michael poured two cups of wine and brought one to her. "You did," he admitted. "And I'm bloody grateful, I'm very attached to Sligo, I'd have hated to lose him. And yes, you were a very good servant. When we got here, I was thinking how much I missed you taking care of my kit and my horses. Surprising how quickly I got used to you."

"You would not have to pay the women for laundry and mending," Ariana said. She was negotiating, Michael could hear it in her voice, and she was making a very good case. "I can do all that. I will not trouble you, I can sleep in the stables."

"You bloody can't," Michael said firmly. "God knows who might find you alone in there and for all your insistence, you're still a lass and a very young one. You can sleep in the kitchen for now, I'll get Jenson to find you some bedding and I'll speak to Mrs van Daan about finding you something a bit better. But brat, this is temporary, you understand. Just through winter quarters, you can't come on campaign with me. I'm hoping by the time we march out again, I'll have found something a lot more suitable for you. And if you follow me after that, I'm sending you back."

She ducked her head in something like a bow and Michael reached for his shoes. "I'm going to speak to Jenson and to Mrs van Daan," he said. "Wait here. God only knows what the rest of the battalion are going to think about me yelling Ariana every time I want my boots cleaned, they're going to think the worst of me."

"You do not have to call me Ariana," the girl said, with unexpected dignity. "I like it when you call me Brat."

***

Paul was almost asleep when Anne slid in beside him and he reached for her, feeling how cold she was. "Everything all right, love?"

"Yes. Poor Michael, he has no idea what to do about that girl. I cannot believe she followed him again, I thought we had her settled with the nuns."

"She's determined," Paul said, enjoying the feel of her snuggling close into him. "Well, she's here now, I'm sure she can make herself useful, we're always short of help. I'll get George to find her a job."

"It appears she already has a job," Anne said. "She's going to continue as a boy and work for Michael."

Paul started to laugh. "I ought to put a stop to that," he said. "Given his reputation, nobody is going to believe she's just his orderly."

"Let's leave it for now, Paul. I've spoken to Michael. I know it's not ideal, but that girl is completely desperate. She's beyond reason, with everything she's been through. The only person she trusts is Michael."

Paul lay quietly, thinking about it. "I think I understand," he said slowly. "He was the person who stepped in and broke the pattern. Until Michael, everything that happened to her ended the same way. He changed it."

"I suppose so. It's odd, but I don't think there's any harm in this."

"No. I'm going to leave it up to Michael for the time being. "Let's give her a chance to feel safe."

There was a wail from the crib in the corner of the room, and Anne sighed and moved away from him to collect her daughter. Georgiana, for all her delicate appearance, was a voracious eater and Paul was beginning to feel concerned for his exhausted wife.

When the baby was finally settled back to sleep, Anne lay back with her eyes closed. Paul studied her. She was unusually pale, for Anne, with dark circles under her eyes which made his heart turn over.

"Oh, Nan, you look so tired. Are you sure you don't want Teresa to try to find a wet nurse? This is going to exhaust you."

Anne opened her eyes and smiled at him. "Don't fuss, Colonel, this is my job, not yours. I think I'll be all right now we're safe and warm and there's enough food. You know how quickly I recover. I'll keep an eye on her and if she's not gaining weight or if I'm not feeling well, we'll look for somebody."

"Is that a promise?" Paul asked, leaning over to kiss her.

"Yes. I'm not stupid, Paul. But I've done this before, and the milk is coming through very well. I'll only have a few months with her, I'd like to make the most of it."

Paul hesitated. He had not intended to raise this with her until they had been settled for a few weeks, but she seemed to sense his intention.

"No, Paul," she said.

Despite his anxiety, Paul grinned. "How do you know what I'm going to say?"

"Because I know you."

"Nan, you could stay in Lisbon for a while. It's very secure now, we have the villa and the children could come out to be with you."

"I'd love to spend some time with them, Paul, but I am not leaving you."

"Love, this campaign has been bloody awful for you and I can't promise next year will be any better. It's so difficult to know what we're getting into, you shouldn't have to…"

"Stop trying to coddle me," Anne said, and there was an edge to her voice. "You once promised me you wouldn't."

"You once told me that I should tell you if your unconventionality was making things hard for me," Paul said.

It was an unfair blow and Paul knew it. He saw her eyes widen in shock and he remained there, looking at her steadily. To his horror, the dark eyes suddenly filled with tears. She raised her hands and scrubbed them away.

"Am I?" she asked, and she sounded suddenly very young and unsure.

261

Paul's resolve melted and he reached to wipe her tears with his own hand.

"No," he said and heard the unsteadiness in his own voice. "Oh God, no, love, I'm just trying to keep you safe."

"I am safe when I'm with you, Paul."

"You might not be. I might not always be there to take care of you, and when I'm not, I am completely terrified of what might happen to you."

His wife studied him for a long time. Then she said:

"How do you think I feel?"

Paul felt himself flinch internally. Anne held his gaze for a long time.

"Girl of my heart, that has always been the lot of women whose men are at war."

"Don't prose at me, Paul van Daan, I know damned well what my place is, but it doesn't mean I have to like it."

"I'm sorry. I'm not being fair, am I?"

"No, you're not," Anne said flatly. "When we married, we agreed we would stay together through it all. It hasn't always been easy, but we've made it work when everybody else thought we couldn't. It was never part of the deal, that I would sit at home with the children and a piece of pretty embroidery while you risked your life on the battlefield."

"I know, love."

"For me, nothing has changed. I love you just as much as I ever have and I want to be here, with you. I'm willing to face anything for that. You're my husband. If you tell me I can't, I'll obey you. But you'll have to make it an order, Paul."

Paul felt slightly sick. He also felt overwhelmingly certain that he was in the process of making a stupid mistake. Reaching out, he took her free hand and raised it to his lips.

"I can't really imagine giving you an order," he said. "I'm sorry, I'm an idiot. And a selfish idiot because you're right. We both worry about each other all the time. It isn't fair for me to ask you to go home to stop me worrying while I'm still here fighting. And I don't want you to. It's just that sometimes I look at you, and what you go through, and I feel so bloody selfish."

"You're not. It's what I want," Anne said. "Where you are, is where I want to be. Can I still have that?"

Her voice was tentative, as though she expected him to be angry and Paul was furious with himself for making her feel that way. He reached out and drew her closer.

"You can have whatever you want. Love, I'm sorry. There is never going to be a time when I don't want you with me. I just feel so guilty when I know I'm putting you in danger."

"You aren't. I am. Let me choose, Paul."

Paul kissed her again. "Always," he said seriously. "Can we forget this particularly idiotic conversation?"

Anne smiled properly. "Gladly. Although I will admit that I am thoroughly looking forward to a few months of comfort here. I love this place;

262

it feels like home. Do you think Patience would bring the children out again this winter?"

"I'll make sure she does, I want to see them. Will must have changed so much. And they'll be able to meet their new sister."

"Grace will go wild about her; she was hoping for a girl," Anne said. "Thank you, Paul. I know I worry you."

"I know I worry you as well, bonny lass." Paul hesitated, and then decided to take the plunge. "Look - there is something you can do to help me."

"What is it?"

"Let Teresa find a nurse for Georgiana. I know you managed with Will, but this year has been so bloody awful. We're both so tired. It doesn't change how much we love her, it just gives you more sleep. And it gives us some time together. I really want that…"

"Yes."

Paul stopped. "Yes?"

"Yes. I'll talk to Teresa tomorrow. She'll ask around, we'll find somebody. If that's going to make you feel happier, I'll pick something else to be stubborn about."

Paul drew her closer. "Thank you," he whispered. "Oh, Nan, thank you."

She had relaxed back into his arms again and Paul could feel the tension leaving her body. He thought, not for the first time, how ridiculous some people might find it, for a man of his age and experience to be so completely invested in the happiness of one woman and then he thought again, how completely right it felt, that he should be so.

"Paul? May I ask you something?"

Paul kissed her gently, and then nuzzled her ear, making her giggle. "Anything, light of my life. It is almost Christmas, and if I could, I'd give you the riches of the world."

Anne slid her body down under his with obvious intention. "I wasn't thinking of that," she said. "I thought I might like to learn how to shoot. It could be very useful when faced with a French hussar with a bad attitude."

Paul lifted his head to look down at her in total astonishment and saw that she was completely serious. After a moment Anne appeared to realise the incongruity of her request at this moment, and she began to giggle. Paul was laughing too, and they lay entwined in the bed, stifling their laughter in the pillows until mirth drifted joyously into lovemaking and onwards into deep and contented sleep.

# Author's Thanks

Many thanks for reading this book and I hope you enjoyed it. If you did, I would be very grateful if you would consider leaving a short review on Amazon or Goodreads or both. One or two lines is all that's needed. Good reviews help get books in front of new readers, which in turn, encourages authors to carry on writing the books. They also make me very, very happy.

Thank you.

# Author's Note (May contain spoilers)

Wellington's campaign of 1812 is remarkable. In twelve months, his army managed to storm two border fortresses, advance into Spain, win a spectacular victory at Salamanca and enter the Spanish capital of Madrid. The French must have wondered what had hit them.

The campaign ended with an attempt on a third fortress city, but Burgos proved too much for Wellington's army, and he was obliged to make a difficult retreat, with the French at his heels, back to the border. It was a miserable end to a triumphant year, but it did not nullify Wellington's achievements. He had given the Allied army an ascendency over the French which it had not had before, and the next campaigning season had a new purpose to it.

I have, as always, taken some liberties with history for the sake of my story. The Light Division was not heavily engaged at the battle of Salamanca, so I have given my fictional brigade something else to do. The skirmish at Alba de Tormes on the day of the battle is entirely of my own invention, although it is true that the Spanish troops holding the town marched out without Wellington realising it. Wellington made much of this in his letters, explaining how the French army managed to escape, but it is hard to imagine how 2000 Spaniards could have stopped the entire retreating French army any more than Paul's brigade could have. Wellington appears to have expected more of the French to make for the fords at Huerta. Even so, darkness and exhaustion made a successful pursuit impossible.

The mistreatment of the French garrison from the Retiro really happened and is recounted in Thomas Henry Browne's published journal. In reality, Browne rode after the Spanish on his own, and records that the French prisoners made it to Bilbao without further attacks, which tells me something about how effectively Browne must have got his point across. I gave him some help in my novel, but it shouldn't take away from what Browne did.

The combat on the Huebra, also known as the battle of San Munoz, is one of those confused skirmishes which sounds different in every account. Even the layout of the river and the fords is hard to establish; I would like to know how much the landscape has changed between 1812 and now. Accordingly, I have used author's licence and created a different ford and a skirmish of my own.

As always in my books, I have occasionally stolen the laurels of another officer or another regiment to give my characters something to do. My apologies to the officer who actually led the assault on the Retiro in Madrid, I hope his ghost will forgive me.

The letter which Paul reads out to Johnny Wheeler at the end of the book is taken directly from Wellington's memorandum, which caused enormous resentment among his officers especially when it was published in the London newspapers. The Light Division were especially angry, since their men held discipline very well during the retreat.

That letter epitomises every reason why his Lordship is such a central character in my books. The man simply will not be ignored.

As with all the new editions of these books, I've included one of my free short stories as a bonus at the end, so that readers who don't spend much time online don't miss out on them. *The Gift* was published at Christmas 2021 and was my own Christmas present to those of my readers who complained that Captain David Cartwright was getting a raw deal in his personal life. I hope you enjoy it.

# The Gift

*1ˢᵗ March, 1812*

*Wanted, for immediate employment. Respectable female to act as housekeeper and companion to elderly lady, living alone in the town of Rye. References required. Apply in writing to Captain Cartwright, via this newspaper.*

*14ᵗʰ March, 1812*

*Dear Captain Cartwright*

*I write to apply for the situation advertised. I am a single lady, aged thirty-four, with considerable experience in housekeeping. Until recently, I was employed in taking care of an elderly relative. I have provided a recommendation from a clerical gentleman and, should this prove satisfactory, I would be free to take up the position immediately.*

*Yours, respectfully*

*H. Carleton.*

*Quinta de Santo Antonio, Freineda, Portugal, November 1812*

Major David Cartwright of the 112ᵗʰ infantry did not generally consider himself burdened by family responsibilities, so it was a shock to find a package of letters awaiting him on his arrival in Ciudad Rodrigo in the November of 1812, giving him news of two bereavements.

The first of them, that of his elderly Aunt Susan, should not have been a surprise. Mrs Everton was in her eighties and had been unwell for so many years that David was amazed she had lasted this long. During her final months her recent memory had faded, and she had drifted into the distant past. She had done so happily enough, according to Miss Forbes, her long-time housekeeper and companion, who wrote to David occasionally with news. David was grateful, but missed his aunt's regular letters, full of acerbic remarks about her neighbours, the current government, and the iniquities of the butcher.

Miss Forbes was elderly herself and had written to David as her own health began to decline, suggesting that it was time for a younger replacement. David, newly transferred into the 112th from a tedious post in the quartermaster's department, had no time to take furlough to attend to distant family affairs. He had taken Miss Forbes' advice and advertised the post, leaving it to the departing housekeeper to select the new incumbent.

Miss Forbes wrote to him just before she left for an honourable retirement with her widowed sister, expressing cautious approval of her successor. Miss Helen Carleton was, in her opinion, young for the post, but appeared very efficient and good with her elderly charge. David grinned at her assessment, since Miss Carleton was apparently in her thirties, but he supposed she seemed young to a woman approaching seventy. Having discharged his duty to Aunt Susan, he thought no more about it until he arrived back on the Portuguese border, exhausted and dispirited after a long and dangerous retreat, to find a letter from his aunt's solicitor informing him that she had died, leaving a simple will making him her sole heir.

David read the letter again, thinking about his aunt. He had last seen her just before leaving for Portugal to join Wellesley's army four years ago and there had already been signs of her deterioration. Their meeting had been hurried, made awkward by the presence of Arabella, David's wife, whom Mrs Everton cordially disliked. David found himself wishing he had made time to see his aunt alone that week, given that it had been the last time he saw her, but he could not have known it.

Mrs Everton was not a wealthy woman, but she had left David her rambling house in the little seaside town of Rye, in Sussex, and a small income from government bonds. Along with a similar income from his deceased parents, it would enable him, should he decide to leave the army, to live comfortably. David wondered what his wife would have thought of that, then dismissed the thought. Arabella would never have been satisfied with mere comfort. She wanted wealth and social status and a number of other things David was unable to give her, and her disappointment had led to repeated infidelity and their eventual separation.

It had been eighteen months since he had last heard anything of Arabella and during the past year, busy with an unexpected revival of his career, he thought of her less and less. Their marriage had been unhappy, and their separation, although painful, had come as a relief to him. He thought of her briefly when he received the news of his recent promotion to major, but he did not think even that would have satisfied Arabella's ambition.

David opened the next of his letters and began to read. After a moment, he put it down and sat very still, staring out of the window into a damp winter morning, not seeing the drizzling rain.

Arabella was dead.

The letter was from a Mrs Hetherington, who claimed to run a lodging house in Shrewsbury where Arabella had lived for five months before her untimely death. She had died on the charity ward of a local hospital and Mrs Hetherington, who needed to let the room, had taken it upon herself to pack up her possessions and had found several letters giving David's name and regiment. She gave the impression of being surprised to discover that her lodger's claim to a married woman's status was true but stated that she considered it to be her Christian duty to inform him. There were several trunks and boxes of Mrs Cartwright's possessions, and Mrs Hetherington would store them until the end of January, when if not collected, they would be sold. David wondered if the rent was unpaid. He was surprised that the woman had taken the trouble to write to him but supposed she had genuinely felt that it was her duty.

David read both letters several times, unable to decide what to do. Eventually, he took his troubles to his commanding officer.

"I'm wondering if it would be possible to take furlough, sir," he concluded. "I'll have missed my aunt's funeral, but I should see the lawyers and work out what's to be done about the house. It's a decent property just on the edge of town, with a big garden. I'll probably rent it out rather than leave it empty. It shouldn't take much more than a month to arrange everything, but..."

"Take whatever time you need, Major," Colonel Wheeler said. "I'm sorry to hear about your aunt, but in terms of convenience, this couldn't be better. We're in winter quarters and are likely to be for a few months yet. If it was the middle of a campaign, I couldn't manage without you but we're not going anywhere until spring."

"Thank you, sir."

Wheeler stood up and limped to a side table to pour wine for them both. David got up quickly and went to carry the glasses back to the table. Wheeler had been badly injured during the recent retreat and could only walk using a cane for support. Wheeler hobbled back to his chair and sat down with relief.

"I keep forgetting," he said. "I'm not accustomed to being waited on. Thank you, Major."

David sipped the wine. "Is it still painful, sir?"

"Bloody painful, but not as bad as when they first brought me in. I can put weight on it now, but Dr Daniels says I should rest it as much as possible. Davy, I'm conscious that I've said everything that's proper about your aunt and nothing at all about your wife. I don't know what to say. I know you were separated and there was no possibility of a reconciliation, but she was very young. I am sorry."

David was grateful. His own emotions about Arabella's death were still raw and too muddled to make sense of, but he appreciated Wheeler's tact and also his bravery in raising the matter where another man would have let it pass. Wheeler had known Arabella during the time she had travelled with the army and knew the full circumstances of her various, very public infidelities. One of her first affairs had been with David's current brigade commander. A recent one had left her carrying a child which could not possibly have been her husband's and had led to their final separation.

"Thank you, sir. I don't know what to say myself. It doesn't feel real. I hadn't heard from her since the day she left, but it's difficult to believe that she's dead. As you say, she was so young, only twenty-seven. And she was always so full of life."

"Do you know what happened?"

"Some kind of fever, according to her landlady. There was an outbreak in the town. She was taken into the local hospital but died within a few days."

"Had she other family?"

"Her father is still alive as far as I know, and there was an aunt. Her mother died a few years ago. I doubt Bella had any contact with her father. When the scandal broke, he wrote to her telling her he never wished to see her or hear from her again. I think I should write to him all the same. He should know she's dead."

"What of the child?"

"I don't know," David said. "I don't even know if it's a boy or a girl, or if it's alive. Possibly not, so many children die in infancy and the landlady doesn't mention it. But I should at least make a push to find out."

"It's not your responsibility, Davy," Colonel Wheeler said gently.

David looked at him, troubled. "I know it isn't. But sir, who else is going to bother?"

\*\*\*

Arriving in Southampton on a bright, blustery day, David made enquiries about the best method of travelling to Rye, which was about a hundred miles along the south coast. There were no direct mail coaches, and David objected to the cost of hiring a post chaise, but he was able to find a place on a carrier's wagon leaving early the following morning. The journey was not particularly fast, but was surprisingly entertaining, as Mr Samuel Rochester regaled his passenger with stories of his life on the road. David slept in small inns along the way and was finally deposited, along with his luggage, at the gates of Oak Lodge just after midday. He had written to inform Miss Carleton of his expected arrival.

The door was opened by a maid in a plain dark gown and white apron. She bobbed a curtsey and stood aside, murmuring that she would call the boy to bring in his box. The boy turned out to be a sturdy manservant who was probably approaching forty. As far as David was aware these were the only two servants apart from the housekeeper.

He stood in the hallway awaiting the appearance of Miss Carleton. A door opened and a young woman emerged from the kitchen area at the back of the house. She wore a respectable dark green woollen gown, with a lace-trimmed cap pinned to very fair hair, and she had a pair of bright blue eyes, a decided nose and an expression which hovered between apprehension and defiance. David, who was hopeless at such things, thought she was probably not much above twenty. The girl approached and gave a little curtsey. David bowed, utterly bewildered.

"Major Cartwright. Welcome home, sir. Harvey will put your luggage in the master bedroom. It's been cleaned and aired, and I'll ask Sarah to unpack for you. Unless you've brought a valet?"

"No, I haven't," David said. "Thank you. Only, I do not perfectly understand…who are you?"

The girl folded her hands at her waist. "I am Miss Carleton, sir, your aunt's companion and housekeeper. You arranged for my employment."

David stared at her for a very long time, then surprised out of his customary good manners, he said:

"I'm not sure who I employed, ma'am, but I'm very sure it wasn't you. The lady who applied for that post gave her age as thirty-four, and I'll be surprised if you're older than twenty. Who the devil are you?"

The girl raised well-marked eyebrows and looked down her slightly long nose. "Well you must be surprised then, Major, because I am twenty-four. And I am indeed Miss Carleton. I have been working here since Miss Forbes left at the beginning of the year, and I nursed your aunt through her final illness. Obviously I am in the process of seeking a new post but Mr Bourne, her solicitor, suggested I remain to keep the house in order until your arrival. And to cook your meals for you, unless you intend to do that for yourself, because neither Harvey nor Sarah has the least aptitude for cooking."

David stared at her open-mouthed. Miss Carleton stared back. There was definitely defiance in her expression now. Eventually David said:

"You lied to me in your application."

"Yes, I did."

"Why?"

"Because yours was the tenth post I had applied for, and all of the others rejected me on the grounds of my age."

"I would have done the same."

"Then it is unnecessary for you to ask why I told an untruth."

"Was any of your application true?" David asked. He was genuinely curious. Miss Carleton lifted her chin with something like indignation.

"Of course it was. All of it, apart from that one small detail. I am a gentleman's daughter, I have been used to acting as housekeeper to my parents, who live in Leicester, and I cared for my elderly grandmother before she died."

David studied her for a long time. "So why were you seeking employment?" he asked finally. "If your parents…"

"My parents do not employ a housekeeper, Major Cartwright, and I was tired of working for nothing. My mother was not grateful for my efforts, I spent my time running the household or visiting my older sisters to help with their children. All my mother's attention was focused on finding a husband for my youngest sister, in the hope that might repair the family fortunes. I was sick of being an unpaid drudge, so I chose to seek paid employment instead. My father called me undutiful, and my mother prophesied that I would ruin my reputation and come to a bad end, but so far, I think it has gone rather well.

Until today, that is."

David could think of nothing at all to say. He stood looking at her, struggling to think of a suitable response. Miss Carleton looked back, daring him to speak. The silence went on.

Abruptly, the girl straightened her back and bobbed another neat curtsey. "Would you like some tea, Major? I can serve it in the small parlour. Neither the drawing room or the dining room have been much used this past year, although I have cleaned the whole house and removed the holland covers. I baked a cake this morning."

"Thank you," David said faintly. "That would be very welcome. No, don't trouble yourself to show me the way. I know the house very well."

The small parlour was situated at the back of the house, overlooking the garden. At this time of year, it was a tangle of damp greenery, but David remembered it as a riot of colour in the spring and summer. His aunt had loved gardening during her younger days.

It was obvious that Miss Carleton had made the room her own. A cosy arrangement of furniture around the fireplace included her sewing box, and a partly darned stocking lay neatly folded on top. On another small table was an inlaid portable writing desk. Against the far wall was a small table and two chairs, which suggested that Miss Carleton dined in this room as well. It was common for upper servants to take meals in the kitchen or in their own room, but Miss Carleton was effectively mistress of this small household and David did not blame her for making herself comfortable.

She returned shortly, shepherding the maid who carried the tea tray. David ran his eyes over it and looked at the maid. "Bring another cup, please. Miss Carleton will be joining me for tea."

The girl did so. David indicated that Miss Carleton should pour. The tea was welcome after his long journey and the cake was excellent. Both improved David's mood considerably. He watched her sip her tea.

"How did you persuade Miss Forbes to collude with your falsehood, Miss Carleton?"

The girl gave him a look. "I did not," she said. "She had no idea, of course, that I had lied about my age. She expressed surprise at how young I was, but once she saw what I could do, she did not mention it again. Why should she? I can cook, I can keep house and I was very good with your aunt. She liked me."

David could not help smiling. "I don't suppose you gave her much choice, ma'am, you're a very decided young woman."

The blue eyes were unexpectedly
misty with unshed tears. "I was very fond of your aunt. Even though she was confused, she was so kind. And she could be very funny. I am sorry she's gone, sir."

"So am I," David said. "I've not inspected the rest of the house yet, ma'am, but I don't need to, I can see you know your work. The place is immaculate. Thank you for your efforts."

"Thank you for acknowledging them." Miss Carleton sniffed audibly.

"I'm sorry I deceived you, sir. It was wrong of me, but I was becoming desperate."

"What will you do now? You mentioned seeking another post, but have you not thought of going home?"

"Not unless I have to," the girl said. "I have written several applications, and I shall continue to do so. I am not sure if you intend to sell the house, Major, but if so, I will naturally leave as soon as you wish me to do so. I am not wholly estranged from my family, they will have me back if needs be. I hope I don't have to though, my mother will be unbearable."

Unexpectedly, David laughed. "Is she really that bad?"

"Yes. She has never got over my father's reversal of fortune. He made several bad investments, and my mother was extravagant. She also had five daughters. Marrying us off successfully has been the aim of her life, and she tried hard to maintain her position in society in the hope that a good marriage could save the family fortunes, but it was not to be."

"But your elder sisters married, I think you said?"

"Yes, eventually. But not the kind of marriage my mother had in mind. They are respectably established, with a collection of children, but none of them could afford to give anything away to my parents. Recently they were obliged to sell Carleton Hall. It has been in the family for almost two hundred years, and it was a great blow."

"I can imagine it was," David said. Now that he was beginning to relax, he decided he rather liked this straightforward young woman. She was easy to talk to, with no affectations or pretensions to grandeur. David, who had married a woman full of affectations and pretensions, had developed a dislike of both.

"Not that they are in any way destitute, you understand," Miss Carleton said. "They own the house in Leicester, and it is a perfectly good house. A little larger than this, and not as old. With the proceeds of the sale of Carleton House and the estate and the income from my father's remaining investments, they could live perfectly comfortably. They could even afford a housekeeper. But my mother still has ambitions. My youngest sister, Katherine is just seventeen and is by far the prettiest of all of us. My mother is saving up to give her a London Season in the hope that she will attract a wealthy or titled gentleman and we shall all be saved. Well, at least, I shall not be saved because I have ruined my reputation by seeking paid employment as a housekeeper instead of doing the same job at home and being paid nothing."

David laughed aloud. "I do hope it is not that bad," he said. "Although now you have explained your situation, I do have some qualms about staying here myself. You are, when all is said and done, a young unmarried lady and…"

"If you continue in that vein, Major Cartwright, I shall not be answerable for what I may do," Miss Carleton said in freezing tones. "I am your housekeeper. Your servant. Your paid employee. Nobody gives a fig about such things with the staff. And if I had not told you my background, neither would you."

David took a second slice of cake. "Well either way, I'm not going to stay at an inn. The cooking here is far too good. Miss Carleton, I have no set plans, but I won't be here for long. I have to see my aunt's solicitor to find out how things stand, and then I have to make a journey to Shrewsbury on a separate family matter. I had not thought of selling the house. I may rent it out while I remain with the army. I'm fond of this place, I spent a lot of time here as a boy, fishing off the quay and listening to smuggler's tales from the grooms."

"I'm glad you said that sir. Your aunt would be happy to think that you intend to settle here one day." Miss Carleton stood up. "If you'll excuse me, I'll be needed in the kitchen. Will you be dining at home today?"

"Yes, thank you. If it is not too much trouble."

"It is my job, Major Cartwright. You pay me."

"You seem keen to remind me of it. I am not sure what your usual arrangements are, but will you join me for dinner? It seems foolish for two people to eat in solitary splendour, and there is nobody to mind."

Miss Carleton studied him for a moment, then smiled broadly. "Do you know, Major, when you arrived and looked at me so censoriously, I decided that you were a very strait-laced gentleman, but I think I was wrong."

David found himself smiling back at her. "I think I was in my younger days," he said. "Army life alters your priorities. Although it is unlikely to change my opinion that you should return to Leicester and make your peace with your parents. At least for the Christmas season."

\*\*\*

Helen found cooking a very soothing activity. The kitchen at Oak Lodge was old-fashioned, but well designed and after almost a year in post, she felt at home there. The thought that she might not be here for much longer saddened her. She had been telling the truth when she told Major Cartwright that she was happy in her position.

Helen understood she had potentially committed social suicide in taking the post as Mrs Everton's companion-housekeeper. It was one thing for a young lady in straitened circumstances to seek employment as a governess or companion, or even as a schoolmistress in some respectable establishment. But cooking and cleaning placed one firmly among the ranks of the upper servants. Helen had accepted the post in a spirit of seething resentment at the constant, unreasonable demands of her family and the complete lack of appreciation for the work she did, but she had not really intended to stay for so long. When the expected letters began to arrive from her family, pleading, cajoling, and castigating her rash decision, Helen had expected she would probably give in and go home. To her surprise, she realised she was happy where she was and wanted to stay.

Taking care of Mrs Everton was not difficult and with two servants to assist her, and most of the rooms in the house unused, Helen's housekeeping duties took considerably less time than when she was living at home. Her mother employed a cook, but Mrs Beech could manage only plain dishes, and when the Carletons entertained, it was Helen who planned elaborate menus and spent long hours in the kitchen preparing them. She enjoyed the challenge of complicated dishes but was tired of being used as an unpaid servant, while her elder sisters clamoured, from their various households, for her equally free services as nursemaid and governess. Her youngest sister Katherine spent hours studying her reflection, dreaming of a titled husband, demanding Helen's help with refurbishing her gowns and pouting when Helen told her shortly that she did not have time.

"You are so grumpy, Nell. It isn't as though you did not choose to remain as the daughter at home. Everybody knows that you had every opportunity to marry and have a home of your own, and you refused two perfectly good offers."

"One offer was from Mr Grant the solicitor," Helen said, trying not to grit her teeth. "He is forty-five and drinks so much port that his nose looks like an overripe plum. The other was from the curate, who informed my father that his interest had alighted upon me because he thought it his duty, as a man of God, to eschew all thoughts of beauty in favour of a plain woman with a light hand for the pastry. He further said that he thought in time he would be able to repress my tendency to levity and teach me to show greater modesty in public. Even Mother thought that was a bad idea."

"Well it is your own fault, Nell. You are not at all plain, you have beautiful hair and lovely eyes. You simply refuse to try."

"I have the Carleton nose, Kitty."

"It is a perfectly nice nose, if a little more prominent than others. If you would look at your wardrobe and curl your hair and learn to flirt a little, you would do so much better. Look at Eliza. Nobody thought she would do so well."

"I have the greatest respect for Mr Ingram, Kitty, but if I had to be married to a man that dull I should expire within a year."

Her younger sister laughed. "Well I shall not care how dull my husband is, dearest Nell, as long as he is rich. Now come and look at my old blue and tell me if you think we can remove the train."

Helen paused in rolling out her pie crust, surprised to realise that there were tears in her eyes. She blinked them back firmly. She missed Katherine's laughter and occasional sisterly confidences, but she did not miss being expected to act as a ladies' maid every time her sister was invited out. She supposed that Major Cartwright was correct, and she should go home to her family for the Christmas season, but she was surprised at how little she wanted to.

It felt strange to sit across the table from the Major at dinner. Helen had never eaten in the dining room. She instructed Harvey and Sarah to remove all the extra leaves from the big table and set out the various dishes on the polished sideboard so that they could serve themselves. Major Cartwright went to investigate the wine cellar and as Helen filled their plates, poured two glasses of cool white wine. Helen eyed it suspiciously and the Major laughed.

"I take it you haven't been raiding my aunt's cellar?"

"I don't think I've ever been down there. She liked a glass of wine with her dinner though, right up to the end. I remember you sent her some, once or twice, and it pleased her very much to receive the gift, though I'm not sure she understood where it came from."

He smiled. "I'm glad she got some enjoyment from it. She and I shared a liking for good wine and when I first joined the army and began to travel, I used to try to send her some local wine from wherever I was stationed. When I was in Naples…"

He broke off abruptly and Helen said nothing. She sipped the wine, enjoying the crisp, fruity taste of it. Her employer did the same. She could see him considering, wondering what he should tell her, and whether it was at all suitable for him to tell a housekeeper anything at all. He would not normally have shared details of his personal life with an unmarried young lady from a respectable family whom he had just met, but then he would not have been dining alone with such a person either.

"I was married," Cartwright said abruptly. "I don't suppose you knew, since my aunt was already very forgetful by the time you arrived. She cannot have told you anything about it. Naples was my first posting after we married. Less than a year and Arabella was already very bored with me and wishing she had waited for a better prospect."

"I know about your wife," Helen said. She saw his head snap up and the brown eyes darken in sudden anger and wished for a moment that she had not spoken.

"Who told you?"

"Miss Forbes. She had been with your aunt for so many years, I think they were more like family than employer and servant. I asked, very casually, if you were single or a widower. I thought it unusual that it should be a gentleman placing the advertisement for such a post. I'm sorry if I've offended you, Major, it wasn't my intention. Miss Forbes was not gossiping, but she said that she thought I ought to know in case I did come across any idle gossip in the town."

"Miss Forbes was probably right. What did she tell you?"

"That your marriage had not been a success and that you were separated from your wife. She told me that Mrs Everton used to say that she thought your wife a fool for not appreciating you."

Cartwright gave a very faint smile and began to eat again. "My aunt was invariably biased in my favour, Miss Carleton. She and Arabella never got on well, they were too different. She tried to persuade me against the match. I had very little money, but when I was younger I was ambitious and thought I could make my own way in the world."

"Have you not done so?"

"Yes, I think I have. But it did not come fast enough for Arabella." Cartwright hesitated, seeming to recollect that he was talking to a stranger. "My apologies, Miss Carleton, this is a very unsuitable conversation. Did you make this pastry? It's excellent, I feel very spoiled."

Helen allowed him to turn the conversation neatly away from personal matters. She asked him about his service in the army and found it unexpectedly interesting. He had served in Italy, in Portugal and in Spain, with a spell in Ireland. He spoke little of the battles he had fought, but a great deal about the places he had seen and the people he had met. There was nothing boastful or vainglorious about Major David Cartwright, but Helen thought that he had seen more and done more than most people of her acquaintance. She did not usually find it easy to talk to people she did not know well, particularly gentlemen, but as they finished their meal and Helen rose to clear the table, she was aware of a sense of regret that it was coming to an end.

"I should get these to the kitchen, sir."

"Let the maid do that. Please, sit down and join me in a glass of port. Or if you prefer, you can watch me drinking it. I feel as though I have bored you senseless with my army tales all through dinner and given you no chance to talk about yourself."

Helen subsided, watching Sarah clear the plates. "I've already told you about my situation, sir. I left home in a temper with my ungrateful family. I remained because I liked it here. But I suppose that unless I find another situation as much to my taste as this I shall have to go home."

"Do you think it will be a problem for you? Socially, I mean?"

"I don't suppose for one moment my mother has told anybody that I have been employed as a housekeeper, let alone a cook. She will have said that I am acting as companion to an elderly lady, which is perfectly respectable, you know. Anyway, I had no social life."

"None at all?"

"I used to go to parties when I was Kitty's age. But I didn't really enjoy them that much. Dancing and trying to flirt and speaking nothing but inanities never suited me."

"I can imagine. That doesn't mean you have nothing to say. I've really enjoyed this. May I...that is, I shall be here for a few days, seeing the lawyers and working out how things stand. After that, I am travelling to Shrewsbury on business. But I would like it if you would dine with me again while I'm here. As you are, even temporarily, my housekeeper."

Helen laughed. "As you are, for a short time longer, my employer, sir, I am at your disposal."

As she rose to leave finally, he escorted her into the hallway and bowed. "Thank you again, ma'am, for the meal and the company. Both were excellent."

"I enjoyed it too, sir, although I'm aware that I've stepped above my station this evening."

"Or back into the station you were born to, depending on your perspective. Look, about earlier. The conversation about my wife. I should tell you, that she recently died. A fever outbreak. It was very sudden."

Helen felt a little shock. "Oh no. Oh Major, I'm so sorry."

"Thank you. I'm going to Shrewsbury to see where she's buried. I want to make sure she has a proper gravestone. There are some things I need to collect, and I'll pay any debts that I can find out about."

Helen studied him for a long moment. Major Cartwright was unexceptional, apart from a pair of very fine brown eyes and a rather nice smile. Helen wondered how old he was. She thought possibly in his thirties, although his self-contained manner may have made him seem older than he was.

"I think that is the right thing to do, Major. I hope you won't find it too distressing. I wish, while you are here, that you would furnish me with a list of what you most like to eat. And if there is anything else I can do for you – laundry or mending or suchlike – please let me know. With your aunt gone, I have so little to do."

Cartwright smiled, and she could see the warmth in his eyes. "Thank you. I'll probably take you up on that. But there is one thing you should do. Write to your family, ma'am, and tell them you'll be home for Christmas, even if it is just a visit."

"What will you do for Christmas, sir?"

"I'll stay here and make do with Sarah's cooking."

"It isn't very good."

"It will still be better than what I ate during the retreat from Madrid, ma'am. Goodnight."

\*\*\*

David decided to hire a post-chaise for his journey to Shrewsbury. He had quite enjoyed his adventure with the carrier's cart, but Shrewsbury was a lot further and David had no wish to spend weeks on the road. He admitted to himself, with some amusement, that some of his desire to have this journey over and done with, was because he wanted to get back to Rye before his eccentric housekeeper left for Christmas with her family.

He had not formally given Helen her notice, though he knew he should have done. He was sure that once she was back home, she would decide to stay, and write to tell him so. So far he had made no arrangements with the lawyer about advertising the house for rent. He had asked Helen, during her remaining weeks, to go through his aunt's personal possessions, dispose of the clothing however she thought best and pack up the rest. When he returned, he would go through the boxes for any small items he wanted to keep and make arrangements to put the rest into storage, along with the contents of the wine cellar and a few of the finer items of furniture. He could manage all of that without the help of the estimable Miss Carleton, but he did want to see her again to say goodbye. He had taken a liking to the girl, and she had made his week at his aunt's house thoroughly enjoyable.

He left Helen indulging in an orgy of cooking and food preparation. Clearly the thought of him spending the Christmas feast at the mercy of Sarah's cooking troubled her mind, and David suspected he would be left with a larder stuffed with enough puddings, cured hams and pies to feed half his company. He wondered if she would have to do the same work over again for her unappreciative family and hoped that her mother had the decency to employ a proper cook for the season, so that her prodigal daughter could take her rightful place as a family member. Then again, remembering the sight of Helen in the kitchen, singing Christmas carols, with flour on the end of her nose and her hair curling in little wisps around her face with the steam from the puddings, David wondered if in fact, Helen might be perfectly happy in the kitchen if her family would just show some appreciation.

David had been to Shrewsbury once before, in the early days of his courtship of Arabella, when she had taken him to spend a few days with her aunt who lived in a graceful eighteenth century house close to the Abbey. He had rather liked the ancient town and had hoped that Arabella might settle there with her child, finding some respectable occupation and using the opportunity to make a new start. Mrs Hetherington's lodging house suggested that she had not managed to do so.

The lodging house was better than he had expected, and Mrs Hetherington was a dark-eyed handsome woman in her thirties, who kept a clean house, served plain food to those lodgers who required it and showed a rather touching reticence at sharing with her widower the details of Arabella's life. David set aside his awkwardness in favour of plain speaking and over a good cup of tea at the big square kitchen table, managed to drag the information from his reluctant informant.

"I wouldn't normally have let a room to a woman like her," Mrs Hetherington said. "Not that I haven't had lady boarders before. Mostly it's gentlemen, though. Music masters and young officers and those fallen on hard times. I don't take the labouring classes, my rooms are too good for that. I even had a poet once. I take the money up front for some of them, mind, being as they come from a class used to paying their bills when they feel like it. Still, I don't have much trouble. The rooms are clean and well furnished, and I've got three gentlemen who have been with me a long time. The ladies come and go. Governesses and the like, between jobs. I feel sorry for them. Nowhere to go and no money for expensive lodgings. I keep the top two attic rooms for the ladies. They can be private up there, and I let them share my sitting room while they're here."

"And my wife?"

"Anybody could see she'd fallen on hard times. And anybody could see that she'd no intention of finding a respectable position as a governess or a companion, although that was the story she told me when she applied for the room. Still, she'd the money to pay and both rooms were empty, so I let her have one of them, providing she paid in advance for the month and didn't bring anyone back to the room. She laughed when I told her that. 'Mrs Hetherington,' she said. 'My gentlemen friends do not frequent common lodging houses. Although perhaps they should, this is the most comfortable room I have occupied for months.'"

David winced and tried not to show it. "She was here for five months?"

"She had the room for five months. She paid me, regular as clockwork and I never had to ask her for it. I wouldn't say she stayed here for five months, mind, she was in and out. Sometimes she'd be here for a week or two. Slept half the day, ate her meals in her room and was out in the evening, dressed up like a duchess. Sometimes I'd see nothing of her for a month. I always imagined, begging your pardon, sir, that she'd found a gentleman friend who was taking care of her."

"I'm sure you were right, ma'am."

"I'd no idea she was truly wed. She called herself Mrs, but they often do."

"We were separated."

"It's a tragedy. She wasn't a respectable woman, sir. She had this way about her, like she was laughing at herself almost. But she was never anything but civil to me."

David remembered the many times when Arabella had failed to be civil to anybody and was obscurely glad. Perhaps in her darker times, she had learned something that comfort, and prosperity had failed to teach her.

"Where is she buried?"

"At St Mary's, sir. The Rector will know the details."

The Rector was surprised but sympathetic. He led David to the plain unmarked grave and left him alone for a while. When David went to find him, he provided sherry and spiritual guidance in the Rectory and gave David the name of a reputable stonemason who could erect a gravestone.

David spent the night at the Lion Hotel, then returned to Mrs Hetherington's lodging house the following day. She led him up two flights of stairs to a small room under the eaves, where a trunk, a wooden box and several bags contained all that was left of Arabella Cartwright's short, tragic life. David sat on the narrow bed and cried, remembering their courtship, the first heady days of their marriage when all he could think about was making love to her, and the first painful realisation that their love was not after all based on solid ground, but on the shifting sands of her discontent and relentless pursuit of something better.

Eventually, David pulled himself together and repacked the bags and boxes carefully, piling them up for collection by the carter whom he had arranged to take them to the Lion Hotel. There was another call he should make, although he was not looking forward to it. It must have been ten years or more since he had last seen Mrs Gladstone, Arabella's aunt, but he remembered the house well from his previous visit. The butler took his card with an expression of surprise and asked him to wait. He returned soon afterwards and ushered David into a panelled book room where a portly gentleman who looked to be around forty came forward to greet him.

"Major Cartwright. This is a surprise and no mistake, you're the last person I expected to see here. On furlough, eh?"

David shook his hand. "Yes, sir, for a short time. I had family affairs to attend to, both here and on the south coast. I was hoping to speak to Mrs Gladstone."

"Can't be done, I'm afraid, Major. My mother died almost a year ago.

Smallpox outbreak. Very sad. Jasper Gladstone, at your service. I don't think we ever met."

"No, I think you were in India when I visited last. It was a long time ago."

"Aye, that'll be right. I left the company service about two years ago and set up in business for myself in Bristol. When my mother died, I inherited the house, so my family moved here. I still keep rooms in Bristol, it's where my offices are. I think I can guess what's brought you to Shrewsbury, Major. A bad business."

"You heard that she died, then?"

"Yes, though I didn't wish to. The Rector took it upon himself to inform me. Damned piece of impudence, I called it. I told him I'd heard nothing of my cousin since she disgraced herself and didn't consider her any business of mine. And frankly, Major, I'm surprised you don't feel the same way."

David did not speak immediately. He had no wish to be hypocritical and he thought that if Arabella's death had not coincided with that of his aunt, he would probably not have asked for furlough to visit her grave. He had tried hard to set aside his feelings for Arabella a long time ago and he almost resented the stirring up of painful memories. At the same time, she had lived as his wife for six years and he did not think he could have dismissed all thought of her as Gladstone appeared to think he should.

"As I said, I had other family business to attend to," he said finally. "Since I was in England, I thought it right to see where she was buried and arrange for a gravestone."

"Women like her shouldn't be given the luxury of a proper burial," Gladstone said shortly. "Sherry, Major? Throw them in the ground and forget about them, that's what I say. The grief she brought to her poor parents, and my mother. And you, of course."

He held out the sherry glass. David took it and set it on the table, having no desire to drink it. "I understand Arabella came here to have her child."

"So I believe. I wasn't here then, of course, or I'd have put a stop to that. My mother was always sentimental about my cousin. I think she had some notion of finding somebody to take the brat and rehabilitating Bella, but I could have told her that wouldn't wash. My cousin was a whore, Major. A bad 'un, through and through. You can't help a woman like that, and I wouldn't have tried."

David's anger was beginning to settle into a cold disdain. "I am sure you would not," he said. "Will you tell me what happened after the child was born?"

"She stayed for a month or two. I wrote to my mother to inform her that we would be unable to visit her, of course, while she had that woman and her bastard in the house. I've children of my own, I couldn't have them exposed to that kind of thing. Once Bella was back on her feet after the birth it went pretty much as you'd expect. She took up with some man again – don't know who he was, some sort of financier I believe, invested in canals and bridges and engineering works. She took off in the middle of the night with all her fine clothing, leaving my mother with the brat on her hands. I don't know how long it lasted, but not long. She wrote to my mother begging to come back, but this time the old lady had the sense to say no, though she kept the brat. Bella had a small income of some kind."

"It was very little, just the interest on her marriage settlement. Pin money only."

"I think she took rooms in town and made up for any shortfall by selling herself to whoever would have her."

David felt very sick. He had guessed the bare bones of the story, but hearing it related so brutally hurt all over again. He hoped his distress did not show on his face, because he did not wish to give this man a present of his feelings. He would not willingly have given him the time of day.

"What happened to the child?" he asked in neutral tones. "Did it contract the smallpox as well?"

"Lord, no. My mother had the nursemaid keep it isolated. No, it outlived her, that's for sure. Probably dead by now, though. Not many of them survive beyond their first year in those public institutions, do they?"

"Public institution?"

"You know. Charity wards. Orphan asylums. Workhouses. Wherever they put the little bastards nobody wants. The Rector might know if you're interested, though I can't think why you should be. It wasn't your brat and I doubt she even knew who sired it. And don't look at me like that, Major. It was nothing to do with me. When we'd buried my mother, I left the whole thing in the hands of my man of business. He paid off the staff, got the house in order and took the little bastard to the Parish and dumped it there. What in God's name was I expected to do about it? She made her bed, my cousin Arabella, and if she'd cared about that child, she'd never have run off again. She's better off dead, where she can't bring any more disgrace to this family, and her bastard with her. Let's drink to it."

David looked at Gladstone, a florid, prosperous-looking man with thinning hair and a substantial paunch, as he raised his sherry glass and tossed back the warm amber liquid. He reached for his own glass, waited politely for Gladstone to finish drinking, then threw the contents of it fully into the man's face. Gladstone gave a squawk of surprise, scrubbing the liquid away with his sleeve as it stung his eyes.

"You…you…how dare you, sir? To come into my house, acting as though your bitch of a wife should matter to me, and then…we'll see about that, sir."

He surged forward. David waited for him to be completely off balance, then punched him once, very hard. Blood spurted from the bulbous nose and Gladstone fell back, clutching his face as he hit the floor with a crash which rattled the glasses on the polished sideboard. David had only taken up boxing a year earlier in winter quarters, under the tuition of a friend in his brigade. He had never punched a man in anger in his life before and he was astonished at how satisfying it was. He stood for a moment watching Gladstone bleed onto what looked like an expensive Persian rug.

"Thank you for your time, Mr Gladstone. Please don't get up. I'll see myself out."

It had started to rain as David made his way back to St Mary's Church. He found the Rector in his study and blurted out his story and his concerns with little regard for good manners. He was too angry to care what the man thought. The Rector heard him out patiently.

"I am sorry, Major Cartwright. I can see this has all been a shock to you. I respect your compassion and your charity in very difficult circumstances but I'm afraid I have no information about your wife's child. Mrs Gladstone was not a member of my church, and I did not know much about her family, although we had met socially on occasion. Naturally…Shrewsbury is not a large town, and there is always gossip. Many people felt that Mrs Gladstone was wrong to have taken in her niece in such circumstances, and I know there was a general feeling that she would never be accepted back into polite society, but no such attempt was made. When I was asked by the Parish to arrange for your wife's burial, there was no mention of any family. I had rather assumed that if there was a child, he or she must have died."

"Is it possible to find out?" David asked. "What would happen to such a child? Is there an orphan asylum?"

"The parishes have combined in Shrewsbury, to fund a House of Industry where the indigent and the sick are tended. Older children have their own facilities and schooling within the House, but it is customary for the Parish to send babies out to nurse in local households."

"I don't understand."

"Women are paid to take care of the child until it becomes old enough to enter the House of Industry. I presume this child would be very young?"

"Around eighteen months, I suppose. There must be records of where such children are sent."

"You should apply to the workhouse clerk, Mr Jackson. Wait, I will write a brief note to him. He knows me and it will probably speed your enquiries along." The Rector reached for his pen, then paused and looked at David. "Major – what do you intend to do if the child is alive?"

David was unable to reply. He realised he had no idea.

***

Mr Jackson scanned the Rector's letter and gave a sigh which blew the papers about on his desk. He got up and went to collect a ledger from a shelf. David watched as he ran a bony finger down a column, muttering to himself. He turned a page, then another, and began a tuneless whistle, peering at the unintelligible scrawl which passed for writing. David wondered if it was Mr Jackson's own writing and if so, why he did not learn to read it more quickly.

"Aha!" Jackson said triumphantly. "Aha! As I thought. Now we have him. Now we have him, indeed."

"Him?" David said quickly.

"Him. A boy. The boy. Delivered to this establishment on the date in question by Gareth Southern, clerk to Mr Timothy Prestcote. It says here...well now. It says the boy is an orphan."

"Does it not say the mother's name?" David asked.

"It does," Jackson said doubtfully, peering so closely that his nose almost touched the page. "Difficult to read it...Cartridge...no, Cartwright, I think. Looks like Billy. Billy Cartwright. Funny name for a female."

"Bella," David said, trying to sound patient.

"Is it? Oh. Oh yes, could be. Yes, I think it is." Jackson sounded pleased. "Bella Cartwright, prostitute. Presumed deceased."

Jackson froze. On his desk beside the Rector's note was the calling card David had given him. David watched as he read the name again and made the connection, then saw his eyes widen. He looked up very slowly and suddenly there was a wealth of apprehension in his expression.

"Oh. Oh, my. Major Cartwright?"

"As I told you earlier."

"Oh my. Oh dear. How awkward. How very embarrassing. I have no memory for names, sir, but in this case I ought to have. Oh my. But this child...he cannot be related to you, surely?"

"I think you'll find he is," David said pleasantly. "Was no effort made to trace his mother?"

"Well no, sir. Not given that she was reported to be dead. I cannot understand...was she not dead?"

"Not then," David said. "She left the child in the care of her aunt, Mrs Gladstone, who sadly died soon afterwards."

"Gladstone? Do you refer to the family of Mr Jasper Gladstone, Major? But this is extraordinary. He is a member of our board. I cannot think how such a terrible mistake came to be made."

"I can," David said briefly. "Am I to understand that the boy is still alive? Where can I find him?"

"Yes. Yes, indeed. At least, according to our records. He was sent out to nurse with Mrs Bonel, and we've heard nothing to the contrary."

"But?"

"They don't always tell us straight away, sir. If the child dies. Sometimes they bury them quietly and keep taking the money. Eventually the yearly inspection comes around and then they'll come forward and claim the death was recent."

David felt sick again. "Annual inspections for a baby that young?" he said. "Is that all?"

"We've not the time or the staff to do more, sir. I can give you Mrs Bonel's address if you want to visit the boy."

David found the cottage easily enough. There was a narrow frontage open to the River Dee, with chickens scrabbling in a fenced yard and a strong stench of excrement and urine. David paused by the door, taking a deep breath.

His stomach was churning so badly, he was worried he might vomit and for the first time ever he felt the urge to flee in the face of the enemy. Before he had the opportunity to do so however, he heard the cry. It was a long wail of misery which drowned out the cackling of the hens and the steady rush of the river, swollen with winter rains.

Inside the smell was stronger, but there was no sign of life in the main living area of the cottage. David walked through to a small doorway at the back and out into a muddy yard, where two pigs snuffled around, splashed with mud, and snorting indignantly. There was still no sign of occupation, but at the back of the yard was a rough wooden lean-to and the wail was stronger, floating out into the freezing winter air. It sounded like a young child. David walked across the yard and went in through the door.

He found the child in a rough wooden cot, little more than a box, built high against the wall of the shed. He was dressed in a linen smock which was smeared with his own dirt. There were several reeking, threadbare blankets in the cot and the child was crying and shivering, his voice high and thin in the chill air. He was thin and pale and his hair was a coppery red.

"There, then, what's that yelling about, it's not nearly time for your dinner, and if you don't shut up..."

David turned. The woman was thin herself, with sharp features and brown eyes, wearing a respectable brown dress and a warm woollen shawl. She looked irritated, but at the sight of David she froze, ran her eyes over him then managed a wholly false smile. She dropped a little curtsey.

"Good day to you, sir. May I help you?"

"Mrs Bonel?"

"Yes, sir."

"I've come about the child. I understand he was put out to nurse last year by the Parish?"

"That's right, sir. A poor little orphan mite. I've looked after him as if he was my own, haven't I, poppet?"

The child had stopped wailing and was staring at David, one grubby fist pushed into his mouth.

David walked forward. He had spent the walk down to the cottage calculating the boy's age and decided he must be around seventeen months, though he was small, probably through poor nourishment. David studied the child and saw Bella's beautiful hazel eyes looking back at him with wary interest.

"What's his name?"

"Whatever you want it to be. He doesn't..."

David spun around in sudden fury. "What name did they give you for him, you slovenly bitch? Any more of this and I'll have the magistrate down here, and if you've nothing to hide from them I'll be very surprised."

The woman visibly flinched. "George. They called him George."

George had been the name of both David's and Arabella's fathers. He looked back at the child. "George? Georgie?"

The boy stared at him for a long moment. Then, cautiously, he shifted onto his knees, reached for the wooden slats of the cot and pulled himself up to his feet. David looked at the streaks of filth on the smock and consciously reined in his anger. He studied the child. The child stared back. After a moment, David reached out and touched one of the tiny hands clutching the edge of the cot. George flinched away as if expecting a blow and David felt an overwhelming wave of protective tenderness.

"He's cold. And he seems terrified."

"It's his own fault, sir, he throws off his blankets. And they're like that at this age. Skittish, like."

David kept his eyes on the child and reached past him into the cot to feel the blankets. As he had suspected, they were soaked.

"Does he have any other clothing?"

"Another gown, but it's wet. I do my best, but I can't keep up with the laundry."

"Then get me a dry blanket to wrap him in. I'm taking him with me."

"Sir, without proper authorisation…"

David turned to look at her. "You will receive authorisation before the end of the day," he said in icy tones. "Get me a blanket for him. Now."

Afterwards, seated in the post-chaise as it rattled its way towards London and then on towards Rye, David looked back over that long day and found it hard to recognise himself. He had been carried on a wave of indignant fury which swept aside all difficulties and opposition. His years as an army quartermaster had given him a talent for organisation and the ability to juggle too many tasks, all of them urgent. David was thankful for the experience since he did not think he would ever have made it into the coach early the following morning otherwise.

He was also thankful for the support of Mrs Hetherington, who greeted his arrival with the child with blank astonishment.

"I know I'm imposing on you, ma'am, but it's only for today. I've nobody else to turn to in Shrewsbury, and I've a great deal to do to be ready to travel with him tomorrow."

"I don't understand," the woman said, studying the crying child. "Who is he? Where does he come from? Dear God, look at the state of him. He's filthy and he looks half-starved."

"He is half-starved," David said grimly. "It's a disgrace, sending a child out to a place like that. She was keeping him in an outhouse, with the pigs and the chickens. I could kill her, and the Parish Board along with her, except that I don't have time."

"Is he your wife's child, Major?"

"Yes. She can't have known where he was, though. She left him with her family. She probably thought it best for him, but when her aunt died, that odorous piece of pig's excrement Jasper Gladstone sent him to the parish. His own cousin's child. When I've got time, I'm going to ensure that his reputation in this town ends up in the sewer. I don't need to be here to do that, I can write letters, and I intend to ask for the assistance of my Brigadier's wife in the matter. She will enjoy the challenge."

Mrs Hetherington looked amused. "And I thought you such a quiet gentleman," she said. "But Major...he may be your wife's child, but surely he isn't yours? A gentleman like you wouldn't have let her take his son away like this. Are you sure you can just remove him from the Parish because you want to? There will be regulations."

"If they try to stop me, I will take their regulations and shove them where they deserve to be. But they won't. They can't. He is my wife's child, born within wedlock. We were legitimately married, that never changed. If I say he is my son, and can prove she was my wife, there isn't a damned thing they can do about it."

Mrs Hetherington gaped at him. "Sir...are you sure?"

George had stopped crying, probably because he was too exhausted to continue. He was watching David from enormous tear-drenched eyes, but David thought that he seemed more relaxed in his arms. He looked back at the child and finally admitted to himself what he had been unable to recognise two years earlier.

"Yes," he said. "Oh God, yes. I should have done it then. I should have gone to her and offered to acknowledge the child. Because I wanted a child so badly that it hurt. Arabella didn't really, and when I found out, I was furious. It seemed so unjust, because I realised that it might have been my fault that we couldn't have children. Which meant I might never be able to have a child." David stopped, realising that he was babbling. "I'm sorry, this is the most inappropriate conversation I have ever had."

"Lord bless, you sir, I run a lodging house. You'd be amazed what people tell me. Leave him with me. I'll get him bathed and fed, and I'll send Sally to the market, if you'll leave the money. There's a booth that sells used clothing, they'll have baby clothes there. I don't know how you'll manage him on the road, mind. He's not clean yet, so you'll need to change his clouts and wash him, and it's not work for a gentleman."

"I'll learn, you can show me. It's only for three days, and once I'm back in Rye I can hire a nursemaid. I'm going to have to write to extend my furlough, but they'll understand. It's winter quarters. Mrs Hetherington, thank you. I will never forget what you've done for me today."

It took longer to reach Rye on the return journey. It was necessary to stop more frequently because of George, and overnight stops were more complicated. David had no experience of taking care of a child, but Mrs Hetherington gave him an emergency lesson in feeding, bathing, and changing clouts in half a day. The journey was a nightmare of a crying child, desperate inn staff and irritable post boys.

After two days of almost constant wailing, and fighting against every attempt to comfort him, George fell suddenly into an exhausted sleep in David's arms. He barely awoke as David carried him into the Swan Inn. The landlord was more sympathetic than on the previous two nights, and sent a chamber maid to wash, change and sit with the boy so that David could eat in peace in the dining room. After two glasses of burgundy, David was almost falling asleep at the table. He went up to his room and found that the girl had just changed George and was settling him into the bed.

"Will you be all right with him, sir? You should have a nursemaid with you."

"She fell ill, and I couldn't delay my journey," David said with a smile. It was the story he had told all along, not really caring who believed it. This girl apparently did and gave him a somewhat misty smile.

"Bless you, sir, I've never seen such a devoted father. Have you much further to go?"

"No, we'll be home before tomorrow evening."

"I'm glad to hear it, you're in need of a rest. With your leave, sir, I'll come back in the morning and get him fed and ready while you have your breakfast."

"Thank you. You've been so kind."

"You're welcome, sir."

David undressed, then checked that there was water in the jug on the washstand and that there were clean clouts available in case of disaster, then he got into bed. The boy lay beside him, long lashed eyes watching him curiously. Over the past days he had seemed to David to see every human contact as a potential threat, and David tried not to imagine the miserable existence that had taught such a young child that nobody was to be trusted. Now, though, he lay wakeful but calm. David looked back at him.

"Are you in the mood for conversation, Georgie? I'm not sure I'll be much use at it, I'm so tired. Still, we can give it a try. I'm your Papa. You don't know it yet, and nor did I until just recently, but we've a lot of time to get acquainted. At least we will have, when Bonaparte is gone, and I can come home to you. In the meantime, we'll need to find you a good nursemaid and a new housekeeper…"

David froze suddenly. He realised that he had forgotten, in the stress of the past days, that his departing housekeeper might well still be in residence when he arrived with a child she knew nothing about. It had not occurred to him to write to Helen Carleton, he had been too busy. Now he realised he should have done so. He wondered if she had already left for her family home in Leicester for Christmas. Part of him hoped she had done so. The other part hoped he would have the chance to see her again, to thank her for her kindness.

He fell asleep quickly and woke in the half-light of dawn. To his surprise, George still slept, curled up against his body, warm in the chill air of the inn bedroom. David lay very still, savouring the moment. Very gently, he kissed the top of the child's head. The colour of his hair reminded David sharply of Arabella and he wept a little, regretting all the things they might have shared.

They arrived at Oak Lodge late in the afternoon, several days before Christmas. George was asleep when David lifted him from the chaise and instructed the coachmen to go to the kitchen for refreshment while the baggage was unloaded. He walked into the house and stopped in the hallway in considerable surprise. The stairs were decorated with greenery and tied with red ribbons. It reminded him of the Christmases of his childhood, and he stood in the hall, the child in his arms, unexpectedly assailed by a rush of memories.

"Major Cartwright."

The girl's voice was astonished. David turned to see her emerging from the kitchen area, still wearing her white apron. She had discarded her lace cap and looked neat and efficient and surprisingly attractive. David quailed internally but took his courage in both hands, remembering that this was his house, and he was her employer.

"Miss Carleton, what on earth are you still doing here?" he asked sternly. "By now, you should be at home with your family, ready to celebrate..."

Helen came forward, ignoring him, and drew back the grubby blanket from George's flushed face. "Is this your wife's boy?" she asked softly.

"Yes," David said. "His name is George. And he is my son."

Helen lifted her eyes to his face. "I'm not going home for Christmas," she said. "I'm sorry, Major, I know I was ordered to do so. But it occurred to me that I might be needed here. And it turns out that I was more right than I knew. Here, let me take him. How on earth did you manage on the journey with him?"

"Very well, ma'am," David said haughtily. He decided not to mention how appalling it had been at times. "I'm an army man, we're very adaptable."

Helen looked up at him, a smile lurking in the blue eyes. "So am I, Major Cartwright. And since I do not think you intend to abandon your profession just yet, that is just as well. I've had a lot of practice taking care of my sisters' children, you know, and we still have a few days before Christmas to get the nursery set up just as it ought to be. He's a beautiful child."

"He's been badly treated. I will tell you everything, ma'am. But just now..."

"Just now, we should take him upstairs. I think he needs changing."

David trod up the stairs in her wake, remembering his resolve of earlier. "I told you to go home."

"I ignored you."

"You cannot remain in my employ if I dismiss you."

"That is very true. I think we should discuss it again after Christmas."

"You are not going to listen to me, are you?"

Helen shot him a look. "Don't you trust me with him, Major?"

David looked back at her steadily. "I cannot think of anybody I would trust more," he said simply. "But Miss Carleton..."

"Major Cartwright, why don't you let me decide for myself? There is nothing more irritating than a man trying to tell a woman how she should think or feel. Just now, let us take care of your son."

\*\*\*

It was frosty on Christmas morning. Helen reluctantly left George in Sarah's devoted charge and went to church with her employer. Inside, she headed towards her usual seat among the tradespeople and upper servants at the back, but Major Cartwright took her arm and steered her firmly into the pew beside him.

Gossip travelled fast in a small town like Rye, and there were sly looks and veiled hints, which over sherry in the rectory turned into open questions about Major Cartwright's new charge. Helen watched admiringly as the Major responded, his replies so bland that eventually even the most avid gossip became frustrated.

"He is my son. My wife and I were temporarily estranged. Tragically she died just as we were planning to reconcile. I am, as you can imagine, heartbroken. Miss Carleton has agreed to remain in my employment as his governess, and to oversee the nursery once I return to the army. I am very grateful to her."

He told the story over and over, varying the words but sticking firmly to the message. Helen felt enormous respect for him. She could not imagine how badly he must have been hurt by his wife, but his thoughts were all of the child. After church, he sat at a table in the hastily furnished nursery, with George on his lap, showing him how to build a simple tower with wooden blocks. George picked up the idea quickly, and then abruptly reached out and pushed the tower over. The hazel eyes flew to the Major's face apprehensively. David Cartwright was laughing.

"Good at siege warfare, I see. Shall we do it again?"

He did so, and this time George gave a crow of laughter as the tower fell. The Major bent and kissed the soft copper hair. Helen stood up, fighting sentimental tears.

"I will be needed in the kitchen, Major, so I'll leave you to it."

He looked around quickly, smiling. "Come back as soon as you can. It's important that he gets to know both of us, but you especially, if you're really going to take on the job of raising him. Are you good at building towers, Miss Carleton?"

Helen smiled, her heart full. "I have three nephews, Major, I am an expert. I just don't want to intrude."

"This is your home too, ma'am, for as long as you choose to stay. You couldn't intrude. And I hope you'll be dining with me as usual. It's Christmas, you cannot leave me to eat alone."

"I should be delighted, sir."

"Was your mother very angry?"

Helen laughed. "Yes," she admitted. "But she is happier that I am now able to call myself a governess rather than a housekeeper, so it could have been worse."

She had received the letter from her mother the previous day. Lady Carleton had expressed herself freely, but Helen felt that the anger was half-hearted. It seemed that Kitty had made the acquaintance of a titled gentleman at a hunt ball, who appeared very taken with her, and who openly expressed his hope of renewing their acquaintance in London next year. Helen had no idea if the attachment was real, but it was a useful distraction for her parents.

They dined on roast goose and traditional Christmas pudding and drank a rich red wine which Major Cartwright told her came from the vineyards around the River Douro and was a favourite of Lord Wellington. He made her laugh with stories of various Christmases spent on campaign and asked her about her family. Helen had wondered if she would miss the noisy family gatherings of her childhood, but she did not. After the meal, they visited George to wish him goodnight, and when he was finally in bed and sleeping, Helen sat beside the fire, in the drawing room, sipping sherry and trying to pretend that this was normal behaviour for a housekeeper who was also a cook and a nursery maid. David Cartwright sat opposite her.

"Do you play chess, Miss Carleton?"

"Yes. I'm quite fond of the game."

"Would you do me the honour?"

They sat with the board between them like a shield and Helen concentrated on her moves and tried not to think about anything else, until he said:

"Do you really want to stay?"

"Yes."

"I'm going to increase your salary, and I'd like you to employ a kitchen maid and a nursery maid. You can't leave it all to Sarah and you'll be very busy with George."

"Thank you, Major. I…"

"I feel as though I ought to send you home, but I don't want to. You'll be so good for him. I want to be here, but I can't. Not yet. Still, it's a huge responsibility, and if you change your mind, please tell me and I'll find somebody else."

"I won't. But thank you."

"Will you write to me with news of him?"

"All the time," Helen said warmly. "There will be nothing of him that you do not know."

"Thank you. I've felt so resentful sometimes, about Arabella but in the end, she gave me something I've wanted for so long. A child. A family. I'm so grateful. It's your move, Miss Carleton."

Helen studied the board. After a long moment, she moved her rook. "I think you are going to lose, Major Cartwright."

"I don't."

Helen looked up in surprise and found that he was looking at her, with a hint of a smile behind the steady brown eyes.

"I'm playing the long game," he explained, and reached to move his piece.

# By the Same Author

**The Peninsular War Saga**

An Unconventional Officer (Book 1)

An Irregular Regiment (Book 2)

An Uncommon Campaign (Book 3)

A Redoubtable Citadel (Book 4)

An Untrustworthy Army (Book 5)

An Unmerciful Incursion (Book 6)

An Indomitable Brigade (Book 7)

**The Manxman Series**

An Unwilling Alliance (Book 1)

This Blighted Expedition (Book 2)

**Regency Romances**

A Regrettable Reputation (Book 1)

The Reluctant Debutante (Book 2)

**Other Titles**

A Respectable Woman (A novel of Victorian London)

A Marcher Lord (A novel of the Anglo-Scottish Border Reivers)

Printed in Great Britain
by Amazon

28367008R00165